AUTUMN OF THE GRIMOIRE

THE SISTERS SOLSTICE SERIES

BOOK ONE

J.L. VAMPA

PHANTOM HOUSE PRESS

AUTUMN
OF THE
GRIMOIRE

WORKS BY J.L. VAMPA

The Queen's Keeper

Stolen Magick

Exquisite Poison Anthology: One Pirouette

THE SISTERS SOLSTICE SERIES

Autumn of the Grimoire

Winter of the Wicked 2023

Midlerea

OBUR

PRAEVAL

HELSVAR

PRILEMIA

Driftho

SORSCHA'S
TREEHOUSE

River Vide

Eridon

CORONOCCO

LYRONIA

Sudern Isle of Coronocco

SACREE
MOUNTAINS

Hiverterre

ISLE OF
BALLAST

WENDOLYN'S
CASTLE

MERVEILLE

MER
NOIR

FOREST
OF TOMBS

MER ROW

AGATHA'S
COTTAGE

SEAGOVIA

Rochbury

LITUR

ISLE
TIAMAT

SELESTE'S
ISLAND HUT

Norð

Ovest ✦ Est

Sud

AUTUMN OF THE GRIMOIRE

For more information, address: jlvampa@jlvampa.com.

First edition September 2022

Cover design by Franziska Stern — www.coverdungeon.com
Instagram: @coverdungeonrabbit
Photography by Alyssa Thorne Fine Art — www.alyssathorne.co
Instagram: @alyssathorne.co

ISBN 9798354186945

www.phantomhousepress.com

FOR ANYONE WHO HAS EVER HAD TO
CLAW THEIR WAY FORWARD.

CHAPTER
ONE

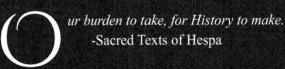

O *ur burden to take, for History to make.*
　　　　-Sacred Texts of Hespa

SHE WAS naked in the murky woods, dripping wet. Agatha frowned down at herself, then up at the full Reaping Moon. Unfortunately, it wasn't the first time—or even third—that she had been summoned in the nude. Though, Agatha was usually dry when she found herself suddenly in a new location, not of her choosing.

With a sigh, she turned to find her eldest Sister glaring, lips pinched and one finger *tap tapping* against ghostly pale arms folded across her chest.

A giggle sounded behind Agatha, and she turned once more to see her second eldest Sister appear in the gloom, also naked and dripping wet. Agatha's head tilted to one side as her brows knit together.

"Why are you both naked and *wet*?" Wendolyn demanded.

Agatha's third eldest Sister appeared out of thin air next to

Wendolyn, fully clothed in swaths of blinding lemon chiffon and cradling an ancient tome. Seleste looked a bit like a black python devouring a canary.

"I was in a bath, Winnie," Agatha answered drily.

Sorscha sauntered forward, her tanned skin glowing under the moonlight. "I was with a girl on the beach."

Winnie shook her white-blonde head as Seleste, her polar opposite in absolutely every way, smiled sweetly at their two dripping Sisters.

"Come along, then." Winnie intertwined her arm with Seleste's, the contrast of their skin bewitching.

Sorscha slapped Agatha on her backside before gliding after their Sisters, content to remain nude. Sister Spring was rarely clothed, anyway.

Agatha plucked a handful of elderberries from a nearby shrub. With a will of iron and wisps of her magic, she summoned a dress of the same colour from her cottage on the far side of the twilit woodland. The cottage with a perfectly delightful bath—now abandoned. She sighed, slipping the bedimmed violet gown over her head.

Agatha wiggled her toes in the fog, contemplating which of her lace-up boots to conjure—crushed velvet or the ones Sister Winter referred to as *sinister*. The cinnamon and sienna leaves felt delicious beneath her bare feet, so she settled for none.

Agatha trudged onward after her Sisters, wringing out her sopping, deep auburn hair and readying herself for what was to come on this eve—her Autumnal Equinox.

The Sisters Solstice gathered around a blazing fire Seleste conjured, each of them facing the flames from whence their magic came: Wendolyn from the Nord, Sorscha from the Est, Seleste from the Sud, and Agatha from the Ouest.

"I'll not sit here starved, Sisters. I worked up quite an appetite on that beach." Sorscha raised a brow coquettishly at

Winnie. "You pulled me away just as things were beginning to take a delightful turn."

Winnie huffed. "I'll gladly provide nourishment if you'll put some clothing on."

Sorscha whispered and snapped. A blood-red chemise—nearly transparent for all the lace it was comprised of—appeared on her sun-kissed body. Sorscha leaned back on her hands and winked at their eldest Sister. Her familiar, Ostara, wound herself around Sorscha's arm and hissed at Wendolyn.

Winnie wrinkled her nose at the snake. She muttered a complicated incantation from memory and a roasted turkey on a spit appeared over the fire, fat dripping and sizzling on the logs. Agatha and Sorscha ripped off the legs in unison. Seleste unsheathed the long dagger strapped to her thigh and sliced off a chunk of white meat. She ran her tongue along the length of the blade before returning it to its rightful place under her yellow skirts.

Wendolyn sat primly upon the Nordernmost rock, eyeing Sorscha and Agatha. She ran a hand down her snow-white owl's feathers as her talons scraped the boulder. Winnie would inevitably comment on the way they favoured one another, Agatha and Sorscha, with their full lips and plain features; their honey eyes and freckles—she always did. Sorscha's complexion was darker, albeit not nearly as dark as Seleste's, who favoured their father most of all with rich skin and hickory eyes. But Sorscha was the perfect blend of their long-dead parents.

Agatha noted the way she and Sorscha held their turkey portions the very same way. They were similar in many ways, but Agatha found Sorscha to be all she was not. Sorscha's body was lithe and romantic whereas Agatha's was curved and soft. Sorscha sat with her shoulders back and chin high, but Agatha was slouched, the heaviness she always carried bowing her shoulders. The wind blew her hair back, whispers of past Autumn nightmares tickling her neck. Agatha wished she'd brought Mabon for comfort, but he had a treacherous habit of trying to eat Seleste's colossal monarch butterfly, Litha.

"Sometimes," Winnie spoke over the fire, "I'd think the two of you identical if only Aggie did not sink into the dark, and Sorscha did not run wild in her brightness."

How very predictable Wendolyn was.

"The pair of you"—she pointed a long fingernail at her Sisters—"do know it is forbidden to be together apart from our meetings."

Agatha snorted. As if Winnie hadn't mentioned that edict four times a year since they were wrenched apart as babes.

"You can join us next time." Sorscha made a crass gesture. Winnie rolled her eyes and Agatha stifled a laugh. "We were not together anyway, *Your Highness*," Sorscha drawled.

"You can see why one would think that is a falsehood, yes? When you both showed up here indecently? And *wet*?"

"If you would simply set a consistent time"—Agatha glowered—"you would not summon us whilst *indecent*."

"You know it's coming, Aggie. Every Solstice and every Equinox we meet. Why is it so difficult to be prepared?"

"What about the time you summoned us at High Noon?" Sorscha egged Winnie on.

"That was *one* time, and it was well over two hundred years ago."

"And the time you waited until the Witching Hour when the Solstice was nearly over?" Agatha added. Winnie opened her mouth, but Agatha kept going. "Just set a damn time, Sister." Winnie's eye twitched at Agatha's disrespect. "Here. I'll set it for you. Dusk on the Solstice, dusk on the Equinox." She sank her teeth into her turkey leg and ripped a chunk off, eyeing her eldest Sister.

Seleste's mouth quirked to the side and she lifted one elegant hand into the air, her many bracelets tinkling. "I second."

Winnie's nostrils flared and Sorscha barked a laugh. She

adored seeing Winnie and Agatha at each other's throats. "I third."

Winnie begrudgingly took a black tourmaline crystal from the pouch at her hip and let it slip from her palm, falling into the fire. A plume of silver smoke billowed into the twilight sky. "It is done. Dusk on the Solstice; dusk on the Equinox."

"Now," Winnie went on. "Our first order of business." She turned to Sorscha. "It appears a young man just outside your village has been…consumed."

Sorscha baulked. "Don't look at me. I haven't drunk a boy's blood in at *least* a hundred years."

Agatha snickered.

"The fact that you have to clarify the last time you drank mortal blood is unsettling." Seleste's words of censure did not match the mirth behind them.

Sorscha shrugged and licked the bones of her turkey leg clean.

Winnie heaved a great sigh. "Please just see to it, Sorscha." Sister Winter turned toward Seleste. "Your Order this Summer went well?"

It bothered Agatha that Winnie phrased it in such a way. Undoubtedly it went well. The Sacred Grimoire delighted in giving her Sisters only Orders of wholesome purpose.

"It did." Seleste's glowing smile warmed the wind a fraction, and Agatha felt a pang of guilt for her resentment. "I was sent to a dignitary in Eridon. His wife was with child and she needed special care for an internal affliction. When it came time for the child to be born, I discovered the babe had the affliction as well." She smoothed her skirts. "A potion distributed methodically to them both, and now lives a healthy mother and a healthy heir." Seleste's eyes twinkled.

Agatha ground her teeth together. Of course Seleste's Order was to heal a newborn babe.

Winnie dropped her chin and eyed Seleste. "And you are certain no one suspected your tincture to be witchcraft?"

For the briefest of moments, a crease settled between Seleste's brows, but she smoothed it away with a sweet smile. "I'm quite certain, Sister."

"Good." Winnie straightened and ran her hands down the sides of her pristine, white bodice. "I trust you are all reading your Sacred Texts daily?" They all nodded, Sorscha with derision and an eye roll. "And you've all had the chance to read Father's journal?" They all nodded again. "Very well. It is time to trade."

Winnie snapped her long fingers and one of their father's journals appeared on her lap. She looked at her Sisters pointedly and they all three snapped in unison. A different, worn notebook appeared in each of their laps, and Winnie gathered them all to redistribute them.

Sorscha blew a stray hair out of her face and irreverently lifted the journal she'd been handed. "Why do we continue to read these things?"

Winnie's eyes widened and Seleste looked at her toes. Agatha felt a sting deep in her bosom.

"They're all we have left of our father, Sorscha. Of our coven." Winnie's gaze bore into Sister Spring. "That's reason enough."

"I'll take yours if you don't want it." Agatha held out her hand and Sorscha dropped the journal into her palm before crossing her arms. Winnie seethed but said nothing.

There was a brief lull, then Sisters Winter, Spring, and Summer turned to look at Agatha one by one. Sister Autumn sagged. "It's time, then?"

Wendolyn nodded. "It is."

Agatha stood and shuffled her way to Seleste, taking the gargantuan Grimoire from her. The weight of it in her arms dragged her heart down to the Underworld—precisely the *opposite* of what it should do.

Part of her thought it best to rush and open it—to see what dastardly deed she would be Ordered to commit this time. Part of her wanted to toss it into the blazing fire. Part of her wanted it to take centuries to walk back across their little fireside circle—everything else did.

Alas, it only took a moment to return to her place.

Her Sisters' eyes were unrelenting fire pokers upon her cheeks as Agatha ran her sharp-tipped fingernail down the length of the worn cover. She unfastened the bronze latch, took up the velvet placeholder—nearly black with time—and opened the Grimoire. The familiar script of Belfry—the first Sister Autumn—spelled out Agatha's name on the page before her eyes, followed by the shortest Order she'd ever received. Certainly it wasn't the full command—it rarely was. The rest would follow soon, and with it bring death.

Agatha slammed the Book shut.

Crippling silence filled the air. A hush permeated the Autumn trees, and the fire ceased its crackling. Even nature knew the Grimoire would not be kind to Agatha.

"Well," Winnie pressed, dispersing the aura of stillness like moths off a corpse. "What did it say?"

"You know exactly what it said," Agatha snapped.

"I do not, Sister. You know we cannot see what is written for another until it has come to pass."

"It says the same thing it always does. Can we move on?"

"What has happened to you to fill you with such disdain?" Wendolyn chastised.

"I'm a three-hundred-year-old witch, Winnie. What *hasn't* happened to me is a road far less dark to travel down."

"We're all witches. Don't be dramatic, Aggie. I simply think you could be happy if you'd let yourself."

"Because you're the picture of bliss, Winnie," Sorscha

pointed out. Wendolyn stiffened, but she kept her eyes fixed on her youngest Sister.

Agatha's jaw clenched as she looked down at the Grimoire on her knees. "What makes you think I'm not happy?"

"Tell me you do not still think of Ira."

Agatha's eyes ticked up at that. Sparks burst from the fire toward the stars at the sound of his name. Her magic would not soon forget him, either.

"Not fair, Winnie," Seleste's sing-song voice broke in.

"It was nearly a hundred years ago," Winnie challenged.

"You know that's just a breath to us," Sorscha added.

"Ah yes, it's all just a breath. An agonising, horrendous, dreadfully long *breath*, suffocating your lungs until you *drown* on dry land."

The Sisters stared at Agatha.

"Thank you for trying to help, Seleste and Sorscha, but I'm okay. Truly." Agatha turned to Winnie. "Yes. I think of him every time the wind blows cold. So, thirteen times since you summoned me right out of my bath."

"We've all lost lovers, Aggie—"

"*Not like that*," Agatha cut her off, the words catching in her throat. "Now, if you don't mind, I have some packing to do."

"I don't make the rules." Winnie's voice was soft. Almost as if she cared.

But Agatha knew better.

"No, you just enforce them with the tender care of a dungeon warden."

Winnie's rigidity surfaced once more as her hand sliced through the air in time with her words. "It is our duty, our purpose, and our *privilege* to honour what the Grimoire says."

Agatha held up the ancient tome, her knuckles white for how tightly she gripped it. "This Grimoire has done nothing for us. *Nothing*. It's just a damned book."

All three of her Sisters gasped. An ice-cold knot of dread knit together in Agatha's abdomen, but she'd already said the words aloud.

"How dare you blaspheme Hespa! She is our Goddess Three."

"Hespa is not a book, Wendolyn."

Winnie took a deep breath before speaking again. "Please do not be difficult, Agatha."

Agatha laughed, mirthless and wicked. She set her eyes on her eldest Sister and curved her lips into a sinister smile. "Who has the Grimoire called upon to incite wars, Sister? To unleash plagues and kill kings? Is it you, or is it me?" She stabbed a fingernail into her own chest. "Because I am quite certain it is *me*."

Winnie stood, towering over her youngest Sister. "We've all been Ordered to do difficult things, Sister."

Agatha lifted her chin. "Oh, and what was your Order last Winter? That's right—to poison the garden of a village healer. How very malevolent, indeed." Sister Autumn's eyes flashed and the fire guttered out.

"*Disparaître.*"

And Agatha was gone.

CHAPTER

TWO

O ur blessed Mother, Maiden, and Crone's imbued
power—the Sacred Grimoire.
        -Sacred Texts of Hespa

AGATHA EXHALED, drawn out and slow, as she materialised in
front of her woodland cottage, balancing her father's journals
atop the Grimoire.

The old sable house sat nestled in maple, oak, and sweet gum
trees dripping with her Autumnal hues. Agatha might prefer
black, but she claimed it was because her trees demanded all the
luxurious brilliance. This time, her lips tipped up as the chill
breeze brushed her cheek and the trees' branches swayed in its
caress. She had to admit, her little corner of the woods was more
devoid of light than most, even in midday—like someone had
taken a burnt amber brush and painted Agatha's abyss in hues of
warm gloom. But that was precisely how she liked it.

The barest tendrils of smoke rose from her chimney—curious, considering the flames had been strong and of magical
nature when she'd left. In her short absence, fog had also begun

crawling in, curling up to her pumpkins and nestling amongst the leaves.

Sister Autumn's Season had truly arrived.

Winnie mocked her abode tucked deep into the Forest of Tombs, but it gave Agatha peace and rest unlike any other place she'd been—and that was not only due to the enchantments placed upon her grounds.

She found the alder and ash trees breathtaking. The maple and birch a life force all their own, dripping with colour. Agatha kept them in perpetual Autumn, and, on occasion, she let Winter befall them as well. Greenery simply did not suit her as it did Sorscha and Seleste.

She had chosen the Forest of Tombs because no one wanted to venture too far from a beloved's gravesite in a place of the dead. Witches had hung from the alder and oak trees that rose between the ancient gravestones; feet swinging and life leaving. No, it was not a place many frequented.

Agatha, however, was all too familiar with death and had tucked her home amongst the graves of the fallen Witch Trial women. They'd been deemed the Hollows by Hespa's Hallowed and Sister Autumn had chosen to keep them company in the woods. Most of the women hadn't even been true witches, the poor souls. Their crumbling tombs had names that were too weathered to make out—though she imagined most headstones were younger than herself. The Trials had lasted a gruesomely long time.

Alas, not a single mortal had darkened Agatha's doorstep in a hundred years.

The full Reaping Moon lit the leaf-strewn path up to her cottage. Agatha was glad for it, since the warm candlelight that usually gleamed in her windowsills at night had mysteriously vanished. Mabon had an irritating habit of blowing out the candles when Agatha wasn't looking. She summoned a black taper and strode through the leaves, relishing their crunch underfoot.

Agatha surveyed the plumpness of her pumpkins as she walked. She drew near to the fattest one and bent down to inspect it, balancing the Grimoire and journals on her knee—if Winnie were to somehow discover she'd placed the Book on the ground, she'd string her up by her toes. Agatha rapped her knuckles on the side of the orange beast, a hollow *thunk* promising its ripeness.

"I'll at least get some food for my travels out of you, deary."

She'd only planted one pumpkin seed, when she was a toddling child. Agatha had found the slimy seeds fascinating when her mother handed her one. Her Sisters had set to making lanterns and pies, while Agatha heard her Season's call and waddled outside. Right in front of their family's cottage, amongst their coven's community in Helsvar, Sister Autumn had planted her first seed in the soil. Since that day, no matter where she'd lived, pumpkins appeared at her home in Autumn. They were the unlikeliest of comforts, but they were also a bit of a nuisance—such is the way with creature comforts and life, particularly a long one.

Agatha could not bear to have even one pumpkin rot like a mortal lost to madness or decay. No, she simply had to make them all into *something*—pies, cakes, bread, butter, soup, pasta, lanterns, votives, poultices, elixirs...

Since Agatha had no inclination as to how long her Order would take, she was bound to return to rotted pumpkins, and the thought depressed her. Certainly, she could keep them in perpetual Autumn like the trees, but Agatha found the over-use of witchcraft to be like the over-abundance of coin—a want for nothing leads only to a bleak existence. It's good for the soul to have something to crave; to tend; to strive for. Therefore, Agatha let most things occur in their natural order without fiddling with them. Regardless, ever-growing and rotting pumpkins would be an unfathomable pain.

Her Sisters would simply transport themselves to their destination, but Agatha relished the trip. If there was one thing she'd learned in her three hundred years, it was that—to enjoy the journey. Or try to. Joy was exceedingly difficult to come by whilst delivering death.

Agatha rose and made her way into the cottage. She let the aroma of *home* wash over her, its familiarity instantly calming the frayed edges of her nerves. The herbs and spices that hung from the rafters of the kitchen, swaying gently in the night air that entered with her. The cinnamon, apple, orange, and cloves simmering in a cauldron within the hearth. The books in every nook and cranny, whose pages were more ancient than Agatha— that distinct parchment scent of knowledge and wonder. The earthy aroma of moss terrariums that dangled throughout the cottage. Lingering potion and tincture balms mixing with the ever-present scents of coffee and tea. And Mabon.

"*Lumière.*"

Agatha's many hanging lanterns yawned to life, as well as the fire in the hearth. Several of her hundreds of candles flicked on, and a fuzzy black form flew at her face. Agatha laughed and nuzzled Mabon before he settled onto her shoulder, leathery wings folded primly in place, his oversized ears lost in Agatha's long hair.

"You blew out all the candles again, didn't you?"

Mabon looked down at his nimble feet.

"I was only gone a short time. How did you manage to get the fire out, too, you pesky little night stalker?"

The bat huffed through his nose and blinked onyx eyes at her, unamused. With the tiniest flick of his tongue against her cheek, he flew off to hang upside down on an ear of corn suspended in the air. Mabon preferred for all his food to float.

Agatha trudged up creaking steps to the second floor, home

to her bedroom and lavatory. She deposited the Grimoire on her bed and tucked the journals under her pillow, hoping her father's words would seep comfort into her as she dreamt. Discarding her dark elderberry dress, she replaced it with a dressing gown the colour of burnt ginger. From the ancient serving tray by her bedside, Agatha poured a generous goblet of mulled wine. A brazier of hot coals had kept it deliciously warm in her absence, but her bath was another matter.

Nearly to the door of her lavatory, Agatha stopped and turned back to look at the Grimoire. It amazed her that something as simple as an old book could be so utterly damning, and she wondered if the rest of her Order was laid out within the pages yet. Curiosity and dread warred within her, creating a tumultuous flurry of indecision. Agatha growled and stalked over to bring the hulking Grimoire to the bath.

Once the archaic tome was poised upon a dark walnut tray positioned across the clawfoot tub, Agatha dipped one finger into the bath.

"*Chaleur.*"

The milky water began to bubble while Agatha drizzled a bit of honey in it and sprinkled black salt from Mer Noir amongst the ripples. She took up an old scrying bowl filled to the brim with bronze and black dahlias, scattering a few to float amongst the creamy bubbles. She let her dressing gown fall to the wood floor and took up a taper to light the candles of her candelabra.

Agatha stepped into the soothing bath and sank to the bottom, submerging herself and allowing the water to envelop her in its embrace. She counted the length of a few breaths and resurfaced, finally prepared to open the Grimoire and see if the rest of Belfry's vision had been scrawled across the pages.

The first Sisters Solstice—Talan, Hissa, Monarch, and Belfry —spent their entire preternaturally long lives penning visions, dreams, and spoken messages sent to them from the Goddess Three, Hespa. The Sisters wrote in parchment and ink spelled with the sands of time. Each word was only permitted to come forth at the proper time for the prophecy, and only visible to the proper Sister Solstice—the one who would use it to mould History. For, anything of note in History has begun at the hands of a Sister Solstice.

Belfry had written only the vilest of Orders for Agatha. Sister Autumn was designed, with her equal darkness and light, to be the brutal hand of Hespa.

During her time with the prior Sister Autumn—a gruelling eight years before she came of age and took up the mantle of the Autumnal Witch—Agatha had questioned *why*. But her questions had long since been beaten out of her. It was an honour. A duty. A holy burden.

She dried one hand on a nearby linen and placed her palm on top of the Book. She felt Hespa daily—at least she thought she did—but Agatha certainly loathed the Goddess' Book. The image of King Caliban's horrified eyes as he bled out on her freshly polished lace-up boots filled her mind. The assaulting memory of children covered in boils, dying on cots in a crowded infirmary followed swiftly after.

Agatha shook her thoughts loose and took another sip of wine, setting it back down on the tray next to the Grimoire. With a deep, calming breath, she took the velvet page marker in between her fingers. Agatha lifted it carefully, the spine of the Book creaking as she began to open it.

The steamy air that clung to her skin suddenly smelled of geraniums and fresh rain. A breath later, a form materialised next to her bathtub, swathed in a nightgown of jade.

"Hello, Sorscha." Agatha let the cover of the Grimoire fall shut with a small huff of dust and sand from Seleste's island, where it had resided all Summer.

"Dear Sister Autumn. You had to know I would check on you after that debacle." Sorscha slid a wooden stool next to Agatha's tub and sat.

"It wasn't that bad."

Sorscha frowned, her chin resting in her hand and her elbow propped on the side of the bathtub. "Do not diminish it, Aggie. Winnie was cruel. She poked and prodded at all your wounds."

"I appreciate your concern, Sister, but Winnie has treated me far worse than she did tonight, and I am quite familiar with how this all goes for me."

Sorscha shrugged, winding her long dark hair over one shoulder. "It is an Equinox, therefore it's *our* night. So why don't you point me to that delectable smelling mulled wine, and I'll join you for a nightcap."

Agatha couldn't help but smile. "By my bedside."

Sorscha raised an impressed brow. "That's a good witch."

She trotted off to pour a goblet while Agatha dried herself and donned a deep plum nightgown. On her way out of the lavatory, she remembered the ominous Grimoire and snatched it up with a scowl. She turned to find Sorscha leaning against the door frame, sipping her wine. Agatha pushed past her and unceremoniously dumped the Book on her bed to be dealt with later.

"You don't have to do this alone, Aggie."

Agatha's responding laugh held no humour. "You know I do, Sister. We all do."

Sorscha swirled her goblet. "I will write you every day and send a raven every Witching Hour with the letter, should you like me to."

Agatha squeezed her Sister's hand once and turned to refill her wine.

"What did the Grimoire say?"

Agatha let out a breath. "It said I am to travel to Merveille and seek out the Grand Magus."

"That's all?"

"That's all."

"Perhaps it will not be so very bad, then, after all."

Agatha smiled sadly at Sorscha. "Perhaps not, Sister."

But they both knew better.

"How will you approach the Grand Magus?" Sorscha pushed a lock of hair behind her ear. "Isn't he rather untouchable and tucked up in the palace?"

Agatha shrugged. "I thought I'd just walk right up and tell him I'm a witch, there to see him."

Sorscha tipped her head back and cackled, coaxing the corners of Agatha's lips upward. "That would be a riot. Can you imagine the *Grand Magus* discovering we still exist? That the Witch Trials did nothing but murder innocents?" She shook her head and lifted her goblet to her mouth. "I'd like very much to see that."

Sister Autumn heaved a sigh. "I truly don't know what I'll say or how I'll even get to him."

"Surely the Grimoire will reveal more before you arrive…"

"Surely so." And it would be menacing, no doubt. "This boy," Agatha taunted, desperate to change the course of their evening. "The one killed outside your village. It truly wasn't you?"

Sorscha put a hand to her chest, scandalised. "It absolutely was *not* me. You know drinking the blood of mortal men was all the rage back then and you three still tease me mercilessly for it! I never *consumed* one." She shivered, her face contorting with disgust.

Agatha laughed, relishing a brief respite from the gloom hovering over her.

"I suppose I really must find out what happened to the poor lad when I return tomorrow."

Agatha started. "Tomorrow? You can't stay here, Sorscha. You know that."

They'd never tried it, staying with one another past the Witching Hour. Not after the hearth tales. The former Sisters told them as children what occurred when two Sisters met outside the Solstice or Equinox. According to the legends, the trees as far as three towns over toppled in tandem. The Autumn Harvest never came—there was nothing left to reap. The moon never told the tide to go back out to sea...

In one of the more gruesome tales, a land of desolation, death, and madness was all that remained—the very centre of which was a small, once-lovely place where two Sisters Solstice of old napped past the Witching Hour on a Summer Solstice. The Sisters? Punished. Never permitted to look upon one another again. Agatha swallowed. That particular tale landed too close to home.

"I don't mean to stay here, Aggie. I have a mortal, aside from the one that was consumed, to contend with tonight." Sorscha smirked. "A memory to alter, and then, if I have my way, a dawn of catching up where we left off before Winnie so *callously* pulled us apart."

Agatha snorted. "You're not supposed to *be* with anyone on a Solstice or Equinox for this very reason. Need I remind you of the Lilith debacle?"

Sorscha had once been summoned to Winnie's mountaintop home rather *intertwined* with Lilith. Though it was a humorous anecdote to Agatha, Sorscha did not relish the reminder of all the memory alterations she'd been forced to spell Lilith with.

Sorscha waved her off. "That's a Rule of *Winnie*," she mocked, "not a Rule of Hespa. Besides, I should like to think the Maiden of our Goddess Three is who bestowed upon me this insatiable thirst I bear." Sorscha dipped a fingernail into her wine and drew it, dripping, to her lips.

Agatha rolled her eyes. "I'm quite certain you're right, Sister."

Sorscha drained the dregs of her drink and kissed Agatha on the forehead. "I must be going. I shall see you at the Winter Solstice when you hand over the Grimoire to Winnie with utter relief." She reached out and caressed Agatha's cheek. "Happiest Day of Birth, Little Sister."

With a whisper of wind and shimmering spell, Agatha was alone with her thoughts once more. And the Grimoire. She moved to pull back her downy bed cover when the scent of the air turned sweet once more and a gentle wind lifted the back of her nightgown.

"Did you forget something—" Agatha turned to find a different Sister than expected. "Seleste, what are you doing here?"

The bits of gold woven into Sister Summer's braids *tinked* as she shot an anxious glance out the window. Agatha followed her gaze, noting the moon's placement in the sky. She was nearly certain she caught a glimpse of Winnie's ghostly image in the glass before she turned back to Seleste.

"I must hurry, Aggie." She rushed forward and took Agatha's hands in hers. "The Witching Hour is upon us, but I couldn't leave you without knowing where you're going. All you said was that you have to pack."

"You know as well as I that we all have detection spells on us to be used *by* all of us. You can find me anywhere I go."

"Yes, yes, I know. But you always insist upon travelling like a mortal and I worry for you."

"I'm a witch, Seleste, I can quite take care of myself."

"You're insufferable, Aggie." Her words were irritated, but her face only read concern and pride for her Sister's stubbornness.

"And you're a fussing mother hen, Sister Summer. I'm to travel to Merveille. It will only take but a handful of days, perhaps only three."

Seleste's eyes softened, her relief palpable. "Very well. Send a raven or Mabon with word of your safe arrival, Sister."

At the very last second, before the bells of the Witching Hour, marking the middle of the night, sounded in all the villages across the land, Seleste vanished.

Agatha slid beneath her covers and took up the Grimoire.

19

Mabon flew in the window, settling himself next to her warmth and snuggling down into the covers with a sigh. Sister Autumn stroked her familiar's head and fought the fear clawing at her insides. Never before had two Sisters come to visit her on the same night. And she couldn't help but think it was a bad omen.

CHAPTER

THREE

T he Goddess' hands of wrath and mercy, to balance History.
        -Sacred Texts of Hespa

AGATHA CAREFULLY PLACED the last of her pumpkin delicacies—bread and pumpkin cinnamon butter—into her saddlebag open on the small kitchen table. Mabon chirped at her from where he was perched atop a floating banana, then took a nosedive, swallowing an intruding moth whole. He swept up and landed proudly on Agatha's shoulder. She scratched him generously between the ears and made her way up the stairs.

"And you wonder why I can't take you to see my Sisters. We can't have you gobbling up Litha or one of Seleste's other butterfly creatures."

Agatha swore Mabon snickered. He spread his wings and flapped away, depositing himself in his hanging enclosure. Agatha watched him take the handle of the wooden door in between his minuscule teeth and pull it shut.

"It appears one of us is ready to begin this journey, then."

Mabon squeaked in response.

Agatha stood in front of her bed and peered into the empty knapsack. One would think after countless assignments and Orders from Hespa—or, rather, the Grimoire—that Agatha would know what to bring to any court in any land. Alas, she never chose correctly.

Black and plum were not fashionable colours in Merveille and Agatha did not own the restricting undergarments of the court women. She did, however, appreciate that the thin band of bronze set with alexandrite and amber encircling her arm had come back into fashion. It was her mother's, and before the rise of the armlet in courts across the continent, Agatha had always left it home so as not to attract unwanted attention, particularly with thieves.

She tucked a portion of her long, wild hair behind her ears and moved to stand before the open armoire. Staring at the dresses had as little effect on filling her knapsack as staring at the sack itself had. Agatha frowned, closed her eyes, and whispered.

"*Inattendue.*"

Three dresses and one pair of riding breeches folded themselves into the knapsack, and Agatha nodded with satisfaction. She took up the four colossal tomes stacked on her bedside table and placed them on the Grimoire before balancing her father's journals on top.

"We leave as soon as Guinevere is saddled," she spoke over her shoulder to Mabon, making her way back down to the kitchen with the books teetering.

Agatha set them down on the table and tapped a fingernail to her chin. There was absolutely no way they would all fit into her saddlebag, and there were three others she'd want to bring along as well.

"*Petits livres.*"

The tomes all shrank to a size befitting Mabon or a sprite. All except the Grimoire. It remained as intimidating as before. Agatha deposited the small books into her saddlebag and reached for the Grimoire. It thrummed under hand as it only did when the next bit of an Order was spelling itself out in the handwriting of one of the First Sisters.

Agatha's throat went dry. Trepidation crawled up her spine, and she couldn't bring herself to read or even open the Book. Not yet. When she reached Rochbury, she would read it. Really, she had no choice, for Rochbury was less than a day's ride from Merveille, and it would not do to enter the capital city unawares. She was still entirely unsure how she would approach the man who sat supremely over all magi; a reigning member of The Order—the ruling council of Hespa's sacred teachers. By many, he was more revered than the royalty on the continent of Midlerea.

Agatha growled and shoved the Grimoire in with the rest of the books, then winced at her carelessness—or was it resentment? Nevertheless, she snapped her fingers, and all her luggage, including Mabon in his cage, floated behind her in procession toward the meager stable behind her cottage.

Just inside the stable, the Great Horned Owl who'd invited herself to live on Agatha's grounds issued a soft hoot.

"What has you awake so late, hm? The sun is already rising." Agatha rubbed a small circle on the owl's head, and she nestled her beak snuggly under one wing, content to stay in the barn until the sun traded places with the moon again.

"Mabon, Guinevere, and I are leaving for some time, Cosette. Be a good groundskeeper, will you?"

Cosette's retorting hoot was laden with fatigue. Agatha had precisely seventeen wards and charms upon her grounds but adding a petulant old owl to the protection certainly wouldn't hurt matters. She retrieved Guinevere's saddle, heaving it up onto her shoulder. Witch or not, the Sisters did well to manage their physical strength and agility.

J.L. VAMPA

Agatha did not have to guess where her black Friesian was when she found the stall empty. She let Guinevere roam about as she pleased and eat anything she liked aside from the pumpkins. The great steed could eat herself ill of the ripened apples on the trees. And that is precisely where Guinevere was as the sun lazily drew back the curtain of night. By the time the horse saw Agatha carrying her saddle—and the luggage floating obediently behind—Guinevere was stomping and whinnying with excitement.

The corners of Agatha's mouth tipped upward in the peaceful way only her creatures could draw from her. She ran a hand down Guinevere's mane and the horse nudged Agatha with her muzzle. "We have a trek to make, Guin. Have you had your fill of apples?"

The horse pranced in place until Agatha chuckled. She ran her hands along Guinevere's back and flanks, whispering an incantation that elevated her baggage and Mabon's cage, ever so slightly, to alleviate any burden for the horse, save for Agatha's weight. She then directed the bags and cage to fasten themselves to the horse with ropes around her middle.

"That about does it, then."

Agatha took one final look over her shoulder at her cottage, melancholy washing over her. By the time she returned—be it a handful of days or years—she would not be the same. She never was.

With a hand on the saddle, she heaved herself up and onto Guinevere. The horse danced underneath her, anxious to set off. Agatha gave her a gentle kick and thus began their journey to Merveille.

The roads from her cottage in Douloureux to the outskirts of Rochbury were little traversed and quite peaceful aside from the occasional embittered squirrel. For that reason, Agatha decided to camp for the first night, just before the roads would turn busy

24

and potentially problematic. With more people always comes more trouble—thievery, sickness, quarrelling and the like.

It was nearing dusk when she found a copse of trees pushed up against a rock face with a generous overhang. Off to one side was a thin stream and a small clearing with the grass of Summer still clinging on for dear life. It did not get any more fortuitous than that. Perhaps Hespa was looking out for her after all, even if Her Book was not.

Agatha dismounted, and Mabon's relentless squeaking rose to new heights. "Cease all your fussing, you ingrate." She unfastened the bat's cage, and he flew off into the bruised sky.

Tired as she was from riding on little sleep, Agatha relished the soreness in her limbs. She often forgot how physical labour could push at the ever-present darkness shrouding her—at least minutely. With that thought, she removed the bags, Mabon's cage, and the saddle with the saddlebag from Guinevere by hand. She pulled out the horse's brush and methodically tended to her mane. She led her to the small stream and took the bit out of her mouth.

"Drink up and graze your fill. You've gotten us one of three days' ride, old girl." She gave the horse a nuzzle and set to gathering brush and branches for a small fire up against the rock face. It was unlikely they would meet any trouble, but she took out her velvet pouch of black salt—made from charcoal charged by the Waning Moon and black salt from Mer Noir—and sprinkled it around their campsite in a circle. After ensuring there were no gaps, she recited the same protection spell her mother had taught her as a child.

Her voice was still as clear as the day she'd last heard it nearly three hundred years ago, but Agatha grasped at the fragmented memories of her mother's face. She stood still, feeling the Autumn wind on her cheeks, and closed her eyes. All that came, as usual, was a foggy wisp of white hair like Winnie's, and a smile just like Sorscha's. Her mother may have been a heretic, but Agatha had loved her fiercely.

She sighed and flung a palm toward her piled logs.

"*Feu.*"

She and her Sisters were far beyond the need of words or tools for their magic—all they needed was a strong will, an even stronger mind, and an element at their disposal—but Agatha found comfort in the old ways. At least those pertaining to her personal practise of magic.

She made herself as comfortable as one can whilst leaning against a giant rock in the woods, curled up in the dirt, and took out her books and pumpkin bread. Sweet tooth mollified a few pages into a tome about the first witch coven led by Talan, Hissa, Monarch, and Belfry, and Agatha took out some dried meat and cheese. With a full belly, sleep beckoned her sweetly. Through eyelids nearly shut, she saw Mabon flit about the salt circle and squawk at her for making it so small—he was a creature of the open night, after all. Guinevere grazed near the circle herself and Agatha drifted off to sleep.

"Please," the man before her begged. "Please don't do this."
He was on his knees, palms outstretched toward her, but he did not blubber as so many often do. "We can arrange whatsoever it is you desire. Please, don't kill me."

Agatha tapped the pointed toe of her beautiful, heeled boot impatiently. Her Order had come that morning. She'd known the night of the Autumn Equinox that she would be taking the life of a king, but she hadn't known which one until she'd been woken by a thrum of magic coming from where the Grimoire rested on her bedside table.

When Agatha saw the name of her own Seagovian King Caliban scrawled out in Belfry's sprawling handwriting, she nearly vomited. He was the only monarch in her long life that she'd considered half-worthy of a throne. Standing in front of the man as he pleaded, she could still see the fire of goodness in his eyes. He'd been the one to end the Witch Trials. He'd been the one to halt the segregation of Seagovia—

Agatha blinked her thoughts away. The Grimoire, the First Sisters, the Goddess Three... They must have known more than she did about the man kneeling at her feet.

But this king had defended the outcasts and imprisoned those that tormented them—

Agatha shook her head. It was best to get on with it.

"I've no choice in the matter, Your Majesty."

Agatha lifted her blade, vaguely wondering why she hadn't thought to simply bring a vial of poison instead. She was bound to ruin her new boots. There was movement from the corner of the dark room, and a distant song drifted in through the window, catching her by surprise. The king took his chance while she was distracted, lunging for her knife, but Agatha was swift. She kicked him back and bound him with silent magic. She had no time to consider her remorse or choice of killing blow, for she didn't know who or what *lurked in the corner. With one hand tangled in his snowy white hair, she drew the dagger across his throat. Blood, hot and sticky, sprayed onto her boots, ruining the black lace as predicted.*

"Merde," she swore and transported herself back to Ira's cottage. The reality of what she'd just done hit her square in the gut and she fainted, only to wake a long time later, cradled in Ira's arms.

27

AGATHA AWOKE WITH A CHOKING GASP, the memory of King Caliban's blood and Ira's worried face burned into her mind. She turned over and violently vomited into the dirt.

She washed out her mouth with water from her water skin and roused the sleeping bat and horse. It was close enough to dawn, and there was no rest left for her after the nightmares—no matter how used to them she was. Weariness settled into her bones. For once, Agatha let her magic take the burden of cleaning up their camp and preparing for another long day of travel.

It wasn't until they were nearly ready to head out that she noticed a raven perched atop the cold fire logs, a small roll of parchment tied to his leg. Agatha stroked the bird's feathers and untied the note.

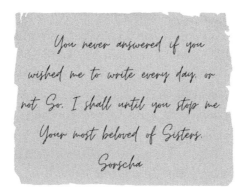

You never answered if you wished me to write every day, or not So. I shall until you stop me

Your most beloved of Sisters.

Gorscha

Agatha felt the tightness in her chest unfurl, ever so slightly, at her Sister's words. She tucked the note into the velvet pouch at her wrist and climbed into the saddle.

The roads grew cumbersome and busy when the sun awoke.

Horses and carts filled with all manner of things clambered past them, tinkers attempted to peddle their wares, and soldiers patrolled up and down the sides of the road. It was a dusty, noisy affair the whole day through, and Agatha was near to murdering the next boisterous traveler or falling clean off Guinevere's back by the time they reached Rochbury.

The surprise that they'd travelled so far in the span of two days jolted Agatha enough to think more clearly. If they were in Rochbury, then it was only a little over a half day's ride to Merveille.

She inhaled deeply with swift regret. A populated area meant rubbish and refuse. But Agatha also smelled the rich scent of roasted meat and a hint of salt in the air from Mer Noir—the sea acting as a menacing castle guardian to its Nord. She'd nearly made it. Both relief and dread filled her veins, her stomach turning in response. Rochbury meant the Midnight Rouge Inn which, in turn, meant a warm bed for her and Mabon, a stable for Guinevere, and a hot meal. But it also meant she had to open the Grimoire. Trotting through the city gates of Merveille without knowledge of what the rest of her Order was seemed irresponsible, even if avoiding it sounded divine.

Agatha found her way to the Midnight with only a minor spat with a drunken farmer and left Guinevere at the inn's stable. Mabon pestered her to let him fly into the deepening night, and she directed him to tap her window *before* morning.

Bag full of books and a crumpled but clean dress in hand, Agatha stepped into the Midnight. She was immediately assaulted by the acrid smell of old ale and unwashed bodies, not to mention the deafening *noise*. Heightened witch senses were not always a welcomed gift from their Goddess Three. Agatha whispered under her breath, and a magical hush softened the din in her ears. She walked to the bar and the old innkeeper jutted her chin out in silent question.

"I would like supper and a room, please." Agatha sniffed the air, loath to find the stench wafting from her own unwashed body as well. "Preferably one with a bath."

The innkeeper regarded her with shrewd eyes. "Ya' got the coin fir it?"

Agatha jingled her heavy pouch, the unmistakable clink of coins turning the crotchety innkeeper into an affable maidservant. She jumped to produce a hot bowl of lamb stew for Agatha and barked at a barmaid to prepare their best room.

Perhaps Agatha had been remiss for drawing attention to herself. *Keep yourself and your magic hidden,* Winnie would have said. *Never draw attention unless to bed someone,* Sorscha would have said. *It's not safe for us,* Seleste would have said. But Agatha was too tired to care, and the stew was too delicious to consider changing course. Halfway into her second bowl, the innkeeper brought a cask of hot apple cider for her to take upstairs.

Nearly asleep in her bowl of stew, Agatha shouldered her bag and hopped down from the barstool. She took up the cask and turned to head toward her room for the night, but a hooded figure bowled into her, spilling the hot cider down the front of her dress. It seeped straight through, burning her breasts and she hissed.

The cloaked man didn't even stop. He merely mumbled an apology and kept walking. She reached out and snatched his arm. "You cannot even remove your hood to apologise to a lady?" she snarled.

The stranger's face was obscured in the shadows of his hood, but his chin dipped as he looked down at where Agatha's hand latched onto his arm. "'fraid not."

She drew her arm back swiftly, her lip curled, and he moved toward the door again. She was exhausted and anxious. The last thing she needed was some arrogant prick ruining her dress. "Goddess' bones but you are a proud one."

The man turned back toward her at that. She could just make

out the shape of his mouth, but barely. "And you have quite the tongue on you for a *lady*."

Agatha flashed a sinister grin. "Apologies, *Your Highness*." Without a response, he turned on his heel and stormed out.

Agatha muttered to herself and swiped at her travel-and-cider-ruined dress. The innkeeper snapped at the poor barmaid to mop up the mess before turning to Agatha and sweetly vowing to send another jug of cider up to her room.

CHAPTER
FOUR

M y Lorelai is with child. I daresay I had not truly known the Goddess Three's love until this day.
-Writings of Ambrose Joubert

AGATHA GRUMBLED the entire way to her room on the second floor. She didn't bother using the key to unlock the door, ramming the tendrils of her magic into the lock instead. She slammed the door shut before stomping to the bed in the centre of the room and throwing her bag down. Unfastening the many buttons on her ruined dress, she took stock of the small space. It was dismal for what was considered the best room, but it was, indeed, far better than the previous room she'd spent the night in at the Midnight. Her heart ached in its familiar way, but the ghost of a smile touched her lips. The room's aesthetic had been the *least* of her concerns on that glorious evening.

Agatha closed her eyes and could almost feel the phantom touch of Ira's fingertips as they ran down her bare back. She could nearly taste his lips as they turned insistent the further she deepened their kiss. Ira had been afraid, until that night. Afraid someone would see them together and harm Agatha for being with a man of his station. A man of his origin. That was the night she defied the laws of her kind for the first time. She told Ira she was a witch and that no one could harm her. They spent the whole of the night with legs tangled tight and her heart swelling. With Ira's breath against her ear and his lips upon her skin, she never could have imagined what a lie she'd just told the first and only mortal she ever loved.

The thoughts ushered in familiar darkness, and Agatha clutched the locket of crystals hanging around her neck out of habit. Now was not the time to surrender to panic. Instead, she looked around the room. The bed took up most of the space, and the bathtub took up the rest. There was a minuscule table, and the only other fixture was a full-length looking glass propped against the wall next to a small window. It wasn't much, but it would do for the night. Agatha fished in her bag, pulling out one of her father's journals.

"*Grandir.*"

The worn, supple leather shifted in her hands as the journal grew back to its normal size. Agatha moved to place it on the table, but her heart longed to open it. If she must read the Grimoire, she needed to juxtapose it with her father's words. She thumbed through the pages, running her fingers along the lines of familiar script, cherishing each of them. Agatha knew her father's writings like the back of her hand, but they never grew old. She flipped to one of her favourite passages.

Four daughters. We're to raise four *daughters. I can scarcely believe our Agatha has come. This child, so quietly fierce, even as a babe. I anxiously await the day we will show her all she is to become.*

Agatha closed the journal and hugged it to her chest before sliding it beneath her pillow. She rose, unbuttoning the rest of her dress and leaving it to hang loose as she wandered to peer outside. The moon was still nearly full and glowing the colour of fresh honey. She lifted her face and let Madam Moon's enchanted beams fill her with courage for what came next.

Agatha padded over to the old, wooden tub with water already in it. She willed the flames to grow higher within a small hearth situated behind the tub and let her filthy dress pool at her bare feet. The water the barmaid had brought up was tepid when she dipped her toe in, so Agatha warmed it with her magic and added a bit of her marjoram and lavender elixir to the water as well. She could use all the peace she could muster. Agatha held the Grimoire safely to her breast as she stepped into the hot bath. Careful to keep it from dipping into the water, she took one last deep, shuddering breath and opened the Book to the marked page.

THERE SHALL COME A DAY, AS THE NIGHTS LENGTHEN AND THE LEAVES HATH BEGUN TO FALL, THAT A DAUGHTER OF AUTUMN SHALL JOIN A SON OF GEM AND BONE. TOGETHER THEY—

THE REST WAS CUT OFF—ABRUPTLY, with a smudge of ink. It was curious. Worrisome even. No Order had ever been cut off haphazardly. Perhaps Belfry's quill had slipped.

Agatha leaned her head back and pondered the half-written call. It wasn't a true Order, and it certainly didn't emit the ominous air so many of hers did. She was the Daughter of Autumn, but who was the Son of Gem and Bone?

She wound a lock of hair around her finger, attempting to recall everything she knew of Merveille from History. The residents traded the finest delicacies the sea had to offer, but they were also famous for braving the violent temper of Mer Noir to provide rare jewels to the rest of Midlerea. If that was what the Order meant about a Son of Gem, it could be anyone in the kingdom.

The country of Seagovia had not seen a true war in their land since King Frederic Peridot took the throne following the death of his childless uncle. King Frederic II married Princess Fleurina of Eridon and they had a son... *Merde*, she couldn't remember his name. Agatha tapped a sharp nail to her chin. Peridot was a gemstone. Could she be meant to join forces with the king? That had little to do with *bones*, though.

Perhaps the Grand Magus would direct her to join forces with a gravedigger. She chortled at her dark humour. It evaporated quickly when the Grimoire thrummed in her hands and Talan's unmistakable penmanship scrawled across the page, strokes tight and slanted. Agatha lurched forward, spilling water over the lip of the tub. Why would Talan have penned an Order for *her*? Autumn Orders had always been penned by Belfry.

AGATHA JOUBERT SHALL ENTER INTO MARRIAGE WITH THE CROWN PRINCE OF SEAGOVIA, HIS HIGHNESS, THACKERY FREDERIC PERIDOT III, BEFORE THE LEAVES HATH ALL FALLEN AND FROST KISSES THE CASTLE GARDEN.

AGATHA CHOKED and dropped the Grimoire in her bathwater. With a gasp, she snatched it out as quickly as she could, only to find it was not wet in the slightest. She threw it across the tiny room toward the bed and scrambled out of the bath, cursing the entire way to the looking glass and leaving puddles of water in her wake.

She touched her hand to the imperfect glass and spoke Sorscha's name. It was a dangerous game to play, but there was no way in the seven realms she was marrying *anyone* without a fight.

Agatha stilled. But could she fight it? Without the fear of punishment? From the beginning of their training, until the time came to take the mantle of a Sister Solstice, they'd each been warned. The result of defying an Order was a Sanction— retribution specifically tailored to inflict the most pain on the offender. They'd never spoken their Sanctions aloud to one another. Agatha wasn't certain her Sisters knew theirs, but hers had been made explicitly clear during her years of indoctrination.

Agatha's second eldest Sister appeared in the glass, holding a stemmed goblet of deep red wine and lounging next to a sleeping Rosemary. Agatha hardly contained the sob bubbling up within her chest. She couldn't defy her Order. Not without losing Sorscha. Agatha gave a quiet noise, but it took three tries before Sorscha looked up and saw her—for the second time in three days—naked and dripping wet.

Sorscha's eyes grew wide and she motioned frantically with her hand for Agatha to depart, pointing down at Rosemary. Agatha's firmly set jaw and silent demand won over. Gingerly, her Sister crept out of bed and took up the looking glass. She set Agatha down in her oversized kitchen, practically alive with vines and plants crawling about. Flowers of every colour imaginable shone in the candlelight, tangled in vines climbing up into the rafters of Sorscha's treehouse. Agatha couldn't wait to sit in her Sister's kitchen come Spring Equinox. The familiar sight calmed her until she remembered the death sentence she'd just been handed. She may never see her Sister's home again.

Sorscha situated her face near the looking glass and whispered harshly, "*What* are you doing, Aggie? Is this even permissible?"

Agatha didn't know. They'd never tried seeing each other this way before, but she was feeling both reckless and terrified. She didn't answer Sorscha. She simply pointed to the Grimoire with a trembling finger. "It says I am to marry the Crown Prince of Seagovia before the leaves have all fallen and the frost comes." It took no small amount of effort to keep the hot tears at the back of her eyes from spilling out.

Sorscha gasped. "*Marry?*"

Agatha nodded.

"The Crown Prince…"

Agatha nodded again.

Sorscha ran a hand through her wavy hair, so like Agatha's own except for its warm chestnut hues, where Agatha's was set ablaze in the light. "Aggie… I—I don't know what to say. You'll be a queen someday?" Her cheeks dimpled as she tried to make light of the situation, but fear lit her countenance as well.

"I don't want to be a queen," Agatha nearly shouted. "If any of us should be a goddess damned queen it's Winnie. She'd wet herself at the prospect!" Agatha shook her head violently. "*I can't do this,*" she whispered, voice cracking.

Sorscha leaned in closely again. "Aggie, don't speak like that." She looked over her shoulder. "You have no choice. The fate of Midlerea, or at the very least Seagovia, could depend on this. You know that. Hespa has commanded this, and I cannot—I *won't* see you Sanctioned for disobedience, Sister."

Agatha couldn't breathe. Sorscha was right. She had no choice. It was either a lifetime—or several—of marital servitude at the command of her goddess, or it was punishment at Her hand as well. No matter what she could manage to do, she would never win against an Order.

It wasn't right. It didn't *feel* right. Why had her Order changed from Belfry's hand to Talan's in such a peculiar way? Talan had only ever written Orders for Wendolyn. Why would Hespa command such a sacrifice from her? Was it punishment for her hatred of all the goddess had Ordered her to do through the Grimoire?

"Aggie," Sorscha's voice broke in. "You will outlive this prince many times over. Once he is dead you could remain Queen of *Seagovia*, the most powerful kingdom in Midlerea."

"For how long, until it becomes apparent that I haven't aged a day?"

Sorscha waved off her words. "Semantics."

She reached up to place her hand on the glass and Agatha did the same, Sorscha's sun-kissed and Agatha's moon-kissed.

"Perhaps this will afford you the freedom and control you've so desperately been searching for, in that title of Future Queen of Seagovia. Perhaps this is a *blessing* from Hespa. A reward for all the things you've done for Her."

A tear slid down Agatha's cheek and she swallowed. A forced marriage to a man she'd never met did not bode well with her as a *blessing*.

"I must go, Sister. I don't know if this is forbidden for us or not, and I can't alter Rosemary's memory any more than I already have or I fear I'll scramble her brain."

Despite herself, Agatha snorted. She didn't see why, after all this time, Sorscha didn't just tell Rosemary who she truly was. Rosemary knew Sorscha was a witch, but not a Sister Solstice. Agatha didn't see the difference. She'd already defied the laws of The Order by telling her anything at all.

"I'll send a raven on the morrow and every night hereafter, whether you wish me to stop, or not."

Swiping at her silent tears, Agatha nodded and wiped her hand across the mirror. It reflected her haggard face and naked body once more. She looked more like a cadaver than a witch in her prime.

"*Merde*," she swore, then went to dress.

Agatha spent the better part of the night shivering beneath the blankets and heating the room to a suffocating level with her magic. Not even the entire cask of hot apple cider the inn keeper had sent up could warm her. The tremors wracking her body refused to cease. She was fooling herself into believing it was just the nights growing colder and the window she'd left ajar for Mabon. Her silken nightgown simply wasn't enough protection against it. But Agatha knew better. The sourness in her stomach and boulder upon her chest were as familiar as her own hand.

She threw the covers off and took out a lavender and chamomile balm, rubbing a generous amount into the bare skin of her chest. Methodically, she drew in deep breaths and exhaled them slowly, calling upon the moon's peace and serenity. For good measure, she retrieved her velvet bag of crystals. With ritualistic precision, she unclasped the filigree locket of her necklace and removed the black tourmaline she'd used for travel protection and replaced it with blue calcite to relieve anxiety. No sooner had she closed the crystal's cage and rested it upon her skin did her burden begin to ease long enough for her to drift into sleep.

Even the purest magic could not ward off her nightmares for long. Agatha awoke with a start, flexing her hand against the haunting fingers of a child plagued with sickness, begging for help. A sickness Agatha had herself unleashed upon their village at the bidding of the Grimoire.

She stared at the ceiling, lying perfectly still. At some point, Mabon had made it into her room, for the window was fastened and he stirred beside her, sensing her unease. He never opened his eyes, but crawled atop her aching chest and curled up, head tucked under one leathery wing. Mabon weighed next to nothing, but the slight pressure eased the greater burden pressing in on her. He always knew when she needed him.

THE WIND TEASED Agatha's hair as she rode. Leaves coiled and danced in Autumn's breeze, and if she were not on her way to be shackled to a stranger, Agatha might have considered it a perfect morning. She looked up at the sun and determined time was drifting into the afternoon. It wouldn't be long before Guinevere trotted them right through the gates of Seagovia's capital city of Merveille.

As the road stretched wider and the air grew thick with city smog and sea salt, Agatha fine-tuned her plan to best locate the Grand Magus without drawing a great deal of attention to herself. The spires of Merveille's cathedral could be seen from outside the city gates—it would not be difficult to find—but the Grand Magus was known for rarely being within its Hallowed walls. She'd have better success finding him in the castle, as he dealt heavily with the affairs of the royal family. He was even rumoured to have his own wing in the palace.

Agatha had not been into the heart of the kingdom in several decades. It was a place filled with nothing but misery for her. The last time she'd set foot within the gates of Merveille was to see the lifeless corpse of a king being buried in the soil. He died of old age and natural causes, but Agatha would not have raised qualms with being the hand to deal that particular man's killing blow.

She'd stood hidden in the lush Summer trees, watching. Once she had seen him lowered into the dirt, Agatha had paid another grave—an unmarked one—a visit before turning her back on the city. That night, she'd left by ship and had spent the better part of a decade away from her cottage—away from everything. She emerged only to answer her Orders. To sow derision between peaceful nations; rain fire on villages; steal coin and precious gems from entire cities; reveal secrets of powerful men to their enemies... Agatha did her duty and returned to solace upon the Isle of Ballast off the coast of Seagovia.

She pulled Guinevere to a stop as the tip of the city gate rose above a hill. Agatha closed her eyes, willing away the screams she could still hear at the back of her skull. The blood she could still see, streaming from flesh ripped down to the bone. She'd not been on this road since. Not in a hundred years. The one time she'd returned, she'd spirited herself right into the city. But it was time she faced these demons and this road head first—head *high*—to the gate.

"There is nothing on this road that can do you harm, Aggie," she whispered to herself. "Not anymore. Nothing is coming for you."

The truth of it settled into her bones and her spine straightened. She kicked Guinevere's sides gently, and the horse walked on. Agatha did not want to rush this. She needed to face each painful step forward, setting her face like flint and refusing to look to either side of the road. To the tree she knew was ahead, with a dead man's bones feeding it life. To the bird etched in the tree's trunk. To the foul phantom voices screaming at her from all around. To the ghost of horror replaying that fateful day behind her eyes.

When she reached that tree off in the distance, the wind kicked up furiously. It swirled around her, lifting her hair on end. Leaves spun wildly and the tree bent its branches to her in a crimson and russet bow.

A smile crept across Agatha's face. She could do this.

As she drew nearer to the gate, a steadiness settled over her as it did when she was answering an Order from the Grimoire. *Your blessing from the Goddess*, Winnie called it. *Your killing calm*, Sorscha called it. *Your iron will*, Seleste called it. Agatha called it her armour.

She'd never met this Grand Magus, but her studies over the years had often mentioned Grand Magus Gerome von Fuchs as a learned man, often in the castle library for ages at a time. It was as good a place to start as any, and Agatha would never begrudge her soul the good fortune of seeing the royal Stacks again. She would most likely have to charm a guard or two to gain entry from outside, but it was nothing she hadn't done countless times before.

The stone castle loomed beyond the gate and memories crashed into her. They were easier to bear with her armour set firmly in place, but no less menacing. Guinevere carried them through, and Mabon squeaked reassuringly. The dirt turned to cobblestones and the city sounds became intoxicating as if the entirety of Merveille were within a wall of magic that kept the din at bay until one passed through the gate. Hooves clomped on the stones, merchants shouted their wares, ladies gossiped in packs, children ran—filthy and laughing. The salt in the air tugged Agatha's heartstrings, and she vowed to stand on the edge of Mer Noir before sunset on her first day in the heart of the kingdom.

"Well, Mabon, it's now or never. And I don't believe 'never' is an option for us, old boy."

Mabon tittered and Agatha urged Guinevere toward the mammoth library on the Ouest side of the castle. The castle itself was so aged that its stones bore the pallor of a cadaver holding up spires hewn by the hands of Lady Death or Lord Night. It was breathtaking. The library butted up against the chapel, its ancient bells tolling the hour ominously and reverberating through Agatha's bones.

She dismounted and tied Guinevere to the post, glad hers was the only horse present. Mabon squawked and squealed relentlessly in his cage. "I'm not letting you out to fly right now," she muttered.

Mabon hung upside down from the top of his cage, a bit of moss brushing against his head, and pointed to the library with a wing.

"You cannot mean to go in there with me. A bat in a library will be frowned upon."

Mabon frowned at *her*.

"Can you be discreet?"

He gave her a withering stare. With a great heaving sigh, she unclasped his cage, and he flew ahead of her.

Just as Agatha reached the first stone step, a lean, stately man came through the gargantuan wooden doors of the library, clad in the golden robes of The Order of Hespa. He nodded to the guards posted on either side. Agatha's skirts slipped out of her hand, tangling in her boots, and she tripped, landing hard with one knee against the sharp stones. Mabon flew back to rest on her shoulder, and she stood to compose herself, hoping against all hope that the Grand Magus had not seen her buffoonery.

When she lifted her head, her stomach dropped to her toes. The Grand Magus had not only seen her, but he was also standing stock-still in the middle of the steps, mouth agape, staring directly at her.

There was simply nothing to do about her unfortunate entry and she'd forgotten every ounce of her prepared introduction, but it mattered not. The only trajectory was forward. She smoothed her skirts and climbed the steps toward the horrified magus.

She dipped into a curtsy. "Grand Magus—"

"It's you," he breathed, a finger pointed toward Agatha's chest and awe upon his face. His eyes darted from hers to her dress, to Mabon, and then up to her hair.

Agatha opened her mouth to say…she didn't know what, but the magus went on.

"She shall come," he recited, "shrouded in black, but not of mourning…" With a continued look of astonishment, he reached out and pointed to her black skirts before looking at her face. "With eyes of the honey moon."

His disbelieving gaze remained fixed, and it was a struggle not to let her own eyes go wide.

"And Autumn in her locks," he continued, watching Mabon use his teeth to withdraw a tiny ruby leaf from where it was unknowingly tangled in her hair. "She will come, escorted by a creature of the night." They both looked at Mabon upon her shoulder. "And a raven shall descend upon her."

The words had hardly left his lips when Sorscha's raven swooped down from the clouds and landed on Agatha's shoulder opposite Mabon. She kept her expression as even as her three hundred years of witch madness had taught her and met the magus' inspecting, flabbergasted stare once more.

"She will come," he whispered. "Our Daughter of Autumn. *Agatha of Helsvar.*"

Agatha bit the inside of her cheek to keep from baulking.

G*oddess-blessed above everyone. Her chosen instrument of sanctification. The magi.*
-Sacred Texts of Hespa

MAGUS VON FUCHS regained his composure long enough to lead Agatha to his study within the castle. Her mind swirled as they walked down the long corridors, the heels of her boots clicking on stone and Mabon hiding in her hair. Every echo of her footsteps sounded more and more like an ominous funeral dirge.

No one knew of the Sisters' existence. Not anymore. They'd been reduced to folklore after the Witch Trials. Helsvar, the Burned City, was no more. Hespa's Hallowed believed witches to be amongst the evil Hollow. There was no reason Magus von Fuchs, Grand Magus or not, should know who Agatha was or that she hailed from a city burnt to ash three hundred years ago. The magi might serve The Order, and in their own way Hespa, but they believed they'd eradicated witchcraft over a hundred years ago. If the magus, or the royal family, knew Agatha was a witch, this Order from the Grimoire could be the worst of her existence. Or the end of it.

She stole a glance at the Grand Magus as they walked, taking in the golden robes of The Order's ranks. His black mantle was embroidered with a nightingale carrying a nightshade blossom, a crescent moon tucked behind the bird—the official emblem of the Grand Magus. His silence was nearly as foreboding as the sharp angles of his face and the plethora of unknowns she was walking into.

One thing was for certain. Agatha needed to decipher how much this magus knew, and how he knew it.

Finally, they reached a door flanked by two of the king's guardsmen. The men dipped their chins at the magus, offering a solemn, "Good Evening, Grand Magus" in unison. They eyed Agatha with curiosity—most likely due to her dishevelled state and the bat upon her shoulder—but they straightened without a word to her.

Magus von Fuchs led Agatha inside before turning to one of the guards that had trailed them into the castle. "To the king," he snapped, tossing a hand toward the open doorway and huffing through his nose.

The guard started, shifting on the balls of his feet, opening and closing his mouth like a fish. "To say what, Grand Magus?"

The magus' lips pursed as he blinked at the young man before turning to Agatha. "If you'll excuse me for a moment."

They moved toward the corridor together, the magus' sharp whispers drifting in through the open door from the hall as he berated the guard for his insolence. Agatha hovered near a chair, unsure if she should sit, and focused all her efforts on willing her hands to stop shaking. Mabon licked her cheek, sensing her unease.

When he returned, the magus straightened his mantle and sat behind the imposing cherry wood desk. He gestured for Agatha to sit and she did, momentarily horrified by her reflection staring back at her from the wood's immaculately polished surface.

Magus von Fuchs rested his forearms on the desk, curling his fingers, intertwined at the tips and resembling a ribcage. Without a word, he studied her, the candlelight casting his worn face in an eerie glow.

Agatha wriggled her toes within her boots, refusing to outwardly fidget before this man's inspection. For, she reminded herself, that's just what he was—a mortal man like any other. She was a powerful witch, and one not easily trifled with.

A servant barged in, drawing them from their heavy silence. He moved about with downcast eyes, and when he mumbled his fourth unnecessary apology within moments of entering, Agatha couldn't help the sickening feeling that unfurled in her stomach. The tea set trembled in his hands as he poured, offering the magus and then Agatha a cup.

"Thank you," she said, wrapping her hands around the warm teacup. The servant was so startled by her words of gratitude that he snapped his eyes to her face, then quickly lowered them and hurried away.

Agatha was still looking curiously after him as the door shut, when the magus spoke. "I must admit, we've waited so long for Our Daughter of Autumn, that I did not expect you to come in my lifetime."

Did that mean he knew she was a witch? Surely they would not be sitting in his study civilly, if so.

She chose her next words with great care. "Sometimes fate can surprise us."

He glanced distastefully at Mabon. "Indeed, it can." The magus leaned back, his chair groaning. "Is not Helsvar destroyed?" Agatha's heart beat hard against her ribs. "The Burned City, it's called, yes? I've often pondered how Our Daughter of Autumn could hail from a place that no longer exists." He eyed her carefully, his shrewd gaze looking down his nose at her.

Agatha fought the urge to squirm. She would not cower under this or any other man's scrutiny. "Yes. Helsvar burned nearly three hundred years ago, yet it has been rebuilt slowly." It was not a lie. Not a full one, anyway.

He levelled her with another stare, then sniffed and went on. "I trust you have been prepared for this?"

Agatha nodded once. "I've been trained for my entire life." Another half-truth. He tapped his fingertips on the thick desktop unnervingly. She straightened. "I know what I am to do, Grand Magus."

His eyes narrowed, ever so slightly. "And that is?"

The air around her stilled, and Agatha could feel her magic swimming through the room, pulsating with every anxious beat of her heart. Her magic had a way of sneaking out to eliminate a potential threat. The magus didn't appear to be aware, but the teapot began to steam, and their cups rattled on the desk.

Just as his eyes left hers to question the oddities, Agatha blurted, "I am to marry the Crown Prince of Seagovia. His Royal Highness Thackery Frederic Peridot the Third." Her magic calmed and she wanted to sag in relief. Alas, she lifted her chin high and kept her back straight. "Before the leaves have all fallen," she added for good measure.

Magus von Fuchs sat as still as a corpse. "Indeed." He made no move to smooth the crease between his brows that had appeared the moment his astonishment with her fled. "And the leaves have already begun to fall in droves."

They drifted into probing silence once more. Agatha was unwilling to offer information or ask anything that revealed how little information she truly had. Regardless of her trepidation, regardless of her unwillingness to marry, she could not leave that study without one question answered: Did the magus know she was a witch?

Mabon tugged at her hair as if to encourage her. Agatha's lips parted to speak, but the magus stood abruptly and lifted a hand toward the door. "Shall we?"

Agatha regarded him quizzically.

"Go and meet with the royal family, but of course."

"*Oh.*" She stood too fast and nearly toppled her chair. She had not expected to meet with them directly upon her arrival. "But my horse, she's outside the library, Grand Magus. And my belongings. I—I'd greatly appreciate a chance at a bath before I meet His Highness—" Perhaps a nerve-calming elixir, as well.

"Nonsense. They deserve to see Our Daughter of Autumn exactly as she entered the city. As the prophecy depicts."

Which was covered in grime and with sleep-deprived eyes, evidently.

Agatha trailed after him, hoping Mabon would behave and that the royal family wasn't squeamish of bats. She stumbled when the magus' words finally hit her frazzled mind. A *prophecy?* That explained how the magus knew information about her, and it explained his mistrust. Anyone aware of a prophecy could attempt to cause it to happen, at least by show.

What troubled her was how anyone could glean what the Grimoire knew before it was ever penned. That was a different beast altogether. No Order from the Grimoire—prophecy or otherwise—had been recorded outside the Book, and nothing within the Grimoire had ever been seen before the appointed time at which it appeared to the Solstice Sister Ordered to execute it.

Agatha was so distracted that she collided with the magus as he halted in front of a large set of wooden doors. He stiffened but said nothing. He must have sent the earlier guard to prepare the king and queen, as well as their son, for Agatha, because raised voices could be heard shouting at one another. She swallowed. Her future husband—and not so distant future, at that—stood behind those doors.

When the guards opened them, silence descended and the magus led Agatha into a large, open room of marble and stone, with windows overlooking Mer Noir. Magus von Fuchs curtly demanded that all servants and guards leave them. The heavy doors closed with an ominous *clunk* that reverberated through the cold room. Agatha tore her eyes from the black waves calling to her through the window, to set them upon the four people standing in the middle of a large dais.

The woman, every inch as regal as the jewels upon her neck, regarded Agatha with awe and wonder. The older man with greying hair at his temples—most assuredly the king by his dress and stature—regarded her with suspicion, very near the magus', but it had an edge of optimism. The other gentleman of around three decades, utterly breathtaking with his sepia skin and green eyes, had no expression whatsoever. Intriguing. But the last man, around the same age, was dishevelled—as if he'd been in the same expensive clothes for days. He regarded her with hatred. Ire at the very, very least.

That must be the one she was doomed to marry, then.

The Grand Magus bowed deeply and Agatha followed suit. "Your Majesties, Your Highness, My Lord." He inclined his head to each of them in turn. "I present to you Our Daughter of Autumn. *Agatha*, of Helsvar."

He gestured to her grandly and Agatha curtsied again, her stomach twisted in knots. When she rose, she looked anywhere but at the prince's face. The queen had her hands clasped in front of her chest with glee alight on her beautiful features. The king and the unknown lord simply stared.

Prince Thackery broke the silence first. "You cannot *possibly* be serious about all of this." His hand was splayed out toward Agatha, but his incredulous gaze remained firmly placed on those upon the dais with him. He was not an ugly creature by any means, tall with tawny skin, dark features, and a strong jaw. He hadn't seen a shave in several days by the looks of him, and the waves of his midnight hair were as chaotic as his wrinkled shirt and waistcoat. The fury twisting his face, though, darkening his cinnamon eyes, was rendering his countenance irksome.

Wedding this prince would be a cumbersome task.

"Grimm, please," the queen addressed her son with a peculiar pet name. "You know the prophecy as well as any of us."

He took a step toward his mother, hand bunching up into an accusatory gesture still pointed in Agatha's direction. She had to fight back a snarl, her nerves swiftly replaced with repulsion and enmity, but she too stepped forward, anxious to hear anything more about the prophecy.

"I cannot marry that *peasant!*" He spat the last word and it took every bit of Agatha's self-control to not recoil or throw her dagger at his princeling neck. "She has a *bat* upon her shoulder for Goddess' sake."

Entitled little prick.

Mabon squawked in a similar response and flew up to the rafters.

Queen Fleurina gave Agatha a half-hearted apologetic smile and turned to her son, speaking quietly. But Agatha's witch senses were sharp. "She is the key, Grimm. Her, a *peasant*, marrying into the royal family will mollify the people. Quiet their unrest. Now their beloved crown prince will know their plights firsthand."

Relief shot through Agatha so swiftly she thought her knees might buckle. Our Daughter of Autumn, Agatha the *peasant*, not Agatha the *witch*.

Prince Thackery watched his mother carefully. "That is how it will *seem*, isn't it?"

Agatha's brows drew together. She hadn't known there was still unrest with the people of Merveille—the people of Seagovia. Perhaps she should not have spent a hundred years as a recluse.

The prince turned to look in her direction and Agatha met his vehemence with a clenched jaw and raised chin. It suddenly struck her that there was something rather familiar about him. She swore recognition flashed across his face as well, but the king shouted, drawing their attention away.

"*Enough!*" he boomed, and all eyes shot to him. "You will marry this Daughter of Autumn before the leaves have all fallen. The prophecy depicts a peasant joined with a prince." The prince opened his mouth, but the king silenced him. "And that is the *end of the discussion.*" As if he'd never spoken at all, the ruler of Seagovia went still, blankness inching across his face until it read boredom.

The Grand Magus preened, and Agatha had to smooth her features before she baulked in disgust at him. He turned toward the door and clapped three times, the sound cracking off the walls. A guard opened the doors and in filed maidservants to hide in the shadows at the back of the room. "A welcome dinner will be prepared for Lady Agatha at sundown."

Wonderful. Now she would miss seeing Mer Noir and be forced to converse dully on top of everything else.

The maidservants curtsied and the queen left the dais to instruct them elaborately about the evening's new agenda.

Magus von Fuchs turned to the prince and spoke under his breath, "I will leave you with your betrothed to get to know one another." He and the king turned on their heels and strode to the door, the magus' golden robes brushing the Seagovian ruler's sapphire mantle as they trailed in their wake.

Near the door, the magus turned back, attention landing on the unnamed lord and prince, both men stiff, their eyes locked on one another in some silent exchange.

"Lord Gaius," the magus snapped. The lord shot one last look in the prince's direction and quickly followed the magus, close at his heels.

The gargantuan doors closed with an ominous clank and Prince Thackery stalked toward her, stopping only a stride away.

"How *dare* you stand there and deign to say *nothing*?" he ground out.

Her nerves bent a knee to her fury at his unexpected outburst. Agatha let a spiteful smile adorn her lips. "And what would you have me do, then? Throw myself at your feet and argue that I *am* worthy to be your bride?"

Surprise flashed across the prince's face at her gall, but he swiftly shoved it away.

She swung an arm out wide. "Or would you have me faint upon the chaise because of my utter *fortune* to be your betrothed?" She took a step closer to him. "Because I will do neither of those things."

His lip curled. "A bit bold for a peasant, aren't we?"

Agatha cursed her cheeks for heating. Perhaps she was a fool not to play the part of a meek little mouse, but she couldn't stop the storm of rage bubbling up inside of her. "I do not wish to marry you any more than you wish to marry me."

A muscle in the prince's jaw flexed. "Then help me fight this madness! Deny the proposal that has been asked without my will."

Agatha snickered. "And risk the loss of my head at the hands of our darling Crown?" She crossed her arms at her chest, matching the prince's stance. "I think not."

He let out an exasperated breath. "I will ensure that does not happen."

Agatha scoffed. "With what power? You wield *none*."

"You forget yourself, peasant," he warned.

"No. You forget *yourself*, prince."

Prince Thackery set his jaw, presumably to quell his rising temper. "They are my mother and father."

Agatha inched toward him, letting her hands drop to her sides and form fists. "*Wrong*. They are *King* and *Queen*. Their duty is to their people, not to you. You heard your mummy. I'm to be the one that ensures the people know their plights are *understood* and their burdens shared."

He did not miss the derisiveness of her words, his smile turning serpentine in response. "You won't fight this because you stand to gain so very much from a union with me. Isn't it every farm girl's dream to fall in love and marry a prince?"

Something about the way his mouth moved with the words made her realise exactly where she knew him from. "Oh, dear boy," Agatha cooed. "Tell me you are not foolish enough to believe a prince could ever marry for love? Or is that why you frequent taverns in Rochbury, hidden beneath your hood and bowling over women you have no intention of properly apologising to?"

The prince snarled. "You know *nothing* of me. Love is not my aim."

Agatha stood to her full height and the room began to heat with her fury. "*Good.* Neither is it mine." She pasted a patronising grin on her face and smoothed her skirts still edged with soot and dirt from her travels. "Now, if you'll excuse me, I have quite the dinner gathering to prepare myself for."

When Agatha exited the room, her hands shaking, two maidservants squealed, nearly falling into the room for eavesdropping at the door. Privacy was going to be difficult to come by at court. They adjusted their aprons with wide eyes and promptly led Agatha to her new quarters.

THE TWO YOUNG women had Agatha stripped naked and in a beautiful copper tub before either one spoke a word. There were fresh roses and lilies on every polished surface and the overpowering fragrance was tickling Agatha's nose. When the stone-faced servant left the lavatory to retrieve a fresh towel, the other leaned in.

"I'm Anne. That's Eleanor," she whispered, gently massaging lavender soap into Agatha's filthy hair. "She's a bit...harsh with outsiders."

Agatha nodded mutely, staring at the brown streaks of bubbles sliding from her hair down her shoulders and chest, as well as the small cut on her knee from her graceful arrival.

Anne smiled sweetly at her, the candlelight reflecting off the tub and dancing on the maid's cheeks in fragmented bits of sunshine. "I, for one, am ecstatic for you and Prince Grimm." Agatha had to fight a snort. That did, indeed, make *one*. "How did the two of you meet, my lady?"

It struck her as an odd thing to ask. Apparently, she had not heard the words within the throne room despite her eavesdropping. Wasn't it common for royalty and aristocrats to have arranged marriages with those they'd never met? Agatha avoided the question. "Oh, Anne, I'm no lady. Agatha will do."

Anne's hands froze, a pitcher of steaming water halfway to Agatha's hair. She grimaced and attempted a nervous laugh, but it came out more hysterical than anything. "My lady, I—"

Agatha turned her shoulders to face Anne, the water rippling. "What is it? Surely no one will punish you for calling me by my name if I've directed you to do so." Anne blanched, and Agatha worried that was exactly what would happen. She shifted, encouraging Anne to meet her eyes. "Will they?"

"It is not worth finding out, *my lady*," Eleanor hissed from the doorway. "Stop your prattling, Anne. We haven't much time before the dinner." Her eyes raked over Agatha. "And *Lady Agatha* has a long way to go to be deemed presentable."

Agatha wanted to slap the snide look right off Eleanor's lovely face. Winnie appeared in her mind's eye. "*Think, Aggie. What are her emotions telling you? Every person tells a story. What is hers?*" Blast her sister for *sometimes* being right.

Agatha watched the two servants bicker under their breath over which dress to tie her up in. Eleanor dealt annoyed expressions as often as Anne dealt delighted ones, but they still managed to ready Agatha just in time. A knock sounded at the door and Eleanor went to retrieve her escort.

Anne spun her without warning to face her reflection in a tall looking glass. Agatha frowned. The gown was atrocious. Never, in all her days, had she worn *salmon*. It did not suit her skin tone, let alone her taste. She looked like an over-baked cupcake spilling out of its tin, dripping too much frosting. Anne tied a ribbon in Agatha's auburn hair like a toddling babe and she considered stabbing both her maidservants out of spite.

"His Highness will be glee-ridden when he sees you," Anne whispered proudly in her ear.

Agatha gave her a tight smile. As soon as Anne turned her back, she summoned her knife and thigh holster to her leg. She'd quickly hidden it with a glamour during the servants' demand she undress. As soon as she felt the familiar weight of the dagger against her skin, she relaxed enough to step forward toward the door.

When she reached the sitting area, her mood dipped even lower. The prince rose and bowed to her as she forced a curtsy. An easy smile, completely at odds with his earlier display, slid across his face.

"Dearest Agatha," he crooned before turning to her maids. "You've done a splendid job of readying her, mademoiselles."

Both servants curtsied. Anne offered a, "Thank you, Prince Grimm," while Eleanor mumbled something about her regrets that they hadn't chosen the taupe gown instead. Agatha was inclined to agree. It wasn't exactly what she would've selected for herself, but it at least had more style than the crime against humanity she currently wore.

The prince offered Agatha his arm and she reluctantly stepped forward to take it, fighting back the urge to roll her eyes as Anne squealed about how precious they were together. *Poor, blind little fool.* If Eleanor's pursed lips were any indication, she was thinking the same thing about sweet Anne.

Agatha forced a coy smile. "I did not expect you to escort me yourself, Your Highness."

"Now, now, darling, you may dispense with proper titles around Eleanor and Anne. They call me Prince Grimm themselves." He smirked and patted her arm, but she did not miss the flex of his jaw or the warning in his eye.

She'd thought he was being facetious at first, but it was a ruse he was playing at. One of familiarity that he wanted her to keep up—at least in front of her maids. Why couldn't this simply be an arranged marriage like any other? Agatha forced her bewilderment from showing on her face. This court was a twisted web.

Heels clicking on the marble floor, they made their way toward the boisterous noise of a full ballroom where they were halted at the entry to be properly announced. When they heard their names shouted by a herald and the crowd's collective gasp, the prince pasted a smile on his face and spoke through gritted teeth, "Look alive, peasant."

The room was stifling hot and stuffed with bodies. They were all dressed as dreadfully as herself, and Agatha thought perhaps Eleanor's comment about a taupe gown had been a slight. Every face of aristocracy in the room was either confused or angry at the sight of her on the prince's arm, the gaudy ladies all tied up in corsets like wasps poised to sting. Agatha could feel their eyes on her, judging. Word had spread quickly about her arrival, indeed.

Out of the corner of her eye, she caught the hint of a cautious smile on a servant's lips. Then another. She found herself scanning the room for those clothed in the black and brown garb of the serving class. An older woman with sparkling eyes and a tuft of white hair set down a pitcher of wine and placed a hand on her chest, bowing deeply. A young man with rough hands and a gloomy countenance saw her and his face broke into a dazzling smile, the flutes on his tray swaying as he bowed.

Agatha swallowed the lump in her throat. Perhaps the queen had been correct about her purpose within the court. Their hope was nearly palpable. A hope she needed to learn more about. Her heart constricted further with each glint in their eyes. Part of her Order or not, Agatha would see these men and women heard.

The prince led her past the gawking people and up onto a raised platform where there was a table loaded with food. Despite her best efforts, her stomach rumbled. No sooner had they rounded the table to their designated seats did the king and queen rise, and everyone else followed them.

"Our guests of great honour!" the king boomed. The crowd broke into applause, but it was the fervent clapping of the servants that Agatha noted most of all. After a brief display of kingly pride, they were instructed to sit. Eat. Enjoy. Sit and eat, Agatha did. The prince sulked, drowning himself in goblet after goblet of wine. If she were being honest, Agatha would have liked to do the same.

It wasn't long before the magus' lithe form stood behind them. He rested a tender hand on the prince's shoulder, but Grimm's face contorted before he shoved the obvious disgust away.

With a smile on his thin lips, the magus bent between them, his grey beard grazing Agatha's shoulder. He spoke in the prince's ear, "They are all watching you, Prince Grimm. No one would see love in the ice chilling between the two of you at present. *Converse*, at the very least."

The prince let out a breath as the Grand Magus strode back to his place at the table. "I suppose he has a point." He turned in his seat to Agatha, his demeanor awkward for the first time since she'd met him that afternoon. "Let us *converse* then."

"The people do not know of the prophecy," she blurted. "They think I'm truly your betrothed."

"You are," he said with a grimace. "I was thinking more along the lines of discussing the weather." He gestured to her dress. "Or the horrifying turn your fashion has taken since this afternoon. Which is saying something."

Agatha took another pull of her wine. Goddess knew she needed it. "I would rather face the wrath of that invasive magus than discuss the *weather* or abominable gowns with you, prince."

"Fine." He leaned in close, resting an arm around the back of her chair. "We can certainly discuss how best to dispense with this predicament we've found ourselves in."

She faced him, close enough for their breath to mingle, and squared her shoulders. To his credit—and most likely the great satisfaction of the magus—he did not move away. "I thought I made it quite clear that I will not defy my orders."

"Orders?" One side of his mouth dragged upward, revealing a slight dimple in his cheek, and Agatha cursed herself for the slip.

"What else would you call my being forced by your king and magus to wed you?"

The prince's eyes narrowed. "What if I were to defy these orders *for* you?"

Agatha scoffed. "Unlikely. You will never stop this marriage. You don't have it in you."

He backed up at that. "You've known me all of a handful of hours and you're so certain?"

"Yes."

The prince searched her face, mirth in his eyes. "Do tell," he prompted.

"You're too rash. You say exactly what you're thinking."

"It would seem you say exactly what you're thinking as well," he challenged.

"You reveal your hand at every turn with your emotional outbursts."

"And if that is exactly my aim?"

She hadn't expected that. Nor did she know what his aim *was*, but that was precisely why she was goading him. "Then you're a fool. The more childish you act and the more you fight this trajectory, the more they will have you watched. You will have no secrets with eyes on you at all times."

"Mm." He leaned back in his chair, taking up a nearly empty goblet and swollowed the dregs. "Right you are, peasant. Perhaps I should rethink my strategy." But he was smiling.

Agatha hadn't time to probe further, for a lord approached and requested permission of His Highness to dance with his betrothed. He granted it with no small amount of amusement.

The dance floor was crowded. And hot. And Lord Urek smelled of sweat and beef. Agatha thought the music would never cease as they spun and she stepped upon the lord's toes. She hadn't danced in ages. Quite literally. When the song's last note rang out and the crowd drew closer together, Agatha slunk toward the door. She snatched a goblet of wine and drank deeply as she slipped out into the castle halls.

As soon as the sea spray hit her face, Agatha exhaled the last few days, letting the moon and the black waves wash them out to sea. The seas were Seleste's domain as much as the Autumn trees were Agatha's, but the water's fluidity had always enamoured her. The way it could ebb and flow; hold unimaginable secrets; its divine connection to Madam Moon; its power through movement. All things Agatha distinctly did not have. Winnie might be the Sister as immovable as a mountain, her powers imbued with their grandeur, but it was Agatha who was forever stuck.

She took a moment to marvel at the slice of rocky, black sand beach set aside for the royal family and their guests. When the castle had been constructed thousands of years prior with Mer Noir as her guardian to the Est, a bit of architectural genius went into ensuring the sea's success at such a grievous task. The reef was too high for a ship's approach, but the waters were deep enough to sail small boats—if an army so dared.

The first King of Seagovia had goliath structures carefully crafted by blacksmiths of the highest order. They laid atop the reef below the water, spanning the full distance of the beach, and fused with vertical structures of the same kind that jutted out into the sky. A net of chainmail, each link as thick as a man's arm, was woven together and fused to the structure. Only tiny fish and the sea herself could make it through that net. Though, to be safe, on the small island just inside the steel net, sat the tallest lighthouse on the continent of Midlerea.

Agatha let her gaze drift upward to the tip of the lighthouse shooting into the stars. The torches remained lit at night, but the post had been abandoned for centuries. No army or pirate had attempted to attack Castle Merveille in nearly eight hundred years.

Agatha felt more than heard a presence behind her. She could sense the sand shifting and the weight of a body upon the earth. Three bodies. Two held back, but one came nearer. *Curious.* She kept her eyes on the darkened sea as a man stopped next to her, a polite distance away.

"Lady Agatha."

She turned and the man inclined his head toward her. Agatha had not the energy to feign surprise or do anything but give a half-hearted curtsy. "Your Highness." When she stood upright, she faced him fully, her sore feet sending a whisper of sand out to sea. "*Agatha* will do."

The lord chuckled. "I'm not one to dispense with titles so quickly, but I take it you aren't one for them at all." He smiled kindly. "You may call me Gaius, if you wish. Except in front of the magus." He twisted his face in a humorously vile expression. "That would be ill-advised."

Agatha nodded once and turned back to the waves lapping at the shore. The tide was coming in and she wished to stand in that spot until it lapped at her toes. Preferably alone.

Alas, Lord Gaius spoke again, taking another step toward her. "You did not enjoy the festivities thrown in your honour tonight?"

Agatha did not look at him. *Her honour* was a rather liberal way to phrase it. "You are correct. I'm not one for titles. I'm also not one for festivities or flocks of people."

They stood in silence a moment more before Lord Gaius moved even closer. Agatha tensed but did not let it show. It would take nothing to disembowel this lord or topple his head from his shoulders. It would be another matter entirely to explain a senseless murder to Winnie.

"You have no guards?" he questioned.

Surprisingly, Agatha did not detect any form of threat in his voice, only curiosity—if not concern. Perhaps this lord would keep his viscera and head firmly in place. For the time being.

"I do," she answered softly. "Two of them. They are not in uniform, and they believe I don't know they exist." They'd trailed her through the halls to where she'd discarded her goblet and heeled shoes, then out into the sand.

She turned to face Lord Gaius again to find his brows were knit together and his hands were clasped behind his back. His shock amused Agatha, so she went on. "One is pretending to be a bored guest of the festivities, skipping rocks to our Est. The other is inching toward one of your guards. Presumably to have a nice little chat about what we might be discussing."

Lord Gaius feigned pointing out a constellation to her in the

Est, his gaze sliding over Agatha's first guard. He let a beat of silence pass before glancing over his shoulder to find Agatha had been correct about the second as well. "My, my, but you are astute."

Agatha hid her satisfaction, instead only lifting one shoulder briefly. *Never reveal your keen witch abilities,* Winnie would chastise. *Bewitch one and all,* Sorscha would say, sending her a wry smile. *Be more careful, sly girl,* Seleste would warn her. But Agatha was still feeling the minute effects of the wine and more than a little antsy to let some of her power *out* before she killed a mouthy prince she didn't want to marry.

Lord Gaius closed most of the remaining distance between them. "Might I speak frankly with you, Lady Agatha?"

"Please do. I've had quite enough of veiled conversations for one evening."

He chuckled. "I can understand the sentiment." His smile faded as he continued. "You do not wish to marry Grimm—His Highness."

Agatha regarded him curiously. "You do not wish to conceal your familiarity with him."

The lord shrugged. "It is common enough knowledge."

Agatha gave a shallow sound of acknowledgment. "Well, *Gaius*, does anyone wish to marry someone they do not know?"

"That's it then? That you do not know him? That can be rectified."

She thought hard about what to say to this lord with so many questions. "Not entirely. But it is all I will say on the matter," she finally answered.

Gaius grew stiff. He spoke in a low voice, eyes darting back toward their guards. "I do not wish for this union, either, for my own reasons."

Agatha saw the challenge in the set of his jaw. But it was the fear in his eyes that he made no move to conceal which gave her pause.

She desperately wanted to hide away in her rooms and request that Anne bring her dozens of tomes and society papers so she could better understand the madness she was entangled in. Her mind spun through what little information she had. There was unrest in the city, possibly the country, *again.* It had remained quiet enough for her and her Sisters to not hear of it. That only meant an outcry was imminent.

The queen thought her, a supposed peasant in their court, to be enough to mollify them. No matter what the issue, there was absolutely no way that would be enough. Prophecy or not. But the servants had hope in their eyes, and the prince was playing some twisted game she hadn't yet untangled. Magus von Fuchs' prophecy held far more information than Belfry's Order— Talan's, she supposed—in the Grimoire.

But was Lord Gaius for the crown or the people? What was he risking by revealing this sentiment to her? It was too much to consider while he stood there looking at her.

There was one thing Agatha was certain of. She could do nothing without her head upon her shoulders.

"I will not defy a royal decree, Lord Gaius."

His face fell, further than she'd anticipated. He nodded tersely and turned back toward the castle. Part of her wanted this lord to succeed in his wishes, whatever that might mean for her Orders.

"Gaius?" He looked over his shoulder, one eyebrow raised. "Why do they want me to think I'm unguarded?"

His mouth twisted in thought. "I suppose they want to see how truly dutiful you are."

Agatha straightened. "I will not run. You have my word, and you may give it to them. But I cannot promise to be *kind* to your prince."

To her utter shock, Lord Gaius' face broke into a wide grin, rendering him alarmingly attractive. "He should only think you quite boring if you were." With that, he strode back to the castle.

Agatha remained firmly in place until the tide soaked her toes. The water's kiss settled her bones and she faced the great stone fortress—her future family's home. A pang of hope shot through her as she replayed the conversation with Lord Gaius in her mind. She entertained it for the briefest of moments before her palms began to feel damp and she reached up to clutch her amulet of crystals. Hope was not a friend to Agatha. She could not risk falling for its lies.

"Come along, gentlemen," she called out, startling both of her not-so-hidden guards to the point of blushing in the dark.

S *earch the depths, know Her will. In the scrying flames all will be revealed.*
        -Sacred Texts of Hespa

HER BACK ACHED from crouching in the tomb of gowns for so long. Still, Agatha attempted scrying again. Stuffed in a closet amidst all her horrid dresses wasn't the ideal place for divination, but she couldn't exactly reveal that she was a witch in a land where magic was only fabled to still exist. She needed a clearer answer. At least a *different* answer. The one the candle continued to give her couldn't be correct.

Agatha called forth fire to the wick *again*. It burned tall and strong, a vivid orange in the dark closet. She closed her eyes in focus, letting the thick magic hovering in the air envelope her in its embrace. Directing every iota of her power toward the flame, she willed it to show her *something* about the predicament she was in. A crystal-clear answer.

The Grimoire had lain cold and unchanging for four days. Eleanor and Anne had shoved Agatha into countless dresses, and she'd paraded about court on Prince Thackery's arm without a moment to speak with the people or even Magus von Fuchs alone. She'd considered seeking Sorscha's opinion, but it was frowned upon—by Wendolyn, at least.

Agatha had scoured the tomes she brought with her and even summoned others—quite rashly. They appeared on her dining table almost right in front of Eleanor. Still, nothing she'd seen mentioned anything about a Daughter of Autumn marrying a Prince of *Gem and Bone*.

It wasn't uncommon for a prophecy of old to go unwritten until it appeared in the Grimoire as an Order, but one given to a magus of The Order of Hespa or the royal family with no other mention in History? That was curious indeed. Where had Magus von Fuchs gotten this information, and why was it kept from the people? They seemed to have no inclination about it whatsoever.

Despite their ordination, magi no longer wielded magic. They had believed such a practise evil for centuries. It was possible the prophecy was older than the Witch Trials, and that would explain why the Grand Magus didn't think it would come to pass in his lifetime.

Agatha ground her teeth in frustration.

Whatever the case may be, she desperately wanted to know what the *people* knew and what they needed. She could not discredit the possibility that it might be her true purpose ordained by the Grimoire.

Agatha exhaled slowly and finally opened her marigold eyes. Twin flames crackled from the same wick. Again. She watched as one shifted from gold to blue, and both flames began to sputter. Again. Agatha sat back on her heels. She could no longer deny the accuracy. She'd scried with the flame five times and each time it split in two—one blue, one gold—and sputtered. Two opposing forces; one of spirit, one of mortality.

She brushed her hair back from her face. It wasn't entirely helpful. Could the spiritual forces be warring with the mortal realm? The spirit and mortality of one person—perhaps herself? And what the Underworld did any of it have to do with her and Thackery? *Grimm.* Agatha rolled her eyes. She would never get used to that foolish pet name.

"Lady Agatha?" Anne's voice was muffled by the closet door and obscene number of gowns surrounding the witch.

"*Merde.*" Agatha blew out the flames and whispered for the smoke to disperse. She stepped out of the closet and sat quickly on the chair in front of the vanity. "In here," she called, trying not to sound breathless.

Anne rounded the corner into the room, Eleanor on her heels, both burdened with armloads of gowns. The servants dumped them unceremoniously onto the bed. Anne smiled kindly at her, but Eleanor stalked to the closet and flung it open. Agatha held her breath.

Eleanor made a disgruntled noise from inside the closet. "These gowns all smell of smoke," she grumbled, bringing out a bundle of them and dropping them on the floor. She threw a hand to her slender hip and scowled. "Surely you know how ill-advised it is to take more than a small candle into a closet." When Agatha didn't answer, the maidservant's lip curled and she pointed at the large window. "Just open the curtains next time, lest you set the castle on fire."

Agatha ignored her entirely, turning instead to Anne. "What is all this?"

Anne grimaced and cleared her throat delicately. "It was declared that you had too much colour in your wardrobe."

Thank the Goddess. "Too much colour?"

Anne blushed. "Well—"

"Only the upper class wear vibrantly dyed fabrics," Eleanor broke in with condescension. "You may be betrothed to the prince, but you are not upper class."

"Yet." Agatha smirked.

If she was to represent the common folk yet mollify them as

well, the pile of fine dresses in muted colours made logical sense. Slight to her station or not, Agatha was grateful the magus had complained.

When the wardrobe had been switched and Anne had donned her in an exquisite olive gown, Eleanor thrust a piece of parchment in her face. "A note was sent with the gowns."

Agatha flipped it over and stared at the seal. It was pressed with the initials TFP. It wasn't the magus insulting her after all, but Thackery. She broke the seal and read the prince's messy, looping script.

> No betrothed of mine can walk about looking like a disgruntled peacock. These better suit your true station.
>
> -G

Agatha snorted. At least he was clever with his insults. She looked up to find her maidservants staring. *Good.* Let them think it a juicy love letter.

There were many unknowns and a plethora of things to worry about, but at least she wasn't in a goddess awful gown. It improved her mood considerably.

Mabon flew in through the window, coming irresponsibly close to Eleanor's face and the woman shrieked.

"Why do you have that infernal creature?" She growled and stormed toward the door. "Anne, you clean its cage. I won't do it." And she left.

Agatha suppressed a small smile. Her mood was indeed *much* improved.

Anne blushed, but Agatha reached out and touched her arm.

"Mabon uses his enclosure only for travel and occasional sleep. You'll not have to clean it."

"I would do it, my lady. You're to meet Prince Grimm in the gardens at the turn of the dial. It is the last promenade before the frost comes."

Anne curtsied and left her alone. Agatha's stomach clenched.

AGATHA SAT ON A BENCH, hidden behind a damnable parasol—of all the horrible things, but at least it was black. She flipped Autumn leaves up with her toes, glad to be in her own shoes. She'd donned the lace-up boots when no one was watching, and they paired nicely with the olive gown.

It was breezy just idly sitting, but they'd hardly made it a few steps before Agatha sent Prince Grimm off to fetch a servant for some cider. She'd been alive long enough to see her fair share of promenades but never had she taken part in one and she wasn't going to begin now. The prince had nearly jumped at the opportunity to leave her side. *Good riddance.*

If she couldn't run back to her rooms and avoid the whole debacle, she would sit in silence and contemplate the twin flames from her scrying. As soon as the promenade was over, she would have to ask Anne to take her into the castle library. There was still the great need to speak with the Grand Magus as well, but he'd sent word to her that they couldn't meet until the following day. She simply needed to bide her time, and then perhaps she could covertly learn more about the prophecy.

Agatha had a sinking feeling there was more to the prophecy he had. That, coupled with the switch in handwriting from Belfry to Talan in Agatha's Order, she did not have time to be sitting around in front of court imbeciles. If there was any chance of getting out of this marriage—or worse, something terrible lurking beyond the surface of it—Agatha needed to know. Immediately.

She tapped her heel rhythmically, determined to find a way into the library by herself. What would they truly do to her if she left the promenade? Behead the prophesied bride of their prince meant to mollify the common man? Hardly. The thought filled her with courage and she rose. She pulled in her parasol, only to find Lord Gaius mere steps away, his intense gaze locked on her.

"Lady Agatha."

"Lord Gaius."

They exchanged shallow dips of their heads and Lord Gaius held out his arm. "I'm not certain His Highness will be returning. What would you say to a turn about the gardens with me?"

Agatha ground her teeth. If she was chastised by the queen for that senseless prat leaving the promenade, she was going to slaughter him in his princely sleep. She sighed and took Gaius' arm. "I would say *why not?*"

He chuckled. "So enthusiastic, Lady Agatha. I feel terribly honoured."

"I apologise. It's not you. Your prince has a way of putting me in a foul mood."

"You would not be the first to say so." Gaius' warm smile nearly drew one from her. "You're not overly fond of promenades, are you?"

"They're a ridiculous waste of time."

"Some would say this is simply an advantageous opportunity to find a suitable marriage prospect, like many other events."

Agatha frowned, glancing at him sidelong. "Precisely."

Lord Gaius' forehead creased, a twinkle in his eye. "You do not believe in love, then?"

"Of course I do, which is precisely why I loathe archaic cattle breeding events meant to allow aristocrats and dandies to manipulate women into marriage."

As they strolled, passersby lifted their brows, Lord Gaius nodding at each of them. "Perhaps you're right about that."

"Yes, I am. That is not love."

He was dashing in his lapis-coloured coat. It did wonders for his dark skin and green eyes. Agatha promptly looked away at the thought.

"I'm inclined to agree." He winked at her and she studied the foliage to hide her heated cheeks.

Curse her for still blushing at a pretty face after three hundred damned years. It was only because he had the cadence of Ira, and she was lonely. That was all. Agatha tensed as the thoughts of Ira flooded in, effectively replacing any heat upon her cheeks with an ice-cold tidal wave—and she was glad for it.

"I take it you've not reconsidered backing out of this marriage?" It would seem the lord's pretenses were all used up.

"No. It's clear to any half-wit that I don't wish to be a part of this, but I rather like my head upon my shoulders and I would assume you do as well."

Gaius pulled them to a halt. "To put it plainly, *Agatha*, Prince Grimm has worked with incredible diligence to uphold his"—he broke off, head tilting to one side—"reputation. This marriage undermines that considerably."

"You mean to tell me your prince has worked with *diligence* to be a pompous arse?"

She expected him to snort, or deny it, but Lord Gaius remained sober and stone-faced. "Yes."

Agatha thought back on her brief conversation with Grimm the night she'd arrived. He'd almost *wanted* the magus' attention fixated on him, and Gaius was standing in front of her declaring the prince's horrible reputation was intentional. It didn't make sense. *What kind of—*

"You see how your presence could create a problem for him?"

"I do not." Agatha withdrew her hand from Lord Gaius' arm. "I see how it could help the people."

She walked back to the castle without allowing him a response, opening her parasol as she went. If the prince could leave the promenade, so could she. Consequences be damned.

Grimm

As THE DOOR OPENED, Grimm dropped his feet to the floor from where they'd been propped on his desk and jumped up. "Well?"

Gaius shook his head, closing himself into the top floor of the lighthouse. "Nothing of note."

Grimm ran a hand through his already dishevelled hair, absently thinking he needed to bathe sooner rather than later. He'd spent every waking moment—which was most, as he rarely slept—scouring the city for a way *out* of this blasted marriage. He shed his crumpled emerald overcoat and untucked the other side of his wrinkled shirt, rolling the sleeves to his elbows. Looking through the window out over the Black Sea as the sun considered setting, he waited for Gaius to speak.

"I think she knows, at least to some degree, that our attempt to discredit her place here is a half-truth."

"That's because there's nothing to discredit, Gaius. That's the point. The *prophecy* depicts a peasant." Grimm turned around and flourished his hands dramatically. "She is a peasant."

"Is she, though? Your average peasant?"

Grimm fixed him with a sardonic stare. "Like Hades she is. She's too damn intelligent and bold. That's what concerns me."

Gaius' mouth turned downward. "We'll find it, Grimm—proof that this is all just a sham. We must."

But he wasn't so certain. Not anymore. He slammed his palm down on the desk, a stack of papers spilling to the floor and several of Gaius' alchemy bottles clinking together at the jolt. The lord rushed to right a tube teetering on the edge before it was sent crashing to the floor alongside the papers, scowling at Grimm as he did so.

"What a fool I've been." The prince sank into a plush chair, pushing away the open books resting on its arm and letting them fall to the floor in a heap. "What a fool to think this day would never come."

"Perhaps," Gaius retorted as he picked up the trail of mess left in Grimm's wake. "But the day never *did* come for the four kings preceding you. You couldn't have known she would arrive in your lifetime."

Grimm ran a hand over his face. He was becoming used to the short beard he no longer had time to keep from growing in. "I thought I was out of the woods. My parents married far younger than I am now. I just thought—"

"I know. We just need to find proof that she is not *the* Daughter of Autumn and you are not *the* Prince of Gem and Bone."

It was the *bone* part that worried him. He looked at Gaius, letting down his mask to reveal the full weight of his despair. "And if we *are* them?"

"No." Gaius shook his head, bronze skin pulled tight across his forehead and censure in his eyes. "Don't you grow cowardly on me now, Grimm. We will find the proof. This cannot be. It will ruin everything we've worked for. Not to mention—"

"I know," Grimm snapped. "Goddess' teeth, I *know*."

CHAPTER
SEVEN

B *orn from ardour, our magic is how we regard Her.*
     -Sacred Texts of Hespa

AGATHA

THE HEELS of Agatha's boots clicked on the stones as she made her way through the labyrinthine castle halls toward the royal library. It had been an incredibly long time since she'd last been in the palace Stacks—as a guest of a duchess from a different lifetime ago—but she could never forget its enormity. A characteristic that she found both enthralling and intimidating.

She had no time to waste and too many questions in need of answers to find herself lost in the vastness of it all. To combat such problematic ambling, Agatha had written a thorough list of possible sections and topics that could contain the answers she sought.

She rounded the corner and frowned at the guard standing

post outside the library entrance. Guards always barred entry from outside the castle, but there had been none inside when she'd last been there. She supposed times change and under different, more fearful rulers, it made sense to take note of those entering. Perhaps the king or magus simply didn't want their learned guests to find illicit lovers mingling in the Stacks.

"Good evening," she spoke to the guard.

"My lady." He gave a shallow bow and held out his gloved hand. "Your papers."

"My papers?"

"Of course, my lady. Your papers granting entry into the library."

Now that went a bit too far. Barring those already within the castle from entry into a library unless they have specific papers? Agatha could think of a dozen new questions she'd have to find answers for.

"Oh, yes." She tapped her forehead, mocking her own silliness. "I have them right here." She opened the velvet pouch wrapped around her wrist with a cord and pulled out Sorscha's latest letter. With a breath and invisible threads of magic, Agatha spelled the paper to read whatever it was the guard was looking for. Pasting on a sweet smile, she handed the letter over.

"Ah yes, there you have it." But Agatha's relief was short-lived. "One moment. It appears you're missing the signature. Must be signed by the Grand Magus or the king, my lady."

The books in that blasted library had better detail world domination with great accuracy if this was the price one paid for knowledge that should be *free*. Jaw clenched, she brought the signature at the bottom of a calling card from the Grand Magus to her mind's eye.

Standing on her toes, she reached over to point at the bottom, the signature appearing instantly. "Oh, it's just there."

The guard blinked twice and shook his head. "Apologies, my lady. I'm not sure how I missed that." He handed her back the paper, neck pink beneath his high collar. "You'll need to present this paper each time you enter the Stacks."

Agatha nodded and entered, her heart in her throat. Not because of the task before her or the minor hiccup at the door, but because she knew the sight of so many books in one place would steal her breath—as it always did, no matter the library.

She had not been wrong. The ceiling rose high above, adorned with a painting depicting the Goddess Three as she formed the seven realms and birthed the thirteen lesser gods in facets of Her likeness. In one section, the Lord of Art danced with Lady Death. In another, Lady War battled Lord Nature. In yet another, Lady Love looked on as Lord Night whispered intimacies to Lady Magic. There, beneath that particularly ravishing Lord and Lady, were four toddling girls—Talan, Hissa, Monarch, and Belfry.

Agatha's heart ached at the sight as her neck strained from staring upward. For hundreds of years, children had been told that those four Sisters of Solstice—daughters of Lord and Lady Magie de la Nuit, blessed by Hespa Herself—were just mortal babes seeking a way to the Goddess Three to become one of her Hallowed. No one knew their names any longer. But Agatha did. Her Sisters did.

She sighed and took in the rest of the space, golden lamplight illuminating rows upon rows of bookshelves with ornately carved wood that reached up three stories. Agatha inhaled the scent of old parchment, worn leather spines, and ink. It smelled a bit like her cottage and it fueled her onward.

She'd settled on beginning with historical records of the royal families, hoping she could compile a list of kings' names and the Grand Magus at that time. She spun in a small circle, at a loss for where a genealogy section might be located. Rather than waste time standing around like a fool, Agatha reached into her pouch and pulled out a crystal compass. She whispered the desired section and the needle spun in furious circles before stopping suddenly and surely.

When Agatha finally reached the genealogy section—its shelves less worn than the more commonly frequented ones—her heart sank. There were thousands of tomes ranging from royal histories to the histories of royal horses and the line of succession to the village smithy. Frustrated, she mumbled curses and dumped out the contents of her pouch onto a small table in the middle of the row. She took up a serpentine stone and whispered for it to show her the hidden mysteries she needed to look upon. It whirred in her hand, pulsing with warmth and spurring her toward a particular shelf. Abruptly, it stopped and went cold. Agatha looked down at it curiously, but the hush of a foot sliding against carpet caught her attention.

She turned to find Prince Grimm running an idle finger around the contents of her pouch spread across the table. She tensed, willing the ink on Sorscha's letter to disappear, just in case he had the gall to open it.

"Are these kernels of *corn*?" He shook his head. "You've a habit of leaving trinkets in your wake like a child. It's most unseemly."

She did have that tendency, though it irked her that the prince had noticed. It sounded more like a bored observation than a downright insult, but it ignited Agatha's fury, nonetheless.

"I hear you escaped the promenade as well," he continued, leaning against the sturdy shelves, arms crossed.

"What are you doing in the library?" she demanded, irritation and fatigue seeping out by way of impolite words.

Grimm lifted an eyebrow. "What does anyone do in a library?"

Goddess, she hated his snide arse. "So late at night?"

"I could say the same to you." The prince glanced at the volumes nearest to him, only just realising which row he stood in. "And in the genealogy section? Interesting." His bewildered smirk was rife with amusement.

Grimm ran a finger slowly along the spines of the books until he landed on a crumbling tome near her head, pulling it off the shelf. "Ah, there it is. Just what I was looking for. *The Natural History of Merveille's Royal Wet Nurses.*" His voice choked on the last words of the title, and Agatha sneered at his foolish lies and discomfort.

"I did not peg you for an intellectual, prince," she mocked.

He opened his mouth to retort, but a staggeringly beautiful woman cleared her throat at the edge of the row behind Agatha. Clearly caught off guard, Grimm stepped back abruptly.

"My lady." The woman inclined her head briefly toward Agatha. "Your Highness." She dipped into a low curtsy, the fullness of her breasts nearly spilling out of her gown. "I'd have a word with you in private, please."

Grimm nodded and she sauntered away, skirts swishing on the plush carpet.

Agatha snorted. "Now *that* makes more sense." The prince's attention snapped to her and his face darkened. He moved to leave, but she barred his exit, unwilling to let him just walk away without a response.

"You don't know the first thing about me," he growled. "And I've had *enough* of those who think they do. Now, kindly move out of my way, or I will forcibly remove you, peasant."

Agatha's mind screamed to keep her mouth shut. To let him go. Shouted that she was supposed to be the demure little bride. But she was not that witch. The entire mess surrounding them was too much and they both knew it. They were each hanging upright by a thread, and she wanted to pull his and watch him topple over.

Agatha raised her chin and stood her ground, looking him straight in the eye. "You don't have it in you, princeling."

She didn't know why she was so intent on challenging him.

Perhaps she just hated him, plain and simple—loathed the fact she would have to tie herself to this moronic prince until he grew old and died. If she didn't kill him first. That would be so much easier than continuing with this charade. Perhaps if they married and she killed him on their wedding night, she would still have fulfilled her Order and wouldn't face her Sanction.

Eyes flashing, Grimm closed the distance between them in one stride and lifted her nearly off the floor. His strong fingers dug into her shoulders as he moved her to one side and pushed her up against the bookshelves, the wood pressing into her back. For the space of a breath, their eyes locked, both filled with fury, desperation, despair. There was a storm brewing behind his stony exterior, and she felt her own tempest echo his. He dropped her to her feet and Agatha barely kept herself from stumbling as he stormed away.

Grimm

EVERY CURSE WORD HE POSSESSED, invented or otherwise, flew freely from his mouth as Grimm moved about the library to find Mila. He flexed his hands into fists and stretched them out again. They burned from where he'd touched Agatha, as if her very skin was on fire.

"*Mila*," Grimm snarled when he found her behind a row of mathematical texts, her pretty lips turned up at the corners. "Quite proud of yourself?"

"You nearly jumped out of your skin, Grimm. I would be rather dull to not find that at least minorly humorous."

"Don't interrupt me when I'm speaking with Agatha," he ground out.

"Oh, my." She put a hand to her bosom, eyebrows lifted high. "His Highness has feelings for his pet, then, after all?"

"Drop it. You know that isn't it."

"Oh, please, Grimm." Mila pushed off the table and inched closer, running an icy finger down the length of his face. "All she thinks is that you have me pressed against these books, my skirts pushed up around my waist, whispering your name." He caught her wrist roughly, irritated at the image that came to his mind—it was not one of Mila.

"You'd better hope that's what she thinks." Something in *him* hoped it wasn't, though Agatha had all but said it was what she thought of him.

Grimm dropped her arm and stepped back. "What did you need to speak to me about?"

Mila flipped open a large tome on the table and pointed. "A new name has appeared."

Grimm hissed. "Why did you bring this here? You could have just told me."

"No." All of Mila's jesting fled, and if he wasn't mistaken, she'd paled. "You needed to see it."

Grimm leaned in to look at the name and sucked a breath through his teeth.

AGATHA

SHAKING off her encounter with the prince, Agatha smoothed her skirts and set to return her scattered items to their pouch. The stone she'd placed on a nearby shelf in her exasperation with Grimm began to hum once more. She rushed over and placed it in her palm.

The stone's vibration turned urgent, kicking up so much momentum it nearly bounced from her hand. She left the aisle, its insistence drawing her forward. "Where are you taking me?" she wondered under her breath.

It led her past six rows of books and into a darkened alcove of the Stacks before it abruptly stilled in her palm. Befuddled, Agatha tapped the stone with her sharp fingernail before looking around. Her eyes were barely adjusting to the darkness when she heard a whimper, immediately followed by a harsh whisper. Agatha's heart kicked up speed and she followed the sound, dread setting her magic on edge beneath her skin.

She slunk through the aisle of tomes, eyes scanning the gap above the books looking into the next row. There, she caught sight of a skirmish of some kind. Agatha inched closer, her nose nearly touching the books, dust tickling. She reached up to cover her nose and mouth, desperate not to sneeze and reveal her sleuthing.

It was difficult to make out details in the low light, but there was a man in a fine purple coat, his back to Agatha. He was rigid and speaking in a severe tone, his words too muffled to make out. He jerked forward twice and another whimper sounded.

Agatha took two steps to the side, attempting to achieve a better angle. She clamped a hand over her mouth when a young woman came into view, her maid's dress askew and her eyes wide with fear. The man shook her violently once more and fury burned in Agatha's hands.

"*Enough,*" she spoke through gritted teeth over the books.

The man twisted around at the sound of her voice, but Agatha was already storming around the corner, her rage spilling into his aisle of cruelty.

"Keep your hands off her," she demanded through her clenched teeth.

The man's shock wore off and his lip curled when he recognised her. "Prince Thackery's peasant. How lovely." He brushed lint off the sleeve of his coat, the woman cowering behind him. "This woman is a servant of mine, and I will do as I please."

Agatha ignored his derision, her blood boiling at the man's narcissism. "Just leave her be. There is no reason to treat her that way."

"You would do well to mind your business." He took a step toward Agatha, but she held her ground. She might need to keep her magic secret, but there were many, *many* ways to harm a man without it.

"She is a human being—" Agatha's words were cut off by another's.

"*You*, Lord Wellington, would do well to mind who you are speaking to." Agatha turned to find Lord Gaius at the end of the row, face set like stone. "This is your future princess, as you well know."

She caught fear flash across Lord Wellington's eyes before he brushed it off. "Of course. Lady Agatha, I apologise that you had to witness the censure of my servant." He dipped his chin to them both and left in a hurry. His servant kept her face downcast, but lifted her eyes to meet Agatha's and offered her the barest of smiles.

When they were out of earshot, Agatha whirled on Lord Gaius with a scowl. "I did not need your intervention."

The lord smiled. "And here I thought you were going to offer me your thanks."

"I had it under control."

"Clearly."

"I thought you didn't want me to be *princess*, anyway," she shot back.

Gaius straightened his coat. "I do not, but I do feel that you deserve respect."

Agatha's temper sparked even further. "A servant does not deserve any less respect than I do." She clenched her fists at her sides. "I can't very well be what I'm supposed to be in this court if your precious prince is such an arse all the time and you're rushing in to *discredit me*."

He raised his hands in surrender. "My apologies. I thought I was helping you."

Gaius looked genuine enough and it softened her resolve. "Why are you here, anyway?"

"Grimm never returned to the promenade and I can't find him. Apparently, that's the theme this evening." He looked pointedly at Agatha and she shrugged, offering a noncommittal noise. "I came here to find him."

"Prince Pride frequents the library, does he?"

"He does, in fact."

She rolled her eyes. "Dark corners to hide his sins like our upstanding Lord Wellington." Gaius observed her curiously. "He went off with a courtier." She pointed behind him. "That way."

The lord looked bothered. "What did this courtier look like?"

"Blonde. *Busty*."

Worry slashed across his face and Gaius cursed under his breath in a language Agatha hadn't spoken in many, many years. It had the ebb and flow of the vibrant Prilemians, which explained his dark skin and sharp features. The green eyes must have belonged to his Seagovian father. She wondered how that had played out—a Segovian Lord marrying a Prilemian.

"I must take my leave, Lady Agatha." With a slight bow, he hurried away.

Grimm

BLOOD DRIPPED on the carpet of his rooms and Grimm cursed, ripping his sodden clothes off. He returned to the window and slammed it shut, not caring whoever it might disturb. The heavy drapes pulled shut, he stalked to his mahogany bar, but the reflection in the looking glass stopped him dead in his tracks.

Blood coated his face, stinging his eyes and running into his mouth. The man had clawed at him, leaving streaks in the gore Grimm's cheek was still slick with. A lump threatened to close his throat and he growled. He was foolish to have involved him in the first place. Alestair and Gaius had both warned him not to, but he hadn't listened. Now he'd gotten one of his comrades killed.

Grimm reached out and slammed the looking glass onto the floor, watching as it shattered and welcoming the pain of the glass slicing into his leg. He turned away and closed his hand around a crystal decanter, the amber liquid sloshing with the tremble of his fingers.

"Cursed hands," he exclaimed as the drink spilled onto the wooden tray. "*Mila,*" he hissed. "Show yourself."

Mila stepped silently out of the shadows behind the lavatory door, looking away from his near naked state. "It's done, then?"

"Of course it is. Why else would I be covered in his damned blood?"

"I'm so sorry, Grimm."

"It is my duty."

"I would have gone if I could—"

"*Enough.* I don't need your pity. Leave me be," he snarled.

Mila's expression hardened, and Grimm closed his eyes for a heartbeat. He hadn't meant to be so harsh. It wasn't her fault. He opened his mouth to say as much, but she had already slipped out into the hall.

It was for the best. He needed to be alone.

M y beloved daughters. Winnie, my fair rose. Sorscha,
my wild vine. Seleste, my radiant sunflower. Agatha,
my fierce black dahlia.
-Writings of Ambrose Joubert

Grimm

GRIMM SHOVED another forkful of fruit into his mouth and sighed heavily at his mother's prattling. He was in no mood to play the self-indulgent prince and every morsel of food felt like lead in his stomach.

Gaius whispered behind his coffee cup, "Professor Ludwig was found murdered this morning."

Grimm pushed a fork through his eggs.

"Are you alright?" the lord pressed.

He eyed Gaius, aggravated. "It never gets any easier. Let's put it that way."

"We've much to discuss."

"We do, but not here—"

"Are you even listening to me?" His mother's shrill voice startled them both. "For Goddess' *sake*, child! You simply *must* change your behaviour! You are to be married in a fortnight. You cannot have a courtier in your rooms, sneaking out in the dead of night like a harlot."

Gaius choked back a laugh and Grimm shot him a look. He wanted to shout at his mother that it wasn't what she thought. He didn't have the energy to keep up the façade. To play the cocky bastard. Steeling himself, he gave Gaius a sly grin before turning back to the queen. "But of course, Mother. I will save all my affection for the darling peasant you bought me."

"I'll pinch that smirk right off your face, Thackery," she warned.

Grimm rolled his eyes dutifully.

HE WASN'T likely to say it aloud, but Grimm thought it foolish that only women were societally allowed to enjoy flowers. He picked a black dahlia and marvelled at the bloom's resplendence. Black dahlias were daring in their shape. He found their colour —so close to coagulated blood—alluring. Their petals were imposing, threatening that they might slice you if they so choose, only to find they're delicately soft. Black dahlias defied the common rules of vibrant flora and pushed through the dirt to bloom in their darkened glory.

Grimm tucked the flower through a buttonhole of his elegant, if not a bit wrinkled morning coat. Why his mother had summoned him to her private arboretum when they'd last spoken just that morning was beyond him. He wandered through the greenery, mind on too many things at once. When he looked up to see Agatha's maidservant, Anne, at the entrance, he knew with a sickening surety why he'd been summoned.

Agatha stepped in just behind the young servant, her mouth forming a flat line as soon as she saw him. He'd expected her to look away and busy herself elsewhere until his mother arrived. Alas, she lifted the skirts of her merlot gown and barreled toward him.

"Do you know what this is about?" she demanded, her brows creased in the middle.

Grimm picked a rose and handed it to her. Agatha grabbed it roughly and threw it in a bush. He chuckled. "I surmise it's concerning our mutual abandonment of the promenade."

Her neck flushed and she cursed under her breath, presumably thinking he couldn't hear. It was an impressive litany, really.

The glass door opened once more and in stepped the *Almighty Queen Fleurina*. She demanded everyone leave them, and—ensuring the door was firmly shut—strode regally to where Grimm and Agatha stood. His mother picked at his unruly hair, attempting to smooth it. "I know that the two of you left the promenade."

She let the words hang in the air as she bent to rub a rose petal between her fingers. Grimm fought the urge to look in Agatha's direction, anxious to gauge her reaction. Instead, he studied his mother's profile. She was a nearly unreadable woman —even for him.

The queen turned her probing attention back to the two of them. "And I know you were found in the library."

Grimm swallowed and felt Agatha shuffle on her feet next to him. Surely Mila had not ratted them out. Had someone heard them fighting and told his mother? He was a damned grown man for the love of Hespa.

He snuck a quick glance at Agatha to see her hands twisted together, knuckles white. His father had done some ludicrous things under the magus' counsel, but Agatha was wrong about losing her head for disobedience. *Surely* she was wrong. Grimm was beginning to sweat by the time his mother sighed heavily.

"Though this turn of affection toward one another pleases your father greatly..." The queen trailed off and stroked another flower. Grimm and Agatha exchanged befuddled glances before quickly turning back to the queen. "If you would like to be *alone* together to explore these new feelings, no one will hold it against you. You are meant to be seen as sickeningly in love. But *please* find someplace more suitable than the *Stacks*. You are royalty, and almost royalty, after all."

She sidled close to Grimm and spoke quietly, but no less stately. "It would have been better to take your betrothed to your room than to call a courtier to take up where she left off."

Grimm fought a wave of nausea. "Mother, please."

With that, Queen Fleurina pursed her lips and walked away, her glass slippers clicking on the stones and the train of her cherry-coloured gown flowing out behind her. When the door shut, Agatha released a breath and the prince sagged.

He opened his mouth to apologise, but stopped himself. Agatha scowled, reaching out toward him—he was certain she'd smack him. To his surprise, she snatched the dahlia from his coat, turned on her heel, and walked away.

He stood for several moments in the garden, hands in his pockets and the previous night heavy on his mind. As he meandered around, he bent to inspect a wilted flower and caught sight of something glimmering in the sunlight. He reached to pick it up, recognising it as the curious stone he'd seen Agatha with in the library. Sliding it into his pocket, he headed for the lighthouse to write Alestair.

AGATHA

MABON TITTERED in Agatha's ear to calm her nerves. It did force a smile to her lips, but quell her anxiety it did not. She'd been summoned to meet with Magus von Fuchs in a matter of moments, but Eleanor wouldn't cease fussing with the hem of Agatha's dress.

"It's fine, Eleanor. It's the tiniest of tears. It can wait until after my meeting with the Grand Magus."

Eleanor spoke around a mouthful of needles and thread. "It is not fine. I plan to attend the queen one day and I will not have tears in the gowns I oversee."

Agatha frowned. "Don't you mean that you plan to attend *me* as queen one day?"

The maidservant's hands stilled. There was a beat of silence before she mumbled, "I suppose so."

Agatha hid her sneer at the woman's discomfort, though it quickly faded. She had no desire to be a queen of any sort. She was meant to be part of the Royal Peridot family in order to bridge the gap between the commoners and the aristocracy, but one day she would find a way to do that without a throne.

Agatha studied Eleanor, certain she was the young woman's least favourite person in all the realms, despite her newly appointed station and purpose. She wondered if Eleanor could simply *enjoy* serving a higher class and not want reformation. It seemed a preposterous idea to her. Unless Eleanor was scared. Considering the debacle in the library between master and servant, Agatha couldn't really blame her if that was the case.

"Where did you get a tear like this, anyway?" Eleanor broke into her thoughts. She rose and stood in front of Agatha with her hands on her hips and nose wrinkled. "It looks like someone took a knife to it."

"I snagged it on a rose bush in the queen's arboretum,"

Agatha explained, partially wishing someone *had* taken a knife to it. It would've been better than the alternative of being humiliated in front of the queen and prince.

One of Eleanor's brows shot up. "No one is allowed in the queen's private indoor gardens unless they are family."

Agatha had her own denials about becoming part of the royal family, but Eleanor's were irritating. "Precisely," she snapped, effectively silencing her.

That is, until Mabon squawked and flew straight at the servant's head. She screeched and swatted at him, but the little fuzzy bat took up a clump of her hair in his clawed feet and pulled.

She did not think it wise or befitting of someone meant to unite royalty with the working class to laugh at the expense of one such servant, but...restraint was difficult where Eleanor was concerned.

"*Erg*," Eleanor growled when Mabon flew away. "You infernal creature!" She swung around to face Agatha, who was hiding her mouth behind a hand. "And *you*. Keep control of your blasted pet or I'll accidentally lose him in the forest." She smoothed her blonde hair and irate face. "Now, come along. And try not to rip your dress again, *my lady*."

Eleanor seethed and Agatha followed her out of the room toward Magus von Fuchs, whom she was very late in meeting with. A rug did—accidentally, of course—bunch up and trip Eleanor along the way, sending the maidservant's scowl down to impossible depths. Agatha smiled. It was worth it.

"Grand Magus," Agatha spoke, returning a book back to his shelf as the magus came in. She wiped her hands on her skirts and moved to meet him.

The magus said nothing, only gestured for her to sit before taking his place behind the desk and folding his hands over his thin abdomen. Agatha sat very still. She'd hoped speaking privately with the magus would push her anxiety away. That perhaps he would explain the prophecy more; explain her duties or offer some deep wisdom concerning Hespa.

Alas, he only looked perturbed, just as he had since the night of her arrival. It shouldn't have come as a shock after witnessing his overbearing nature and peculiar sense of authority, but who else could answer her questions? Sitting in front of him, it no longer seemed wise to voice them to this man at all.

"Our Daughter of Autumn," he mused, expression unreadable. The Goddess Three pendant on his long chain glinted in the sunlight that drifted in through the open windows. The image was strangely unsettling.

Agatha schooled her emotions, took three measured breaths, and touched a hand to the stones encased at her throat. Lepidolite for emotional balance and lapis lazuli for vision beyond the seen. Her questions only compounded as she waited for the magus to speak. But Agatha waited for no man—Goddess blessed or otherwise—and she couldn't sit mutely.

"I have so many things I wish to speak with you about, Grand Magus." She let childlike excitement fill her voice. One, because, despite her mistrust of this man, she wished to hear the tales of a mortal so in communion with her Goddess after the magi's fall away from magic. And two, because she wanted this mortal magus to think her naïve enough to deem her no threat. The deadliest monsters are the ones who don't appear monstrous at all.

The Grimoire might have remained silent since her arrival at the Midnight in Rochbury, but it would toll its bells of death sooner or later, and Agatha would be Ordered to deal a killing blow.

"I have much I wish to discuss with you as well, Agatha."

Her eyebrow twitched at the lack of title. A title she did not want, but for how much they all cherished this *prophecy*, they certainly had no qualms with shoving her station in her face.

"First," he went on, "how about a spot of tea?"

Agatha could do without formality but nodded. The magus rang a small bell, its tinkling reminding her of faeries. All images of folklore died a gruesome death in her skull when she laid eyes on the maidservant who brought in the tea tray. The blood drained from Agatha's face as she took in the battered cheek of Lord Wellington's servant from the library.

The woman averted her gaze and Agatha clamped her mouth shut in an effort to not openly gape at the purple bruise marring her eye and the deep gash along her cheekbone. Someone had taken a knife to this woman.

Oh, gods…I caused this.

When the woman placed the tea set before them and Agatha turned back to the magus, he was watching her reaction like a viper. He said nothing as the servant poured them tea, but Agatha was no fool.

The servant was a warning.

"Thank you kindly, Miriam," he spoke as she gathered the tray, his eyes never leaving Agatha's. "You're free to return to Lord Wellington now."

Agatha ground her teeth together painfully. This was an abhorrent man. If he held divinity of any kind, she wanted no part in it.

A flash of Sorscha being permanently ripped from her slashed violently through her mind. The image was nearly enough to double her over. Her time locked away in the woods with the previous Sister Autumn had taught her all too clearly what would happen if she chose to walk away from her duties. Her Sanction would debilitate her. Agatha eyed the magus, swallowing the bile at the back of her throat and smoothing out any alarm on her features.

For Sorscha. For Miriam.

"Now," Magus von Fuchs spoke once Miriam left, his face suddenly brightening and jarring Agatha deeply, "we must discuss the *Royal Wedding.*" He clapped his hands together once. "The entire kingdom is talking about it."

Agatha kept her mouth shut.

He stood and rounded the desk. "Plans are well under way, but you needn't worry about those until the *fittings.*" He narrowed his eyes, glancing down at Agatha's full figure. His distaste vanished from view as quickly as it had arrived. "Those should begin in a handful of days as the ceremony will be during the full moon."

Agatha choked. "That's less than a fortnight away, Grand Magus." She was finding it increasingly difficult to breathe. She'd known the marriage would come before the leaves had all fallen, but a date was too solidifying to handle.

"Why of course. The first frost could come any day, and we simply cannot risk it."

The magus prattled on about the ceremony, Agatha hardly hearing a word until he placed a list in front of her.

"What is this?"

"This is the list of duties you are to fulfill prior to the wedding. Queen Fleurina has aided me, so graciously, in compiling it."

"*Appear at the docks and give out vouchers for extra grain,*" Agatha read aloud. "*Visit small shops along Gemme Road. Purchase ribbons at Gregoria Holeman's...*" Agatha flipped the list over and made a face. "What does this have to do with me or the prophecy? How will this mollify the people? If I'm to visit shops, shouldn't it be on Mer Row where the commoners shop?"

Magus von Fuchs had the audacity to look horrified. "Mer Row is for the Blacklisted of our fair city. Those that are no longer worthy of having a shop on dignified streets such as Gemme Road. You are *not* to associate with them." He stabbed a finger at the list of petty errands, his coldness returning. "This list is your concern, and *this list* is what you will do."

THE GRINDING of her teeth kept time with her furious pace as she marched down the hallway to the library.

The *Blacklisted*? What could they have done that was so very terrible it warranted being labelled as *unworthy*? Like Hades she wasn't going there now. It had taken all of her self-control to ask that duplicitous magus to issue her library papers, but she'd done it. Agatha couldn't risk any of them finding out she'd fabricated her way into the library the first time, with or without magic, and there was *no* chance she would ask the king.

The Grand Magus had denied her at first, but she demurely claimed it was for royal wedding etiquette research. Since she was *but a peasant*, she needed all the help she could get to represent the royal family well on her errands and make them proud at the wedding.

She'd nearly gagged on her own words and rolled her eyes just thinking of them. He'd bought it, though, which was what she needed in order to figure out what in the seven realms was going on. They were using her as a pawn and Hespa was content to stand idly by.

Agatha slowed and blew stray strands of hair out of her face before approaching the library door. It was a different guard standing post, and Agatha withdrew her papers.

"Lady Agatha." The guard bowed deeply.

"Good afternoon." She inclined her head and made to hand him her papers, but he was already opening the door for her. "Oh, don't you need to see my library papers?"

"No, my lady. We've been instructed to never bar you from the library, no matter the day or time."

Agatha's head tilted to one side. "Who gave you this order?"

The guard shifted on his feet. "Our captain, my lady."

"And who gave it to him?"

The young man blushed but kept his head high. "Apologies, but it is not my place to know such matters."

Agatha regarded the young man in front of her and walked through the door, turning back. "What is your name?"

The guard smiled wide. "Lotrum, my lady. Augustus Lotrum."

"Thank you, Augustus."

CHAPTER
NINE

M ore than magic, or duty, or blood, may love be what
binds us.
    -Writings of Ambrose Joubert

AGATHA

THE RAVEN SQUAWKED and Agatha untied a parchment from its leg. He pecked gently at her hand, awaiting his treat. This particular raven was quite the lover of treats, and he was so fat it was a wonder he could make it all the way from Sorscha's treehouse. Agatha took a mango from where it had been floating for Mabon, holding it for the bird to pick at. He had no intention of ceasing his gluttony any time soon, so Agatha set it down on the windowsill and unfurled Sorscha's letter.

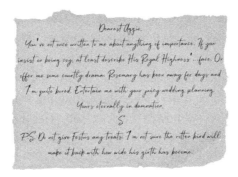

Agatha snorted and snatched the fruit from Festus. She opened the window and out he flew, Mabon entering in his wake. The bat gave Agatha a small lick, nuzzling her cheek before flying to the rafters and snuggling in for the day.

She and Sorscha usually wrote in a code of sorts. Though Agatha was certain her Sister truly wanted every morsel of court detail, and to know precisely what the prince's *face* looked like, she knew what her Sister was really asking. Agatha wanted to tell her everything, but writing it was too risky, and she hadn't sorted things out enough to even begin to explain.

She pulled the Grimoire out of its spelled hiding place and took a deep breath before opening to the marked page. Nothing. Marry the prince and then…nothing. Still.

Agatha drummed her fingers on the desk, chewing the inside of her lip. Perhaps speaking with Sorscha could help her sort through it. Her Orders had always been heavy and brutal, but they'd never been so tangled. Possibly against her better judgement, Agatha was willing to test the boundaries of their rules and contact her Sister directly again.

She took up a bit of black chalk and scrawled symbols invoking silence as well as privacy, and barring intrusion. When she was done, Agatha dusted her hands and pulled out her onyx scrying mirror.

Though witchcraft had all but disappeared from the continent after the magi lost their potency and kings began fearing it,

Agatha thought it wise to not use objects in her rooms that weren't *hers* for magical purposes. One could never be too careful.

She held her hand above the mirror and whispered her Sister's name three times. When the roiling fog within the mirror cleared, Agatha swallowed back a sob. Her beautiful Sister Spring lay sunbathing in the lush grass below her sprawling tree-house home in Prilemia.

Sorscha refused to let another Season encroach upon her little oasis. Agatha watched as her Sister turned over onto her stomach and picked an orange blossom so bright it made Agatha's soul burn. She smiled, watching Sorscha set it in her hair and take up Ostara, who slithered upon her arm.

"Sister Spring," Agatha cooed, quite pleased when Sorscha jumped.

"Aggie, you peeping witch! How long have you been there?" She stood and sauntered over to the black orb of magic with Agatha's face in it. Ostara coiled her body around Sorscha's arm as she sat down naked and graceful in the grass.

"Not long enough to see anything incriminating." Agatha smirked.

"Well, you wouldn't have had to wait long. I think I might set up my stall in the village market and terrorise some poor soldiers this afternoon."

Agatha's brow furrowed. "Prilemian soldiers?"

Ostara flicked her tongue at Sorscha's puckered lips. "No. Seagovian soldiers. I would've thought you knew they've moved into nearly every land on the continent."

"I did not."

"Hm. Well, what did you break the rules to tell me this time, Sister, since you refuse to write to me properly?"

Agatha sighed. "I'm not even certain how to formulate it all. I thought Grimm was just an arse, but he's clearly up to something—"

"Who?" Sorscha interrupted.

"Oh." Agatha looked at her hands. "Prince Thackery. He's called Grimm by most."

Sorscha snickered. "Fitting match for you, then, Sister Sunless."

Agatha blinked at her and trudged on. "The Grand Magus...I thought I would glean much from him about Hespa. At least how She speaks with the magi now." She shook her head. "But he seems only irritated by me and he appears to hold as much power as the king does. He's a disgusting excuse of a mortal for all the abuse of the lower class he turns a blind eye to." Sorscha's eyes were going wide the more Agatha said, but she kept on. "*And* I don't understand how he heard a different version of all this than Belfry did...or I guess Talan—"

Sorscha baulked, setting Ostara in the grass and letting her slither away. "Hold on. Go back. A different version? Of what? Your Order? No one should know anything about your Order... and what do you mean about Belfry and Talan?"

"Right. The Grimoire stated that I, by name, was to marry the Prince of Seagovia. Actually—" Agatha's nose scrunched up. "No, that's not entirely true, either. I opened the Grimoire and the Order was in Belfry's hand as usual—*a Daughter of Autumn would one day join with a Son of Gem and Bone*. Then, the second half was in Talan's hand, calling me by name to marry Prince Thackery Peridot III." Sorscha looked almost frightened, but Agatha explained further. "I thought it odd, that Talan had any Order for me, but perhaps Belfry grew ill and Talan had to finish it." She shrugged. "When I arrived at the castle, the Grand Magus recited a prophecy similar to my Order. It didn't mention Thackery, and they all seemed surprised at my arrival, but it had even more detail—details about me and what I was wearing, even Mabon and your raven—"

"*Stop.*" Sorscha held up a hand and Agatha clamped her

mouth shut. "I'm sorry, Sister. That—I don't think this is good. At all."

"Clearly. That's why I'm here—or not here—speaking with you. I need help. I didn't think it was quite as dreadful as the look on your face warrants, though. I haven't even told you the worst part, so why do you look as if you've seen a ghost?"

Sorscha squirmed. "I will not get into it, Agatha." She flinched at her Sister's use of her full name. "But, once, a long time ago, my Order changed from Hissa's hand to Talan's."

"*Truly?* Perhaps it's more than Talan just filling in for Belfry, then. Why did you not tell us?"

"I—I'd rather not think about it. We've all had to do some dark things, Aggie. Even if they've not been as bloody as yours. I must go, Sister. You have knowledge beyond measure and countless books at your disposal. You will figure this out."

Sorscha stood, whispered a word, and the mirror turned black in Agatha's hands once more. But she did not miss that someone was approaching her Sister's hidden home. She hoped with all her might it was friend and not foe.

Quickly, Agatha hid away her mirror and washed all traces of the chalk marks from the door before making her way to the library. She didn't have long before Anne and Eleanor would arrive to take her on her first ridiculous errand from the queen and Grand Magus.

This time, she was prepared. She'd spent the last two library visits scouring the catalogues to find specific titles of interest. With her list and spelled compass in hand, she flitted about the library only to find that every book on her list was missing.

"You're not buying that hideous thing."

Agatha frowned at Eleanor. "I like it." She turned back to the looking glass to admire the wide-brimmed dusky hat upon her head. It was a glorious piece of fashion. She had to admit ,the shop itself was a surprise. Being on Mer Row, Agatha had expected it to be shabby. Instead, it was modest, though baroque and very tasteful.

"You look like you're in mourning. Or a farmer." The maid-servant looked about the shop with nervous disdain. "I don't even know why we're *here*," she whispered sharply. "This designer is Blacklisted."

"And why exactly is that?"

"No one knows," Anne broke in while fussing with the brim of Agatha's hat. "I could add a lavender ribbon around it," she offered. Eleanor shot her a glare and Anne turned to busy herself with a nearby dress.

"We're here because I want to be." It had taken all her efforts to convince her maids to visit Mer Row, and she was glad she had. "And I like this hat. I have my own coin to purchase it."

"Nonsense. His Highness was clear that we are to use his line of credit in all the shops," Anne said, fluffing Agatha's hideous skirt.

The prince had a line of credit at shops on Mer Row. *Intriguing.* Agatha glanced over to the men's side along one of the deep evergreen walls. Some of the items did look like something Grimm would wear—if they were wrinkled and rolled up at the sleeves.

Eleanor crossed her arms and Agatha thought, not for the first time, that she'd be incredibly beautiful if she didn't scowl quite so often. Not that she was the epitome of cheerfulness herself.

"This is ridiculous," Eleanor huffed. "You should be ashamed to be seen here."

Agatha crossed her arms. "Of course. And next, I'd like to attend High Tea at the whorehouse and gossip my wits out."

Eleanor's mouth fell open and Anne giggled.

"My my my my *my!*" All three women turned to find the shop's owner, Monsieur Tindle, with his hands on either side of his face in astonishment. "If you are not the most beautiful creature I've ever beheld."

Agatha looked at Eleanor, certain he was speaking of her, but Tindle rushed forward and bowed low in front of Agatha. He was either a liar or a brown noser, for Agatha knew quite well after three hundred years that she was, in a word, plain.

"Lady Agatha. No wonder our dear prince is so smitten with you. And this hat." He tsked. "The most incredible statement! Here you are, bridging the gap for us all and bringing your own fashion sense into court." He held his sharp-angled chin in one hand, inspecting her. "If I had a whit of your courage. I'll say, the other ladies will all be wearing such daring hats within a day."

Agatha forgot how to speak. She was not used to being fussed over—or being a leader in fashion, despite her adoration for her own style. She contemplated putting the hat back, but a thought occurred to her. If the other court ladies did begin to mimic her fashion, would not it mean that the gap was truly shrinking—that they were seeing her as a leader for *them*?

"Thank you so very much for closing your shop for us, Monsieur Tindle. You did not have to do such a thing on my account. I'm no better than anyone else."

Tindle beamed. His tanned, bald head was gleaming in the light and his brown eyes were amongst the warmest Agatha had ever encountered. "His Highness certainly picked the right bride. Take it as a personal thank you, from me." He put a hand to his chest with sincerity. "My own way of honouring you."

Agatha curtsied, because words had well and truly failed her. The initial opinion she'd formed of the man before her had been wrong. He had not been issuing her false compliments. He was viewing her through the eyes of hope.

Agatha wasn't sure if she deserved to be seen through such

eyes, but she vowed to do everything she could to live up to it. First, she would speak with everyone else possible on their little outing. Knowledge did not only come from books.

"MY FEET ARE GOING to fall off the end of my legs. Are we quite done yet?" Agatha complained.

Eleanor had managed to briefly drag her away from Mer Row, but Anne was leading them back that direction on their way to the castle. They'd meandered into so many frilly shops she thought she'd scream.

"Goddess, but you are a frail thing for growing up on a farm," Eleanor mumbled.

It was the first time Agatha had heard that bit of supposed information about herself, aside from cruel remarks from the prince, but she thought she should lean into it.

"On the *farm*, we don't amble about cobblestone streets in heeled shoes and corseted gowns."

They stopped in front of a shop and Anne smiled. "Perhaps this will lift your spirits, my lady."

Agatha did dreadfully need a lift in her spirits. Although she'd forced Eleanor to purchase everything to her taste—despite the maidservant's revulsion—her conversations with the people had revealed nothing. Their faces lit as she strode past, and they offered too-deep bows, but it was as if a veil fell over each person once she tried to speak with them.

Determined to try one more time, Agatha veered away from her entourage. She ignored Eleanor's shrill complaints directed at her back and approached a young mother. The woman's face brightened as Agatha neared and she dropped into a low curtsy.

"Madame, would you mind terribly if I purchased a treat for

your daughter?" Agatha smiled kindly at them both. The little girl gasped and jumped up and down. Her mother was grinning ear to ear and began to nod her agreement. Suddenly, a jolt of bewilderment shot through the woman and Agatha stepped backward. She and her daughter both went a bit rigid, their faces drooping, then they walked away without a word.

Agatha was still reeling when Anne came up and grabbed her arm, pulling her away. "This is Prince Grimm's favourite pâtisserie," she explained, pointing at a cheerful confectionary.

Shaking off the strange encounter, Agatha took note of the sign, *Dulcibella's Pâtisserie,* as they entered. She wasn't likely to ever turn down a sweet pastry or a hot cup of coffee.

As soon as the door opened, the aroma of the shop greeted her. The delicious warmth of the bakery kissed her cheeks like an old friend, cinnamon, nutmeg, rich butter, and a hint of honey enveloping her first. With all the high class of a farm girl, she gaped at the rows of sweets. The baker stood smiling at her with a hand on one hip. She was a woman well-on in years, but the vibrancy she exuded was breathtaking.

"My Lady." She handed Agatha a large, pink box. "Fill it." She winked and Agatha instantly felt her a kindred spirit.

"You do not have to tell me twice, Madame."

Fill the box she did, with cinnamon buns, crêpes, chocolate-dipped madeleines, brioche, honey cakes, croissants, macarons, and—of course—pumpkin muffins. She bit into one and it tasted so much like home that her heart ached.

"Thank you, Madame. These are delicious," she spoke around a mouthful. "I presume your name is Dulcibella?"

Her rich skin and sloped eyes told Agatha she'd hailed from the Sudern Isle of Coronocco, but her name spoke of Lyronia. The two countries sat just to the Nord of the Isle, and Agatha was pleased to see that the populations had mingled since her sabbatical from life a hundred years ago.

"It is, my lady, but you may call me Dulci. Here." The vivid woman turned to her confections and placed more madeleines and a few chocolate croissants in another box. "His Highness' favourites." She winked again and Agatha made a mental note to visit Dulci again, tout suite.

Grimm

GAIUS POPPED a bite of croissant in his mouth as Grimm paced the limited interior of the lighthouse watchroom. He'd been sneaking away to the lighthouse since he was a boy. Eventually, it had become a hideout of sorts for him and Gaius. Grimm had the only key, an ancient thing, and it was clear no one cleaned the place—aside from Gaius on very rare occasions.

Something brown was bubbling inside alchemical beakers in the corner Gaius vacated, and Grimm went to sniff it. "What is this?"

"That"—Gaius swallowed his pastry—"is what the draught boils down to."

"Which is?"

An impatient grunt sounded in Gaius' throat. "I haven't deciphered that yet. I...needed Professor Ludwig's insight."

Grimm ran a hand through his hair and sat. "We've lost our footing."

"We've not. Not yet," Gaius shot back. "You didn't see who killed him?"

"I didn't. They were cloaked. It could have been anyone. My assumption is a hired assassin."

"The magus?"

Grimm's mouth formed a thin line. "I wouldn't put it past

him, but I don't think so. He's even overseeing my meals now. Thankfully, he's remained so focused on me he's no idea what you or Alestair are up to."

In truth, he was becoming nervous about Alestair. There was a very good chance he shouldn't have sent him out, regardless of their need for it. He'd only been a child when Grimm noticed his knack for stirring up trouble, and barely a man when he'd asked him to join forces with him and Gaius.

GRIMM REACHED out and snatched the little ruffian by the collar as he ran. He turned the boy around and held his shoulders gently, bending down to eye level. "If Cook finds out you stole that biscuit, you're in for a lashing. You know that, right?"

The scruffy little boy beamed. "That's why she won't catch me."

"Do you know who I am?" Grimm didn't mean to pull the prince card, but he liked this kid's spirit. He was met with a withering stare and Grimm laughed. "Tell you what. If you can sneak yourself into my mother's tea party and come back with three valuable pieces of information that are new to me, I'll make you my apprentice." He expected the little scoundrel to mock him, but his face brightened.

He'd come back with five secrets. Lady Olivia was with child, so late in life. His mother had hidden a note in the folds of her skirts. Duchess Corinne slipped something smelly into her tea. Eleanor was the new maidservant's name. And another servant had read the letter before handing it to the queen.

"I'm still concerned Alestair will only meet stone walls for all this draught is doing," Gaius broke into Grimm's reverie.

Grimm's chest rumbled his agreement. "Precisely why I sent him past our borders."

After a moment of silence, Gaius changed the subject. "When did you meet with Dulci?"

"I didn't. She sent croissants to me this afternoon. They were in my rooms when I returned from the library."

"Ah. She must want to speak soon, then."

"And I quite expect an earful."

AGATHA

A letter sat against the vase of fresh flowers by Agatha's bedside table when she arrived back from her shopping excursion. She was to attend afternoon tea with Prince Grimm and his courtiers. Signed and sealed by the Grand Magus.

Agatha groaned, crumpling the letter and tossing it into the flames of her fireplace. Anne walked in just as the flames roared exceptionally high with a bit of magic Agatha had spat into it. The maid jumped back with a mouse-like squeak. Adrenaline sparked through Agatha as she tried to decipher how long Anne had been there, unbeknownst to her.

"Did you add parchment to the fire, my lady?"

Agatha nodded mutely.

"Ah." Anne carefully laid an armload of laundered dresses on the chaise and took up the fire poker. "The ink on parchment can sometimes make for a misguided fire."

"Right." Agatha let out a breath.

"Is everything alright?" Anne stood and wiped her hands on her apron, leaving soot smeared across the linen.

She'd been so foolish to use magic at all within the castle. It was such a strange thing to keep herself concealed in front of people after she'd spent so long in isolation. Agatha missed her solitary life in the Forest of Tombs. There were no *teas* or corsets or annoying princes. No meddling magi or battered maids.

"Yes, why?" Agatha lied.

"Letters that contain good news aren't generally hurled into fires." Anne's gentle smile made Agatha's heart twinge. Perhaps some parts of the court weren't so bad.

"I have to attend a tea and dinner with…far too many people for my liking, that's all."

"It's a different realm in those rooms for the likes of us, isn't it?"

Agatha nodded. If only there were more people like her precious maid in existence.

Anne reached out and squeezed Agatha's hand. "Thank you for doing what we can't, even if it's simply being in rooms we're not allowed in. I know it isn't easy."

Blast her. Agatha swallowed down the lump in her throat. She didn't see how teas and suppers would bring lasting change, but she could handle a few miserable hours for the likes of Anne.

That afternoon, Agatha sat tapping her nail against the teacup she'd hardly sipped from, beholding the bright, open parlour of marble and uselessly gilded grandeur. All the lords and ladies sat in little groups dispersed throughout. None of them spoke to her.

Truthfully, it was preferable, but it dug the splinter of classism deeper. She didn't want to *blend in* with these waspy ladies tied up until their bosoms burst from their bodices. All *they* accomplished was luring milquetoast men into boring conversations. Agatha would not be like the rest of them. True reformation would come not from blurring lines between the aristocracy and the lower class, but from erasing them altogether. Agatha could not do that single-handedly, Goddess-Ordered or not, and she couldn't do it by becoming anything like these courtiers.

She was contemplating hiding in a corner with a book when Miriam walked in carrying a tray of frosted tea cakes. Agatha jumped from her seat and moved toward her. "Miriam." She dipped her chin to the servant. "It's lovely to see you this afternoon." Miriam's attention darted every which way, and her hands began to tremble. "I wanted to apologise for—" Miriam nearly dropped the tray, and Agatha reached toward her to keep it from tipping, but the servant startled backward, eyes wide.

"Please, my lady," she whispered, eyes still skittering around the room. "I would appreciate it if you didn't address me. You've done enough."

Agatha's lips parted, but the servant rushed away, depositing her tray on a table next to Grimm—who sat speaking with Gaius and Mila—before she dashed from the room. The prince caught Agatha's eye, face solemn, but she looked away. Guilt dripped over her like oil, heavy and sodden. In her periphery, she saw Grimm finally pull his attention back from her and say something to Gaius in a hushed tone.

She needed some air.

Agatha rushed out into the hall, the events the day emotionally and physically weighing on her. Her mind felt foggy and she didn't know which way to turn just to find some damned *air*. She calmed herself long enough to take out her guiding stone, but it wasn't there in her wrist pouch. Cursing, she dug through it, dropping bits of Mabon's treats and a sprinkle of dried leaves onto the stone floor.

Exasperated, she growled and reached up to the black sapphire encased in its filigree locket at her throat and whispered.

"*Respirer.*"

The stone hummed in its cage and she began walking, letting it lead her. The sound of boots scuffing against stone came from behind her and she stopped.

"In need of a break?"

Agatha met Lord Gaius' piercing seafoam gaze. "Very much."

He glanced over his shoulder at Agatha's guard and the two others that spilled into the corridor to watch them. "Come on. There's a place where they can see us, but the sea drowns out conversation."

Gaius led her to a balcony built into the towering black rock jutting out over Mer Noir. The air off the sea was too cold for the thin, chestnut gown she'd selected, but it did instantly calm her anxiety. The guards hung back, just inside the castle. They were mere feet away, but the crashing of the waves hit the stone walls and bounced back toward the water, cocooning Agatha and Gaius. She owed the lord a hefty favour for showing her this place. When she turned to thank him, she found he was already looking at her.

"Court intricacies can be overwhelming."

Agatha huffed a small breath through her nose. "Understatement of the realm." She hugged her arms around herself to stave off the chill. "What happened with Miriam..." She trailed off shaking her head.

"It wasn't your fault. Wellington is a monster."

"She practically told me it was my fault." And Agatha wasn't convinced *Wellington* was the one who had maimed Miriam further, anyway.

Gaius turned toward her. "She's just scared."

Agatha wasn't certain how much was safe to say to him.

He'd taken her to a pretty place, but who was to say his kindness wasn't an agenda? The thought made her guilt over Miriam melt into resolve.

She squared her shoulders and shifted so they were face-to-face. "I will simply find a way to raise the people without endangering them."

Lord Gaius looked out to sea then back at Agatha. "I don't think that's possible, Lady Agatha."

"Funny, I didn't ask what you thought." Agatha turned on her heel and left, pushing past the guards and leaving Gaius out in the cold.

CHAPTER
TEN

D uty first to the Crown, for she bows to none. Our
Seagovia.
      -Seagovian Royal Edict

AGATHA

THE SUNSET over the waves was dazzling, its indigo and azure
bruising the sky, bleeding into gold just over the water. A breeze
off the sea lifted Agatha's hair, and she inhaled deeply, listening
to the music of Mer Noir. Tilting her head back, she marvelled at
the stars just beginning to sparkle at the crest of the sky. Her
mighty waves crashed against rocks jutting out into the water,
creating a symphony that settled Agatha's weary bones. The
trees, kissed deeply by Autumn, rustled in the cool breeze, some
leaves flitting inland and others bravely wafting out to sea. If not
for the sullen prince walking at her side, it would have been a
perfect moment.

He'd been in a foul mood all through dinner. They both had

been, really. Once the queen had noticed, she'd snapped at them and commanded they go for a walk along the beach to correct their vile tempers. "The people must see you in *love*," she'd chastised under her breath.

Agatha's temper heated at the thought and she directed her mind to Mabon's growing disdain for Eleanor to cool her cheeks. Alas, it backfired, for she let out a small involuntary snicker. She clamped her mouth shut, but Grimm had already turned his head, watching her with one brow arched.

"If you've seen something amusing, please share with the class. I'm nearly dead from boredom out here."

"My sincerest apologies for not being the sort of company you normally keep," she bit out. "I don't know that you would find it comical, anyway."

"Try me."

Agatha smoothed her hands down the sides of her dress and felt something. She patted it for a moment, digging through the folds of the fabric. Grimm stopped walking and eyed her curiously.

Agatha gasped. "This gown has pockets!"

The prince snorted, shoved his hands in his own pockets, and ambled forward. "I grew tired of your embarrassing and endless trail of trinkets everywhere you go. Stones you carry, letters, filthy leaves you find pretty...morsels for the *bat...*" He shook his head. "I instructed Anne to ensure all your gowns have them. Now you won't leave a mess in your wake." He gestured to her skirts. "Pockets."

She would have almost thought it a kindness, though she knew better. "Mabon is actually what I found humorous," Agatha offered.

"Who?"

"My *bat*. Mabon." The prince kept walking as he waited for the rest of the story, his profile illuminated by the setting sun's reflection off the waves. "He's decided my maidservant,

Eleanor, isn't to his liking, and he flew into her hair yesterday in a huff."

To her utter surprise, the prince tipped his head back and laughed in earnest. "Oh, I would've paid handsomely to see that." He shook his head, chuckling still. "Eleanor is a frightful thing."

Agatha nodded her agreement and silence descended once more between them, awkward and uncomfortable. She wanted to retreat to her rooms and write Sorscha about her discussion with Magus von Fuchs. Or lose herself in the Stacks now that she'd mysteriously been granted open admission. Frankly, she'd rather wade into the black depths of the sea than stand out in the cold with Prince Grimm any longer.

"Gaius showed you the Balcony of Deafening Silence this afternoon?" the prince asked abruptly.

Agatha glanced at him sidelong, wondering why it came up. "He did."

Grimm nodded. "It's one of my favourite places in the castle."

Agatha said nothing. She merely watched him with suspicion. He'd never spoken to her so civilly before.

"Did you grow up in Helsvar? I'd heard a rumour that it was being rebuilt slowly."

Agatha stiffened. He was certainly full of questions, and it unnerved her. "No."

"What made you want to keep a bat as your pet?"

Agatha stopped dead in her tracks. "Why are you interrogating me all of a sudden?"

He looked exasperated, lips in a flat line. "I'm not *interrogating* you, Agatha." He pointed down the beach to a few people milling about. "Two of those women are my mother's maids. They report *everything* to her. We need to keep up pretenses, do we not?"

"*Please.* Those nasty gossips have followed us for days." His eyebrows furrowed and he frowned, but she trudged on. "Their presence never caused you to question me before."

"Goddess, Agatha." He ran a hand through his wild hair, shifting on his feet. "I'm not *questioning* you. If we're to be married in less than a fortnight, I'd at least like to know something about you."

"Your and Lord Gaius' plans are failing then, are they?" She was shocked by the amount of hopelessness she felt at the realisation. The desire she'd been harbouring to see the marriage fail was deeper than she'd thought. Agatha wondered what that meant about her devotion to Hespa. If someone else stopped the marriage, would she still lose Sorscha? Dread coiled in her middle and she pushed the thought away.

Grimm glanced at the ground briefly before turning his gaze out to sea. "Not failing, per se, but I would not say it's going as well as I'd like." He stopped abruptly and touched a hand to Agatha's arm to halt her as well. "I've had enough of despair and gloom today."

The sincerity in his voice landed like a strike against her chest. Noticing that he still held her arm, he promptly let go and resumed walking. Agatha reluctantly followed.

"Let's make a game of it, hm?" Grimm said. "Three inquiries each. We both have *one* chance to pass on answering an inquiry, but the others must be answered."

Agatha thought for a moment. Most assuredly, it was a clever trick to try and undermine her presence there—prove she wasn't worthy of marrying him. Though, perhaps she could twist the game in her favour to learn what *she* needed to know.

"Fine."

"As a show of goodwill"—the prince mocked a bow—"you may go first, my lady."

Despite the thousands of questions peppering her mind, Agatha found it best to begin small. "Why are you called Grimm when your name is Thackery?"

Grimm clasped his hands behind his back as they walked. "As a boy, my father as well as my tutors incessantly chastised me for being too stoic, too serious, too *grim*. Eventually, it became what I was known for, and as any other pet name originates—what I was known *by*."

Agatha considered his candour as well as the intriguing look into his life, still so foreign to her. "Your turn."

"If not Helsvar, where did you grow up?"

He did not pose it as a probing question, but Agatha was certain it was. However, he'd been quite forthright in his answer, so she thought it would work to her benefit to do the same. "I grew up in a place called Drifthollow with my three sisters." Never mind that it was a half-truth. She'd only had her Sisters for a few moons after Helsvar burned before they were wrenched apart and raised by the former Sisters Solstice —separately.

"*Three* sisters," Grimm marvelled. "I assume that provides a plethora of intriguing anecdotes."

Agatha did not miss the way he phrased his response, so as not to use up another question. Still, she smiled wistfully, thinking of her Sisters, and nodded.

With only two questions left, she needed to delve deeper, but not too deep. "What do you think the people *see* when they think of you and me? Of our sudden engagement and what it could mean for them?"

Grimm's breathy laugh escaped in a burst. "Gloves off already, hm?" She expected him to pass, but he did not. "I think *hope* is what they see."

It was so at odds with what Agatha had expected. She couldn't fathom why the prince was being so candid unless his aim was to urge her to be just as forthright. She wondered how he could be so callous as to want to squash their hope by preventing their marriage. Though, she surmised, if he sat under the teaching of that despicable magus... Guilt trickled in then—

she had wished, not moments ago, to see the marriage fail as well.

Agatha braced herself for his next inquiry.

"I do find your bat intriguing," Grimm said instead of asking anything.

He smiled warmly and she furrowed her brow at him. She'd originally thought him a handsome idiot. Prideful and spoiled. And he was those things still, but she hadn't expected him to be so calculated in his pursuit to discredit her. He wasn't dim-witted —she'd grant him that.

"You're not so very *grim*, you know."

Grimm laughed openly, certainly giving much good news for the loose-lipped maids to report to the queen as they passed by. "You are."

Despite herself, Agatha's lips turned up on one side. "I suppose you're right about that."

They reached the end of the rocky beach and turned back, black sand scattering underfoot. They'd gone several steps before Grimm asked, "Why do you think we've been forced into this?" His tone did not read anything aside from genuine curiosity, and that unnerved her more than a downright interrogation.

Agatha swallowed. "I'm the peasant girl foretold in a prophecy, of course."

Grimm stopped and turned to face her. "Do you believe that?" His last inquiry used up, his good humour vanished and his usual headstrong pride lit his eyes.

"Do you?" Agatha challenged.

"*Pass*," they said in unison.

They stared at one another, Grimm's jaw flexing and unflexing, camaraderie entirely evaporated.

"Final question, peasant."

Agatha's thoughts spun in a frenzy. Curse her doubts for making her think he was anything but calculated with this farce of a game and curse him for playing the bastard prince so well.

"When did you learn of the prophecy foretelling our marriage?"

He did not so much as blink. "When I was fifteen."

They were back at the entrance to the castle where Anne stood with Agatha's guards, waiting to escort her back to her rooms. Grimm slid his hand into hers, interlacing their fingers and sending a shock roiling through her from the contact of their skin.

He leaned in, his breath tickling her ear, and she could hear the grin in his voice. "I'll let you have this one. Let you slide with only two questions answered. I will not be so kind next time." He pulled back and pressed a chaste kiss to her hand before dropping it.

"Goodnight, prince," Agatha spoke sarcastically under her breath and curtsied.

"Sweet dreams, peasant," he whispered right back.

Agatha's hands were trembling, and not from the cold, but she smiled to herself as she walked with Anne down the corridor.

It didn't matter what the prince thought of their little game. He'd given her two valuable pieces of information. For a surety, he was more than just a spoiled princeling. What he was playing at she didn't know, but there was more to this man. And, best of all, he gave her a timeline to better search records for the original prophecy—the year Grimm was first told of it.

ELEVEN

T here comes a time when what is deemed right *differs from what must be done.*
                    -Writings of Ambrose Joubert

AGATHA

IT TOOK three days and no small amount of manoeuvring to lose her guards and servants, but Agatha found the book—the one housing the mundane court records taken during Grimm's fifteenth year. It dated back thirteen years, almost exactly, and she marvelled at the dreadfully boring things a young boy had to sit through to be the prince.

Growing impatient, she began to skim the pages, leafing through them until she saw the word *Autumn* and halted. When the word *prophecy* also stared back at her, Agatha nearly yelped.

ON THIS DAY, THE FOURTH OF THE WANING CRESCENT OCTEN, IN THE YEAR OF OUR GODDESS THREE, 1694, HIS ROYAL HIGHNESS, PRINCE THACKERY FREDERIC PERIDOT III, WAS READ IN FULL THE PROPHECY OF OUR DAUGHTER OF AUTUMN.

THE NEXT ENTRY was that of Grimm holding his first court session. Agatha slammed the book shut, a cloud of dust assaulting her.

She needed to find that blasted prophecy in full. It struck her as odd that it had only the mention of Our Daughter of Autumn, not Grimm. Of course, if it had mentioned Grimm, the magus wouldn't have been so shocked when Agatha arrived. She recalled the prince's outrage and disbelief the day she'd come to Merveille as well.

Frustrated, she stormed out of the library, making her way to find her maids. In her haste, she rounded a corner and bowled into Gaius and Mila. The lord's face brightened as he caught her by the arm, but Mila stared daggers at her. Irritation flared within Agatha when she realised they'd been walking alone together in the dark halls.

"Apologies." She swallowed her sneer. "If you'll excuse me, I must be getting back to my rooms."

Gaius opened his mouth, but she kept walking, disappearing around a corner.

There was far too much afoot to agonise over what tangle Mila and Gaius might be in together. Agatha still had questions in need of answering, and she knew just who to ask—if she could work up the nerve.

"YOU CERTAINLY HAVE GROWN fond of these confections," Eleanor grumbled, dodging a gaggle of children running down the dirty sidewalk.

Agatha was indeed fond of Dulci's sweets, but her reason for visiting the pâtisserie every day was a far cry from a sweet tooth. The first few visits, she purchased treats and made small conversation with Dulci. For this visit, Agatha had different plans. When she'd come the last time, the old baker informed her they needed to speak privately about something important. She couldn't fathom what that might be, but she'd had an inkling since first meeting Dulci that this particular encounter was inevitable. For that to happen, though, Agatha needed to lose Eleanor.

"They're delicious. If you'd have even a morsel, you'd see that."

Eleanor scoffed. "You'll be lucky to fit into your wedding gown."

Agatha's stomach flipped at the mention of her impending wedding, but she shook it off. "I've not even begun fittings yet, so it's no matter."

Eleanor's eyes slid over Agatha's figure and she wanted to snort at her maidservant. She'd clearly never been comfortable enough in her own skin to not pity those she thought less beautiful. A true shame. Agatha shrugged and bit off another chunk of the turkey leg she'd procured a few shops down the lane. The merchants of Gemme Road, in all their finery, had absolutely nothing on Mer Row. She could see why the prince quietly had credit in the shops on the Row.

As they rounded the corner to Dulci's pâtisserie, Agatha pointed across the way to the cobbler she'd strategically ordered boots from two days prior, so they'd be ready on this day. "Eleanor, be a dear and pick up my boots from the cobbler while we're in Dulci's. I'd like to make it back to the castle in time to visit the library before dinner."

Eleanor huffed but made her way across the street, shouting violently at a horse and carriage that narrowly avoided hitting her.

Anne, and Agatha's two guards, followed her into the pâtisserie. One of her usual guards, Clark, had recently been replaced with the kind guard from the library—Augustus Lotrum. He and Porthos held back, but only slightly. Anne, however, stood dutifully by Agatha's side, a sweet smile adorning her pretty face.

Dulci greeted them warmly and Agatha turned to address Anne. "Pick a few things for yourself." Anne began to protest, but Agatha squeezed her hand. "I want you to enjoy them *with* me this afternoon." Anne's smile lit the room. Agatha would have felt poorly for distracting her if it hadn't also been the truth. She was beginning to cherish her peaceful camaraderie with Anne.

Dulci dusted sugared and floured hands on her apron. "My Lady. Four days in a row you grace me with your presence. You've the nastiest sweet tooth I've ever encountered"—she lowered her voice—"or you've more than confections you're seeking." She winked.

"Both are correct, Dulci." Agatha let her eyes drift to her guards and back to the baker. "Eleanor is detained, but I'm afraid ridding myself of everyone is difficult."

Dulci narrowed her eyes, but her lips turned up knowingly. "Porthos," she called out to one of the guards, shocking Agatha that she knew his name. "There's a fresh pan of lemon-berry savarin in the back." She inclined her head toward the kitchen and both guards raised their eyebrows at Agatha in question.

She chuckled at their child-like behaviour. "It's fine with me. I'm perfectly safe."

"Anne," Dulci offered as the guards barreled past them, "I see that twinkle in your eye. Go."

Anne looked to Agatha, and she nodded. "I'm fine, Anne. Go."

When they were alone, Agatha gave Dulci a curious stare. The baker shrugged. "Lemon is Porthos' favourite. And *Augustus* is Anne's favourite." She winked at the realisation dawning on Agatha's face. She'd been blind to any attraction her maidservant had for her new guard.

"You need to open your eyes, my lady." Dulci was unnervingly intuitive, but Agatha only wanted to soak it up. She'd been correct. There was more to this woman than baking.

"What have you gotten me alone here to say?" Agatha glanced toward the door Anne and her guards had just vanished through.

The woman's face was weathered with age, wisdom in every line etched across it. "You've been coming here for days, sitting on the verge of asking *me* something. I didn't think you'd ever actually ask me if I didn't tell you to do so." Agatha frowned. She wasn't wrong. "Now, what is it, Lady Agatha?"

She twisted her hair around and let it drape over one shoulder, unsure of where to begin. Dulci was little more than an acquaintance—a Blacklisted one, at that. Asking her outright if she knew anything about the prophecy the royal family kept close to their chest was foolish. Agatha wasn't fond of the prince, but—despite her own vicious thoughts of maiming him—she didn't want to risk him undeserved harm. She couldn't have a loose tongue with a baker on Mer Row she had a *feeling* was a friend and not foe.

She selected her words carefully. "I take it that by now you are aware of the circumstances surrounding my betrothal to His Highness?"

Dulci squinted, suppressing another astute smile. "And what might those circumstances be, my lady?"

Agatha took her time, chewing on the inside of her lip. "That I am not high born."

She watched as the older woman nodded and crossed her arms. "No, you are not. Which begs the question *why* our pious royals would allow such a thing." The woman's gall took Agatha by surprise, though she saw no fear or worry of retribution on her face. "Is it because they truly wish to do away with their classism?" Dulci chuckled darkly.

Of course not. Agatha fiddled with a crystal in her pocket, its properties doing little to quell her rising anxiety. "You don't believe that to be so?"

The wrinkles on the baker's face deepened with her responding laugh. "The people do," she said when her mirth trickled away. "The people might feel ill toward their king, but they would fight for their prince if they could." Dulci wiped at the flour-dusted counter and went on. "The prince within the castle is not the same man outside of it. *Open your eyes.*"

Agatha shook her head; she hadn't come there to speak of Grimm. "You truly believe they would fight—the people? They are afraid to stand up against injustice, surely." She could painfully identify with a want to defy authority and a greater fear of doing so. "I've seen some severely mistreated for small infractions. I can't imagine there is much room for them to do anything to fight back. For *us* to fight back."

"It's true. But the fact remains, they are very tired of waiting for Grimm to become king, and we've all grown restless."

Agatha wondered at Dulci's abandonment of Grimm's title but said nothing. "They feel Grimm would make a better king?" She struggled to keep the disgust and disbelief from her voice.

"King Frederic used to be a good man." Dulci frowned. "It wasn't until he married Fleurina that he hardened. The people *hope* Prince Thackery will be a better king. He was their only hope, truthfully, until you came along."

Agatha swallowed hard. Sister Solstice—witch or mortal— that was a tall order. "Is the Grand Magus from Fleurina's former court, then?"

"No, he was brought in by one of the king's advisors before they married. King Frederic was quite young, not even into his second decade, and Queen Fleurina was hardly even a woman. Their advisors and the magus made decisions for the kingdom for quite some time."

It certainly seemed like the magus still did. "I've only spent mere moments with the king. He speaks little and seems content to let the Grand Magus parrot for him."

Dulci nodded. "You are an observant young thing." Agatha nearly snorted at the thought of being *young*. The baker leaned up against the pale blue counter and dusted cookie crumbs off one of the brightly dyed fabrics resting beneath the goods. "In the time of my ancestors, Merveille was ruled by King Frederic's great uncle, King Leopold. His cousin, King Caliban was on the throne before him, working with The Order of Hespa to dispel the class system and put the painful turmoil between the people of Merveille and the immigrants of Coronocco and Lyronia to rest."

Agatha's chest ached. She knew all too well the unrest in those days; the vicious treatment of those that were different. And she knew all too well what Dulci would say next.

"But King Caliban was murdered, and Leopold, next in line for the throne, did not share his views." Dulci looked at the wall of confections, though Agatha knew she saw only the past behind her eyes. "It was difficult to be an outsider to the aristoc-racy—a common man—but it was another thing altogether to be a foreigner or a halfling. Our very lives depended upon keeping our heads down, taking positions of servitude, and never, ever speaking out of turn to a person born of Seagovia." Dulci fiddled with a loose string on her apron. "My grandmother used to tell me she wondered why her parents had ever come here at all."

Agatha swallowed back her tears. She'd let herself walk away after what they did to Ira. She'd let herself turn her back on these people because of her own blinding pain. Perhaps that was why Hespa had sent her back here. To finally be able to end what had been caused by killing Caliban on the horrible night that had blackened her soul.

"It wasn't until King Frederic II took the throne at seventeen that the hatred calmed. He was marrying an immigrant—a woman from Coronocco."

Agatha's eyes grew wide. She'd never read this. Never heard this. As far as she knew, her Sisters had no hand in it, either, but it was a monumental moment in History. Or it would've been. Queen Fleurina hailed from peaceful Eridon, a small country on the far inland reaches of Seagovia. She had been a princess, and was about as opposite of a Coronoccan woman as one could be with her fair skin and lilting, lyrical accent.

"What happened?"

The bell over the door chimed and Dulci waved at the patron before turning back to Agatha and speaking under her breath. "No one knows. But the moment the marriage was called off and Queen Fleurina came about, the people grew restless. The king's advisors and the newly appointed Grand Magus urged him to put curfews in place and to close himself off from the people. It was a downward spiral from there." She lifted a tuft of curly, salt-and-pepper hair out of her face. "Riots began in the streets, servants refused to work...before we knew it, we were being shoved back and—" Dulci shook her head. "The people all of the sudden quieted, all but a very few of us. The quiet and complacency lasted for a long time—decades. When it wore off, the crown found new ways."

The curious veil that dropped suddenly over some people. "*You* don't seem complacent, Dulci."

She shook her voluminous hair, face set like a warrior. "Never. There are a handful of us in agreement. And, if I'm honest, I think there are many more that are beginning to open their eyes, quietly waiting for a chance to act." She began filling a box with treats.

Agatha's pulse surged. Was she speaking of a secret faction? "Why are you telling me this? Trusting me with it?"

Dulci had no chance to respond. Anne, Porthos, and Augustus burst through the kitchen door then, and Dulci shoved the box in Agatha's hands. "For His Highness."

At the door, Agatha turned back, locking eyes with the old baker. Dulci nodded once and turned back to her work.

Agatha and her party meandered their way back down the row of dilapidated merchants and past the shops of Gemme Road, the castle looming at the end of the sparkling street. Eleanor walked in front, head held high, while Anne lagged behind. She was speaking with Augustus, a bashful glow upon her cheeks. Agatha wondered how she could have ever missed Anne's clear feelings for the guard. Dulci was right, she needed to open her eyes.

She brushed a stray strand of hair out of her face and lifted the wide brim of her hat to better see her surroundings. She bit back a hiss at the sun's brightness, but when her eyes adjusted, she took in the world around her. The streets bustled with people of a multitude of races, dressed in the vibrant fabrics of the rich. Horses clomped down the cobbled street and shopkeepers shouted their wares and swept their stoops. It was such a normal place. The people seemed to be intermingling, but she noticed almost no one wore the dark and colourless clothing of the common folk. Curious, she asked Augustus—a descendant of Lyronia—to take them the long way to the castle, past his childhood home. He blushed but obliged, only momentarily put off by Eleanor's scowl at the request.

The group wound through the streets, Agatha analysing the clear descent from clean and proper to the slums. The people wore the hardened faces of those bent by life, along with the distant look Dulci had alluded to, but they'd *stayed* in Merveille. Despite how they'd been treated and how their ancestors had been treated, they'd not run as Agatha had.

"This is the home I grew up in." Augustus' voice was thick with emotion as he pointed to a worn house half the size of Agatha's small cottage in the Forest of Tombs. The roof was partially caved in and the entire structure tilted to one side. A multitude of cracks ran the height of the structure, and three windows were broken. "When Prince Grimm instated me as a guard, I saved my coin for years to move my mother and my sister there." He pointed a few streets over to a beautiful but modest area on the crest of a hill.

Agatha didn't know what to say. "Thank you for showing me this, Augustus."

As they wound back toward the wealthier part of town, nearing Mer Row once more, a thought struck her, and she stopped. "If the shopkeepers of Mer Row are Blacklisted, how do they have such beautiful wares when their patrons are..."

"The lower class?" Eleanor finished with scorn.

Anne spoke, her voice as bright as the sun assaulting Agatha. "Rumour has it that a secret benefactor provides their supplies and wares."

Agatha's eyes widened and Augustus popped into the gossip. "I heard a mysterious hooded man paid rent for all the homes in the slums for a *year*."

"That can't be true," Agatha said as Anne gasped.

Eleanor folded her arms, frowning. "It's true." They all turned in unison to look at her, even Porthos. She sighed and rolled her eyes. "My gran lives there. A man came a fortnight ago."

"And no one has any idea who?" Agatha asked, but something familiar caught her eye, distracting her.

It was her hat. A woman was wearing her hat. The very one she had on her own head. A breath caught in her throat as she saw another. And another.

Monsieur Tindle had been right.

Agatha lifted her skirts and ran for the dressmaker's shop on

Mer Row, guards on her heels and her ladies' maids shouting after her. She flung herself through the door, the little bell above it chiming delicately.

"Monsieur Tindle!" she called out.

He came around the corner and put a hand on his hip. "It's just Tindle, darling, *please*. What's all the fuss?"

"Have you seen them?" she asked, breathless.

"Seen what?" His coy smile told her he knew precisely what she meant. Anne and Eleanor stumbled in, heaving.

"The hats. *My* hat. They're wearing my hat. Just like you said."

Tindle picked a piece of lint off his elaborate coat. "I sold four just this morning. Two of them to court ladies." Agatha's eyes widened as Anne put a hand over her mouth. "They're rallying behind you, my dear. What shall we do next?"

Agatha looked around the shop, contemplating. A surge of hope she hadn't felt in hundreds of years bolstered her, and she gave Tindle a wicked little smile. "*Boots*. Black leather. Laced intricately up the shin, with a tall, squared heel." Tindle looked positively ready to burst. "And send a slash down all my new skirts so the boots can be seen."

Tindle put his hands on either side of his face. "You're sinister and I adore you!"

"No one will wear those boots or cut their skirts like a harlot," Eleanor interjected, receiving a scowl from everyone at once.

"It's not harlotry, Eleanor. It's *fashion*. And it remains to be seen what the people will do. If they do wear it, we will know."

> *The magi lead with grace and honour, aiding the flock in setting their worship upon Her.*
>
> -Sacred Texts of Hespa

Grimm

"YOUR HIGHNESS." The Grand Magus bowed to Grimm, barely bending at the waist.

"Von Fuchs," Grimm spoke, smirking as the magus' nostrils flared at his disrespect.

They stood silently in the throne room for a few brittle moments before the magus turned to him. "You look ill at ease, Your Highness. Wedding jitters?"

Grimm was in no mood to deal with the snivelling bastard. "You know all about those, don't you, magus?" It was foolish to play a card he'd held close to his chest for so long, but he was just so damned *tired*. Perhaps Agatha had been correct. Maybe he did show his hand too easily at times. But his barb hit home with the magus and the result was horribly satisfying.

His face darkened. "I don't know what you're insinuating—"

"I'm insinuating nothing. But wouldn't it be a damned shame if your plan failed?" He lifted an eyebrow at the man.

"*My* plan?" Von Fuchs barked a humourless laugh. "Oh, dear prince, it is beyond even my power to cause a *prophecy* to come to fruition."

Grimm turned to face the magus, as much to gauge his reaction as to watch the door for his mother's approach. "Or is it?" he challenged. "You don't benefit from appeased sheep in your pews?"

The magus' neck reddened and his jaw flexed. "So help me boy, if—"

"Good afternoon, Mother." Grimm smiled pleasantly.

The blood drained from von Fuchs' face, but he hid it with a low bow. "Your Majesty."

His mother was many things, but she had never once expected Grimm to bow to her. She was not just his queen. Agatha had been wrong about that. His mother smoothed his lapel and took a seat on her throne. "Are the two of you at odds?"

"Of course not, Your Majesty," the magus replied quickly.

Grimm watched as his mother eyed them both at length. Finally, just as von Fuchs was beginning to squirm, she spoke. "The plans for the wedding are coming together beautifully."

Grimm ground his teeth together. He did not have time for wedding planning.

"But I've called you both here to inform you that the king has requested the presence of the Empress of Coronocco and King of Lyronia to attend the wedding as a show of goodwill. They have both accepted."

Grimm furrowed his brow even as his heart began to pound

hopefully within his chest. "Why should they need such a show of goodwill? We've been at peace for hundreds of years."

"It would seem, though Our Daughter of Autumn has done much to appease our own people, her presence is causing quite a stir elsewhere on the continent." She paused, and Grimm fought to keep from inching forward in rapt attention.

"There have been many countries dealing with...unpleasant feelings toward their leaders now that we've become so forward-thinking."

You mean you appear *so forward-thinking.* Farce. The damned thing was a farce, but it was working.

"They've grown agitated and are trying to come here."

"That's preposterous." His words were strong and came out too loudly, but Grimm could scarcely breathe. They'd finally done it. *Alestair* had finally done it. His men had finally incited an uprising—one spanning the *continent.* Or had it really been Agatha's presence?

"It is preposterous," his mother responded, examining a fingernail. "The king"—she glanced briefly at von Fuchs— "thought it best to send soldiers to contain the people. The rulers of some lands are not pleased."

"Hence the olive branch," Grimm finished for her.

"Precisely. Prepare yourself for a few uncomfortable encounters with the rulers and their courtiers." She clapped her lily-white hands together. "Now, the last order of business. Is there anything in particular you would request for your wedding day, my son?"

Grimm caught von Fuchs' snide smile out of the corner of his eye. "I could not care less, Mother."

She frowned. "Very well, then. You're both dismissed."

Von Fuchs bowed and hurried away, most likely to rob some poor elderly woman out of her last coin donated to *Hespa,* but Grimm lingered. A thought had occurred to him, completely unbidden. When the throne room door whispered shut, he turned back to his mother to find her face anticipatory.

"On second thought, Agatha appears to be fond of a dressmaker named Monsieur Tindle on Mer Row. I would request that her gown be designed by him."

He hoped to Hespa that she wouldn't inquire how he knew such a thing.

But his mother only smiled. "On Mer Row, hm? Bold choice." Grimm worried he'd made a grave error, but the queen nodded once. "I'll see that it is done."

He turned to leave, forcing a nonchalant pace. He needed to speak with Gaius immediately. They could no longer attempt to put a stop to this wedding. But first, he had to ensure the names of his men out across Midlerea had not appeared in the Book.

GAIUS' ecstatic grin faded. "Why do you look so dejected? You were elated a moment ago." The lord stepped forward and placed his hands on Grimm's shoulders, shaking him. "We've done it! We've rallied the *nations* to our cause."

Grimm shook his head, a ghost of a smile tugging at his lips. He scrubbed a hand along the back of his neck and moved to stand behind his desk in the lighthouse. "I don't know. I'm happy we're making progress, but this doesn't feel right. It isn't fair to Agatha."

"No one wants to marry a person they don't know, but this is *working*, Grimm."

"Is it? I think it's *her* that's working. They believe in *her*. That damned hat?" He threw his arm wide. "It's everywhere and the magus is furious—" Grimm's words broke off and he sat. "They think I chose her."

Gaius grew serious, crossing his arms over his chest. "Then choose her."

Grimm's head jerked back as if Gaius had slapped him. "No. Out of the question."

"She's not quite so terrible once you get to know her."

"And you've gotten to know her so well?" He loathed the petty jealousy that crept into his voice.

"I've had more real conversations with her than you have," the lord shot back.

Grimm wondered for the first time if his friend had developed feelings for Agatha. Not that it mattered—they'd both agreed, long ago, to keep the mission first at all costs.

"The answer is no, Gaius. If the enemies we've made think, for even a moment, that I care anything for her, they'll kill her, at the very least. Probably worse. And there are far worse things than death."

"If that's the case, then she's already in danger. The whole of Seagovia thinks you're madly in love with her."

"But *von Fuchs* does not. I've been extremely careful about that. His information will travel to whomever he's cavorting with."

"That's been our hope, but we don't know that for certain. Agatha could be an *ally*."

"Many of the people are fond of her, and she's intelligent— I'll give her that—but she's a peasant. She's not familiar with politics. She's not even court-trained. Have you uncovered anything about *Our Daughter of Autumn* that paints her as anything but a peasant?"

"You do believe she's *the* Daughter of Autumn, then?"

"Damn you, Gaius. I don't *know*."

"Grimm, this marriage is happening whether you like it, or think it a good idea, or not. We've tried to prove she isn't the Daughter of Autumn. We've tried having you play the bastard prince and pushing her away. We've tried to find anything to discredit her… Perhaps it's time to make her our ally."

AGATHA

A QUILL POISED between her teeth, Agatha sat hunched over several open tomes in the library. She'd come to continue searching for the full prophecy, or at least information concerning the strange cancellation of a proposal no one in the current day knew of between King Frederic and a foreigner. Alas, a novel had caught her eye on the shelves and she'd given into temptation.

The light from her oil lamp began to sputter, just when the book was reaching a pivotal moment. She lifted the lamp and held it close to the pages, unwilling to tear her eyes away long enough to turn the light up. A whispered *pssst* startled her and she jumped, spilling oil all over the books and sending the light skittering away.

She spat out the quill and cursed, "*Merde*." Agatha turned around to steal a lamp from the table behind her and looked around for the whisperer. She was alone in that row of the Stacks and thought it must have been someone speaking in hushed tones a row or two over.

Seeing the mess she'd made of the books, Agatha ran her hand over them, willing them to dry. She was halfway through the process when she heard it again.

"*Psssst*."

Agatha froze, listening. She could have sworn it came from *under* the table. She bent down, and the whisper grew louder.

"Psssst. *Aggie.*"

Mumbling that she would throttle her Sister, she remained bent under the table and shoved her hand into her pocket, withdrawing her scrying mirror. "*Sorscha.* You blasted fiend. Anyone could have heard you."

Sister Spring grinned at her through the dark glass. "Only if they have witch ears. In that case, I'd surely like to meet them."

"What do you want? I'm in the library."

Sorscha rolled her eyes nearly to the back of her skull. "Then *leave* the library."

Agatha suppressed her flash of irritation, immensely grateful that her guards and ladies' maids had gotten caught up chatting a few rows over. It was vastly unprofessional, but she'd relished the space, even more so with Sorscha now conversing in her pocket.

Agatha slipped through the aisles toward the back of the library where the lanterns were cold and blackness shrouded the shelves. When she reached the far corner and put her back against a tapestry hanging on the wall, she felt a doorknob press against her back. Curious, she lifted the thick tapestry and twisted the knob, but it didn't budge.

She let the hanging fall back, frowning as she reached into her pocket to pull out her mirror again. A voice sounded just on the other side of the mysterious door, and Agatha jumped across the way to ensure she was behind it if it opened.

"*Masquer.*"

A glamour of shimmering magic rendered her invisible within a bubble only Agatha could see, obscuring her in silence.

The door did open, and out stepped the Grand Magus from behind the tapestry with two magi of the cloth Agatha hadn't seen before. They spoke in low voices as the magus locked the door behind them, the wall hanging concealing it from view, and they made their way toward the front of the library.

She'd read that the magus was known to keep long hours in the library, but behind hidden, locked doors seemed a little unnecessary. What could possibly go on in there? What sort of reading material might the magus need to keep hidden? Agatha could hear Sorscha cursing in her pocket, so she pulled the mirror out.

"I can hardly see you. You didn't even leave the library."

"My guards and ladies' maids are in here." Agatha held her borrowed lantern up so Sorscha could see her in the dark.

"You have guards? Gods, that sounds awful."

Agatha gave a weary shrug. "They're not so bad."

"What were you reading? Or are you still looking for the prophecy?"

They both wound their hair around and around before draping it over one shoulder in unison. "I intended to look for it, but I found a novel by Marlowe I hadn't yet read. The one about Lady Magic's faerie realm."

Sorscha perked. "Oh! I've read that one. It's delightful."

Agatha squinted. "I know. I *hadn't* read it because I let you borrow it and you gave it away."

"Oh, please. That was a hundred and fifty years ago."

"It was a new release!"

Sorscha snorted. "You stole my favourite shoes and ruined them."

"You never even wear shoes, and I stole them because you burned my damned house to the ground."

Sorscha scoffed, throwing her hands up. "One time. It was *one* time."

"That's an awful *lot* of times to burn someone's home to ash."

"It's not if you consider how many homes you can have, you crotchety old hag."

Agatha laughed outright. "I miss you."

"And I you. Terribly."

"Has anything dreadful happened since we've been meeting like this?"

Sister Spring blew out a long breath. "Yes, but I don't think it has to do with us speaking this way."

"Are you alright? You didn't quite seem yourself when we last spoke."

"I know, I'm sorry for that." She ran a hand down her face. "The boy Winnie has me looking into—the one that was eaten. It has me spooked and I've been having night terrors, and Rosemary is still away..."

Agatha wished desperately to be allowed to hug her Sister. "Have you found out what happened to him, then?"

She shook her head. "No. Everyone is so close-lipped about it. I had to dress like a lady of the cloth to get anyone to speak with me, and even then, all I uncovered was that he lived in a monastery. He was hardly even a man and had given his life to Hespa to one day be one of the magi."

"What mage in training goes out into the woods and finds himself eaten by something if it's not a simple animal attack?"

"That's what most say, but I don't think they believe it, and it certainly doesn't sound right to me." Agatha nodded along, but Sorscha waved a hand. "Never mind all of that. Your plight is more important. Is there a date yet for the wedding?"

"The full moon." Agatha's throat felt tight as she swallowed.

Sorscha tried to grin, but it fell flat into a grimace. "That's not far off. Less than a fortnight, yeah?" Agatha nodded. "Is it terrible there?"

"No. I don't wish to be *married*, but I think there's a chance I might be helping the people. There is unrest here, still, as there was when I lived here before. The Crown and Grand Magus are using me as a common peasant to mollify the unrest."

Sorscha hissed. "Fat lot they know."

Agatha snorted. "It's backfiring on them, though. The people seem to like me. It seems to be giving them confidence instead. They even mimic my fashion choices."

Sorscha's face lit in pleasant surprise. "People will always follow someone they can believe in, Aggie, and there is no one better to follow than you."

Agatha did not find a shred of truth in such a statement, but she loved her Sister for thinking it.

"You'd better go before your *guards* and *maids* miss you." She rolled her eyes and smiled wide before wiggling her fingers in farewell and the mirror went glossy black once more.

Agatha deposited the mirror back into her beloved pocket, ignoring the pleasant feelings for the prince that arose in doing so. She glanced at the ominous door tucked into the tombs of the Stacks, considering. Thus far, she'd played it safe—*too* safe. She tapped a sharp fingernail to her chin.

The Grand Magus will have nothing to hide, Winnie would foolishly say. *What's the fun in being a witch if you cannot sleuth out filthy secrets from the* pure? Sorscha would say. *If it will help the people,* Seleste would say. Agatha moved the tapestry and spelled the door to unlock, flinching when the bolt slid out of place loudly.

"Furtivité."

Magic began to flow around her, seeping into every nook and cranny Agatha neared, muting sounds as if they were submerged in water. She nodded, satisfied, and slipped inside, the silencing tendrils of her magic standing sentry.

The room was thick with inky darkness, more of an oppressive aura than the absence of light. Agatha conjured a flame, wrapping her protection charms around herself like a cloak. The warm light glittered in her palm, doing little to ward off the eerie chill in the space. She turned in slow circles, taking it in.

It was no extravagant suite, not like the Grand Magus' study. This room was hewn right out of the castle's stones, tucked away —a secret nook no one was meant to find. She wandered to the desk, littered with papers that appeared of no real importance. Decrees, letters, ledgers. Agatha pulled open a drawer and shuffled through its contents, disappointed when all she came up with were quills and bottles of ink. Some parchment at the back grazed her finger and she flipped her hand to feel it. There was something stuck to the underside of the desk.

Agatha gently pulled at it, heart pumping as she realised it had been purposefully hidden away. When it came loose, she gingerly pulled it out and held it up to the light of her flame. An exquisitely lifelike rendering of a young woman stared back at her. She was beautiful, with thick waves of hair and kind eyes. Perhaps it was a rendering of the magus' mother or his sister. But why would he hide such a thing away?

She returned the peculiar sketch back to its hiding place and moved about the rest of the room. It was a small space, but there were countless books stuffed into shelves along two of the walls. Agatha approached, itching to see what sort of reading material the magus, content to lock away knowledge, would keep further hidden from those even granted access to the library.

As light caressed the spines of the thick leather tomes, she noticed a glint at the bottom of each book.

"*Lever.*"

Cautious not to disturb any dust, Agatha let her magic lift one of the tomes to her. As it slipped off the shelf, a thick chain unfurled from behind it, tethering it to the wall. Agatha sucked in a breath. Caution be damned. She commanded all the books leave their place.

Every one of them was chained to the stone.

Her mind swirled, taking in the titles as they hovered all around her. Some were in languages long lost, and she contemplated removing one and taking it with her. Keys rattled on the other side of the door and Agatha held her breath, snuffing out her flame.

"*Rendre.*"

The books slid back upon their shelves, chains rattling too loudly. She was grateful her silencing spell stood in place.

"*Casser.*"

Her magic broke the chain of a tome at random and delivered it to her.

"*Disparaître.*"

Agatha opened her eyes in her closet, clutching the book to her chest and heaving great gasping breaths.

O ne must take pains to remember that life deals in
greys. What is white to one might very well be black
to another. It matters not who is right or wrong, but
how we mutually treat one another in the midst of the grey.
  -Writings of Ambrose Joubert

AGATHA

"MONSIEUR TINDLE." Agatha curtsied, only to rise and find the
designer watching her with pinched lips.

"Darling, if you don't dispense with the *monsieurs*, we're
through." He marched to the plush velvet stool near a four-paned
looking glass, depositing a basket of needle and thread on it. He
turned to face her, fluttering his hand impatiently. "Stand up on
the platform," he commanded.

Agatha obeyed, albeit unnerved by four reflections of herself
staring back. Even with the disconcerting reason for being called
to Tindle's shop, she was pleased to be there. Despite her odd

sense of fashion and loathing for shopping, she did appreciate a lovely item of clothing as much as the next witch. And, she had quite a fondness for the man of small stature and gargantuan personality that stood before her, paper measuring tape looped around his neck.

Tindle's lips puckered and twisted in thought. "What do you envision for this? For your wedding gown?"

"Oh." Agatha baulked. "I—I don't know. None of this is—" She stopped herself, but Tindle's warm eyes urged her on. "None of this is really what I would have chosen. Or how I would do things."

"Of course, it isn't." His words had an edge, but not of censure or judgement. Perhaps the cadence of passion. "This wedding is not for you, my dear. Or the prince. This wedding is for the *people*."

He let that sink in while taking a few measurements, jotting them down on parchment with a gilded crow quill. He took up several bolts of fabric—some lace, some sheer, some pale, some ominous—and set them on the table next to her. Agatha eyed the darkest of them: a deep, burnished gold and nearly black lace. *That* is what she would have chosen.

"Now. What do you want to say to the people, Lady Agatha? *Your* people. For you may not hail from this city, but they are *your* people." His gaze burned intensely as he studied her reaction to his words. "It is no small thing that the prince chose a peasant. It is no small thing that you've been granted permission to select the designer of your choice."

Agatha dared not correct him on the former, but the latter gave her pause. No one had asked her which designer she'd like. The queen had simply stated she was to come to Tindle's for a fitting. In truth, she'd hoped her fashion choices of late had led the queen to change her mind about Tindle, but she'd assumed it was just another slight to her peasant status.

"I may be the greatest designer in Merveille," he went on,

"but I am indeed Blacklisted, therefore I'm bound to the Row. Yet, here stands the soon-to-be *Princess of Seagovia* for me to design her *wedding* gown." He tsked. "No, it is no small thing indeed, my darling." Tindle clutched a bolt of sheer, luxurious fabric the colour of champagne, holding it up to Agatha's chest. "So, go on then. What do you want to say to your people?" he pressed.

Agatha shook her head, looking at her reflection in the mirror. She could feel in her bones he was not asking about a *dress* or a wedding, but she still had no answer.

Sensing the tumult behind her eyes, Tindle took her hand and squeezed gently. "Darling, fashion is an art form. It is meant to be seen. Admired. *Imitated.*" He let two breaths pass before continuing. "Fashion makes a statement. And this gown is your first *act* as Princess of Seagovia. What do you want it to spoke?"

"Defiance," Agatha said fiercely without thinking.

A fire lit behind Tindle's eyes. "*Of?*" he urged.

"Oppression. *Su*ppression. Inequality." Her hands formed fists at her sides. "Of being shoved into a shell of yourself at the hands of what someone else tells you is right."

Tindle gave her a small, powerful smile. "The prince, it appears, has not failed us."

The reality of what Tindle did not know—that Grimm hadn't selected her at all; that he was trying with all his might to *not* marry her—doused her ferocity like the crashing, Winter waves of Mer Noir.

"I should not have said those things out loud."

Tindle cocked his head to the side, eyes narrowed. "Then do not say them. *Wear* them."

WITH BOTH THE wedding madness and the queen's *list*, Agatha hadn't found the opportunity to do more than glance at the stolen tome from the Grand Magus' hideaway. The book kept taunting her. She'd at least spelled the chain off and given it a different, innocuous cover.

The library was just about the only place no one interrupted her, so she took the old book there and curled up in a plush chair beside the fire. It was a peaceful spot and Agatha was so cosy that she chastised herself for always selecting the uncomfortable wooden chairs at the tables. Granted, one could only balance so many open books in their lap. She currently had five.

Agatha flipped to another useless page of the magus' book and groaned. The entire blasted thing was in ancient Coronoccan. She hadn't even read the modern tongue of Coronocco in over fifty years. Frustrated, she slammed the tome shut, disturbing the other four on her lap and spilling them all to the floor with a series of thuds.

Cursing, she bent down to pick them up. Polished boots stepped next to the fallen books and Agatha looked up to see Lord Gaius crouching down to assist her.

"Marlowe, hm?" He glanced at the cover and held the novel out to her.

She snatched it from his hand. "You know Marlowe?" Agatha scoffed, but she was impressed, truthfully.

"Of him."

Her, Agatha corrected mentally with a sense of pride. Marlowe's success was one of her life's greatest joys as a Sister Solstice.

"Grimm has all of his works," Gaius finished.

Agatha's mood instantly soured. "How wonderful."

Gaius handed her the magus' tome and she was immensely grateful she'd thought to put a glamour over the cover. He stood and fidgeted, something she'd never seen him do. "Look, I just wanted to say that…" Gaius traced a thumb along a button of his coat. "No one should ever be forced to marry someone they don't want to. But, for what it's worth, I—I think I was wrong before. I believe you might turn out to be truly wonderful for this kingdom."

Agatha's lips parted and she blinked mutely at him. Gaius' kind words left her feeling terribly morose but optimistic at the same time. He offered her a gentle smile that didn't quite reach his eyes and walked away before she could respond.

AGATHA HAD SENT everyone away after dinner, shocked that Anne and Eleanor had gone away with them. Augustus and Porthos trailed behind her down the beach, but left distance as the guards used to when they thought she was unaware of them.

On the eve of her wedding, she did not want the comfort of the sea. She sought the solace of the woods. The Grimoire and Hespa had remained silent, and Sorscha's letters had been short and trivial. Agatha knew she had much to deal with in her search for information, but she desperately wished Sister Spring was with her, at least by post.

Agatha felt utterly alone. Usually, that was precisely how she liked things, but she'd always imagined the eve of her wedding to be one of blissful anticipation. The night before she'd marry Ira. After he died, Agatha never thought she'd have a wedding, let alone one of obligation. It seemed like a cruel jest, well-intentioned to help the people or not.

Agatha stepped off the cool black sand and into the mossy woods, relishing the crunch of the crisp leaves under her sand-dusted toes. She lifted her eyes up to the canopy of giant trees, so alive with vibrant, dying leaves. The irony had always struck a chord with her. A macabre display of artistry.

Augustus came close as she paused. "My Lady, I'll give you space if you desire it, but it's dangerous in the woods. I ask that you don't stray too far." Agatha nodded slightly, turning back toward the trees, but Augustus spoke again. "Are you alright?"

His concern cracked a piece of her heart. A piece she'd barely held together with the cobwebs making up her rib cage. "No, Augustus. But I will be."

He nodded once and stepped away. Keeping his word, he stayed closer than before but left her room to remain somewhat alone.

She dropped her boots to the ground and tucked herself up onto a fallen tree trunk thrice as thick as her body, folding her legs under her flowing, corset-less gown—the newest idea of Tindle's. It captured her essence more than anything else she'd worn since arriving, its row of pewter buttons descending from the high collar all the way down to her waist. The blackened aubergine fabric cinched in at the wrists, dark lace weeping over her hands. Eleanor had said it looked like a widow's nightgown, and that was precisely when Agatha knew it was perfect.

This was not the part of Brume Forest she'd frequented with Ira, stealing kisses—and much more—away from disapproving eyes, but it looked so similar that her soul ached. Agatha knew that if she didn't face this ghost now, she would fall apart on the dais before all of Merveille.

She took out a small leather notebook and sharpened charcoal. With it, she wrote two letters to Ira. One as if it were the eve of their own wedding—the one they'd spent countless nights planning—and another as she truly was. Agatha wrote to him of her fear, her shred of hope, and her utter despair that it wouldn't be him meeting her at the altar.

She wrote to him of how it pained her heart that Hespa would ask her to do such a thing as marry. That her Sisters couldn't be there with her. She wrote of how wrong it all felt that her life would turn out this way when she knew in her bones the Goddess Three was not a villain—

Agatha drew in a sharp breath. It wasn't until she wrote it all to Ira that she realised how strongly she felt about the contradictions—what she knew Hespa to be and what the Grimoire had made her do for the last three hundred years.

"My lady." Augustus peeked around the tree he'd stood behind to give her privacy. "Apologies, but it's growing rather dark. I think we should venture back toward the waterfront now."

Agatha nodded. "Give me one more moment."

Augustus moved back behind the tree, and Agatha peeled up some moss from the trunk she sat upon. She turned her back to where her guards were hidden and ran her thumb over the moss, feeling the tender bit of earth flood her body with power. In a blink, small black flames lit on the moss and Agatha held her letters to Ira until they burned to ash, drifting off in the breeze like otherworldly moths.

The flames winked out, and Agatha called for Augustus and Porthos to follow her on the long walk back to the castle.

Near the entrance, she couldn't bring herself to go in. "I'd like to sit outside a while."

Porthos shrugged and walked away, but Augustus nodded kindly. "Of course, my lady."

"Augustus," she spoke, and he turned back. "Why did you replace Clark as my guard? Is he well?"

"Yes, my lady. Clark is quite well. Prince Grimm personally asked me to look after you."

With that, Augustus slunk back against the castle walls beside Porthos, and Agatha sat in the dark sand, looking out over the even darker waters and wondering why Grimm would do such a thing.

A moment later, a deep voice broke into her thoughts. "Would you like some company?"

She looked up to find her betrothed standing over her. Without waiting for a response, he sat down in the sand and Agatha wondered how she hadn't noticed his approach. But she was much too melancholy to care. They sat in silence for a very long time, the sea's waves crashing against the shore. It was curious how comfortable it felt with their shared misery linking them. The thought made her wary.

Agatha turned her attention to Grimm, taking in his profile. She did have to admit he was handsome in his own tousled, unkempt right. He looked over at her and she could see a torrent of unspoken words within his eyes, but there were too many shadows to make them out.

"Three inquiries?" she asked, surprising them both.

Grimm

GRIMM GAVE AGATHA A TIGHT SMILE. "If you'll pull your punches, just this one time." He couldn't play games tonight. He couldn't be the scoundrel. Be the liar, the defector, the philanderer. Not with what faced them both on the morrow.

She dipped her chin. "Alright."

He watched her look out over the sea, wishing he didn't find her beautiful in her darkened mystery. Wishing he didn't find her fascinating for her sharp mind and daring fashion sense. And wishing he weren't the reason she had such anguish in her eyes.

"What is your favourite time of day?"

Curse her for making his heavy heart lighter with that one simple question. "Dawn," he said without hesitation.

She furrowed her brows, the wind off the sea lifting her

waves of hair out behind her, the dying sun revealing more gold and red than he'd known was hidden there in her dark tresses. "That would not have been my guess. I've heard tell of you spending many a night gone until dawn."

A low rumble sounded, unbidden, from Grimm's chest. "Yes. But the nights are often very difficult for me. I'm pleased to see them over. To let the sun chase the monsters away."

She beheld him thoughtfully and he forced his eyes not to drift to her lips. He knew he should put the mask back in place, that it was a mistake to answer her so honestly. Her doom would be sealed before the next sunset, and it was his fault. "What is your favourite time of day, then?"

"Twilight." Agatha's lips turned up and she might as well have squeezed his insides. He'd not once seen her genuinely smile. "When the moon and sun war for control of the sky."

She turned back to take in the sun, nearly drowned by the sea. "I know your favourite sweet treat is a chocolate croissant." A cocky smirk tilted her lips and it sent his heart thudding against his ribs. "But what is your favourite savoury food?"

Grimm hid his sudden nerves with a laugh. "Dulci has revealed my great weakness, I see. I have heard tell of your insatiable sweet tooth as well." He leaned back on his hands and gently pushed her shoulder with his, eliciting the smile he'd found himself in want of.

"She's a wonderful woman," Agatha offered.

"She is," he agreed. "My favourite savoury food..." He pulled his bottom lip between his teeth. "I would have to say a large slab of juicy beef."

Agatha snorted. "Says every man who ever lived."

Grimm shrugged. "We all used to be hunters, after all. Well then, what is *your* favourite of Dulci's confections?" He already knew she'd say something with pumpkin.

"Anything with pumpkin."

Something about his accuracy lit a flame in the dark caverns of his soul and he had to look away. "Not a bad choice."

They drifted back into silence as the sun finally succumbed to the water, the impending day looming heavy before them both. Neither of them needed to acknowledge it. They uniquely knew how the other felt, as no one else could.

"Are you alright?" Agatha finally asked, using up her last inquiry.

No. Not even a little. He was very likely dragging her to an untimely death with the last vestiges of her life spent chained to a man she hated for a cause that wasn't hers and a prophecy that probably didn't have anything to do with her. All because he'd failed, over and over.

"Pass."

She nodded and looked back out to sea.

Grimm swallowed. "Do you know that I'm sorry?"

Her eyes snapped to his. "Is that your question?"

He dipped his chin.

"I'm...beginning to see that, yes," she answered finally.

"I am sorry, Agatha. For all of this. I never would have chosen this for you."

They sat without words until the stars sparkled overhead, and then Agatha spoke. "Do you think our union will truly help the people?"

She sounded genuine, her shoulders were slumped with defeat, but there was defiance in the cut of her brow and her gaze out over the water. If this was her pulling punches, Agatha Joubert was a formidable opponent yet.

"You're plum out of questions, peasant," he teased, and—to his delight—she smiled. "But, yes." She looked at him fully then. "I think it's already begun."

Agatha opened her mouth, but sand murmured behind them and they both turned to find Mila. Grimm's heart dropped, and not just for what he worried Mila had interrupted them to say, but because of the hurt that flashed across Agatha's face and the coldness that descended upon her. She rose and walked away without a word.

"Grimm, hurry," Mila whispered.

With a look over his shoulder at Agatha's retreating form, he followed Mila as quickly as he could to a shadowed alcove of the castle's courtyard.

Concealed and alone, Grimm squared his shoulders. "Who is it?"

A flash of movement caught his eye, and Gaius rounded the corner, hardly a shell of himself for the look on his face.

"*Who is it?*" Grimm demanded, looking between them, terrified of the answer.

Tears spilled out of Mila's eyes. "It's Alestair," she choked out.

It was a punch to the stomach. Grimm's legs buckled and he slumped against the stone wall, raking a hand through his hair. It was impossible. He couldn't take the life of his friend, his comrade-in-arms. He was still just a young man. It was his fault Alestair was involved at all.

"When?" he spoke, voice raw and strained. Mila's lip wobbled and Gaius looked at his boots. "*When?*" Grimm shouted, pushing to his feet.

"Moments." Mila handed him the Book.

Grimm didn't waste time looking at the name, the location, or time. He rested his hand on the Book and spoke his true name. In a flash, he was shooting through time and space, breaths from being wherever Alestair was.

"*My Lady!*" he roared against the blur of time.

He felt Her wrap around him in a shroud of inky fog.

"I seek permission to go as I am for this one."

There was a beat of silence before Her dark clouds fell away from him, as did the grotesque decay of his own form, his features returning to those of Thackery Peridot.

"Hurry," She whispered, the sound coming from all around him. "You haven't much time."

Grimm's boots landed in a room just as an assailant slunk from the shadows, cloaked and unidentifiable. Alestair sat, asleep in his armchair, the one Grimm had rested in so many times himself. The one he'd circled not two moons prior, as Alestair watched the fire and Grimm argued with him that he needed to go out again. That it would work this time.

Grimm wanted to scream at his friend to turn around. *Run.* But he wouldn't hear him, not yet. Not until the man slinking toward his prone form issued the killing blow.

Grimm watched as the assailant moved forward on silent feet, Alestair softly snoring. A gloved hand rose up, the firelight glinting off his blade, and Grimm sucked in a breath as he watched the blade come down hard into Alestair's chest.

He saw Alestair's essence flicker and he rushed forward, sliding on his knees to a stop in front of his friend who had woken to meet his end, wide-eyed and gasping.

"Alestair," Grimm murmured, knowing he still couldn't hear him yet; couldn't be seen yet. The assailant's knife rose again and blood poured from his chest, hot and sticky, spraying Grimm's face. "Alestair, I'm here my friend."

The knife pierced him again, the lifeblood leaking to the floor, warm on Grimm's knees. Alestair's essence shot out in a blur of light, but didn't make it far before being dragged back in. Dorian Alestair was a fighter to his bones.

"*Alestair.*" Grimm's words tore from his hoarse throat. "I'm here to take you where no one can ever hurt you again. You've won, my friend. We're *winning.*"

The assailant withdrew his blade and exited through the window, unaware Grimm was there at all.

"Let go," he urged. "It's okay to let go."

His friend turned, his terrified gaze fastening onto Grimm as he choked on his own blood. If Alestair could see him, it was almost time.

"I'm here."

Alestair's eyelids fluttered shut and his essence poured forth from him in a rush. Grimm jumped up and took it in his arms, pulling him to his chest. "You're free, my friend."

Grimm released him and took a step back. He locked eyes with Alestair, placing a fist against his own chest in salute. Then, the prince dropped to one knee and lowered his head—a bow of tribute to his fallen comrade. When he rose once more, he put an arm around Alestair's shoulders, turning him away from his torn body crumpled in the chair. "Come. I've somewhere to show you."

CHAPTER
FOURTEEN

T he greater good will always be the path less traversed.
Let it be mine.
                        -Journal of Thackery Peridot III

AGATHA

TINDLE STEPPED BACK, his eyes misty. "Darling you look incredible."

"If I do, it is only because of your dressmaking wizardry." Agatha kissed him on both cheeks, refusing to peer in the looking glass quite yet. She knew she would need to be very much alone for that moment. "The queen has not seen this gown?"

Tindle shushed her. "No. You might very well get us both killed, but I did as you asked and showed her a decoy gown. The over-skirt of this, without the"—he waved a hand—*"embell-ishments."*

"Thank you, Tindle." She reached out and gently squeezed his arm. "Be sure to tell Queen Fleurina and the magus that I requested last-minute alterations and you were forbidden from telling me no. I'd like to make sure all blame for this is laid directly at *my* feet."

"Oh darling, that ship has sailed halfway to Coronocco by now. If we burn, we're burning together." Tindle winked. "Knock that pretty prince on his royal arse when you walk down the aisle."

With that, Tindle kissed both Agatha's cheeks and left her alone. She had only moments before Eleanor and Anne would return from the false errands she'd sent them on. With a few steadying breaths, she turned to the looking glass. Forcing her eyes to rise from the floor, Agatha took in her reflection.

A small gasp escaped her lips at the sight. She had not been prepared. Her gown was a masterpiece befitting Lady Death or Lady War, and Agatha thought for the first time perhaps that was exactly whom she would be summoning in the moments to come.

She was, by way of tradition, encased in white likened to the fresh snow of Wendolyn's mountain home. But the pure white was slashed through to reveal black and gold underneath. When she moved, the ardentness of the servants and the majesty of the gods raised their voices in defiance. Gold filigree wound up the bodice of the gown, accentuating her ample curves and whorling down her arms. Clasped around her neck and cascading behind her was a cloak of raven feathers, the underside the hue of fresh blood.

Tears welled in her eyes even as courage and indignation filled her heart. Let her silent roar bleed into their very souls until it reminded them of the burned witches, the brutalised outsiders, and the abused peasants. Let it remind them that their time of oppressing others was *through*.

Agatha wore the colours of the Sisters Solstice: White for Winnie. Red for Sorscha. Gold for Seleste. Black for herself. And the four witches did not go down without a fight. Despite their Orders, they left their own mark upon the world. And that was exactly what Agatha planned to do.

A rustling whispered behind her, and Agatha startled at the reflection in the looking glass next to her own. She twirled around, dress billowing out to reveal the extent of her defiance.

"Winnie," she whispered, flinging her crow cape behind her. "What are you doing here?"

"I'm not *here*, per se." She hadn't taken her eyes off of the wedding gown, but they ticked up to Agatha's then, just as a bird flew through the window.

"Goddess, Winnie, are you in the Netherrealm? Is that Lady Death's bird?"

Wendolyn shooed it away. "There's no need to worry unless She sends more and they tear my soul to shreds."

Agatha frowned.

"Sorscha wrote to me and told me about your Order."

Agatha looked at her feet. "Are you here to rub it in, then? My marrying the prince?"

Her Sister Winter looked as if she'd been struck. "Do you truly think so little of me?" She stepped forward, reaching out for Agatha before realising she could not touch her from the Netherrealm. She let her arm fall back to her side, weariness in her eyes. "I'm here because if this were a travesty to any of us, it would be you, Aggie. This is..." She shook her white-blonde head. "This is unfair. I'm so sorry. I'm sorry for what I said on the Autumnal Equinox. This— It should've been Ira—"

Her words broke off as a sob tore from Agatha. "It's all wrong, Winnie. It should be midnight, the moon bathing us in her magic. It should be on the Solstice so you can be there. So Sorscha and Seleste—"

"*Aggie.*" Winnie's voice grew stern. "I don't want you to run from what's been done to you any longer." Agatha raised red-rimmed eyes to her eldest Sister. "Do you understand? I don't want you to lock your fury away this time. I want you to *unleash it.*"

Three more birds appeared behind Wendolyn then, and another flew in to land on her shoulder—a warning.

"I have to go, but I brewed you this. Hold out your hand."

Agatha obeyed and a vial of glowing purple liquid appeared in her palm. "Cry your tears for Ira. Cry them for *yourself.* Then take this. It will dry your tear ducts. You are to be queen one day, and you will not cry in front of them, Aggie. You will change this world."

Tears streaked down Agatha's cheeks as Wendolyn backed away. The birds were many now and tearing at her hair, her clothes, but still she stayed. "Winnie, *go.*"

"I should have stopped this, Aggie."

Sister Autumn could scarcely believe the tears that fell from her Sister Winter's eyes as well.

And then she was gone.

Grimm

GRIMM CLENCHED one hand in and out of a fist, yanking at his collar with the other.

"Stop fidgeting," his mother whispered in his ear.

They were seconds away from making the procession down the aisle and he was very certain he was going to be ill or sweat through the lovely black and gold coat Tindle had made for him.

160

"Father," Grimm addressed the king, "I can't remember, do you stand with me or sit?"

"We've been through this." The Grand Magus pushed past them. "The king and queen enter first. They sit upon their thrones. You and I go in and stand on the dais, under the arch of flowers. Then Lady Agatha enters. Per tradition, she will take off her cape of black to turn it over to pure white. She will then walk down the aisle of rose petals and I will instruct you for the rest. Understood?"

Grimm nodded mutely.

An orchestra began to play.

His mother kissed his cheek.

The magus pulled on his arm.

The next thing he knew, he was standing under an arch of roses with too many eyes on him and one resounding thought.

Agatha hates roses.

"It is time," von Fuchs whispered.

The orchestra shifted into a song as old and boring as time. The massive oak doors were the only thing left between his betrothed and her doom, and they were opening. Grimm fought a wave of nausea.

Agatha stepped in, and everyone in the ceremonial hall gasped in unison, including his mother. Grimm dared not even breathe.

She was riveting. Ethereal. He wanted to run to her. Scream for her not to take that first step. It was wrong. It was so utterly *wrong*. Agatha deserved better. She *was* better. But she took that first step toward him and his lips parted involuntarily. His soul begged her to keep coming toward him, even as his mind screamed for her to flee.

He watched her hands drift up to her neck as she walked. He couldn't remember correctly, but hadn't von Fuchs said she would turn her cape *before* going down the aisle?

Without so much as a pause in her step, Agatha unclipped the cape of...*raven feathers* and flipped it around behind herself to reveal not white, but blood red. He risked a glance at his parents, expecting them to be radiating fury. The king looked a bit bored, but the queen wore a mask of pride Grimm didn't think was entirely for show. His mother's eyes suddenly widened and a collective intake of breath echoed through the hall. The magus tensed next to Grimm and the prince flung his attention back to Agatha walking down the aisle.

Their reactions instantly made sense. With every sway of Agatha's white bridal skirts, black peeked through, and golden ceremonial bands of the gods trailed intricately up her bare arms.

Her eyes landed momentarily on each one of them upon the dais, locking lastly on Grimm's as she ascended the steps. Grimm couldn't help it, his lips turned up in an astonished smirk. Her attention flicked to his mouth then she lifted her eyes to his once more. A sinister grin spread across her face, igniting the spark she'd set into a full inferno.

It was likely they were both dead, as the magus was nearly purple with repressed rage. But it was *certain* that Grimm was in far deeper than he thought with this riveting creature.

The Grand Magus commanded them to face one another and join hands. Agatha's were cold, and she flinched ever so slightly. Grimm looked at her face, his heart sinking to his feet when he saw all her bravado had melted away when she'd stepped up to join him. She did not cry, but there was a sadness behind her eyes that made him squirm. It was something deeper than being promised to someone she didn't love. Did Agatha wish someone else was standing in his place?

A crack shot through him at the realisation.

The rest of the ceremony was a blur. Words—*oaths*—were exchanged. The king and queen bestowed their blessing, albeit through gritted teeth. And the Grand Magus of The Order of Hespa anointed them with the tears of the Goddess Three.

Grimm's mind cleared enough to snort at that one, and Agatha's eyes cleared long enough to glare at him for it.

"Your rings," von Fuchs instructed.

Grimm had forgotten about the ring—the one he'd had specially crafted for her like a fool. He wished with all his might that he could halt time and rush back to select a plain band like any other, or that he'd just sent Anne to do it.

With trembling fingers, he withdrew a velvet pouch from his pocket and dumped the ring into his palm.

Von Fuchs instructed, "With this ring, I thee wed."

Grimm took Agatha's hand, grateful she did not flinch again and wished his palm wasn't so clammy. "With this ring, I thee wed." He slid the gold band with an onyx stone over her finger, and she sucked in a small breath only he could hear.

Her expression cleared, and she repeated the same words, sliding a plain gold band onto Grimm's finger.

Magus von Fuchs lifted their joined hands into the air and shouted, "His Royal Highness Prince Thackery, and his bride, Her Royal Highness Princess Agatha Peridot!"

The room erupted in deafening noise, and all Grimm could think was how very grateful he was that his people believed 'you may kiss the bride' to be crass and undignified. Together, he and Agatha—his wife—walked back down the aisle and into whatever traps awaited them.

AGATHA

AGATHA COULDN'T *BREATHE*. "Gods, Anne, get this dress off me! Tindle said there is a second gown in the armoire."

They were taking a brief pause after the ceremony to *collect themselves*, which was code for 'they don't let us kiss up there, so we'll do it in the bridal suite.' In their case, it meant running away from one another to process what had just happened.

Anne appeared with a traditional cream gown, it's only spot of colour the large peridot gem. Gold filigree surrounded the gem where it was set into the waist. Just below it, the tight bodice jutted out into skirts. As Anne helped her into the dress, Agatha caught another glimpse of the exquisite ring that was expected to permanently mark her finger.

Upon further inspection, she would have bet her life that the mount was a gilded set of tiny bat wings. And the band was a link of golden bones.

A Son of Gem and Bone.

Agatha shook her head, thoughts rattling loose. "Anne, who selected my ring?"

Anne blushed. "Oh, your husband, of course." Agatha baulked. "He had it specially made. He and Lord Gaius went to pick it up themselves just yesterday."

Agatha looked at the ring again. It was beautiful, that much was certain. But it was the opposite of Seagovian tradition, where a plain band adorned the fingers of the aristocracy. Had he meant it as a barb to her recent fashion mayhem? An insult?

When the reception was dipping into lewd drunkenness all around, the queen sweetly—and with wine-soaked lips—told the newlyweds to *go, enjoy their night.* Grimm had visibly stiffened.

Their rooms were lavish. Beyond anything Agatha had stayed in, in all her three hundred years. The walls were a stately, deep indigo, gilded to the point of obscenity. Thick, ornate rugs trimmed with gold lay so plush beneath Agatha's silk slippers that they begged for her to sink her bare feet into them. Floor-to-ceiling glass doors framed with velvet curtains of burnished gold led out to a balcony overlooking Mer Noir.

Beside the hearth—as tall as Grimm and wide enough to house a faerie village—was a lovely table and chair set, a chaise situated behind them. And there, in the middle of the far wall, sat a dark wood bed draped with a delicate cream canopy. In any other circumstance, the imposing bed would be what dreams were made of. At present, it was more of a taunting nightmare than anything else.

She wandered momentarily while Grimm watched her as if she were prey about to devour him whole.

"They're going to expect me to stay here all night," he said in a low voice.

"Stop twisting that button on your coat before you pop it off."

He lowered his hands to his sides and scowled. "You take the bed. I'll sleep on the chaise."

Agatha pursed her lips. "Don't be ridiculous. You're much longer than me. You take the bed. I'll sleep on the chaise."

"I'm very tired and I do not wish to argue with you," he growled.

"Just turn the lamps off so I can change into my bedclothes."

"Why don't you go behind the partition or into the lavatory?"

Agatha sighed and stomped away only to come back out moments later, fuming. "I can't undo all these blasted ribbons and buttons on my own." She stopped in her tracks when Grimm turned around shirtless.

"I'll call Anne for you. She was supposed to attend you until you were out of your dress—" His words broke off and he shifted his weight uncomfortably.

Agatha looked dutifully at his feet, finding them bare and—strangely—equally as intimate. "Just undo the damned things, *please.*"

Grimm cleared his throat as she turned her back to him. He unlaced the ribbons with no harm done, but when he reached for the top button, his finger brushed against her shoulder, and she shuddered. Her throat went dry as a crackle of sparks shot through her and chillbumps spread across her back as his hand pulled away.

"Are you cold? I could build up the fire if you like."

"I'm fine," she snapped, holding her dress up and stepping away as the last button came undone.

After much argument and awkward lumbering in the dark, they both managed to make it into bed. Agatha lay on the plush mattress while Grimm made a pallet on the floor.

Agatha winked the last lamp out and snuggled into the sea of covers, staring up at the beautiful canopy.

"Agatha?" Grimm's voice drifted through the dark.

"Yes, dearest husband?"

She could hear the faint smile in his voice as he said, "Three inquiries to pass the time?"

There was very little chance she was going to sleep, anyway. "Alright."

"Who was it you wished was up there with you today, instead of me?"

All traces of humour had left him, and Agatha wondered if this was the thought that had been drawing his brows together all evening.

When she didn't answer right away, for fear she might weep, Grimm spoke again. "I could see it on your face. The pain." He waited a heartbeat before adding, "I'll not hold it against you to pass."

She wanted to speak of Ira on this night. At least in some small way. It only seemed right. "He was my lover many moons ago. But he is long since dead."

The air in the room was stiff, stuffed with tension. Grimm let out a breath, and his voice was barely audible. "I'm so sorry, Agatha."

"So am I."

He most likely thought the game was over, and perhaps it should have been, but Agatha needed her mind reined in.

"Are you afraid to be king?" A heavy hit for a heavy hit.

"Yes," he answered without pause. "I'm terrified."

Agatha's heart constricted at the cadence of his voice. She pulled the covers tighter to her chest, wishing Mabon would fly in through the window to comfort her.

"Will you tell me about him someday? Your lover?"

She closed her eyes against the tears, but they spilled down her cheeks unmoored. Apparently Winnie's potion only lasted so long. "Perhaps."

Her next question surged up before she could think of how scared she was of the answer. They both must have been too raw from the day. "My ring," she said. "With the black stone. Did you mean it as an insult? A mockery of my station?"

Grimm sat up, a mere shadow in the dark. "What?" She felt more than heard him moving closer.

The lamp next to the bed flickered on, illuminating him. She looked away from his bare chest and swiped at her tears.

"Agatha, no. Absolutely not." He looked everywhere but at her, and she pulled the blankets up to her neck. "I—" He ran a hand down his short beard. "Everything about this was thrown on you against your will. Not only did you have to marry someone you didn't want to, but nothing about the wedding was something you would have chosen for yourself. You hate roses, and I didn't know what dress Tindle would make for you. I thought—" He chewed on his bottom lip. "I thought the one thing that you were to wear always, with it sitting on your hand as a constant reminder... I just thought there should be *one* thing you might have selected for yourself, and you seem fond of black. And bats."

Agatha's lips parted in surprise, despite herself. The prince snuffed out the lamp without another word and returned to his pallet on the floor. A few moments of silence passed, and Agatha thought he'd fallen asleep until he spoke again.

With hardly a whisper, he asked his final inquiry. "Do you like it?"

"I do." She twisted the obsidian ring on her finger and sleep dragged her under before she could think of her own final question.

FIFTEEN

G hosts of ancient magic whisper that a storm is nigh.
      -Writings of Ambrose Joubert

AGATHA

AGATHA CRUMPLED up Grimm's shirt from where he'd tossed it onto her vanity and threw it on the floor. She hadn't even seen him, not really, since their wedding night. Aside from dinners they'd been forced to attend, she only saw him when he slipped into their rooms after he thought she was asleep. Some nights, it was just long enough to change clothes. Other nights, he slept a handful of hours on the floor or chaise before disappearing before dawn.

"Are you upset, Your Highness?" Anne's cheerful smile lit the room more than the rising sun that flitted through the curtains she'd just pulled open.

Agatha swept tangled hair out of her eyes and shuffled to sit at her vanity without answering the question. Instead, she let her elbow rest on the back of the chair and turned to watch her maid. Since the rings and exchange of, "I do," Agatha had felt trapped in more ways than one. The magus was clearly irritated with her display at the wedding and had essentially confined her to the castle without actually saying the words. He'd demanded her presence at countless frivolous, *pointless*, court events filled with so many wasp ladies and daft lords that she thought her eyes would burst right out of her skull. She did not come to Merveille, Ordered and bound in matrimony, to be shoved in a corner and told to *heel*.

"Anne," Agatha finally said as the maid stoked the fire, "what do you *really* think of my marrying into the royal family? Of my bridging the gap between royalty and the people?"

Anne paused briefly, then returned to her stoking. "That is not my place to say, Your Highness."

"It is, Anne. I value you and your thoughts and opinions. *Please*."

Anne chewed on her thumb nail, returning the fire poker to its stand. "I—" She looked at the door, then at Agatha. "I think what you're doing with Monsieur Tindle is a start. You're giving us a way to stand up, to support what you stand for without having to use our own voices." She came and crouched down next to Agatha's chair, looking up at her. "If we do anything on our own, or you single us out..." Anne looked away with a grimace.

"Miriam."

Anne nodded, and Agatha reached out to rest a hand on her arm.

"I won't see you end up like Miriam. I didn't know that would happen."

"It wasn't your fault, Princess Agatha." Her heart nearly stopped with Anne's decision to finally let go of the ridiculous title of *Your Highness*. "But—" Anne continued, looking at her hands, then fully into Agatha's eyes—something she rarely, if ever, did. "But I think you can do better—*more*, in time. Without risking harm by singling any of us out." Anne's face dimpled with a smile meant to soften her words, but Agatha was glad for them.

"Thank you, Anne."

She glanced at the door and inched closer, lowering her voice. "I've had an idea, actually."

"I'm listening."

"The tea you're scheduled to attend this afternoon is another in honour of our guests, Empress Amira and King Rashidi."

Agatha had forgotten about the Cronoccan and Lyronian royalty in their midst.

"Everyone who is anyone will be there, including their servants. And servants *always* talk." Anne's face lit with a conspiratorial grin. "I think you should make a toast."

Agatha's face broke into an impish smile. "Anne, you're brilliant."

TINK. TINK. TINK.

Agatha stood, teaspoon still poised against her empty champagne glass. She did not have to feign a blush or the tremor in her voice as all eyes landed on her. The eyes of the most powerful leaders in all Midlerea, and those of their servants. Agatha took a deep breath and spoke, her voice echoing through the stone courtyard more clearly than she'd anticipated. "Our wedding day was such a whirlwind that I never got a chance to properly thank my king and queen." She turned her attention to where they stood stoically and raised her glass. "Thank you for welcoming me into your kingdom, your castle, and into your family with such honour." Her heart hammered against her ribs as the Grand Magus' face purpled.

"Without you and His Highness Prince Grimm's benevolent ability to see past social class, I would yet be in the fields, bent over and heartbroken for the loss of love." The king's gaze was on her, but his eyes sat vacant. The queen, however, lifted her graceful chin. "To *you*, for paving the ways of change for our great country."

Someone shouted, *"Here, here!"*

Agatha's eyes roved over the courtyard, but it almost sounded as if it came from somewhere high above. The servants echoed it with fervour and the aristocracy with reluctance.

Agatha hoped this would work. Hoped it would place the king and queen in hot water and force their hand to make some changes, even small ones. She hoped the servants would spread the word like wildfire that their peasant princess had stood in front of the aristocracy and spoken in *their* honour.

Finally, she raised her glass higher. "To our most enlightened and progressive king and queen!" She almost grinned, sinister and wicked, at the vein popping in the Grand Magus' forehead.

"Here, here!"

AGATHA SAT down to look through her herbs and crystals in order to ensure she had what was necessary for her newest plan. Things were going well with the minor fashion defiances mimicked by the people, but it was only a start. With no more word from the Grimoire or even a whisper from Hespa, Agatha needed to formulate her own plan.

Queen Fleurina had thus far turned a blind eye—for the most part—to her quiet disobedience. The king kept silent as usual, but the Grand Magus' temper with Agatha was growing thin. She found it fairly amusing but knew she'd reached the end of his patience when a summons arrived along with her breakfast.

Her next action as princess would be to make a bold request. Because Queen Fleurina remained kind to her—even after her daring wedding gown and toast—Agatha would give her a chance to agree to her proposal without spelled influence. If she refused, or the magus attempted to stop her... That would be a different matter entirely. Influencing the will of another was a tricky bit of sorcery, and to do so without dark magic was unstable and short-lived at best. It was definitely a last resort.

Mabon squeaked from his perch, upside down on a floating bushel of grapes, and Agatha looked up to see a raven tap at her window. She let in Edina, one of her own. Stroking her blue-black feathers, pale sand trickled down and Agatha knew where Edina had flown in from. She took the parchment from her leg and once the raven was relieved of her parcel, she squawked once and flew away. Edina was not one to loiter.

Agatha unfurled the parchment, anticipating Seleste's signature monarch sketched at the top—identical to her precious familiar, Litha. Sorscha had written the night after the wedding, but not since, and Agatha had to admit she felt a pang of sadness that the letter was from Seleste instead. Though, she was still glad to hear from her Sister Summer.

Dearest Aggie,

Winnie wrote to me of your plight. Though I know you no
doubt made an absolutely ravishing bride and will rule
Seagovia with unmatched ferocity and grace, I cannot help but
feel sorrow for your hand being forced in this, Hespa's words
in the Grimoire or not. Please, Sister Autumn, know that
I am ever on your side, and you are ever on my heart.

Yours Always,

Seleste

Agatha swallowed her tears and incinerated the letter. Seleste was, without a doubt, her most selfless Sister. She was kind and nurturing, but it left her too trusting. Anyone could have intercepted that letter, and Agatha found it foolish to be so open in correspondence.

Seleste also viewed Agatha through some rose-coloured vision of her own making and had since they were babes. Alas, Sister Summer's words had the effect they always did—they warmed the cold caverns of her dark heart.

Without warning, the vanity began to tremble under her hands. Agatha looked frantically for the cause as the rest of the room remained completely still. Peering in the drawer, she found the Grimoire shaking violently. Never in all her years had she seen it do such a thing. When she took it up, the ancient Book instantly calmed in her hands. Agatha flipped it open to see the last letters written, still glowing gold beneath the black ink.

TOGETHER THEY—WILL CHANGE THE COURSE OF ALL THINGS.

TALAN'S PREVIOUSLY CHOKED-OFF calligraphy was filled in by Belfry's hand. Although, her usually strong, purposeful strokes were frenzied, clipped—forced, even. Her Order had begun with Belfry, per the norm, shifted into Talan's hand, and back to Belfry's. An image of the Sisters standing over the Grimoire, pushing one another back, fighting to write, passed through Agatha's mind.

She picked up her quill to write Sorscha about the strange encounter, but a bell tolled the hour. It was time to meet with Their Majesties.

Grimm

"WHERE IS YOUR DARLING WIFE?" Dulci questioned, handing him a scone right out of her personal oven.

If one more person asked him that, Grimm was going to break something. He didn't know where in the Underworld she was, and though he probably needed to keep some sort of tabs on her for the purpose of her continued safety, he wasn't fond of doing so. For one, he didn't want her to feel like she was in a cage, even though he supposed she was. Secondly, he was finding it much easier to be *away* from her, without knowledge of her comings and goings. Soon, his mother would ask the same question Dulci had, and it could become problematic.

"The last time I saw her, she had her nose buried in a book."

Dulci made a derisive nose at the back of her throat and tied a band around her greying hair. "Sounds familiar."

Grimm did not wish to discuss Agatha. They'd only been married a handful of days and being forced into her presence was a strange sort of torture. Conversing about her wasn't much better.

"And together they will change the course of all things," Dulci recited.

Grimm blinked at her, lips tight. Dulci was the only member of their faction, aside from Gaius, that knew of the prophecy and what Agatha was really doing in Merveille. Unfortunately for Grimm, Dulci sided with the prophecy.

"Together, Grimm." She kept her voice low, so the others wouldn't hear as they filed into her small apartment above the bakery.

"Thank you, Dulci. I know what it says. We have come together, considering we've just been *married*, and we *are* changing the course of things."

"Have you? Come together?" When her eyebrows raised suggestively and Grimm caught the meaning behind her words, his chest rumbled with a suppressed growl.

"Dulci, you are like a mother to me, and I don't wish to have this conversation with you."

The old baker held up her hands in mock surrender. "I'm simply saying you should think on that portion of the prophecy."

"Do you think I don't? That I haven't thought about every syllable of that prophecy since the moment she showed up here?"

The squint of her eyes told him he was in for an earful, but Gaius stepped closer and the baker clamped her mouth shut, walking away to speak with Tindle.

"I agree with her," Gaius said behind his steaming cup.

"I know that. What I don't know is *why*. You don't believe this damned prophecy any more than I do."

The others were beginning to get antsy. The grief of Alestair's death burdened them, but it warred with the hope sparked by the recent strides that had been made. Tindle looked pointedly at Grimm, and he knew they'd have to begin soon.

Everyone awaited the appointment of who would take Alestair's place.

"Of course not," Gaius spoke under his breath, "but what this prophecy has *caused* is working. Despite the control, the people still follow her defiance. I think Agatha makes a suitable asset to you."

"She's not a blasted tool, Gaius," he snapped.

Just then, Augustus burst through the door of Dulci's home, distracting them both.

"If you are here," Grimm addressed the guard with thin patience, "who is protecting Agatha?"

Dulci huffed a laugh through her nose and Grimm glared at her.

"Porthos is with her as well as Anne, but you might want to return rather quickly." He looked nervously around the room.

Ice was slowly building in Grimm's gut. "Why is that?"

"Erm. Her Highness Princess Agatha has been called to a private meeting with the king and queen. It was called by the Grand Magus."

The string of curses that flew from Grimm's mouth made one of the ladies blush as he snatched up his cloak and stormed out.

AGATHA

HANDS TREMBLING, Agatha cursed herself for being so nervous in front of these monarchs who were mere infants compared to her. It never felt that way, though. As the people around her grew older, she grew wiser yet stayed perpetually the same. She had centuries left before she would see grey in her own hair or wrinkles drawing lines through her skin.

Agatha wondered how long the king and queen in front of her, and her own husband, would lie in the grave with worms feasting on their flesh before she saw that first crow's foot adorning her eye. She wished she could trade them.

Her heart stuttered at the thought. She hadn't had that particular notion since Ira died. She hadn't thought of life much at all after Ira. For those first years, death sounded so much easier. But since arriving in Merveille once more and meeting people like Anne and Tindle and Augustus, Agatha had found she'd begun to envy them again—the mortals.

Though she and her Sisters were far from invincible and not quite immortal, the exchange for their gifts was the curse of watching everyone they cared for grow old and die before their very eyes. If she were being honest with herself, the first pang of that realisation had come from the thought of Grimm dying while Agatha had to rule an entire country in his stead—without him.

As if she'd summoned him with her thoughts, Grimm strolled into the throne room, the rapid rise and fall of his chest the only indication that he wasn't the perfect picture of ease he appeared to be.

"Ah, good," he said with an easy smile. "You've not begun without me."

"We're still waiting on the Grand Magus," Queen Fleurina spoke primly, inspecting her bejewelled hand.

"Did you run here?" Agatha spoke under her breath to Grimm as he took his position next to her, standing far too close.

"It turns out that it slipped my wife's mind to inform me we were meeting with my very own parents this day." His lips curved into a bitter smile.

"If you were ever around, I might possibly be able to inform you of such things, *darling*."

Grimm barked a laugh. "Miss me, do you?"

The queen couldn't hear their words, but her eyebrow rose in pleasant surprise at whatever she assumed was passing between them. Cursed prince, always playing a game with his masks. And curse her for the one moment of weakness she'd spent thinking she might mourn him if he died. Seleste's sentiments must have left her weak and emotional. No more.

"How can I miss someone that's never around? But I'd be happy to stab you and see how I feel once you're gone."

His returning gaze sent a shiver through her. "I'd love to see you try."

The heavy doors of the throne room opened and in stepped the Grand Magus. He strode to the dais, robes billowing behind him and chin lifted high.

"Why are we here?" Grimm whispered.

She fought the urge to fidget. "I don't know." Her best guess was her recent matrimonial wardrobe display, the wide brim hats flooding the streets...oh, and her delightful little toast. Regardless, she would follow through with her coming plan no matter what happened in the meeting.

The silent king sat next to his wife, inspecting what looked like a dust mote, and the Grand Magus sat upon a golden chair next to their thrones.

"Good afternoon," the magus spoke, voice echoing off the marble floor and stone walls. "You've been summoned here today to discuss your rather *inappropriate* display at the wedding and the mayhem that has ensued in your wake." His lips fell into a thin line and Agatha glanced at the queen. Her face was devoid of emotion, but one of her fingers was tapping furiously against the arm of her throne.

Agatha felt Grimm tense beside her, but he kept his mouth shut. "And what display is that, Grand Magus? What mayhem have I caused?" she asked.

His jaw clenched and Grimm shifted on his feet. "You defied

our customs and made a mockery of the wedding ceremony, for one." He chopped one hand with the other. "You were to show the common people that someone of their station has climbed the social ladder and they needn't worry any longer, not parade about like a harlot."

"I *thought*," she spoke sharply, words laced with poison, "that I was to erase the lines of inequality, Grand Magus, and that means bringing *my* ways into the court."

The magus' pompous face darkened with spite and Agatha caught the barest of smiles upon Grimm's lips out of the corner of her eye.

"And your toast?" Magus von Fuchs' face scrunched up like he'd eaten a lemon. "How dare you?"

"How *dare* I toast my king and queen for being the progressive, equality-driven royals you claim them to be by *allowing* their son to marry me?" Agatha raised one eyebrow. "A travesty indeed." She was walking a fine line but finding it difficult to guard her tongue.

Grimm snorted and the queen's pursed mouth slid into genuine amusement. She spoke before the magus could respond, "Though I relish the fact that my obstinate son has an equally stubborn wife he must contend with daily, I'm inclined to agree with the magus." Her response set Agatha's teeth on edge. "Your displays are making the people restless, more than"—she trailed off, waving an elegant hand as she thought—"*soothed* by your position in this court."

Good, Agatha thought. *Let them rise. Let them revolt.*

A door opened, two sets of light footsteps tapping against the marble as Anne and Miriam approached with trembling trays of refreshments. When the Grand Magus smiled at Agatha, she thought she'd be sick. Biting the inside of her cheek to steel her nerves, she tried to ignore the silent implication meant to unnerve her. Her hands were overheating. She needed to calm down, but damn this court for being so vile, toying with *human beings* to get their way. Toying with *Anne.*

Agatha turned to the queen. "Your Majesty, how are we to appease them without allowing a bit of their culture into yours?" Grimm glanced at her with what she could have sworn was pride.

When she looked up at the queen's expression, it mirrored that of her son's. "I will consider your proposal."

The Grand Magus turned sharply to the queen, indignant, but said nothing.

Queen Fleurina paid him no mind. "You're dismissed," she cooed to Agatha and her son.

"You've nerves of solid iron," Grimm whispered out the side of his mouth as they walked away.

"If the magus harms Anne, I will slaughter him myself," she hissed.

Grimm's eyes abruptly landed on her face. After a beat of silence, he murmured, "We are in agreement, then."

"THIS IS A DREADFUL IDEA, and you know it," Eleanor snapped, frowning at the muck caked on the bottom of her shoes.

Agatha ignored her and dipped to one knee on the broken cobblestones in front of a little girl in tattered clothes. "Aren't you the loveliest thing I've ever seen?" She tapped the darling girl on her nose and she giggled. "Here is a bag of grain for your mummy." Agatha handed her a burlap sack, followed by another. "And here is fabric for a pretty dress for you." The girl wobbled a curtsy and bounded off to her mother where she was selling eggs on the dirty corner. Agatha's heart swelled at the sight of the woman wearing a more cheaply made version of her hat.

"You're going to get someone hurt. Or worse." Even Eleanor's whisper sounded on edge.

Agatha straightened, her guards flanking them. When they'd arrived at the edge of the worst neighbourhood in the slums, it took a moment for people to note her presence. They were all busy selling and trading what they could, just to make ends meet. Once a young boy saw the palace guards and his excited shout echoed off the rough stone buildings, it wasn't long before Agatha was recognised.

Within moments, hundreds more people had gathered in the mire, pushing to get closer to her. Many were wearing her fashion designs and it spurred her on. It began as a chance to meet their new princess, but now that she had begun passing out gifts, the crowd was pressing in, dangerously close to rioting.

"I told you not to come, Eleanor."

Agatha was playing a perilous game. The magus already knew how to get to her, and she did not doubt he would. She'd finally convinced Anne to keep far away from the charade, but Eleanor had refused.

The people had begun wearing her and Tindle's creations to an astounding level. She'd made a private request of the queen that no one yet knew about—to throw a ball in celebration of the Eve of Hallows—and had received a surprising yes, but only because the queen hadn't suspected her intentions. Handing out gifts in the slums as a show of goodwill, on the other hand, had been a mistake.

Agatha had known it would turn ugly. If there is not enough for all, the desperate will do what it takes to win what's offered —no matter how wicked.

She had moments, maybe less, before it became a bloodbath. Of course she'd wanted to offer the people something, how could she not? But the point of the outing was to rouse the slumbering giant and force the king and queen to act. With or without the Grand Magus' consent.

A young man shoved forward, sending a woman flying into Agatha. Augustus wedged himself further between Agatha and the crowd. Everything was a blur of skin and rank smelling clothing. Their demanding voices coalesced into an indistinct roar in her ears.

"Eleanor, you need to leave," she demanded when Augustus was pushed backward into her, his scratchy uniform pressed against her face.

"I'm not going anywhere without you, you half-wit. *We* need to leave."

"She's right, Highness." Augustus had his hand on the pommel of his sword. He was a good man, but Agatha knew he'd protect her first, whatever the cost.

"Alright." She turned to Porthos. "Tell them the royal family will have grain, wine, and fabric delivered to anyone who wants it. Find some parchment and get me a list of names."

Porthos nodded as Augustus shielded Agatha and Eleanor both, leading them to their carriage. Augustus helped them in and slammed the door shut just before the crowd could get to them.

CHAPTER
SIXTEEN

K indness is a strength all its own. Peace and tranquillity should never be misinterpreted as meek or feeble.
-Writings of Ambrose Joubert

AGATHA

AGATHA'S EYES SHOT OPEN. Instinctively, she slid a hand under her pillow and withdrew a dagger, her vision adjusting to the soft darkness of the chambers. She dared not move for fear of losing the element of surprise. If they approached, she could slit their throat. Agatha inhaled and let her protection spells know she needed them up and alert.

The bed dipped behind her prone form and Agatha stiffened. She slid the dagger out slowly, preparing to attack. Until she heard a familiar sigh of exasperation.

Agatha returned the dagger under her pillow and flipped over, yanking the covers toward herself. "What in the seven realms are you doing?" she hissed.

She couldn't see Grimm's expression with the curtains drawn and dawn still contemplating her approach, but the low growl that issued from his chest gave Agatha a clear idea of the look on his face.

"Your delightful servants have informed my mother that I'm rarely here when they come in at dawn, and when I am, I'm on the chaise or asleep at the desk."

Agatha smiled in the dark, remembering the time Eleanor startled him half to the grave and he'd jumped up from the desk with parchment stuck to his face. She felt him turn his attention toward her, as if he'd known she'd smiled.

"So, here you are."

"So, here I am." Grimm's foot began rotating back and forth under the covers and Agatha could hear his fingers drumming on his chest. "When do they come in? How long is it until dawn?"

He did not sound himself. She'd never seen him so ill at ease. "You sound like a nervous child, Grimm. You've been here half a moment. If you look like you're going to come out of your skin, no one will believe this ruse. Just calm yourself and quit fidgeting."

She kicked him, her foot connecting with his bare leg, and they both froze. For some reason, she'd expected him to have pants on. Though, that didn't add to the illusion that they were in the throes of young married life. She inched further from him. "They should be in soon. It's starting to lighten up outside."

Grimm let out a breath and stilled his wiggling foot, but his fingers kept their time on his chest. "Tell me something interesting," he said softly.

Agatha glowered. "I'm not playing one of your mind games before the sun is up, prince."

She could almost hear his eye roll. "I'm passing the time, Agatha. Attempting to make this a fragment less unsettling."

He had a point. *Fine.* "Augustus tripped yesterday, attempting to show off for Anne." Despite herself, she snickered into the greying light. "He didn't *quite* fall, but nearly, and his teetering near-topple was amusing."

As the room continued to lighten, she could finally see the planes of Grimm's face, looking at her with his fingers still. The corners of his mouth turned up. "Augustus has had eyes for Anne since we were children."

It intrigued Agatha that Grimm had known these servants and guards his entire life—known things about them. But Augustus had said Grimm appointed him to the palace guard himself when they were older. How had he known them all in such an intimate way as a prince when Augustus grew up in the slums?

"Why did you replace my previous guard with Augustus?" Agatha asked. "He told me, so don't even try to deny it."

"*Snitch*," Grimm muttered. "Who's playing mind games now?" His smirk dimpled one cheek. "I trust Augustus with my life. I can't say that about most, so I knew I could trust him with yours."

Anne's signature soft knock sounded from the entry. Without warning, Grimm slid his arm underneath the small of Agatha's back and hauled her closer. Her breath caught in her throat when her cheek connected with his bare chest, her bust pressed up against his side.

"Just for a moment," he whispered against her hair and heat coursed through her.

Anne bounced into the room, her countenance as bright as the sun. "Oh, if you two aren't the sweetest thing."

She flung the drapes open, and they both winced at the blinding light. Agatha wondered how servants ever got used to walking in on half-naked aristocrats. She supposed it provided them with loads of embarrassment or cannon fodder for the rumour mill.

"Forgive my intrusion. I'll just get your fire burning hot again and let you get up."

Agatha did not need any help in that department. She was quite hot enough as she was.

Grimm's heartbeat thundered underneath Agatha's ear and lighting sparked through her at the feel of him against her. She laid very still, willing Anne to light the fire more quickly. In doing so, she realised her hand was flat on Grimm's stomach and his was cupping her hip. Agatha gasped, pulling away. She jumped up from the bed, looking around for something to cover herself with. Grimm averted his eyes.

"Your Highness!" Anne rushed over. "Are you alright?" She looked between the two of them.

"I'm fine, Anne. I wasn't expecting it to be quite so cold out of all those blankets." And away from Grimm.

Her maidservant draped a dressing robe over Agatha's shoulders. "That's why I was building the fire up *before* you got out of bed."

Grimm cleared his throat and Anne nodded, leaving the room as swiftly as she'd rushed in. Agatha turned to him, wondering what he possibly had to say in that horrifying moment, only to find him rising from bed. It occurred to her that, as indecent as he was, the clearing of his throat had been meant for her to leave the room as well. Or at least avert her attention. Agatha shook her thoughts loose and stormed for her closet.

When she came out, Grimm was gone and Anne was laying out a tray of food.

"For you to eat while I comb the knots out of your hair, Your Highness."

The implication that her hair would have more knots than usual after Grimm was found in her—*their*—bed left Agatha in a sour mood.

Tugging on a particularly stubborn tangle, Anne dropped the silver brush. When she crouched down to retrieve it, something made of glass fell out of her apron pocket, *tinking* when it rolled off the carpet onto the hardwood floor. Without thinking, Agatha bent to pick it up for her. Surprised by what the item was, Agatha held it up to the light. She examined the small amber vial before handing it back to Anne. A fierce blush had spread across her maidservant's cheeks and crawled up her neck.

"Anne, are you feeling unwell?"

"No, Your Highness," she answered too stiffly. "I assure you, I take my draught every day as expected. I simply ran late this morning and dropped it into my pocket to take once I had you ready for the day." Anne pulled out the small cork. "See, I'll take it right now." She downed the draught in one swig. "See?" She beamed a mad smile.

What in the seven realms was in that vial?

Anne deposited the empty bottle into her apron. "Now, what would you like to do this morning? Should you like to go to the library as usual?" She bobbed up and down on the balls of her feet, babbling. "Or perhaps to the woods again to look at the Autumn trees before the leaves have all fallen?"

Agatha studied her jumpy maidservant. It seemed like she was desperate for Agatha to know she *does* take it, not embarrassed as if it were something simple, like a woman's tonic.

"You know," Agatha answered, "I think I would like to see your rooms, Anne."

Anne blanched. "Your Highness...Princess Agatha...I—I don't think a member of the royal family has ever gone down into the servants' quarters except—never mind."

"You forget that I *am* one of you," Agatha pressed. "Think of it like giving me a little bit of home here in this gargantuan stone crypt."

Reluctantly, Anne nodded. Agatha didn't want to deceive her friend, but she needed her hands on a full vial of that draught. Besides, she did want to see how the servants lived, as well as have an opportunity to better get to know this particular servant.

Agatha linked arms with Anne, something very against her nature to do with anyone other than Sorscha, but she knew it would ease the girl's nerves. Her face lit into a beautiful smile and they made their way through the castle, Porthos silently trailing behind.

"Where is Augustus today?"

Anne's cheeks went pink again. "Prince Grimm asked Augustus to spar with him as soon as he left your chambers this morning. He said something about needing to be rid of some restless energy." Anne's dimpled smile widened at the same time Agatha's stomach flipped. "Augustus is the only swordsman that can keep up with Prince Grimm, aside from Lord Gaius."

As they walked the corridors, the heels of Agatha's boots clicking on the stones, Anne pointed out various paintings, explaining who they were. At the start of a long row of kings and queens framed in gold, Agatha paused in front of King Caliban. She peered into his crystal blue eyes, remembering how they looked when the light left them.

"Who is this?" she asked, her voice betraying some of her emotion, but it was lost on Anne.

"That is King Caliban." She sounded sombre herself and Agatha looked sidelong at her maidservant. "The greatest king Seagovia has ever seen."

Agatha swallowed and nodded. "I've read about him."

"He was ushering in a new and better age, freeing the people from oppression, and then—"

Agatha's heart sank. "And then he was murdered."

Anne nodded. "It was his cousin. I just know it."

Agatha watched Anne's expression. She'd spent decades studying historical documents of Caliban's murder. She told herself it was to be sure her name was never mentioned, but she knew it was truly a way to remind herself of what she'd done. Hespa's will or not, it was the greatest regret of her lifetime.

Not once had History mentioned Caliban being killed at the hands of his cousin who stood to inherit the throne should he perish. Agatha knew something like that, even if it were true, never would have made it into the books written by Crown-approved scholars. It was why so many of the books she studied had been written by ostracised scholars and hedge witches. Perhaps she'd been remiss to spend so much time in the castle library. If she wanted to find out more about Merveille and the prophecy, she would need to find books the royalty would burn if they ever learned of their existence.

"Anne, do you know any scholars in the city proper? I would enjoy finding some literature outside of the library."

Anne's face fell. "One. Professor Ludwig. But he was recently found dead."

Her phrasing made Agatha nervous that it was no mere illness or old age. "What happened?"

"I'm not sure." Anne shook her head and kept walking.

Agatha was very certain Anne was lying, or at least suspected foul play herself. But why?

They turned toward a hall Agatha had never been down, and she marvelled at the intricate gold details winding up and into the curved ceiling, even in an area traversed by only servants. The corridor began to narrow, and the torches along the walls became few and far between. Despite the ominous feel of it all, Anne wore a small smile on her face. It occurred to Agatha then that Anne was proud of who she was, and if their time together had told her anything, Anne was not nearly as sunshine daft as she led others to believe.

Just before they reached an archway leading toward Anne's rooms, her maidservant linked their arms once more and leaned in, resting her temple on Agatha's shoulder. "I'm immensely glad you're here, Agatha."

Agatha let her cheek briefly rest on Anne's mousey-brown hair, words failing her.

They walked in comfortable silence the rest of the way until Anne opened a door and ushered Agatha inside. It was a small space, no larger than Agatha's closet, but its simplicity was comforting. Two narrow beds sat pushed up against opposite stone walls, vanity and washbasin situated between. Two small chests of drawers butted up against the foot of each bed, and a wardrobe barely the size of a bookshelf stood on the far wall. There were no windows, and judging by the dampness in the musty air, they'd traversed farther down into the castle than she'd realised.

"Who shares this with you?" Agatha asked.

"Eleanor, of course." She pointed to a bronze bell above the wardrobe. "That is connected to your rooms."

Agatha had never once rung the bell they'd shown her when she moved into the castle. And unless she was in dire need or near death, she never would.

"Anne, I spoke with the queen about hosting a ball." Her maidservant, who was fluffing Eleanor's pillow, turned to Agatha in surprise. "I plan to incorporate my own ideas and invite the merchants from Mer Row."

Anne's grin was nothing short of radiant. "I think it's brilliant."

Another maidservant Agatha had never met stuck her head in then and gasped, dropping into a low curtsy. "Your Highness, apologies. I saw Anne's door open and came to close it."

"No need for apologies. I don't believe I've met you." Agatha moved toward her and the woman's eyes went wide.

She spotted the servant's boots peeking from underneath her simple, taupe gown. They were nearly identical to Agatha's, only less finely crafted. At her request, Tindle had given all his sketches to trusted clothiers in town, so those with even less coin could still procure the items.

"What is your name?"

"M-Mary, Your Highness."

"It's a pleasure to meet you, Mary."

"Oh, Mary!" Anne jumped, bustling toward her. It warmed Agatha's heart that Anne felt comfortable enough around her to ignore formalities. "Do you know who won the sparring match? Augustus or Prince Grimm?"

Mary blanched and looked between Agatha and Anne. Agatha chuckled. "I'd like to know as well."

Mary looked at her feet, but said, "I was there a bit ago and it was evenly matched. They'd moved to fists, though."

Anne's face brightened in a way that led Agatha to think her maidservant knew quite well what an equally matched fight between two men might look like, and the clothing they might discard in the process.

Agatha laughed in earnest. "Go, I'll be right behind you." She was anxious for a moment to search Anne's rooms.

Anne giggled before running out after Mary.

It wouldn't take long for Porthos to come check on her, so Agatha rushed to Anne's chest of drawers and opened them, whispering a spell to silence her movements. In the top drawer, she found four identical vials to the one from that morning, but Agatha worried taking one would be obvious with so few. Anne shared the room with Eleanor, though, and if they were to take the draught every day, Eleanor would most likely have a stock-pile—prepared as she was.

Agatha rushed to her drawers and slid them open. There, in the middle drawer, rested three rows of vials. Bless Eleanor's rigid soul. Agatha slipped one into her pocket, returning the drawers to their position just as Porthos knocked and stuck his head in.

"Your Highness? Are you alright?"

"Quite well, Porthos. Could you lead me to the sparring match between His Highness and Augustus?"

As they walked through the castle and out into the courtyard, Agatha's temper heated. Whatever the vial contained, she didn't like it. Her magic could feel the sinister cadence of it where she clutched the draught within her pocket. She didn't care what sparring match Grimm was in the middle of. She would speak to him immediately.

"Oh," Porthos spoke before Agatha even realised they were at the practise field. "It looks like they're gone." He snagged a guard by the collar, hardly even old enough to be considered a man. "Lamen, where is Prince Grimm?"

"Left, sir. He was late for a council meeting."

Grimm

IT WAS A FOOLISH PROPOSAL.

"Wonderful thinking, gentleman," Grimm said instead. *Daft lot of moronic lords.* "What better way to appease our irritable neighbours and cool the tension building against our peace treaties? Let us send in more soldiers and, of course, invite the rulers to a *ball* after all the tea sandwiches we've stuffed in their faces." He didn't even add the sarcastic lilt to his words. It would have been lost on them, anyway. It was best they think him as asinine as they were, bending to the magus' every whim. The half-wits all smiled at him. Though Gaius' was of pure, unadulterated humour.

Wellington, however, who looked particularly bothered, spoke up with a sneer plastered on his oily face. "Yes, what a grand idea our new princess has had, indeed."

Oh, gods. Agatha's idea? What in all the realms...

Grimm locked eyes with Gaius, whose brow was raised, and fought to school his features before addressing Wellington. "Why, yes. My wife is quite the breath of fresh air, is she not?"

Wellington had barely opened his mouth to respond when the

door to Grimm's meeting chamber flew open and crashed against the wall. Agatha rushed in, her cheeks pink with what he could only assume to be rage, judging by the look in her eyes. That was, until she noticed all the lords standing one by one, staring at her from around the table. She stiffened, one hand hidden within her pocket.

Curious.

They all gave her rapt attention as she dropped into a small curtsy. He'd told her a hundred times she needn't do that any longer. "Grimm," she spoke, her chin high. He hid a smirk, hoping to conceal the staccato his heart took up when she didn't use his title. "I'd have a word with you." Her eyes roved over the men in the room and landed on him again. "Now."

Her tenacity was infuriating but curse him if it didn't make her so alluring.

Grimm winked at her before standing and inclining his head as the lords did the same. "Already my wife makes such open demands of my time." A couple of the lords coughed to hide their amusement at his implication. "Anything for you, my darling wife." His tone was saccharine and the colour of her cheeks dipped into a lovely shade of scarlet. He hoped the men thought it out of embarrassment, but Grimm knew it was fury. He did really, *really* enjoy making her angry.

They entered the hallway, the door softly shutting behind them, and she whipped around to face him. "Do you take this?" She thrust a small amber vial in his face.

Grimm closed his hand over hers, looking up and down the hall. Where was Porthos? He leaned in, whispering harshly, "Put that back in your pocket immediately."

Agatha made no move to do anything of the sort. Grimm clenched his teeth and pried her hand open, awareness coursing through him as he remembered her pressed against him, that hand on his abdomen. He took the vial and closed the remaining handbreadth between them, looking down at her furrowed brows and pinched lips. Sifting through her skirts, he located her pocket and slipped the vial in. He measured his breaths to keep them even, noticing her chest rising and falling more rapidly than usual.

Agatha scowled up at him, neither of them backing away. "Answer me."

"Agatha, we cannot have this conversation here," he spoke under his breath. Behind her, Grimm caught sight of the Duchess of Ramhurst approaching with her guards. Agatha was near to the wall and without warning he put a hand on her waist, pushing her the rest of the way against it, ignoring her sharp intake of breath and what it did to him. He rested his forearm on the wall above her head and leaned in close. "Someone's coming." His lips were nearly brushing hers, and if he hadn't thought it a breach of what little trust they were forming, he wouldn't have been able to stop himself. "We can't be seen fighting, wife."

AGATHA

AGATHA COULD SCARCELY BREATHE with Grimm so blasted close. His hair was still damp from a hasty bath after his sparring match with Augustus, and she thought of reaching up to touch it. Mercifully, the duchess approached, her face tight as Grimm peeled away from the wall nonchalantly.

"Lady Olivia," he purred as she curtsied to him. "You are looking lovely as always."

"You are too kind, Your Highness." The duchess lifted her skirts and began to walk away.

Agatha watched as an intense fury darkened Grimm's

features, but he quickly smoothed his face and called out the duchess' name. When she turned back, Grimm was smiling, but it was a viper's smile.

"I know my wife is as ravishing as these sculptures"—he gestured a hand toward marble renderings of kings and queens of old—"but I'm certain someone such as yourself couldn't *possibly* mistake her for one and miss this exquisite woman standing here with me."

His hand snaked around Agatha's waist and he pulled her to his side. Time slowed for half an instant, and Agatha was acutely aware of every place where their bodies touched. He smelled of clean soap, musk, and coffee. It was the perfect storm and it left her head foggy.

The duchess looked between the two of them, her face set in a barely concealed sneer. She dipped into a low curtsy to Agatha. "My apologies, Your Highness. I did not see you there."

Grimm watched her go, muttering something about *a wretched old hag* under his breath along with a few other choice words Agatha stored for later use. When the duchess and her guards rounded the corner, he untangled himself from Agatha.

"We can't discuss this here. Meet me at dusk in our rooms and we'll go somewhere more private. Until then, I suggest you return that vial to whomever you swiped it from *immediately*."

AGATHA PACED BACK and forth in the rooms she supposedly shared with Grimm. Mabon squawked at her for placing his orange inside the enclosure, but dangled upside down licking it, nonetheless. "I can't exactly have your food floating about in here when Grimm comes in," she snapped at the bat.

Mabon put his back to her in response. Agatha blew a tuft of stray hair out of her face and glanced in the looking glass. Her dress was crumpled and her hair rivalled a bird's nest. There were smudges of ink dotting the arms of her cinnamon-coloured gown, and she considered changing, but the door flew open.

"Come along then, wife."

Agatha snorted. "You look like the Underworld held you hostage all afternoon, dearest husband." He'd apparently had as restless a day as she had since their confrontation that morning. Agatha had spent all afternoon in the woods, wondering if she'd made a mess of things requesting the coming ball, or if it would ignite something more. Only time would tell.

He grinned. "Who's to say it did not? You don't look much better."

"Your mother will give us an earful if she sees us like this. Perhaps we should change."

Grimm leaned on the open door, his hand braced on the knob. "You let Tindle dress you in finery equivalent to a mouthy stance *against* my mother and suddenly you care what she thinks?"

He was right. That wasn't why she wished to change. "I don't want to be detained," she lied.

Grimm stalked over to where her cloak hung near the fire and tossed it to her. "It'll hide the worst of it." He went into their bedchamber and returned with a fresh cloak of his own. "Come on, then."

Agatha took his arm, as was their growing custom in public, and she reluctantly let him lead her through the castle and out onto the beach. As they reached the marina, her tense nerves coiled ever tighter. "What are we doing?"

A rich laugh rumbled in his chest. "We're getting in a boat."

"I can see that, you oaf," she snapped. "*Why?*"

Grimm huffed. "Agatha, do you want to discuss this thing you so *desperately* needed answers for, or not?" He took off his cloak and tossed it in the small wooden craft.

She scowled at him but put one foot in the boat. He dropped an oar to the pebbled black sand and took her arm to steady her, but she shook him off. She could get in a damned boat on her own. It rocked as she did so, but her boots and hemline remained dry. Grimm climbed in, facing her, and pushed off the dock. He began rowing and Agatha pulled her cloak tighter against the chill.

"You're not going to toss me into the sea, are you?" There wasn't a grand bit of the sea before the gargantuan steel net and chains, but it was getting dark enough he could attempt to drown her without witnesses if he wanted.

Grimm simply watched her, unnerving Agatha nearly as much as the shirt that pulled tight against his chest as he rowed. He gave her a sly smile and finally broke eye contact first. "There are messier ways I could think of to rid myself of you. But no, not tonight."

That was fortunate. Agatha didn't need the blood of a prince on her hands, no matter how much she wished to be done with him most of the time. "We're going to sit in the boat out on the freezing water, then? Discuss things with our teeth chattering?"

"It's not that cold. And you will warm up if you'd help me row."

Agatha had rowed her fair share of boats, seeing as Winnie continually summoned them to Seleste's Solstices in the middle of the damned sea, but she was not inclined to do anything Grimm commanded her to do.

"Perhaps if you ask nicely."

Grimm

CURSE HER FOR THAT haughty look that made his body overheat.

"Princess Agatha," he let his voice dip low and sultry, "my arms grow weary without your valiant aid." Her lips were turning up in a reluctant smile, so he took it a step further. "I beg of you to relieve me of the burden of bearing this task on my own."

She bit her lip, but he could still see humour dancing in her eyes. "Come off it, prince." She took up the other set of oars and dipped them into the water. It did not take long for her to remove her own cloak, and Grimm swiftly regretted not just rowing by himself after all, as he tore his gaze away from the straining buttons on the bodice of her dress.

"That was quite a toast you gave, infuriating von Fuchs like that."

Her attention snapped to him. "You didn't even deign to show up."

"Did I not?"

She glowered at him. He'd heard every word from his hidden perch on a balcony overlooking the courtyard. Anne had set to spreading the word that *Her Royal Highness Princess Agatha,* intended to give a toast at tea, and when it reached him where he sat bent over far too many droll court documents, he'd rushed to hear it.

"I've also heard a lovely rumour that you handed out gifts in the slums." Agatha only scowled at him. Despite how close to death she had them dancing, he almost grinned at the look on her face. "You nearly caused a riot." Still, she sat silently, eyeing him. "And now she wants to throw a ball..." He tsked, unable to keep the smirk off his face any longer.

"I'm doing what I'm meant to do here."

"You could run a few things by me first, you know. Like the

list of people you plan to send *more* items to." Her eyes narrowed. Apparently, she'd kept that bit of information to herself, or so she'd thought. "I wouldn't let the magus find out about that one just yet."

"And if I'd like him to find out?" She tilted her chin up. "He's not the damned king, you know."

Grimm snorted and Agatha frowned, turning to look out at the approaching lighthouse.

"We're headed there." He inclined his head toward it.

"The lighthouse? But it's been abandoned for centuries."

Grimm cocked his head to one side. "Has it?"

He studied her. How the moon glinted on her dark russet hair. The set of her cheekbones, tiny freckles dusting the tops like stars over the Sacrée Mountains. The ever-present line between her brows that he was discovering came not only from anger but curiosity as well.

What kind of peasant knew so much history of Merveille and spent as much time in the library as she did? Most didn't even know how to read. Yet, here was this supposed prophesied peasant with enough wit to regularly give Grimm pause. And none of them knew what had *really* brought her there.

Agatha said nothing, but he could sense her earlier trepidation shifting to excitement about the lighthouse. He didn't know why he was taking her there when Gaius warned him not to. He'd planned to talk out on the beach, but his feet carried him to the marina. It was foolish. He was beginning to throw caution to the wind where Agatha was concerned and one day it could lead to a heap of trouble. Perhaps it was a mistake after all.

AGATHA

GRIMM'S MOOD had taken an abruptly sour turn. Hard lines set in his face as he tied the boat to the lighthouse and hauled Agatha out without warning. She wanted to inquire about his sudden shift in mood, but they'd had enough painfully intimate moments for one day. Instead, she silently followed him up the winding steps and waited as he unlocked a weathered door with a skeleton key.

Agatha had not expected what stood before her when he opened the door. The octagonal room was worn and grey, old beyond even herself. It was the very essence of what she'd discovered about Grimm, all shoved into one space. Not the act he played as the prince, but the secret things she'd pulled from her time with him when he thought she wasn't paying attention.

Stacks upon stacks of haphazardly placed books lined nearly every inch of the room. A worn leather chair sat nestled into a corner. Maps, quills, and parchments with half-written thoughts littered a large desk and part of the floor. Several discarded shirts and empty goblets sat abandoned wherever he'd dropped them.

He might fault her for leaving trinket trails, but Grimm was *chaos*.

"So, you do enjoy reading after all." Agatha played coy, poking at him for catching him in the library with Mila, but she'd seen him reading by the fire in their rooms at night, and Gaius had mentioned he owned all of Marlowe's works. He was often writing as well. She'd seen the ink stains on his fingers, and once even his lip.

"I do. Mostly for academic purposes, but I've been known to enjoy a novel if it's done properly." He folded his arms across his chest, eyes tracking her movements.

Agatha walked around the room, noticing a strangely vacant table with wet spots of a peculiar colour. Upon further inspection, there were trails of drips from the empty table all the way to the door. Someone had recently been in to hastily remove a sopping mess, or something she wasn't meant to see.

"This is where you hide out, then?" What she meant was: This is the real Grimm, then.

"It is."

His tone remained clipped, and she considered that this might be the equivalent of inviting him into her cottage. She couldn't really fault him for perhaps thinking that bringing her there had been a mistake, and she wondered if that was the source of his mood's decline. A jolt of unease reminded her why she was there in the first place.

"The draught, then." She turned abruptly to face him where he stood next to his armchair. "Do you take it?"

Grimm sat on the arm of the chair, folding his hands in his lap. "I do not."

"Why?"

He ran a hand through his dark hair, leaving it somehow more dishevelled than usual. His eyes moved around the worn floorboards at his feet as he calculated how to respond to her. "Because I am high born," he finally said.

Agatha gaped at him, leaning back against the edge of one of the three desks crowding the small room. "What is it?" she demanded.

"Would you like a drink?" Grimm ignored her question and rose to pour a dark amber liquid into a crystal glass, hovering over a second as he awaited her answer.

Goddess knew she wanted that acrid drink to calm her, but she needed a level head. She declined and took hold of the lepidolite crystal within her pocket instead.

"Suit yourself." Grimm shrugged and dropped into the armchair. Agatha opened her mouth, but Grimm spoke. "I know, Agatha. I've not forgotten your question." He looked to the ceiling and back at her with a heavy sigh. "Can I be frank?"

Agatha snorted. "For the first time ever? By all means." He'd given up some personal information about himself in recent weeks, but never anything about the court or Crown. His mouth turned down at the edges, and she could see the dark circles beneath his eyes. He was bone-tired. Agatha could use that to get necessary information. She almost felt bad for thinking of it, though. Almost.

"I'm trying to decide what to tell you. I've been debating all day, actually."

"Why can you not just tell me all of it?" she pressed.

"Agatha…" He let out an exasperated sound and set his drink on the side table with a loud crack. "The less you know, the safer you are, alright?"

Agatha might have staggered back a step at his honesty if she hadn't been leaning on the desk. She searched his eyes as they seared into her. It was always so irritating to pretend she needed anyone's protection. If she wanted to, she could squash a man like a fetid slug between her long fingernails.

Fists clenching in the pockets of her skirts, Agatha gritted her teeth. She was sick and tired of knowing nothing because she wasn't a born *royal*. Grimm was the only blasted person she could ask unless she wanted to shame him by taking up with Lord Gaius.

"Perhaps I should be asking Lord Gaius about all of this instead." His eyes narrowed, but she dug the barb in deeper. "Or Mila."

"*Enough*," Grimm growled, rising to his feet. He stalked toward her, his boots thudding on the floor. "If you want to ask Gaius or Mila, you go right ahead." His jaw clenched as he looked down into her eyes.

"What I want, Grimm, is for *you* to answer me."

His eyes fluttered shut for an instant before he backed away and retreated to stand behind the armchair. He cleared his throat and spoke. "The draught is known to the people as a medicinal elixir meant to prevent disease that could easily spread in blighted areas." His hands gripped the back of the chair, the leather protesting. "The slums."

Agatha scoffed. "And the elite are immune to disease, then, tucked up in their mansions? Do the poor have a *choice*?"

His eyes slid up to hers. "No."

"What is it *actually* for?"

He took up pacing, scratching the dark beard at his jaw.

"If you cannot answer that, can you at least tell me why I'm not safe if I know these things?"

"Because not even I am supposed to know them, Agatha."

She stood upright and crossed the room to stand in front of him. "Grimm, *please*. I need you to understand that I'm utterly alone in this." His face darkened at that. "I might be a peasant girl, but surely you can tell by now I'm not content to have a peasant's knowledge. How can I rule by your side someday when I know nothing? I was sent here against my will and bound to you with no knowledge of what's really going on. I've fought tooth and nail to make sense of it." She put a hand to her chest. "I can do some-thing for the people. For this kingdom. I don't have to just *look* like I'm doing something with hats and dresses and frivolous things."

Grimm let out a long breath. "I should have told you about this sooner. Now that we're married, and especially since you and Tindle *do* continuously make these fashion choices"—he gestured to her gown—"and you go about infuriating the magus on purpose. They'll trick *you* into taking the draught any day now."

Recent events clicked into place suddenly and surely. Dulci's comments about control, the vacancy in the people's eyes... "Grimm, does it control the people in some way?" It had to be magical if so, not medicinal.

He nodded sharply but did not meet her gaze. What was he

risking by telling her this? A sickening feeling in the pit of her stomach told her it was everything.

"Why do the people still mimic my fashion, then? Why did they have it in them to nearly riot? Shouldn't they be incapable of doing anything that potentially defies the Crown?"

Grimm chewed on his bottom lip. "Until your hats and boots began showing up all across Merveille, it was more of a...heavy-handed suggestion to take it. After your toast? A decree went out that it was mandatory. After your outing to the slums…" He fished in his pocket and pulled out a torn and dirty piece of parchment. "These went up all over the kingdom today."

WINTER IS NIGH. SICKNESS AND DISEASE WILL NOT RUN RAMPANT IN MERVEILLE. DO YOUR PART. TAKE YOUR DRAUGHT DAILY. IT HAS BEEN SO GRACIOUSLY PROVIDED BY OUR GENEROUS KING AND QUEEN WITH NO CHARGE TO YOU, THE PEOPLE. FAILURE TO TAKE THE DAILY DOSAGE WILL NO LONGER RESULT IN A FINE, BUT IMPRISONMENT.

SIGNED BY THE GRAND MAGUS. The paper heated in her hand until one corner singed with a spark. She blew it out, as if it were merely dirt marring the words and shoved it into her pocket. "How does this work?"

"I've been asking myself the same thing. I've been research-ing, doing everything I can. But I still don't entirely know how it works. I just know that it *does*." He surprised her by surging forward and grasping her hand. "Agatha, you need to not take it. Please. Whatever they tell you, *don't* take it." He dropped her hand as quickly as he'd taken it up.

"I would think you'd want me pacified, prince." She hoped her attempt at humour would ease the guilt she could see creeping onto his bent shoulders. He was letting his guard down, and she didn't know if it terrified or thrilled her.

A hint of a smile crossed his lips. "You would be far less enjoyable, were that the case."

Agatha was beginning to feel wretchedly warm. "Does this window open?" She walked toward it.

"It does, but the latch gets stuck."

She fiddled with it for a moment before she felt Grimm behind her. He reached up and forced it loose. Shoving the window up, his chest grazing the back of her shoulder. Chill-bumps ran up her back just as they had when he'd unfastened her wedding gown. Agatha rested her palms on the windowsill and thrust her head out, drinking in the Autumn wind that cooled her face.

When she pulled her head back in, Grimm was reclined against a desk. All that had transpired between them in a single day felt too deep. He was watching her like she was the villain, able to destroy him with one word. Agatha supposed he would be right about that. How was he to know she would not run to the king or the Grand Magus and rat him out? Or turn to Gaius? Or seek out the truth about Mila?

Agatha swallowed, knowing that what she was about to say was reckless and pure folly. "Grimm." The look in his eyes when she said his name made her palms sweat. "A secret of yours is a secret of mine. I need you to know that. We have a common enemy in this. I think we can at least agree on that."

She turned away before she could see his reaction, trailing a finger down the stacks of books lining the tables—and chairs and floor—while examining the titles. Agatha halted mid-step when one caught her eye. *The Lineages of Grand Magi of The Order of Hespa*. Then another. *The Gospel of Hespa According to Magus Luc*. Agatha moved more intently through the stacks, finding every title on her list that had been missing from the library, save for one. She spun to face Grimm, finger thrust out in the direction of the books. "Why do you have all of these?"

Grimm raised an eyebrow. "Why should I not have them?"

She noticed an ancient tome spread open on the desk by the window and went straight for it, knowing it had to be the last book on her list. The one she needed most.

Grimm straightened and rested his palm on it. "Agatha, don't."

She grabbed his hand and pushed it away as he winced, shaking it out as if she'd burned him. She probably had. Her magic tended to act particularly wily when she was under distress.

"Agatha, please."

She looked down at the page and her breath caught in her throat.

THERE SHALL COME A DAY, AS THE NIGHTS LENGTHEN AND THE LEAVES HATH FALLEN, THAT OUR DAUGHTER OF AUTUMN SHALL JOIN THE SON OF GEM AND BONE. TOGETHER THEY WILL CHANGE THE COURSE OF ALL THINGS.

THAT WAS IT. Agatha flipped the page over, reading the back and the next three pages, but there was nothing more about the prophecy.

"Why is my name not here?" She stabbed a finger at the book. There was nothing of what the Grand Magus knew of her listed there, either. Grimm's name was distinctly absent as well.

Grimm's gaze was intense. Studying. "How did you know to come to Merveille?"

Agatha stiffened. So, this was how it would go. "Three inquiries?" she ground out.

"With pleasure." All traces of guilt and congeniality had vanished from him. The guard he'd let down was formidably back in place, and Agatha made moves to do the same.

"Why are neither of our names here?" she asked.

"Because that is the original prophecy, dating back a thousand years." She thought he would stop there, with a non-answer as usual, but he did not. "Your name was written in just over three hundred years ago. Mine never was."

Her name was written in. What did that mean?

Grimm crossed his arms. "How did you know to come to Merveille?"

"*Pass.*"

Grimm smiled wide, wolfish. "That was a foolish mistake to pass so soon."

Agatha feared he was right. "Who wrote this prophecy?"

"I don't know yet." He gestured around them. "That's why I have all these books." He tipped his head to one side. "Who sent you to Merveille, Agatha?"

Her heart hammered against her ribs. She could say Hespa— the Goddess Three. *Should* say Hespa, but she felt it would be a lie. "My ancestors wrote of this prophecy." Grimm's eyes sparked and Agatha jumped to ask her final inquiry. "You're a Son of Gem as the Prince of Merveille, and your name is Peridot. What then is the significance of bone?"

"No one knows for certain."

"You do," Agatha challenged.

"I'm afraid your questions are all used up, peasant." His eyes roved over her face before he spoke again. "What are the names of your ancestors who also penned this prophecy?"

"I don't know their true names." It was not a lie. "They always wrote under the names of their animals." Agatha breathed a sigh of relief that she had not slipped and said *familiars,* and that he could not ask any more questions. Though, there was nothing stopping him from seeking those pen names at a later time. Agatha vowed she would be ready.

They stood, studying one another for a long moment. Agatha couldn't tell what he was thinking, but she knew his mind was calculating something, as his bottom lip was tucked in ever so slightly. Then, out of nowhere, something like rage flashed in his eyes and his jaw flexed. If she hadn't been watching him so intently, she wouldn't have seen anything at all for how quickly he hid it.

"We need to leave. Immediately." He stood straight, casual but for the tightness in his shoulders. "I have to gather a few things. I'll meet you at the boat." Agatha watched him shuffle through items on the desk. When she didn't move, he looked over his shoulder at her.

"And what if I row away without you?"

His lips tipped up on one side. "Then how will I return to sneak into our bed?"

Grimm

HE'D SAID it to anger the intruder behind him, but the flush that went up Agatha's neck at his words made Grimm's heart beat furiously in his chest. She said nothing, only turned and walked out the door. When the latch clicked behind her, Grimm pushed her from his mind and turned toward the window, his fury filled to the brim.

"*Mila*," he hissed.

She materialised, arms crossed and disgust written over her face. "You're growing reckless with her, Grimm."

He bared his teeth, not caring for a second if the short leash on his fury would reveal to Mila the decrepit creature of bone and shadows underneath his skin. If anyone wouldn't flinch from him, it was Mila for how many times she'd seen him unfettered, but Grimm needed her to know he was not playing games.

He dipped his voice low. "If you ever again so much as *consider* stepping into a room, *seen or unseen*," he snarled, inching closer, "that is occupied by Agatha and myself in private, I will return you from whence you came. And I will not hesitate." He clenched his teeth so tightly he thought they might shatter. "*Do I make myself clear?*"

Mila said nothing. She only nodded once, her own rage churning with his. Ice skittered across the window. A glass of water froze too quickly and burst, shards scattering across the desk and floor. She blinked, her cherry lips set in a hard line, and then she was gone.

CHAPTER
SEVENTEEN

*O*ne must remember, the Sisters' duty is to the Grimoire, and none other.
        -Sacred Texts of Hespa

AGATHA

"WHAT ABOUT THIS ONE?" Eleanor held up a mulberry gown.

It was lovely, but Agatha was in a foul mood. She shrugged and pushed a piece of fruit across her plate with her finger.

Eleanor heaved a sigh and swatted Agatha's hand. "Stop touching your food with your hands. You are not a pauper, you're Princess of Seagovia."

Agatha scowled at her bold maidservant. "Surely you wouldn't treat any other royalty this way, like a fussing mother hen."

"You're not just any royalty. Now, get up and get this gown on."

Eleanor couldn't be much past her second decade, a good

211

eight or nine years younger even than Agatha appeared, but she had the soul of an old crone. "You're awfully snippy this morning."

"And you're awfully glum and irritating me," Eleanor shot back.

That gave Agatha a sardonic smile. "Are you ever happy?"

"Are *you*?"

"I don't have to bounce around like a buffoon to be happy." Agatha stood.

To her surprise, Eleanor snickered. "Precisely. Nor do I."

"Am I the buffoon you speak of?" Anne leaned against the doorframe, arms crossed and a coy little smile playing on her lips. Agatha grinned. Her maidservant was growing surer of herself by the day, and Agatha adored her. She wondered if it had anything to do with Augustus returning her affections. They'd certainly been spending a lot of time together.

"You're the ray of sunshine that softens our stone hearts, Anne."

Eleanor laid the gown on the bed and left the room, but Agatha didn't miss the reluctant tilt of her mouth, as if she might agree with Agatha's statement of affection toward Anne.

Anne approached and handed a letter to Agatha. "This just arrived for you. It has the queen's seal."

She waited until Anne had finished buttoning up the high collar of her gown before carefully opening the queen's seal—a cardinal resting upon a branch.

"She wants to have tea this afternoon," Agatha explained.

"That's good, right?"

Agatha shook her head. "I'm not sure. I suppose we shall find out."

Grimm

GAIUS LEANED IN, fork halfway to his mouth. "Mila came to my rooms last night."

Grimm peeked over his coffee cup at his mother, who was pretending not to eavesdrop as she perused the society papers. "I'm certain she did," he responded to Gaius around a mouthful of biscuit. "Did you have a lovely time?"

Gaius glared at him. When the queen turned to say something to her servant, Gaius leaned toward the prince. "She's upset."

"With good reason."

"Grimm. You threatened her."

The prince set his fork down with a clatter. "She snuck into where I was holding a private conversation with Agatha." Gaius' eyes darted away at the mention of him being alone with Agatha, but Grimm ignored it.

"She can't sneak up on you. You know the second she arrives."

"Does that matter? It was a breach of my trust."

"She's scared."

"She's *jealous*."

Gaius baulked. "Of *what*?"

Grimm stretched his tense neck. "Of Agatha. Because Agatha has accomplished more in a moon than she and I have in our entire lives." He shook his head and took another sip of coffee.

"You're not wrong, but is it really all Agatha? The people

love her to be sure." Gaius chuckled. "And that riot she used to back the monarchy into giving out royal gifts was something else. However, *we* began this movement."

"We'd accomplished nothing."

Gaius rested his forearms against the table. "Grimm, the slums haven't seen a hard Winter in ages because of *you*."

Grimm eyed him angrily. He never should have let even Gaius in on that. "We saw no real *progress* until Agatha arrived."

"We saw no progress until *you* sent Alestair out."

"And look where that got him." Grimm swallowed his rage, barely stopping his fist's trajectory toward the table. "Agatha is the only reason the people of Seagovia still want to follow me at all."

Grimm pushed a grape around his plate with a fork as Gaius considered what he'd said.

"I noticed you removed all signs of your alchemical endeavours from the lighthouse."

Gaius frowned. "I knew you'd take her there, despite my opinion on the matter."

"I thought you rather enjoyed Agatha." He sipped his coffee indifferently. Gaius simply stared. "You wanted me to have Agatha as an ally, at least," Grimm pressed, keeping a watchful eye on his mother. "Clearly it's something to consider."

"Yes, but *slowly*." Gaius shifted in his seat, hands splayed. "You took her into the very place that houses everything we've worked for. We don't know how much we can trust her yet."

Grimm stabbed the grape with his fork. "Perhaps I'm finally willing to find out."

AGATHA

ELEANOR TUCKED AGATHA'S hair back into her bat wing clip for the hundredth time. Agatha pushed her hand away. "It's not going to stay, just leave it be."

"I can't believe you're wearing this wretched clip in front of the queen, anyway."

That was the point, but she was tired of explaining things to Eleanor. She still didn't know where the maidservant stood, despite the beginnings of warming up to her. "You're more nervous than I am, Eleanor, just go sit down." With a tsk and a huff, she mercifully left Agatha to contemplate her thoughts alone.

She'd been invited to the queen's private park: a small copse of trees fantastically lit with the remaining hues of Autumn, a pathway of faerie lights and floral-covered arbours, and, at the end of the path, a pergola of twisted vines.

Nestled under the bower was a small table fit for two and a tea set befitting the queen rested primly on top. The teapot was hot, but the queen was not present.

When her nerves were beginning to get the best of her, Queen Fleurina finally drifted around the corner and down the pathway toward Agatha, her wisteria-coloured gown floating behind her. In another realm, Agatha was certain she would be Queen of the Faeries. Agatha stood and curtsied.

"Agatha." The queen's eyes flicked to the hair clip and back to her face. At that moment, she wished very much that her powers allowed her to read minds.

"Your Majesty." The queen did not move to sit, and Agatha shifted on her feet, trying not to tug at her dress.

"I take it my son has informed you that the Eve of Hallows ball you suggested throwing will be in honour of Empress Amira and King Rashidi." He had done no such thing. "I will have an integral part in planning it, as well."

Agatha's grand plan was was suddenly shifting into her waking nightmare.

"I also want to thank you for doling out quaint gifts to those in the slums." Agatha stopped breathing. "What a simple way to quell their anger. I should have done that ages ago." The queen lifted her voluminous skirts. "I have other matters to tend to. Namely, dousing the fury your act of kindness has aroused in our dear magus." She motioned to the table. "Sit. My son will take my place for tea."

Queen Fleurina's lips turned up in a smile distinctly like that of an opponent winning a match, and she strode away. Agatha was considering bolting when Grimm strolled into the park, hands in his pocket and a carefree air about him. He nodded to Eleanor as he approached and she curtsied briefly, eyes averted.

"Shall we?" he said as he approached, gesturing to the table.

Agatha huffed. "I'd really rather not."

"My mother has demanded I have tea with you. I'm having tea with you."

Agatha crossed her arms. "And here I thought you were a grown man. Do you always do everything your mother tells you?"

Grimm shrugged. "I generally put my own spin on it to irritate her, but usually, yes. She is queen, after all."

"Does she tuck you in at night as well?"

A lazy smile slid across his lips. "Oh, I do that all on my own."

Lips pursed, Agatha stared at him as he plucked a finger sandwich from the platter and bit into it.

"Come now, dearest wife. We're here, these minuscule sandwiches are delicious, the Autumn trees are ravishing, and my company is unmatched." Grimm sat and poured her cup of tea first. "Sugar?" She glowered, and he dropped in two cubes. "We have to keep that sweet tooth of yours sated."

Agatha looked up to the trees, their leaves thinning as they were, then down at the blanket of colour beneath her boots. It was a lovely afternoon. She sighed and sat across from him with very little grace.

Grimm wiped his hands on a linen napkin and leaned back, tea in hand. "Three inquiries?"

"I'm not particularly in the mood for your mind games, prince."

"Nor am I. But I hardly know anything about you, Agatha from Helsvar, then Drifthollow, with three sisters." He smirked at her scowl. "Three simple questions, to better acquaint ourselves."

She sipped her tea, wondering what had gotten into him. Glancing over, she found Eleanor reading and Porthos talking with Augustus, who'd just arrived. Grimm tipped his chin to the guards and turned anticipatory eyes back on Agatha. She lifted a shoulder carelessly. "Fine."

Grimm smiled wide, rendering him alarmingly handsome without all the sullen tension he usually carried, or the masks he wore. "Are your sisters older or younger than you?"

Easy enough. "I am the youngest." She took another sip of tea.

"Pinky up, wife," he teased, demonstrating with his own cup while he took a sip.

She flung her littlest finger up with as much ire as she could muster.

"Very good." The low cadence of his voice sent an unexpected jolt of lightning through her.

"What is your favourite subject to study?" she asked.

Grimm's brows rose and he chewed on his bottom lip. "Is *all of the subjects* a poor answer?" Agatha suppressed a smile and nodded. He sucked a breath through his teeth. "Then I suppose I must go with Social Sciences. No. History." He shook his head. "Can't I just say both?"

Agatha laughed outright, drawing the bewildered attention of even Eleanor. Grimm's eyes sparked, and she dropped hers to the plate of tiny sandwiches.

She could still feel his gaze on her as he asked his next inquiry. "If you could go anywhere, *right now*, where would you go?"

"To see my Sister. My second eldest Sister." She did not have to think on that one at all.

"You miss her." Grimm's face softened in earnest and that familiar tension crept into his jawline.

"I do." But Agatha found she wanted to erase any weight that fell upon him. "Have you ever had a pet?" It was the most innocent thing she could think to ask.

To her immense delight, he relaxed again, an easy smile playing at the corners of his mouth. "I have a horse. He's been mine since he was born. His name is Nuit."

"I wonder if he has made friends with my horse in the stables, Guinevere." He looked pleased she'd offered a morsel of information freely, and she wanted to tug that thread. "I've not seen her since I arrived, actually."

"Then we will go riding tomorrow. I've not seen Nuit in a long while, either."

Grimm contemplated his last question and Agatha sipped her tea, wondering if he would delve deeper or keep it light.

"Tell me of a memory from your childhood."

Deeper, then. His gaze was so genuine and interested that she couldn't have passed if she wanted to. The first memory that came to mind ached. It was one she'd never explained to another soul. For an inexplicable reason she could not name, she wanted to tell Grimm.

"When I was a little girl, my eldest Sister—Winnie—" She stumbled on the name, afraid to divulge too much, but strangely wishing to do so. "She took my Sisters and me to a travelling carnival—a cirque." Agatha smiled and Grimm's face mirrored hers. "There were performers, exotic animals from Coronocco, acrobatic dancers, unimaginable food and drink—"

Agatha could still picture Sorscha pulling Wendolyn in every direction, chattering the entire time; Seleste's enamoured little face as she watched the dancers, and Winnie actually *laughing* with them. It was the first time since their parents had died—since their entire coven burned—that they'd allowed themselves joy. It was also the last time they'd been together before Winnie came of age and they were no longer permitted to see one another. Despite her best efforts, a lump crowded Agatha's throat.

"There was a man there in tattered clothes," she continued. "He was filthy and hardly skin and bones." Agatha shook her head, the memory weighing on her. "But he had one of the delicacies—a stick of bread dipped in butter and rolled in cinnamon and sugar."

Tears filled her eyes and she couldn't look at Grimm, but she knew he was listening intently. "I remember watching him and thinking how it broke my heart in the sweetest way that this man, who probably saved or stole or begged his way to this delicacy, got to have it."

Her voice began to waver, but she trudged on. "Then, a bird swooped down and stole it from him, and I wept. Not for the treat, but for what was taken from that man. His moment. His brief respite. The culmination of his sacrifice snatched right out of his hand in the blink of an eye." A tear slid down her cheek and Grimm reached out to take her hand in both of his. "I'm sorry," she huffed a laugh. "That's dreadfully sad."

"It's you, Agatha." His eyes held such intensity she had to look away again.

"Dreadfully sad?" She tried to smile.

"No. That moment—it's *you*, in essence. Unafraid to

encounter the dark. To sit there with those who are overlooked. And willing to be moved enough to fight for them."

Agatha looked at Grimm then, truly looked at him. She couldn't believe how deeply he'd understood *her* from such a simple story. She'd never even realised that truth about herself until he'd said it.

"Did anyone else notice that man?" he asked. Agatha shook her head. "And how many times have you thought of him since?"

"Countless," she breathed.

"Thank you for telling me something so precious, Agatha." And she knew he meant it.

Agatha swallowed, looking out at the trees and noticing then that they were alone. When the others had sensed it was time to leave the two of them to some privacy, she wasn't sure, but she hoped it was before her tears had betrayed her. "Will you tell me about a memory from your childhood, then?"

Grimm squeezed her hand and let go, leaning back in his chair. Instantly, she felt his absence and curled her fingers into her lap. "When I was a boy, I was carefully watched just as I am now. I was commanded to do and *be* so many specific things, and I was not allowed to question anything. Nor was I offered answers for anything at all.

"One day, when I was still just a babe, someone very dear to me took me to Dulci's bakery. I prattled on in my way of *how, why, where...*" His eyes grew wistful. "Dulci answered every last one of my questions. In fact, every day, she let me ask a number of questions corresponding to my age at the time, and she answered every one."

His throat bobbed as he swallowed. "I became very skilled at replicating a sleeping boy with pillows and sneaking past guards and servants so I could go be tucked in by Dulci—to have my hardest questions answered." Grimm breathed a laugh and shrugged. "I can name the number of nights I spent in my own rooms as a boy, but I've long lost count of the ones spent at Dulci's. It's always felt more like home."

Agatha wondered if that was where he went most nights—not the lighthouse—but she hadn't the chance to ask.

"Prince Grimm." Augustus rushed forward. "Lord Gaius has requested your presence immediately."

Grimm locked eyes with Agatha—apologetic eyes laced with fear—and abruptly stood, knocking into the table. Agatha watched as he strode briskly across the garden with Augustus trailing behind and the ease of their teatime drifting away on the wind.

In his absence, Agatha looked within her teacup to read her leaves. All the breath rushed out of her lungs at the sight of a crescent moon and a bone, both encased in an unbroken circle. She stood so quickly her chair toppled and rushed to look at Grimm's tea leaves, only to find they were nearly identical.

CHAPTER
EIGHTEEN

I f I must be the villain, the black knight, so be it. I'll see my
people freed, no matter the cost.
   -Journal of Thackery Peridot III

Grimm

"THIS IS an obscene amount of that poison."

Gaius grunted his agreement with Mila.

Grimm stood solemnly, hands shoved deep within his pockets as he stared into the enormous vat of golden liquid. What the vat itself contained was enough draught to supply the city of Merveille and its outlying communities for a month. And yet, there were hundreds of barrels, each filled to the brim, all across the old shipyard warehouse and two more buildings next to it.

"Perhaps they need the people to take a higher dosage?" Mila looked at Gaius.

"No." The lord shook his head at her. "It's potent enough

already, and the fear they've incited in the people is enough to ensure they're taking it at this point. At least most of them."

Mila scoffed. "Agatha certainly seems to have an effect on them."

"*Her Highness*," Grimm interjected, his gaze still firmly locked on the vat before them. But he did not miss Mila's sullen stare.

"True enough," Gaius spoke. "I'm not certain it's an indication of the draught's ineffectiveness, though."

"Maybe they've changed ingredients," Mila offered.

"It's possible. I'll take a vial back to the lighthouse to be sure, but I highly doubt it's changed. What concerns me most is why it can just sit in these barrels like ale."

Grimm watched Gaius as he approached the vat. It looked innocuous at first glance—alluring, even. Like honey awash in the sun's glow on a Summer's day. The taste was just as sweet.

"What concerns *me*," Mila said, stepping up to the vat and resting her hand on it, "is why it glows in this vat while it's brewing."

Grimm shut them both out. It was all concerning—every bit. He fixed his attention firmly on the potion spinning, sliding down the sides of the vat like an elixir from the gods. Gaius and Mila nearly froze in place for how slowly they moved. He wasn't strictly *supposed* to use his time-slowing power outside of its intended purpose, but the guards would only remain unconscious for so long. Whatever Gaius and Mila had drugged them with would eventually wear off, and Grimm needed to *think*. He'd only alter a few breaths.

He examined what they knew. Sifting, sorting through information like wading through waist-high grass in search of a lost coin. The people took the draught once a day and it left them...malleable; pacified. One of their own, Jasper, had let Gaius study him taking and not taking the draught, alternating back and forth. To their knowledge, the effects were the same, and the potency remained. There wouldn't be a need for the people to have *more* unless it would give the magus—and whomever he worked for—more control. But that went against what they knew about medicine.

Gaius had discovered several of the ingredients in his alchemical study of the elixir, but he'd come up short on a few—every time. *"It's as if they use materials from another realm. Materials that don't exist here."*

Grimm chewed on his bottom lip and walked forward, Mila's movements slowed in time drawn out like saltwater taffy strung long and thin. With the vat spinning so slowly, he could see the particles of the draught in the way one sees dust in the sun's rays, or bubbles in the deafening deep of the sea.

Sliding one hand from his pocket, Grimm rested it against the glass. He sucked in a breath as soon as it connected, his skin prickling with the feel of it. It was alarmingly similar to the way his hands sometimes felt when he touched Agatha. A thrumming, searing heat. To be fair, he'd attributed it to his growing desire *to* touch her, but now he wasn't so sure. Grimm stepped back and shoved his hand back into his pocket as he pushed thoughts of Agatha away.

Even with a double dose for each citizen, this was still far too much. If it couldn't sit in the barrels without spoiling, it was far too much to be just for the kingdom. And yet, there was even more being brewed as he stood there watching it. This wasn't Merveille's store. So, what was it?

Mila had floated around the space in search of ingredients, even a formula, but had come up with nothing.

Unbidden, Agatha slipped once more into his mind. He wanted to ask her what she thought. She knew of the elixir and his opinion on the matter, so what would be the harm in asking hers? He very nearly wanted to bring her to see it. She was somewhere with his mother, though, planning that ridiculous ball that would accomplish nothi—

It hit him like a battering ram. He blinked and time corrected itself.

"It's for the people of Coronocco and Lyronia," he breathed.

Gaius and Mila traded alarmed looks.

"You're certain?" Gaius asked.

Grimm nodded slowly. "The hand of friendship is a farce. This ball is a farce."

"But the ball was Agatha's idea, was it not?"

Grimm shook his head violently. "Not the idea to throw it in honour of Empress Amira and King Rashidi—that was *von Fuchs'* idea." He ran a hand down his face. "Think about it. Our soldiers are *in* their lands. That's already a cause for war, and yet an invitation to my wedding and a ball in their honour appeases the rulers?" He snorted derisively. "The people are trying to enter Seagovia, and we haven't the room for them. The Empress of Coronocco and King of Lyronia cannot lose their people. Their countries would suffer."

Grimm couldn't believe he'd missed what was happening. "They came to seek this." He pointed a finger at the spinning vat of liquid mind control. "They're going to ship all of this out to Lyronia and Coronocco. Mark my words."

Mila covered her mouth. Gaius pulled out an empty vial and filled it from the vat's nozzle. A noise sounded beyond the door, and he shoved a stopper in the vial.

"The guards are stirring." Gaius grabbed Mila's arm and pulled. "We have to go."

AGATHA

GUINEVERE NICKERED AND SNORTED, warming Agatha's cheek while her forehead rested upon the horse's own. "I missed you as well, sweet girl."

She silently chastised herself for not coming to visit Guinevere sooner. She'd only inquired twice about the old girl's wellbeing. It wasn't like her.

"She is a lovely thing." Agatha turned to find Grimm leaning up against the stall's door. "Nuit is her neighbour after all." He pointed to the sleek black horse in the stall next to Guinevere's.

Nuit stamped his hoof and whinnied as soon as he recognised his master's voice, and Grimm's chest rumbled with a laugh. "Alright, alright. Let's go, then."

It was strange to have Guinevere saddled by someone else, but both horses were fully tacked by the time she and Grimm had arrived. Perks of being a royal, she presumed.

They led the horses out into the grass and mounted. Agatha had chosen a dress with wide skirts, easy to manoeuvre in the saddle with, but she'd not thought about selecting black to wear on her black horse. She looked at Grimm and stifled a snort. He was also dressed in nearly all black, perched atop his own black steed.

"And what is so amusing?" he inquired.

"Anyone who sees us coming will think death has come to chase them." She gestured to their mournful attire and foreboding looking horses.

Grimm smiled, but it didn't reach his eyes.

"Where are we going?" Agatha asked, Guinevere dancing beneath her.

Grimm's eyes flicked to the excited horse and back to the path ahead of them. He gently urged Nuit forward. "I wanted to show you something."

"You're gifted at non-answers, prince, but that is the best one yet."

He smiled wide and her anxiety dropped a few notches. "Fair enough. It is a place I used to go when I was a boy. It's somewhere I've never shown anyone." He glanced at her. "Does that satisfy you?"

"I suppose that will do. How did you manage to rid us of our shadows for this excursion?"

"It's not hard to convince a guard to leave you be if you want to be alone with your wife."

Agatha's cheeks heated. "It's difficult to convince Eleanor."

Grimm laughed outright. "Right you are, but it's not difficult to convince *Anne* that Eleanor needs to be distracted so one might woo his wife."

"You're too good at this."

Grimm shrugged. "I know how to get what I want." Something about the way he said it sent fireflies bouncing around in her stomach.

They rode in silence for several moments, the fluidity of Guinevere's gait filling Agatha with peace. The forest was serene as they travelled deeper into it, under the sprawling canopy of Autumn trees still clinging to the last moments of their glorious decay. Most of the leaves were on the ground, crunching beneath their horses' hooves as their breath clouded out in front of them. Agatha inhaled the crisp, clean scent of her Season. She could smell the faintest hint of Winter—of her Sister Winnie—and knew the first frost would come any day. She had nearly two moons left before the Winter Solstice, and still no further answers or commands from the Grimoire, other than what Belfry had scribbled out. That she and Grimm would *change the course of all things*. As far as descriptive instructions went, it was dismal at best.

Though she'd ruffled some feathers and suspected Grimm was up to many things on his own, not much about their relationship was actually *together*. At the very least, they'd breached the subject of the draught and had at least one common enemy.

"Will you tell me what you know about the draught? Who makes it?"

Grimm raised an eyebrow at her. "I was waiting for that." He adjusted his position in the saddle. "It's partly why I wanted to bring you somewhere alone. I—" He paused, chewing on his bottom lip. "I know our predicament wasn't selected by either of us, and I would much prefer you had a way *out* of it, but—"

Grimm gently tugged the reins to halt his horse, and Agatha followed suit. He shifted to look at her, whatever he wanted to say warring within him. "Agatha, I think we need to play on the same side. I want to erase this line we've drawn in the sand."

Agatha twirled a lock of her hair and considered him, this prince before her whose mask continued to slip. He seemed content to let it fall away entirely. Something inside of her, completely against her will, trusted him. And something warned that the prophecy held some sort of truth for them, even if she felt it was laced with depravity. Erasing their line drawn in the sand didn't mean letting their guard down entirely. It simply meant a hand of friendship. A hand of allies.

"What is your goal, prince, in erasing this line in the sand? Your goal as Prince of Seagovia?"

He studied her intensely. "What do you think it is, Agatha?"

She spoke without considering her words. "I think you're more of a sympathiser with the people than you want anyone to know. I think *you're* the secret benefactor handing out wares on Mer Row and coin in the slums." His jaw flexed and she went on. "I think you're rash and foolish as an act to hide your diamond mind. I think you want what I want—the oppression of your people erased."

Her heart pounded in her ears. It was the truth she felt, but it was chock-full of accusation. Allegations that, if she was wrong, could land her in a terrible position.

"And that is what you want as well?" It was the most admission she would get. She nodded once, and his countenance grew ever more severe. "How much do you want to know?"

"All of it."

He shook his head, a wayward curl falling over his eye. "What I tell you cannot be unheard. Once you know it, you know it. Are you prepared for that?"

She wanted to roll her eyes and tell him she'd incited wars and slit throats—she could handle a devious crown. "Yes." Her voice was resolute.

"Can I trust you?" The pained lilt of his voice made her heart seize. She wondered how many people had betrayed him. How many he had to play the daft, spoiled prince in front of. How long he'd wanted someone besides Gaius he could trust.

"Grimm." Agatha looked down at her onyx ring and back up into his burning eyes. "I have a sickening feeling there might come a day when I'm the *only* one you can trust." The thought terrified her, but she could feel it in her bones and all around, like a whisper from Hespa through the trees. She knew in that instant that they were going to need one another, and that she was going to have to let in this prince she'd unwillingly married —at least a fraction.

She saw his chest heave and he kicked Nuit's sides, leading them off through the woods once more. After some time of silence full of all he had yet to say, Grimm sighed.

"The Grand Magus is in charge of the production of the elixir." That was exactly what she'd expected him to say, but it still nauseated her. "He uses a portion of the people's offerings and the royal coffers to fund it."

Why was she not surprised? "And your parents are fine with this?"

"For the most part, my mother just does what he says. She's more concerned with court affairs and keeping up appearances.

My father—" Grimm shook his head. "My father hasn't been himself since I was a very small boy."

Line in the sand or not, Agatha was taken aback by his candour. "What do you mean by that?"

"He's just...*not* himself. That man who silently watches butterflies and only speaks when it deals a heavy blow is not the man who sang me melodies and read me books as a little boy." The emotion was thick in his voice. "Not even Gaius will hear me on that one."

Agatha considered his words and what they could mean. It all had a reek to it—one that unsettled her to her core. "Where does the magus get his ingredients for the elixir? His formulation?"

"That, I don't know yet. Gaius has studied the draught day in and day out since we discovered its use several moons ago. He's deciphered many of the ingredients, common enough things, but there are a few he can't quite figure out. Things he's never encountered before."

Unsettling, indeed. Personally, she knew of nothing natural, even combined, that could control a person outside of dark witchcraft. "What sort of control does it cause? My small defiances have continued to be mimicked…"

Grimm snorted. "And von Fuchs hates you for it. As I mentioned in the lighthouse, it was more of a suggestion than a demand until the people began to follow you." He shrugged. "We do have a small group of individuals working with us, and one of them has willingly taken, and then not taken, the elixir as a matter of study for us. The best we can tell is it…" He rubbed his chin in thought. "It blocks impulses to a certain extent."

"What do you mean?"

"'*Block*' might not be the correct term. It's more like it softens the edges of impulses and renders people…calm, content. Unaware they're actually trapped."

"Like a lotus blossom."

Grimm mulled over her words briefly, patting Nuit on the neck. "As in the hearth tale?"

"In theory. Think about it. In the tale, those that partake of the lotus blossom each day become comfortable in their misery, unaware that they're actually dying in a parched desert. What if..." This was dangerous ground. It was the closest she was willing to toe that line gone from the sand concerning her magic. "What if they're real, or something like them? You said there were ingredients Gaius had never encountered or heard of before."

Grimm's eyes drifted off in thought as they rode. "I'll not discredit any theory at this point. It does manifest strangely, though, at times. For example, all the soldiers that left our borders and entered Prilemia, Lyronia, and Coronocco, they just...left."

Agatha frowned. "Soldiers do as they're ordered, don't they?"

"Not in the middle of the night out of a dead sleep they don't."

Any doubt she'd entertained that this draught wasn't magical vanished into thin air. "I didn't realise the soldiers would take it, even if they're not high born."

"They didn't use to, but it's the only thing that makes sense. I even saw Captain Dubois with a vial of it recently."

Agatha blew out a breath. "Soon they'll have everyone taking it, won't they?"

Grimm nodded solemnly. "I fear that might be so."

Silence descended as they each considered the implications of such a thing.

"Do you have any other examples?" she asked finally. "What can the elixir do to control people?"

Grimm didn't answer immediately. Instead, he rode on, brows knit together as he contemplated how to answer. "Von

Fuchs has been attempting to get it in my food for moons. Since before you came to Merveille."

Agatha shifted in her saddle, the trees rustling as if they too couldn't believe his words. "I warned you that your foolish outbursts would garner unwanted attention."

He scowled at her. "I would much prefer his attention remain firmly placed on me, rather than—" His words broke off and he glanced away. "Anyone else."

"How did you discover this was happening?"

"One day, I introduced a document to the court that I have no recollection of writing. One that barred anyone from the library —from *knowledge*—without permission papers signed by my father or the Grand Magus."

"You came up with that ridiculous rule?" Agatha accused.

"No, I did not," he snapped. "That's my *point*. I erased it for you, anyway, so unruffle your feathers."

Agatha blinked. So it had been Grimm that commanded the guards to give her free rein of the library.

"What I'm saying is, I never wrote that decree. I don't even remember presenting it, or my father signing it into law. It wasn't until the effects wore off and Gaius told me of the decree that I noticed it at all. I've had an insider in the kitchens ever since. I won't be anyone's puppet, and I won't stand by while others are, either."

This prince was a far better man than she'd ever given him credit for. The realisation fanned hot cinders in her soul, threatening to light fire anew. Perhaps she wasn't entirely alone, after all. A warmth she hadn't felt in a hundred years began to seep through her and Agatha hoped it didn't show on her cheeks.

"And I've begun to have your food watched as well."

Agatha cleared her throat, as it was feeling a bit thick at present. "The effects do wear off, then? Wouldn't more people realise they're doing strange things if so?"

The prince grimaced and visibly tensed. "From what we can

tell, it doesn't wear off for others. If they realise they've done something peculiar, it's softened by the continual use of the drug."

Agatha's eyes squinted at him. She swore he squirmed. "It only wears off for you?"

"That we know of."

"You are rather pig-headed."

He barked a laugh. "Thank you, wife."

Agatha ran her thumb over the smooth leather of the reins, thinking. "Surely the Grand Magus knows you aren't getting it, what with your outbursts and raging temper all of the time."

Grimm scoffed. "You're one to talk. I do think he suspects, but I've played it carefully enough that I think he's labelled me as unpredictable. Selecting to dine elsewhere, rather than eating what's brought to me by servants." He paused momentarily before continuing. "It gets worse."

Agatha groaned.

"The Coronoccan Empress and King of Lyronia are here to oversee the draught being taken into their lands."

Agatha inhaled sharply. "I don't understand. The magus is pompous and on a power high, of a surety, but I don't see how he could mastermind something like this…"

"He hasn't. Von Fuchs is a sadistic fool, but he *is* a fool. He's just the eventual scapegoat and false face of something much, much larger."

Now that made more sense—and it was terrifying. "Which is?"

Grimm halted Nuit and dismounted, reaching up to help Agatha off Guinevere. "That's what we're working to find out."

Agatha sensed his mood shift, and her theory was confirmed by the mischievous glint in his eye when he smiled and took her hand. "I want to show you that *something* I brought you here to see." To humour him, she let him help her down from the horse.

Agatha could hear waves crashing against the rocky shore as

they walked through the moss and leaf-strewn woods. The horizon fell away just ahead of them, and Grimm led her down slippery black rock to the water's edge.

"At a certain point each day, the tide recedes just enough to slip into this…"

He guided her into a crack along the base of a steep crag of rock. It was a tight squeeze, barely wide enough for him to fit through, and it smelled of ancient salt and stone. Once through, he pulled her along with him. The darkness was utterly blinding after the midday sun, and Agatha fought the urge to summon a flame. Grimm let go of her hand, and she soon heard a stone striking flint. A spark sputtered long enough for her to see the planes of his face, but it faded as fast as it had appeared. Grimm struck again and a sturdy flame lit a torch high in the cave's wall.

Agatha gasped as the warm light flooded the sea cave, illuminating hundreds of slumbering bats. The walls glimmered with unmined gemstones, their reflections dancing across the barest pool of sea water glittering on the ground beneath their feet. Grimm took Agatha's hand again and led her to the far side of the cave where a little ledge jutted out over the sea. She looked around with no small amount of awe as the prince's lips bent up in a grin and he discarded his boots. Though she'd seen —and touched—more of Grimm than his bare feet, something about the gesture was intimate enough that she felt it in every inch of her body.

He sat and dangled his feet down into the cold water. When he looked up at her, Agatha had to force her breathing to slow. She'd always thought him handsome—some things simply couldn't be denied—but the longer she knew him, the more she thought *handsome* or *dashing* to be foolish, childish terms for him. Too inconsequential and not nearly deep enough to grasp the scope of *him*. Agatha shook her thoughts loose. Their line erased from the sand did not mean allowing herself to have feelings for him.

But then Grimm's face broke into the smirk she'd come to learn he only offered to her, and he patted the ground beside him. Agatha discarded her own boots and sat next to him, welcoming the icy sea against her flushed skin.

Grimm

GRIMM SAT *with his feet dangling over the edge of a cliff, his heels barely brushing the calm, cool water. The sound of the drips echoing off the cave walls and the bats chittering with one another did not give him their usual comfort after what his mummy had just told him.*

It wasn't fair. He didn't care that he was a prince, or that everyone told him he was too grim. He hated being shoved in fancy jackets and told what to do. At least she hadn't said it was Gaius he couldn't see anymore. But that was the part that didn't make sense. He ran away from mummy and his guards before they could tell him anything else.

Grimm felt the silent wind and smelled the familiar scent of night jasmine. She always came when he was sad.

"Hello."

"Hello, my little one."

Grimm finally looked up from his hands and sucked in a breath. "I can see you!" She usually came shrouded in dark clouds, but he could see Her face and She was beautiful.

She smiled lovingly at him. "I thought you might need to today. Now, my darling, why is your countenance so downcast?"

Grimm turned his lips down in a glum pout. "My mother says I cannot play with my friend anymore."

"Oh, my darling..." She sounded pained. "And why is that?"

"She says we're different. That our classes should not...enter mango."

"Intermingle?" She corrected gently.

"Yes, that."

She scooted closer and took Grimm's small hand in Hers. "My sweet, can you listen very closely to me?"

"Yes, of course." He looked up into Her violet eyes before dropping them back down to his swinging feet.

"Your mother is teaching you what she has learned." She took his chin gently in Her icy fingers, turning him to face Her. "Listen carefully, little one. Just because something is learned, does not mean it is right*." She let it sink into his young mind briefly. "You"—She pressed a finger to his chest—"must decide in your heart what is right. Take care to mind your mother, but forge your* own *path."*

Grimm didn't know what She was talking about.

"You have lived many lives, Thanasim. You are here to begin again. Use what is in your heart, in your essence. Think, long and hard, about what you see around you."

She stretched out her legs and set Her feet into the cave's corner of the sea. "I am not permitted to tell you anything from your former lives, but you asked me to remind you of something." She sighed, a strange sound coming from Her. "Your friends are no different than you. And I selected you so very long ago to be one of mine because your compassion is unmatched. You are a protector, Thanasim." She leaned over and kissed the top of Grimm's head. "That is all I can say, my little one."

And then She was gone in a cloud of darkness.

"GRIMM," Agatha's voice broke into his reverie. He was never going to get used to the jolt that went through him every time she said his name.

"Yes, wife?" He felt her smile next to him and he turned his head to look at her. He'd sell his soul for that smile. He was suddenly very sure of that.

"Three inquiries?" She dealt him the sweetest of smiles. Too sweet...

Grimm laughed. "Sinister or sweet?"

Her grin turned mischievous. "Somewhere in the middle." Grimm splayed a hand, inviting her to begin. She thought only briefly before asking, "What is your greatest pride?"

His heart constricted. "My greatest pride and greatest failure are unwelcome bed fellows, I'm afraid."

"As is often the case. The moon has darkness in her midst, and she is more majestic for it, is she not?"

The muscles in his jaw flexed as he considered how only Agatha could turn darkness into something beautiful. "One of my greatest friends. My comrade... I sent him out on what I suppose you could call a duty. He succeeded, but he died for it."

Agatha watched him intently. "Yet he died with honour?"

Grimm nodded. "But he should not have had to die at all. If it weren't for me, he wouldn't have." Unwilling to let silence fall between them after that confession, he plunged into his first inquiry. "What is *your* greatest pride?"

She immediately looked down to the gentle sea at their feet. "I don't think I have one." Her voice was too quiet, and when her eyes met his, they were glossy. "But I hope that I'm rectifying that now."

He wanted nothing more than to run his thumb over the dusting of freckles across her cheeks.

"How did Nuit come to be yours?"

He smiled wide. "I relentlessly pestered my mother for a puppy, and she finally told me that the only proper pet for a royal male was a loyal battle steed. I spent much time in the stables as a child—anything to be away from the castle—and Nuit was born the next day. I immediately claimed him as mine. One can do that as a spoiled prince." He winked and she snorted. "Tell me your perfect day."

"Oh, that's easy. Reading in my cottage back home. Possibly some baking, and of course snuggling with Mabon. A bath and some mulled wine wouldn't hurt, either." She looked down at the water again and he wondered what she was thinking. "What do you think of all of this? The draught; the magus. What do you think it has to do with the prophecy?" she finally asked.

Grimm let out a long breath, resting his weight on his hands behind him. If he moved, just a fraction, their shoulders would brush. But he didn't trust himself alone with her in a cave once he touched her. "I don't know. But it all feels eerily connected, don't you think?"

Agatha nodded and adjusted her skirts. When she settled, her arm was touching his ever so slightly. Grimm reached up without thinking and brushed a stray strand of hair back from her face. Agatha shivered and he knew they needed to leave soon.

"What do *you* think of the Grand Magus?" he asked her, using up the final inquiry.

"I think he's a snake desecrating the name of Hespa."

Grimm's eyes roved over her face. He adored when that defiant look came over her. "Then we are of one accord, wife." Their eyes locked and he knew it was *definitely* time to go. "Come on." Grimm stood and helped her up. "I asked Anne to pick up some pumpkin bread for you from Dulci's. We should head back."

AGATHA

AGATHA HELD out a nibble of pumpkin bread for Mabon and he gobbled it up from her palm. She chuckled and scratched his little head.

It was almost time for her final meeting with Queen Fleurina concerning the ball that would take place the following evening, and waiting around for it had her nerves frayed, especially after an afternoon spent alone with Grimm.

Granted, some of her nerves were for the tricks up her sleeve. Agatha had a few ideas she'd been keeping to herself, and not everything she presented to the queen at their tea would be exactly how things would go on the Eve of Hallows.

Queen Fleurina was already irritated that Agatha insisted on asking the servants for their preferences as they began the decorating and chastised her relentlessly for putting her own hands to work alongside them. She'd settled on asking for forgiveness rather than permission. Although, asking forgiveness for the Blacklisted guests that arrived without the queen's knowledge… could be tricky.

Agatha drummed her fingers on the desk, considering writing to Sorscha to fill the time when the air carried a beautiful song toward her. She'd had never heard anyone playing the piano in the drawing room down the hall.

Curious, she rose and went to investigate. As she drew closer, the refrain hit her soul so deeply she had to pause and rest a hand against the wall. The song reached its elegant tendrils within her and squeezed the breath right out of her lungs.

It was haunting.

Ethereal.

And familiar.

She inched closer, chasing the notes down the hallway. The door was ajar and she peered in, sucking in a breath when she saw Grimm at the piano, his hands gliding effortlessly over the keys. Agatha watched him until the song ended, and she felt as if something had been painfully wrenched from her, leaving her cold and empty. She stepped in and wiped a tear from her cheek.

"What song was that?" she whispered.

Grimm spun on the bench to face her, seemingly unaware anyone had been watching. He swallowed. "It doesn't have a name."

"I've heard it before," she mused.

Grimm huffed a laugh and stood. "I don't see how. It is my own, and I've not played it since before you arrived here."

"You play beautifully."

"*What* are you doing here?" Eleanor snapped from the doorway, dutifully ignoring Grimm's presence.

"I was playing the piano and she found me," Grimm said, forcing Eleanor to look at him. She dipped into an awkward curtsy.

"Apologies, Your Highness, but Princess Agatha is late for a meeting with the queen."

The song's melancholy lingered in her ears, resounding the longer she held eye contact with Grimm. She smiled apologetically and followed Eleanor out.

CHAPTER
NINETEEN

T he spectrum of emotion is meant to be felt in full. It is
the corresponding actions that must be disciplined.
        -Writings of Ambrose Joubert

AGATHA

AGATHA ADJUSTED THE NAPKINS—DEEP plum linen traced with
golden swirls. It would be a matter of moments before the queen
ushered in the first guests and saw Agatha's ball in living colour.

To be fair, there wasn't much by way of bright *hues* adorning
the vast ballroom. The Eve of Hallows was not a celebration of
the living, but of the dead. A moment to slow the sands of time
and remember those that had passed. Even in Seagovia, where
magic was all but deceased itself and the magi no longer prac-
tised; where the fabled Sisters Solstice were nothing more than a
rejected myth, it was still widely accepted to celebrate the Eve of
Hallows in earnest.

On the Eve at her cottage, Agatha would have lit hundreds of pumpkins in her forest. She would have mulled cider with the fragrant spices of her Season, filled a tankard with it, and packed a basket with foodstuffs from the last of her garden's harvest. Next to her coal-black woven blanket, she would slip in black, white, and red candles. Dressed in the stygian, high-collared dress she always wore on the Eve, Agatha would have taken her basket, as well as Mabon, to the gully behind her home.

There, a place setting would be laid out for her mother, father, and Ira with care. Candles lit, she would have filled her glass to the brim with mulled cider and recorded what the stars told her within her worn leather journal. Mabon would dine on corn, and then, as the veil between the Netherrealm and the mortal realm grew its thinnest, Agatha would have attempted to summon one of her three ghostly guests.

They'd never come, and they wouldn't have come on this Eve, either. *It's foolish to try*, Wendolyn told her. *Only the restless come*, Sorscha told her. *They're already surrounding you, you only need to look*, Seleste told her. Agatha was relieved to break her tradition of heartache.

She ran her hand along one of the delicacy tables, dripping with gauzy ash and mulberry cloths, taking up a leaf the colour of mulled wine and cinnamon. She'd gone out with the servants that afternoon to collect baskets full of fallen leaves and sprinkled them out across the tables herself. The sconces and chandeliers were left only halfway lit, illuminating the ballroom in a twilight glow.

Upon each dark wood table rested a hollowed pumpkin, overflowing with queen of night tulips, black baccara roses, blood ranunculus, and weeping purple fountain grass. Agatha absently took one of the kitten-soft fluffs between her fingers, examining the place settings. She'd not told the queen what she planned to do with them, but it was a risk she was willing to take. Each place had a name scrawled in gold ink upon a black, scalloped card. Next to each seat lay an amber plate, an empty name card, and a crow feather quill waiting to be dipped in the pot of golden ink. With it, each guest would be instructed to select the ghost of their heart to immortalise on the name card. There were unlit candles placed in front of each place to light in their memory. It was either too far, or precisely enough. Agatha didn't care which it was, it felt *right* to her.

The doors opened and four musicians entered the ballroom to take their places in the corner. Their strings, woodwinds, and percussion filled the vast space with a melancholy song befitting a Queen of the Dead. Agatha thought it would irk the Queen of the Living, but in her own eyes it was perfect. Queen Fleurina bustled through the door then, the train of her blood-red gown gliding behind her. She stopped in front of Agatha, glancing briefly at the morose musicians.

"Agatha, this ballroom is exquisite. Truly you've stolen my breath." She looked back at the musicians, her eye twitching. "This music is fit for a funeral procession, though. They must pick up the tempo." Agatha nodded reluctantly. "Grimm will be in any moment. The two of you are to lead our esteemed guests to their places on the dais after the others arrive." She kissed Agatha on both cheeks—something she had never done before—and rushed out the back door of the ballroom toward what Agatha assumed were suites.

Agatha instructed the musicians to liven things up, *slightly*. They did so—slightly—and Grimm walked in, soaking up the ballroom. Agatha took the opportunity to unabashedly take him in. His coat was the colour of moonlit fog. Underneath, he wore an obsidian shirt with a slightly ruffled collar and topped with a waistcoat the exact hue of Mabon, pewter buttons running down to his belt, where she forced her eyes to move back up.

His dark hair was swept back neatly in place, and Agatha wanted to muss it up. It was devastatingly handsome, but unlike him. When he caught sight of Agatha and smirked, he finally looked like himself. He strolled toward her, hands in his pockets, and Agatha's breath caught raggedly in her throat.

"You've outdone yourself." He looked up at the sweeping perennial vines that hung languidly from the rafters. "I've never seen my mother throw a ball without nauseating colour."

"It was a struggle." Agatha looked around at her handiwork. When she turned back, Grimm's eyes were sweeping over her. It was becoming exponentially more difficult to dislike him. The prince took her hand and led her toward where his mother had flitted off to. "We're to wait in a suite with Empress Amira and King Rashidi until the others arrive, then announce them as our honoured guests." Agatha gave an involuntary groan and Grimm chuckled. "Play nice, wife."

After their discussion days earlier regarding the elixir, as well as the empress and king's desire to see their own citizens take the controlling drug, the last thing Agatha wanted to play was *nice*.

But Grimm was correct. They very well could be the only ones fighting against the dastardly rulers, and they needed to ensure they didn't act rashly. Despite her three hundred years, Agatha was learning Grimm was the level-headed, patient one, while she had to rein in her fervour and wild schemes.

It was likely the rulers had no inkling that the draught wasn't what the magus claimed it was—an elixir to ward off disease—anyway. There was no sense in treating them with hatred.

Though they'd had formal dinners with the rulers, there had been very little by way of conversation. Agatha's first impression of the empress had been one of awe. Her vividly emerald eyes were stark against her umber skin, the planes of her face sharp and beautiful. She'd worn her voluminous ringlets down with a sheer, marigold fabric delicately poised on her head and secured with a jade clip. Every movement she made had been exotic and mesmerising.

Agatha had always felt rather plain, but next to Empress Amira, she might as well have been a stone grave marker. She nearly snorted at the irony. The most fascinating thing about the empress, though, was the intricate ink that crawled from her fingertips all the way up her arm and one side of her face. It bent and twirled, covering every inch of skin like climbing ivy in incredible, tawny filigree.

Grimm opened the door to a suite, and, regardless of her repeated notions that it would do nothing but harm to lash out, it was only Agatha's three hundred years of schooling her emotions that kept her from snarling at the traitors that stood before her. She tried, *again*, to remind herself to give them the benefit of the doubt. Perhaps they *weren't* out to destroy their own people.

Grimm

GRIMM BENT IN A LOW BOW, pulling Agatha down with him. The Coronoccan Empress and Lyronian King dipped into bows of their own, and Grimm snuck a glance at Agatha, nearly snickering at the look of contempt upon her face that she probably thought she was concealing.

"Your Graces," he drawled as they all righted themselves. "Empress Amira." He squeezed Agatha's hand and dropped it, gliding forward to the empress. "You are an absolute vision." He took up her soft fingers and kissed them gently, as was the custom of her country. He stepped away, glancing at Agatha again.

Empress Amira smiled—amused and feline. "You say that, and yet it is still Her Highness Princess Agatha that you cannot tear your eyes away from."

Grimm stiffened, unsure if it was a slight to him—or perhaps Agatha. "Ah yes, my wife *is* irresponsibly distracting." He let his eyes rake over Agatha, partly for the show and partly because he relished an excuse to do so. Her responding blush sent a shiver up his spine.

"I find it interesting," the empress went on, "that a man of your potential and station would select to marry for love."

Grimm ticked through his thoughts quickly, assessing the empress. They'd never shared a conversation without his parents or the Grand Magus present. She seemed inclined to make her views known, and he wanted to make the most of it. She hadn't sounded precisely condescending, as her words would suggest, but she was difficult to read.

"I aim to surprise, Empress Amira. I find love to be a formidable force, don't you?" King Rashidi scoffed under his breath, and Grimm shoved a clenched fist into his pocket, turning his attention to the overfed man. "King Rashidi, I do hope this ball will be to your liking."

The man crossed his arms and said nothing. He'd heard that the king refused to speak in the common tongue of Seagovia. There was nothing polite he wished to say to the man, anyway.

"Princess Agatha," the empress broke in, "Queen Fleurina tells me you have outdone yourself assisting her in the preparation for this ball. Considering your"—she ran her eyes up and down Agatha's form—"*upbringing*, how did you fare so well in the planning? Surely there are not many balls where you are from."

Grimm ground his teeth, watching the empress. She sounded like him when he attempted to insult Agatha and fell short.

Agatha smiled sweetly, but he could sense the poison beneath it. "It does not take a royal eye to know beauty, Your Grace. I find those less *fortunate* are more apt to find it all around than those choking on a silver spoon from birth."

Goddess, she drove him blissfully mad with that sharp tongue.

"I suppose you could be right about that," Empress Amira murmured.

A guard poked his head in and instructed them that it was time to enter the ballroom. King Rashidi pushed to the front, following the guard, but Empress Amira hovered near the door.

"Prince Thackery," she spoke, keeping her voice low, "it has come to my knowledge that you are quite the connoisseur of baked goods." Grimm's attention snapped into focus. It was the beginning of a code—the one Alestair had set in place moons ago.

"I am, Your Grace." His throat was suddenly very dry.

She nodded simply and Grimm felt Agatha's curious eyes on him. "Would you, perhaps, know where I might find the most delectable croissant in your fair kingdom?"

And there was the rest of it. "But of course, Empress Amira." Grimm bowed low. "I will have the location sent to you this very night."

Grimm introduced the empress and king as the esteemed guests of his darling bride and himself. The ballroom erupted in applause, distracting from the doors that opened, ushering in not one or two, but *six* Blacklisted merchants from Mer Row.

The prince fixed his attention on Agatha, who had a coy smile playing at her lips as she watched them slip in, dressed to the hilt. Dulci looked across the ballroom and winked at Agatha.

The Grand Magus snarled next to him. "Who let them in here?" He took a step toward the merchants, but the queen rested a hand on his arm, pointing to where Tindle held out six pieces of parchment to a nearby guard.

"It appears they have been cordially invited."

The magus stormed off, muttering, and Grimm watched his mother carefully. Her face was unreadable, but he would have bet his life she was watching Agatha with pleasant surprise.

As soon as all eyes left them, Agatha hauled him to a table positively overflowing with food. He watched her load a plate full, marvelling at how lovely she looked in her swarthy, flowing gown scattered with dark gems—like a goddess of the night. He suspected some of her intense allure at present came from being in her element. Not a party. No, not that to be sure, but within a place of her own design, surrounded by things so inexplicably *her*. He wondered very much what her own home looked like. With a shake of his dark hair, Grimm pushed away the constant guilt he bore for taking her from it.

All Grimm had wanted since their afternoon in the woods was to pull her away from everything and take her back to where there were no eyes on them. No one to hide from, and no one else to be. In truth, he hadn't seen her much since that day—what with his duties and planning a draught heist—and here she was, shoving a pumpkin tart in her face like no one was watching. He couldn't take his eyes off her.

AGATHA

AGATHA'S TART protruded from her cheek, and Grimm was staring at her.

"Do peasants know how to dance?" he asked with a crooked grin.

Agatha swallowed and tilted her head to one side, her tongue dragging across her lips to collect stray crumbs. Grimm's eyes followed the movement. "Would you like to find out?"

"Very, *very* much." He pulled her toward the over-fluffed and stuffed bodies dancing in the centre of the ballroom.

Grimm took her by the waist with one hand and spun her away, holding her fast with the other hand. Pulling her back in, he settled his palm on the small of her back, and Agatha was certain she could feel the roughness of his fingertips through her bodice.

She looked up into his sparkling bronze eyes. "You're in an exceptionally good mood tonight, prince."

His eyes crinkled at the corners, but he said nothing. He only bore into her with that intense gaze she was prone to becoming lost in as of late.

"It's almost terrifying," she prodded.

Grimm broke into a full smile and laughed. At the sound, a heady warmth slid down her chest and settled low in her belly.

"I've received some good news of sorts," he explained.

Agatha raised an eyebrow. "Good news? I'm glad for it." And she was. "It seems you tend to only receive bad news."

"Ah, yes." He pulled her closer and her breath hitched. "It would seem that *some* of that bad news has turned out not to be as dreadful as I once thought." He inched her ever closer so that she had to look up at him where he peered down at her with an intensity that made her toes curl.

"Is that so?" The bodice of her dress was feeling abominably tight. The low cut of it wasn't doing either of them any favours to cool the building heat at that moment, either.

Seleste insisted a dance was the only way to know if one was truly compatible with another. For the first time, Agatha wondered if she was right.

Gods, she wanted the handbreadth between them erased. As if reading her thoughts, the tips of Grimm's fingers dug into the lowest part of her back, just where the bodice of her gown began to drift off into delicately soft fabric at the curve of her bottom.

He hadn't broken eye contact with her in several moments, and when his gaze flicked to her mouth, she thought she'd burst. He locked eyes with her once more, desire palpable and unhinged. Grimm bent his head down toward her and she tilted her chin up. His hand left hers and he ran the back of a finger along her cheek, sending shivers down her spine before slipping his hand behind her neck, pulling her toward him with the one around her waist until their hips collided.

His lips were a whisper away when the ground shook. A deafening boom sounded behind Agatha and Grimm clutched her to his chest. She could feel his heart thundering against her, his muscles taut and his grip on her bruising, but the only sound she heard was a ringing in her ears.

Agatha twisted in his arms to see debris shooting in every direction, a gargantuan hole in the far wall opening up to reveal the charred suite they'd stood in not half an hour before. Without warning—or perhaps she just couldn't hear him—Grimm spun her away so quickly she turned several times before coming to a dizzying stop.

"*Maintenir.*"

Agatha's protection spell wrapped her in its embrace and time slowed to a crawl. In awe, she took stock of the broken wall, the twisted, bloody bodies of the guests, some crumpled on the floor and others dragging slowly through the air as if weightless. Broken glass and debris littered the ballroom as it hung suspended in the air, glinting in the light and reflecting refracted bits of the horror.

The chaos slowed like sap dripping down a maple tree and Agatha launched herself into it. She knelt before a court lady whose face was twisted in agony, the bodice of her dress slowly soaking through with blood. Putting a hand to the woman's chest, she whispered and commanded her wound to mend. As she rushed to a broken lord, his leg twisted and bone protruding, a haunting refrain permeated the still air. Time had all but halted —there should be no sound. She looked around feverishly, and that was when she saw him.

Agatha stood and watched as Grimm moved about the gory

mess, the song she'd heard him play—the song she *knew* —pulsating from the prince. In that setting, magnified by something ethereal, the refrain was so beautiful it physically *hurt*. Her chest ached to the point of rendering her motionless. She gaped as Grimm plucked a servant from the stand-still time and pulled her close to his chest. He whispered into her ear and, with grief alight on his face, he laid her gently on the ground. His attention shot to a flickering light in the air next to the woman, and he spoke to it before moving on to Lady Olivia. He took her up in his arms to dance, and spun her—just as he'd done with Agatha —far from the blast that crawled toward them in the frozen air. He moved from her to Tindle and she thought his knees might buckle with the relief that washed over him when he took the dressmaker's hand, spinning him away. Agatha trembled as she watched him move with determination to Dulci. He pulled her in and danced with her beautifully, his throat bobbing as he spun her away.

Agatha's hands shook as Grimm danced to the devastatingly beautiful song with every person in the ballroom. Servant or aristocrat. Blacklisted or courtier.

A shard of glass she hadn't noticed coming sliced across her cheek slowly as Grimm spun a servant away from a piece of wood that would have impaled him. But many—too many—he laid down tenderly on the marble floor, coated in red. Laying them down for a ceaseless slumber. Tears burned behind her eyes.

His mother he held preciously close, then spun her elegantly away. Agatha did not see the king or Grand Magus, she realised absently. Grimm's pace slowed when he reached Eleanor where she stood with Gaius. He reached up and touched her cheek gingerly, then held her fiercely—without dancing—and Agatha stopped breathing. The ones he'd laid down did not stir any longer—they were too still, even in the drawn-out moment. A sob choked from Agatha's lips as Grimm spun Eleanor away and moved to Gaius. Relief lit his features, and she watched his chest heave. Grimm hugged his closest friend and pushed him away with incredible force.

He began to search frantically around the room, his panic tangible. Was he looking for her? He found Agatha, and their eyes locked. The haunting music came to a jarring halt. She watched as his lips parted and he swiped at his forehead with bloody hands, smearing it across his face.

Agatha's breath came out in quick bursts through her nose as she walked toward him, tears blurring her vision. A hook sank deep within her heart. A string pulling taut. And she desperately needed to follow the tether.

Grimm searched her face, standing eerily still in place. Agatha waded through time, her steps sluggish. His eyes were fearful and relieved all at once. When she reached him, Agatha lifted a quivering hand to touch his cheek. Who was this man that could slow time and deal death? Her heart thundered, warning her she already knew. Somewhere, somehow, she already knew.

"Wh—who are you?"

Grimm's breath hitched.

He took her by the arm, cursing, and hauled her through the ballroom. As soon as they exited the doors, they each whispered something and then shot one another a look of suspicion. Time corrected itself and Grimm pulled Agatha into a room, shutting the door against the screams sounding from the ballroom. "What did you see?"

"*What are you?*"

His face darkened, a storm brewing behind his eyes. "We don't have time for this, Agatha," he ground out as he stepped forward, breathing hard. "*Tell me what you saw.*"

"I saw you dance," she shot back. "I saw you dance with everyone in the room." She looked around, eyes unfocused as she struggled to find words to explain it. "Some of them you spun away and others you laid down on the floor. Time slowed and there was this haunting song...the one I heard you play on the piano." She gasped, suddenly realising why she knew it. She'd heard it as she left King Caliban's rooms a century prior, his blood on her boots. Her petrified eyes lifted to Grimm's. *"What are you?"*

"You saw *me?*"

"Yes," she bit out.

"As I've always appeared to you?"

"I think I know what you look like, Grimm. What in the seven realms *are you?*"

He let out a long breath. "I am a Marchand de Mort."

Agatha staggered back. "You're a *reaper?*"

Grimm's lips pressed together firmly. "Death Dealer is the proper term."

"But you're—"

"Crown Prince? Yes. It complicates things."

Agatha had no words. Her mind spun at dizzying speeds. "I need to sit down."

She did, and Grimm knelt before her, wiping away a drip of blood oozing from the thin cut on her cheek. "Agatha, how did you see me?"

"I don't know." She tried desperately to shake her shock loose. She couldn't *think* in shock.

"Like *Hades.*" He glanced toward the door, his tone urgent. *"Why* did you see me, then?"

Agatha grasped the crystals within the cage at her neck. "I —" *Goddess*, she couldn't tell him, could she? She looked up from her lap and into his eyes.

"Agatha, no one has a deeper secret than I do, and you now hold it fully within your hands. I would like to know *why.*"

"I put a protection spell in place around me."

Grimm stiffened, but only briefly. "You put a spell in place. As in...*magic?*"

Agatha hardly managed to get her chin to dip once in a nod.

Grimm stood and raked his hands through his hair, smearing blood in it. He looked at his gory palms and wiped them on his pants. For a long moment he studied her, seeking silent answers in her face. "My wife is a witch," he finally breathed out.

She almost thought she saw the barest hint of amusement. Surely not. "I—" *Mistake. Mistake.* Her mind screamed. *Stop.* "I'm a Sister Solstice, actually."

Grimm gaped openly and shook his head as if he could dislodge the notion from his brain. "But the Sisters are just folklore."

"So are reapers."

He blinked. "Touché."

Shrieks grew closer, and someone screamed Grimm's name.

"My mother. They're looking for us." He searched the room. "The blame could be laid at our feet if we're not in there."

Grimm took Agatha by the waist and whispered into her ear. "Hold on tight, witch." And then they were moving so fast she lost her breath, too far gone to even scream. Moving with her magic felt like nothing of the sort. In a blink, they were on the floor in the wreckage behind a toppled table.

Agatha jumped up, anxious to aid the injured even without her magic. Grimm grabbed her wrist and she turned back. "We have much to discuss. I'll meet you in our rooms when this is over." Agatha's pulse quickened further—if that were possible—but she nodded. He let go, and she rushed to the nearest fallen person as she saw Grimm do the same.

Once the palace began to calm and soldiers aplenty lined the halls, Agatha went in search of Anne and Eleanor. She'd seen Grimm twirl Eleanor away and her assumption was—based on body count and what she'd seen—that Eleanor had survived. But she hadn't seen Anne since before the ball.

Agatha searched the halls with feverish desperation, halted at every turn by guards instructing her to lock herself in her rooms.

She peeled off into a linen closet and magicked herself to an alcove she recalled from her trip to the servants' quarters. To her relief and equal dismay, there were not but two guards in that portion of the castle.

"*Idiots*," she murmured. The culprit could easily hide out down there.

She rushed to Anne's rooms and flung the door open, startling Eleanor half to death.

"Where is Anne?" Agatha demanded.

Eleanor pushed up on her elbow from the bed, scowling. "No concern for me, I see."

"You're *fine*. Where is Anne?"

"I last saw her sewing up a lord in the kitchens."

Agatha's knees buckled with relief and she sat on the edge of Eleanor's bed. "Shove over."

Despite herself, she started to tremble, the evening settling into her bones. Agatha leaned back, lying down to rest her head on the pillow beside Eleanor. Her maidservant sighed and wrapped a reluctant arm around her. Agatha leaned into her empathetic—albeit rigid—embrace.

"You're tougher stock than this, princess," she said, not unkindly against Agatha's hair. "Weep now and dry your eyes before you leave this room." It was nearly identical to what Winnie had said to her on her wedding day, and Agatha buried her face in Eleanor's shoulder.

Tears shed, she dared ask Eleanor the question that had been burning within her since Grimm ran a finger down the maid's cheek before spinning her away. "Why do you dislike Grimm so much?"

Eleanor went very still for a moment. "I do not dislike him." She fidgeted and Agatha rose to sit, watching her. "He was once my closest friend when we were children. Before he was forbidden to see me any longer."

Eleanor had been wounded by the elite, just like the rest of them. When her maid offered no further information, Agatha stood.

"You'd better see what else you can help with, princess." Eleanor's tone held no mocking tone and she looked Agatha directly in the eye. "No more tears."

Agatha squared her shoulders. No more tears; only strength.

For Miriam.

For Anne.

For Eleanor.

IT WAS A LONG TIME LATER, dripping into the early hours of the morning, before Agatha made it to her chambers to wash the gore off herself. She paced the rooms in her nightgown for longer still before she could no longer stand and went to lie in bed.

The sun was peeking above the horizon when Grimm finally entered their rooms. He hardly made a sound, probably assuming she was asleep. He discarded his ruined waistcoat and bloody shirt before washing his hands in the basin. Agatha watched him sit on the chaise, his outline foggy in the dim light of morning, but there was no mistaking the despair in his bent posture. He hunched further, resting his face in his hands, and her heart ached.

"Good morning, reaper," she said softly.

His back went a fraction straighter and he huffed a laugh, turning to look at her with the barest of humour in his tired eyes. "Good morning, witch."

He rose and came around to her side of the bed, lowering himself onto the edge next to her. Agatha sat up, leaning against the plush pillows. She took in the set of his jaw and his weary posture. The night they'd faced, and the realisation he'd had to face about the wife he hadn't chosen, was enough to crumple anyone.

"I'm sorry, Grimm."

"For the attack that exploded the ballroom or for being a Sister Solstice?" He lifted her cold hand and kissed it, his lips soft and gentle on her skin. "Neither of those things are your fault."

His affectionate gesture should have sent her reeling, but it did not.

Trauma bonding, Winnie would call it. *A chance worth taking*, Sorscha would call it. *Let yourself find happiness*, Seleste would say. Agatha felt that string between them pull tighter.

"Who do you think attacked?" she asked to school her thoughts.

Grimm sighed heavily. "I immediately sent Captain Dubois, Gaius, and Augustus out with three separate groups to search the castle and the kingdom. When I left them just moments ago, there were still no answers. My father was irate. I haven't seen him show true emotion in...I don't even know how long. It was a small mercy in this mess, to see him as himself, even if only for a moment."

"He wasn't in the ballroom when it happened. Neither was the Grand Magus."

Grimm nodded. "King Rashidi was with them in a suite adjacent to the explosion. Empress Amira was found in her rooms already out of her finery. She was waiting for a letter from me, thank the goddess. Her portion of the dais was the closest to the explosion. Perhaps Amira was the intended target. She would have been sitting there if I had not spoken with her of Dulci's prior to the ball."

"I thought that was an odd conversation to have about croissants."

Grimm looked down at their joined hands. "My brother in

arms, Alestair, he was our boots on the ground. The one I told you about in the sea cave. He set up a code to spread amongst sympathisers before he died. Alestair thought I would find the code about croissants amusing." The barest of smiles touched his lips before fading into weariness. "The empress had been trying to speak with me privately for some time, but the magus was always present until last night."

Agatha twirled the ring around her finger. "I set her place there on the dais."

Grimm stilled before sliding his eyes up to hers. "Do you think someone wants you blamed for this?"

She really didn't know. It was certainly possible. "Perhaps." A thought struck her. "You sent out three separate parties to search out the castle?" Grimm nodded. "There were only two guards below the castle in the servants' quarters."

The prince baulked. "I specifically sent Captain Dubois to deploy a whole host of men down there myself. When was this?"

"I went to ensure Eleanor and Anne were alright not long after the attack, and I didn't come back up until just before dawn."

Grimm shot up from the bed and took up pacing. "Who were the two guards, do you know?"

"No, I'd not seen them before."

Grimm snatched a clean shirt, never mind that he was still caked in dried blood. "I have to see to this immediately." He moved toward the door but turned back and stalked toward the bed, bending down to look into her eyes, golden flecks like embers burning in the brown of his irises. "We've still much to discuss, witch. But perhaps this will do for now."

Grimm's lips found hers, one hand coming up to the nape of her neck. The taste of him was beyond the sweetest delicacy imaginable. His hands tangled in her hair and Agatha struggled to breathe. His own breath was ragged and he deepened the kiss, tongue slipping into her mouth. Just as she was sure the heat coursing through her would cause her to combust, he pulled back.

His chest heaved up and down as much as Agatha's own, and she could see the longing burning in his eyes. He ran a thumb over her bottom lip and she shivered. "I'll be back as soon as I can."

TWENTY

L *et the cry of all creation be resounding peace.*
        -Writings of Ambrose Joubert

Grimm

"Gaius! Thank the Goddess."

Gaius' face contorted in confusion as he walked into the prince and princess' chambers, shutting the door behind him.

Grimm flung a hand toward Agatha. "Please talk some sense into my *wife*."

"You spew that title like it's a curse," she spat, crossing her arms.

Grimm's head snapped toward her and he snarled. "Perhaps I mean it as one."

They'd been at odds since the day following their kiss. Agatha had immediately begun plotting ridiculous matters without thinking them through first. At least she was letting him in on them now, but that didn't matter if she wouldn't blasted *listen* to a word he said about it. Agatha bared her teeth at him before they both looked at Gaius.

The lord's brows rose high in his forehead and he held up his hands. "I don't want to get involved in a marital dispute—" The look Agatha gave him could have curdled milk and Grimm *almost* felt bad for him. "Though, perhaps I could lend an ear," Gaius amended wisely.

Grimm did not give Agatha the chance to speak first. "She wants to wear a pin—"

"A *brooch*."

He clenched his jaw and shot her a glare before turning back to Gaius. "She wants to wear a *brooch* that is just plain treasonous, and the magus will have her head."

"He's being dramatic." Agatha rolled her eyes as Gaius looked between the two of them.

"It does sound a tad dramatic, Grimm."

"*Un*believable." The prince threw his hands up in the air. "Well, show him the damn thing, Agatha." They hadn't yet revealed to Gaius that she was a witch, but he feared they would soon be obligated to.

She haughtily retrieved a small velvet box from the table and held it in front of Gaius, opening the lid for him to peer in, its hinges creaking.

Gaius barked a laugh and tucked his lips into his teeth, shaking his head. "You can't wear that." He closed the lid, the loud snap cracking against the walls, and they both watched as Agatha radiated anger.

"It's a brooch, for Goddess' sake, not an act of treason."

"Treason is a bit of a reach"—Gaius' attention flicked to Grimm, then back to Agatha—"but this is…" he trailed off with a grimace.

"A statement," Agatha finished for him.

"Agatha." Gaius stifled a laugh. "You replicated the Grand

Magus' seal exactly, but replaced his nightingale with a *bat*. Surely you can see how this could go poorly, especially in light of recent events."

"*In light of recent events*," she mocked, "it's exactly what needs to be done. The people need something to rally around. They're worried."

"Well, it's not this."

Grimm crossed his arms when she turned to him, and he gave her a smug smile because he'd won Gaius to his side of the argument.

"Goddess' *teeth*!" Agatha snapped. "This is why the two of you hadn't accomplished a damn thing until I arrived. You're too fucking scared to do anything that takes an iota of courage!"

Gaius stepped backward at her outburst, face amused. "Merde, Agatha. Do all peasants have such a mouth on them?"

Grimm watched with no small measure of pride as Agatha stood straighter. "Only the good ones."

Goddess, she was a captivating creature. Grimm blinked. For the life of him, he could no longer recall why he was so angry with her. He might have been detained in countless meetings in the days since the attack, but their kiss had not left his mind for a second. Nor had they been given the opportunity to repeat it, what with her arguing with him every spare moment.

"That's another reason you lousy lot need me," her tirade went on. "You might sympathise with the common folk, but you're locked up here in this castle and have spent your whole lives with a silver spoon in your mouth and a stick up your arse."

Grimm observed her as she continued shouting at Gaius, their words drowned out by the roar of his blood beginning to heat. It was intriguing to watch her direct her anger at someone else. His gaze strayed to the moss-coloured gown perfectly high-lighting her curves and golden eyes. Agatha had the kind of curves that sent boys running for the hills but made men ache. He wondered what it would unleash within him to release those tantalising curves from the cage of a corset. He wondered what her hips would feel like against his hands as he pulled her on top of him.

Grimm determined right then and there that he would make it his mission to find out what brought her the most pleasure, and he would do it repeatedly. If they could just use all their mutual fury to worship one another's bodies instead of—

"*Grimm*," Gaius' voice broke into his filthy thoughts. The lord gave him a look that told him he knew precisely what he'd been contemplating, and to school his thoughts.

Agatha's countenance remained heated. When she turned that impassioned attention on Grimm, he cleared his throat and folded his hands in front of him, lest the full extent of his thoughts became apparent. She tilted her head to the side with a simpering smile and the memory of his thumb against her lip assaulted him. He needed to do something with his hands, quickly. It was a very fortunate thing that Gaius was present.

Grimm took up a pitcher of water and poured, setting the glass down without taking a sip. "Wear the brooch. It's your head. We're late for our meeting."

"I'm coming with you," she demanded.

He needed to be *far* from her before he ripped her dress off. "No."

"Stop pretending you don't need me."

They squared off and Gaius stepped between them. "She might be helpful, Grimm."

Agatha preened.

"Traitor."

"Let's go, then." Agatha walked into the hallway, leaving Grimm and Gaius in the dust.

"You don't even know where you're going," he called after her.

She turned and scoffed over her shoulder. "Your council chambers."

She wasn't wrong. She did have enough sense to let him and Gaius enter before her, at least. Though, it might have been amusing to watch the captain's reaction to his princess being presented as Grimm's equal—as she should be. He tucked that notion away for later.

Captain Dubois was already present. "Your Highnesses; My Lord." He bowed to each of them.

Grimm clasped his hands behind his back and waited. His patience with this captain had worn very thin. He'd sent the man to dispatch a group of guards below the castle the night of the attack, and Agatha had said there were only two down there that night.

Upon questioning, Captain Dubois stated he'd specifically sent ten men down. The likelihood of Agatha missing that many guards was slim. The likelihood of guards going down and missing Eleanor and Anne's room entirely during their search was even less likely. Captain Dubois gave him the names of those ten guards and Grimm had questioned them himself. Each one stated they'd gone, but the glaze over their eyes as they'd said it told him a different story.

"There is no news, Your Highness."

It was unacceptable. "None, Captain? And who, precisely, is searching the city? The castle?" He reached into his pocket and roughly pulled out the list of names Dubois had given him, the paper crinkling in his fingers.

The captain's jaw tightened. "My men can be trusted, Your Highness."

"You'll forgive me if my trust in this *particular* set of guards is frail at the moment."

"You questioned each of them yourself." Dubois shifted his weight on his feet, eyeing Agatha with disdain. "If they say they were there, I believe my men more than some—"

Grimm held up a hand. "Let me stop you right there before

you find yourself saying something that I might not be inclined to forgive."

Dubois quieted but took no pains to hide his irritation. Grimm let the air hang heavy with tension for a moment longer before turning to Gaius. "Lord Gaius, see to it that all the men deployed within the kingdom and the castle are brought together and re-dispersed into new factions of your choosing." Gaius nodded. "General Dubois, you are dismissed."

He bowed once and left without a word.

When the door shut, Gaius spoke angrily, "It's not Dubois' fault, Grimm."

"Of course not. But I can't very well let him know that, can I? And von Fuchs knows precisely who Dubois would group together."

"We don't even know if von Fuchs is the reason the castle was attacked—"

Augustus slipped through the door then, out of breath. "Your Highnesses, Lord Gaius. Apologies for the interruption, this couldn't wait."

"What is it?"

"I've overheard something in the hall." His cheeks flushed. "You see, erm, Her Highness was with you"—he gestured to Agatha—"so Anne...I was off duty this morning...so there was some free time and—"

"Augustus. I don't care what closet you and Anne found yourselves within. Please get to the point."

He scuffed his boot across the floor. "Right. We overheard two people discussing a shipment of some kind. They didn't mention what it was, but it was to be split nearly in half. One part would ship by sea and the other by land."

To Coronocco and Lyronia.

"Do you know who you heard?"

"The Grand Magus for certain. The other man had a thick Lyronian accent, but it was not King Rashidi."

265

"You're certain?" Grimm hadn't heard Rashidi use more than two words in the common tongue.

"Very certain, sir. I heard the king berating a guard of his, and this man had a very different cadence to his voice."

"When is the shipment leaving?"

"Two days' time."

"Did you hear anything else?"

"I— No, sir. I didn't want Anne to worry, so I erm— distracted her and missed the rest of the conversation."

Grimm smirked. "Good man. Find out all you can. Gaius, see to the guards." He looked at Agatha and held out his arm. "I'm overdue for luncheon with my wife."

AGATHA

"WE HAVE TO STOP THOSE SHIPMENTS," Agatha whispered as they walked down the corridors.

"I know that. But we can't do it right now, and we have several things to discuss." Grimm stopped and buttoned the onyx encrusted closure of her cloak at the hollow of her throat.

She looked up at him as he did so. "I suppose we do have much to clear up."

The prince let one of his knuckles brush against the smooth skin of her collarbone before removing his hands from her cloak. "Yes. Although I thought for certain I cleared *some* things up." He looked pointedly at her lips, then into her eyes, a lazy grin playing at the corners of his mouth.

Agatha swallowed. "Yes, well, the clearing of only *some* things just leads to more questions."

Grimm chuckled and placed her hand upon his arm. "Then let's go clear them up."

He nodded politely to the fawning courtiers and busy servants they passed. The corridors had been a flurry of chaos since the attack. Everywhere they turned there were guards posted, workmen rebuilding, court ladies and gentlemen whispering, and gossips drinking their fill. Agatha wondered briefly if they should be listening in on the chatter to find the culprit, instead of sending out more guards.

"Where are we going?" she asked.

"Mer Noir," was Grimm's only response.

When they reached the marina, Agatha broke the heavy silence. "Anne can be trusted, you know. And she doesn't need Augustus to protect her from the truth."

Grimm took her hand and helped her into the boat. "Of course she doesn't, but Augustus loves her. He wouldn't be worth her heart if he didn't make moves to protect her." Grimm held onto Agatha's hand, his face stern and brows pulled tight. "A woman may not have *need* of a man, but if he does not take care of her anyway, he is no man at all." He let go and climbed in across from her. "As for trust... Yes, Anne can be trusted. I would never place you in the care of someone I don't trust myself, but that does not mean she needs to know everything yet. Augustus doesn't even know everything."

"Who knows about *you*?" Agatha questioned.

Grimm's eyes narrowed, but one side of his mouth turned up. "Can't even wait until we row from the dock, can you? Only Gaius, Mila, and you, little witch."

"Mila knows?" Her voice betrayed her irritation, and one of Grimm's brows shot up as he pushed them away from the dock and took up rowing.

"Mila belongs to Lady Death."

Agatha scowled. "She's a reaper as well?"

"*Marchand de Mort*, and no. Mila is my handmaiden. Death

Dealers such as I are reserved for gruesome deaths of passion. We alone possess the ability to bend time, so we can make it there in time to collect. Mila collects the souls of those that depart slowly. Old age, sickness—that sort of thing."

Agatha considered his words. It did little to ease her distaste for the woman.

"Agatha," he spoke, his voice tender as he inferred her emotion. "Mila is a wraith. A ghost."

All the damned fairytales were proving eerily true. She'd always thought if the Sisters were real, all the goblins, faeries, Druids, and other such fantastical creatures could be as well, but she'd never met one. Until Grimm and Mila. Agatha wondered idly who else she'd encountered with otherworldly secrets she knew nothing about.

Grimm rowed, watching her face. "Wraiths are women that died horrific deaths at the hands of men. Lady Death selects them Herself and employs them as handmaidens. It gives them some closure and peace. Restless souls often roam the realm, unwilling to come with me, or even Lady Death. Once She gives them a purpose, a way to ease the suffering of others, they often take it."

"The Goddess of Death sounds kind."

"She is. Mortals come up with a plethora of things to fill their ignorance. Lady Death is incomprehensibly misunderstood. Death is not to be feared. It is not evil or torturous. It is life that deals those things. Lady Death offers a reprieve."

"She is the sister of our ancestor. Mine and my Sisters'."

His eyes narrowed. "You're truly descended from Lord Night and Lady Magic, then?"

Agatha nodded. "Lord and Lady Magie de la Nuit."

Grimm blew out a breath. "I thought it was all a myth, the Sisters Solstice."

"We've been written over as legend and penned as simple followers of the lesser gods in search of a way to Hespa."

Grimm dipped his chin. "I've studied the subject, though I must admit not thoroughly. I'm not a man of much fiction."

"I would think you'd consider all the hearth tales as possible truths, considering," she teased, gesturing to him.

He made a noncommittal sound. "What are you, truly, you Sisters Solstice?"

Agatha wound a strand of hair around her finger and Grimm set the oars in the boat. It rocked on the gentle waves as she contemplated her answer. "We are the authors of History. Anything of note in History has a Sister Solstice tangled within its midst. Hespa spoke to the first four daughters born of Lord and Lady Magie de la Nuit extensively. They penned Her words —those that came directly, and those that came in dreams and visions—into a Grimoire. The words come forth at the appointed time and are visible only to one Sister in her Season. The one to whom they are entrusted to see through to fruition." Sorrow filled her suddenly and she fiddled with her thumbs.

"The prophecy. The original Sisters wrote it in your Grimoire? They are the ancestors you spoke of in the light-house?" She nodded, still staring at her hands. "Agatha." He inched forward, the boat creaking, and lifted her chin so her eyes would meet his. "Why do you look so sad?"

"History has been full of horrors, Grimm." Tears filled her eyes and when one spilled, he brushed it away with his thumb. "For the last three hundred years, I'm the one that has set them in motion. Not my Sisters. *Me.*"

Grimm studied her, but she didn't fidget under his gaze. If anyone could understand the painful existence of being the hands of gods and men, it was a reaper.

"Three hundred years? You truly are an old crone, then?"

Agatha sputtered a laugh, despite herself. "Curse you for swiping that admission away with a jest."

Grimm grinned. "It worked, didn't it?" He picked up the oars and began rowing them further out. "I'm no saint, Agatha, and

I've seen unimaginable things myself. Done things I'm not proud of. I can't fault you. And that sorrow I see in your eyes is enough to confirm the person I *know* you to be. The world is cloaked in grey, not black and white."

His words reminded her of something in one of her father's journals and she swallowed the lump in her throat. "How old are *you* then?" she asked, desperate to change the subject. The time-line in the records showed one thing, but she wanted to be certain.

His eyebrow lifted. "This time?"

"*This time?*"

Grimm chuckled. "We have many lives, Marchands. I've been in this body for twenty eight years."

"And before that?"

He shrugged. "I've had dreams and memories since I've been in this body that I know I did not experience in this lifetime, from at least six different others. I would say I'm more decrepit than even you, witch."

His simple words scabbed over a gaping wound she'd had for so long she thought it would never do so.

"And how does a reaper age?" Her heart beat frantically against her ribs, surprising her. She was terrified of the answer. Agatha did not want to watch this man grow old and die, despite their forced marriage.

"Marchands are not immortal in the traditional sense. We can be killed in the body we reside in. However, if we remain unharmed and the body does not sicken, we select how long we live and how quickly, or slowly, we age after we reach adult-hood." He looked out over the dark waters. "It's another kind-ness from our Lady Death. She's a romantic at heart and knows well the pain of being separated from a lover over formalities."

Agatha could not deny the unimaginable relief that pulsed through her. Nor could she deny the possibility that Hespa had blessed her after all. Fear flashed across her then, chasing the relief away like the shriek of a banshee. Having feelings for this reaper was one thing. Admitting that their life could be more than dutifully bound was another thing entirely.

"You are a descendent of the previous Sister Autumn?" Grimm asked after a moment.

"Not exactly. Lord Night and Lady Magic had four daughters together: Talan, Hissa, Monarch, and Belfry. But they birthed many other children in this realm with other lovers. When a descendant of Lord Night joins with a descendant of Lady Magic at the appointed time, they have four daughters, each born on a Solstice or Equinox. When each new Sister reaches the age of sixteen, the previous Sister dies. The Grimoire comes to whichever new Sister is born first, when she comes of age, and History begins to be dealt through a combined set of Sisters until the youngest comes of age and the whole new set takes up the mantle."

"You're truly the hands and feet of History, then?" Grimm was chewing on his bottom lip, and the glint in his eye was that of lust for knowledge.

"We are indeed."

"Copernicus' Treaty?" he challenged.

Agatha smiled, true and contented, at that look upon his face. "Wendolyn gave him the idea over several clandestine meetings in a gentlemen's club, illusioned as a man."

Grimm's grin went manic. "The rise of Alejandro the Great?"

"Seleste led the band of soldiers that took control of the Lyronian fortress."

"The Plague of the Ages?"

Agatha's face fell. "Yours truly. I set it free like fireflies out of a jar in a village not far from here."

He reached out and took her hand. "The alchemical discoveries of Kothe?"

"That was actually Kothe himself, but he had quite the muse in the form of Sorscha. He was brilliant and Sorscha insatiable."

Grimm chewed on his bottom lip again. "Who found Elion Fawkes plotting to destroy half of Merveille?"

"Ah. That was Greta. Sister Winter before Wendolyn."

"Cortada's rise to fame?"

The barest of smiles graced her face. "That was me as well. One I'm rather proud of. I found him on a boat off the coast of Coronocco. I'd never heard the likes of his mystical music. I took him to my connections in Obur and the rest is, as you say, *History*."

Grimm resembled a child in a confection shop, wide-eyed and hungry. If Agatha ever needed to dazzle him, all she'd need to do was reveal secrets of History. It was not lost on her that she was a piece of History, herself. Though she supposed he was as well.

"Are there any other musicians or artists that have made History by your hand?"

"By the hand of Hespa, really, but there was a dancer by the name of Giselle Russo from Prilemia." She watched his brows rise—there was not a soul alive that had not heard of Giselle Russo. "Berlusconi—"

"The *poet*?" He leaned forward, engrossed, and she laughed.

"The very same. Also, a painter in the mountains of Seagovia —Hugo Varilla—and an author and playwright on the Isle of Ballast I brought to Merveille. Her name was Eva de Leon, but you most likely know her as Gregor Marlowe."

Grimm's eyes were positively twinkling. "Marlowe was a woman?" He ran a hand over his jaw, shaking his head. "*Brilliant*."

Silence, comfortable and sweet, fell between them for many moments as he began rowing again.

"Are we going to eat on this luncheon cruise of ours?" Agatha looked about the small boat, noticing for the first time that they'd not brought any food.

Grimm laughed. "I need to start keeping morsels on hand for you, I suppose. We'll eat when we get to Dulci's."

"And we're not going to the lighthouse? We're just going to sit in this boat?"

"My, my. You're suddenly of a bad temper, little witch. No, we're not going to the lighthouse. I don't exactly trust myself *alone* with you."

Agatha stilled. "I'm not going to put a spell on you, reaper."

Grimm's chest rumbled with a deep sound of acknowledgment, making her ache for him to come closer. "The problem is you've already bewitched me. Thus, it's best I keep you with other people around."

"You were alone with me this morning."

"Because you insist on wearing that infernal pin."

"It's a brooch."

"Let me see that thing." Dropping the oars into the boat, water sprayed her skirts, and he moved toward her, granting her silent plea. He reached to unclasp the brooch upon her bosom and the needle nicked him. Grimm withdrew his hand as a plump dot of blood welled up.

Agatha tsked and took his hand in hers. "Poor reaper." She brought his finger to her mouth and pressed her lips to it, letting her tongue rest on the wound to stop the bleeding. He stilled beneath her intimate touch.

Agatha knew precisely what she was doing, and how lovely her décolletage looked in her dress, sitting right underneath his line of sight. If he wanted distance she'd just have to torture him.

He sucked a breath through his teeth. "You are very, very fortunate there are other boats on this water right now."

Agatha smiled against his finger and pulled back. "Am I? Or am I dreadfully disappointed?"

Grimm's breath went ragged. "You really shouldn't tempt me so, witch."

"And why not?" Agatha ran a finger down the palm of his

hand and looked up at him from beneath lowered lashes. "It's no crime to kiss your wife, you know."

Grimm came undone. His lips crashed into hers with enough force to nearly tip them into the water. Agatha silently commanded the boat to stay afloat, unwilling to let the moment be ruined. His teeth snagged on her bottom lip and she let out an involuntary gasp. A low rumble came from him in response and his hands roved over her waist, dipping lower. When his mouth left hers, she felt desperate to get it back, but he only unsnapped her cloak and moved his lips to her neck, travelling to the tender skin of her collarbone. Agatha's back arched, sending her hips into his and Grimm growled, pulling back.

"You overestimate my self-control, with or without these other boats around," he said around heaving breaths. "We have to get to Dulci's."

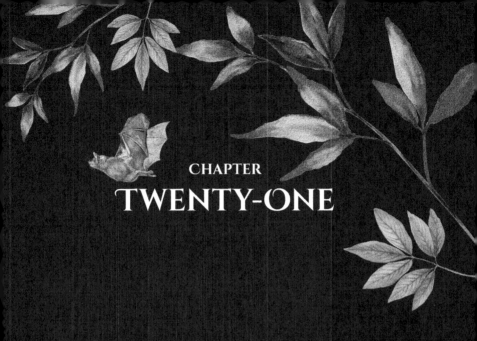

CHAPTER
TWENTY-ONE

N ever allow the disbelief of the Hollow to be
entertained by the Hallowed.
-Sacred Texts of Hespa

AGATHA

DULCI CLOSED AND locked the door behind them, pushing them
to the stairs at the back of her shop. "It would have been nice to
know who exactly you were sending into my home," she spat,
cuffing Grimm on the back of the head.

"I'm sorry, Dulci, but you know all of my correspondence is
read unless it comes from one of our own."

"You've had days to inform me you were planning to send
the empress here, and that's your excuse? You couldn't find a
loyal messenger?" She crossed her arms.

"No, my excuse is that the castle's ballroom exploded. Does
that suffice?"

They stood toe to toe, Grimm a good foot taller than Dulci,

but no fiercer than the old baker. Agatha wondered what it would have been like to be a bat in the rafters during their conversations when Grimm was a boy. He was nothing like the king and queen, but she could see much of Dulci in him.

"I'm sorry to have put you at any risk," Grimm finally conceded.

"Risk to me? Do you think that's why I'm angry? Boy, you could've gotten the Empress of Coronocco *killed* by sending her here." She spat the words and Grimm's jaw clenched.

"Has something happened? You know I have security measures in place."

"No, but you sent her here alone."

"I did no such thing. She came here alone?"

Dulci nodded. "Not a guard, not a lady-in-waiting —nothing."

"How did she get away from her guards?" They both turned to Agatha when she spoke. "It's no easy task. I've tried it many times." Grimm frowned at her and she shrugged.

"She's been here a while, but hasn't said much," Dulci said. "She was waiting for you."

They followed Dulci to the back room and up a narrow staircase, the wood protesting under their weight. It opened up into a small sitting room, kitchen, lavatory, and a closed door Agatha assumed would lead to a bed chamber.

At the table against one wall, Empress Amira slid her chair back and stood slowly. She wore a plain, homespun dress and her hair rested in a severe bun at the nape of her neck, but there was no mistaking the regality of her gait, let alone the intricate ink along her hand and face.

To Agatha's surprise, no one bowed. They all stood silently observing one another, and she thought it must be some unspoken nuance amongst royalty that Dulci knew and Agatha did not. Or perhaps there was very little trust to be had. The silence stretched on too long as she wondered what the three of them were measuring that was more easily deciphered with eyes than conversation.

"Prince Thackery," the empress finally spoke, inclining her head. "Princess Agatha."

Agatha curtsied, but Grimm still did not bow. He'd been excited about the empress' potential involvement until they arrived. Surely something so simple as the fact she'd arrived alone hadn't changed that.

"Empress Amira. We no longer have time for games and pleasantries. Explain why you sought me out, and how you knew to do so."

She clasped her hands in front of herself. "I believe you are acquainted with a man named Dorian Alestair. Is this correct?"

"It is."

"He broke into my court and set fires of discord amongst my people."

Grimm's face read nothing, but Agatha could tell he'd tensed the moment Amira said Alestair's name. "Any fires of discord were there long before anyone could have infiltrated your court, Your Grace. Perhaps you simply could not see them until they were fanned."

"Do you think I am so blind?" She stepped forward, so regal that she was completely at odds with Dulci's simple kitchen. "I am the one that handed him the matches. I am the one that told him where to fan. I am not your *foe*, Prince Thackery."

"Why are you here?"

"I do not want that *poison* distributed to my people. I'm certain you know of which I mean."

"Why seek me out?"

She pursed her lips, her eyebrows knitting when Grimm continually offered no information himself. "Dorian told me to find you, whatever the cost. He said once I got you away from the magus, I needed to inquire about croissants."

Grimm crossed his arms. "How did you come to trust a man

277

in so little time? Alestair did not enter Coronocco until two moons ago."

"I—" Empress Amira looked away. "His confidence caught my attention the very night he appeared at my dinner table. The invitation was forged, and yet it was so masterfully done that only I noticed its falsehood. It was unnerving at first, that my counsellors and guards could be so foolish, but he intrigued me. I grant it was my own foolishness, but I called for him to walk with me the following day."

Agatha's respect for this woman and her lack of formality grew, but it did not appear Grimm felt the same way, judging by his rigid stance and the vein throbbing in his neck.

"He fed me honeyed words, expertly digging to find out...something. I never deciphered what. After the Grand Magus' man visited to offer me a vat of elixir and Dorian immediately dumped it over the side of my balcony, I trusted him implicitly."

Her words hit the cobwebbed corner inside of Agatha's soul where she kept her past with Ira and her growing feelings for Grimm. Alestair had loved the empress.

The click of Grimm's throat as he swallowed lent her to believe the empress was speaking quite truly about Alestair and the kind of man he was. "Why not assume Alestair the enemy and not the magus?"

"The Grand Magus is but a pawn in this realm. And Dorian —" She set her face, chin raised. "I had no reason to think ill of him."

"Alestair is dead," Grimm's voice was so soft it almost didn't carry.

A slight furrow of the empress' brow—quick as lighting— was the only indication that the information came as a shock to her. "He was very much alive when he left my home."

Silence stretched as Grimm thought of his friend and the

empress of her loss. Dulci sat quietly in a corner, chewing on her thumb nail.

It still troubled Agatha why Grimm had gone from hopeful about the empress to complete mistrust. The only new information had been that she'd come alone to Dulci's. Though that was a strange fact, it seemed to Agatha it was better that way. Unless the guards found her missing from her rooms. She'd been at Dulci's for quite some time before they arrived.

"How did you escape your guards?" Agatha blurted. They all looked at her, faces set in hard lines.

"I do not keep people around me that I cannot trust."

It still didn't sit right and she saw Grimm's brow twitch as if he might be thinking the same. No guard in his right mind would let his empress wander off alone in a foreign kingdom.

Grimm shoved his hands in his pockets. "What is it you're asking of me, Empress?"

He had given her absolutely no information, and aside from agreeing he knew Alestair, he hadn't confirmed anything she'd said, either.

"I want you to stop the shipment of that poison from entering my land."

Grimm laughed. "And why do you think I would be inclined to do that? To go against my Crown and Grand Magus to do such a thing?"

The empress only stood straighter, her shoulders pulled back. "Because *you* are the Son of Bone." She turned vibrant eyes on Agatha. "And you are the Autumn Daughter my people have waited a thousand years for."

Dulci swore and Grimm took Agatha's hand. It wasn't until he did that she realised there was a tremble in her fingertips.

"How could she know that?" Gaius demanded. He and Grimm took turns dramatically pacing the lighthouse.

"She said her people have spoken of it for centuries," Grimm explained.

"And why did Alestair not mention her? At all? It's a huge step forward to be in the presence of the other rulers. Why would he not mention it?"

"He did." Grimm cursed. "He sent me a heavily coded message just before Agatha arrived and I just—" He looked up at the ceiling and squeezed his eyes shut. "It didn't make sense until today."

Gaius sighed. "We have to stop those shipments."

"Clearly. But who will we send?"

"Augustus can take the ship and I'll take the carriages."

"Like blasted Hades, Gaius. We need you here, and Augustus would lose his head."

Agatha was only half-listening to their bickering and hadn't realised they'd stopped until she caught Grimm eyeing her with one brow raised. "You've been awfully quiet."

"Something isn't right. She's hiding something—Empress Amira. No one in their right mind would leave their empress alone in the streets of Merveille, or anywhere else for that matter. Not willingly, anyway."

"My sentiment exactly. I don't trust her."

Agatha stood and took up pacing where the prince and lord had left off. She tapped the crystal in her necklace with her fingernail, stopping in front of Grimm. He was rubbing the back of his neck, deep in thought. "And Alestair left you a heavily coded message, just before he died?" Grimm nodded. "Didn't you say you...reaped?" She left off mid-sentence for clarification.

Grimm snorted. "Collected."

"Right." She took up pacing again. "You collected his soul the night before our wedding?" Grimm nodded again. "But didn't the empress say he'd been in Coronocco all that time with her? It's not a short trek all the way across the continent to where her palace sits. Alestair must have travelled here with her."

"He could have. But it's no matter, I can travel anywhere in the blink of an eye to collect a soul if it is mine to collect." Agatha's face contorted and he sighed. "There are many Marchands de Mort. I preside over Seagovia, my handmaidens are dispersed throughout. Although…" Grimm stood and leaned against a desk, taking Agatha by the arm and pulling her down to lean against it next to him, ignoring when Gaius looked away. "You are right. Alestair was in his home that night. Asleep in his chair right here in Merveille."

"I didn't realise that," Gaius piped up. "Why would he not come to see us the moment he returned from Coronocco?"

"I don't know. Something is amiss."

A gasping form fell out of the air in front of them, covered in blood. Too much blood. All three of them surged forward as Mila struggled to stand, trembling all over.

"I'm sorry," she sobbed. "I'm so sorry. I had to." A bloodied dagger clattered to the floorboards next to her.

"What? You had to do what?" She fell against Grimm and he held her in his lap.

"He knew. It wasn't real—it was a trap. He knew your name." Mila looked into his eyes, petrified. "He knows what you are. *Who* you are."

"Who, Mila? Who is it?"

"The name was Pierre. It was a lie. He wasn't dying. He wanted to lure you in. But I stabbed him, Grimm. I had to. He's dying now." She handed him a leather tome as old as time itself. "You have to collect him."

Grimm handed Mila to Gaius. "Get home, Mila. Immediately. Lady Death will come calling." He flipped open the Book, cursing. He whispered something Agatha couldn't hear and was gone.

Grimm

STAB HIM, Mila had. The man was coughing up thick rivulets of blood where he clutched his stomach on the filthy floorboards. They were in a brothel in the slums just outside Mer Row. A mouse skittered along the wall and there were more than a few distasteful insects quite at home in the space.

The room was nearly dark, save for an oil lamp, its light flickering and dim. It was afternoon, but the curtains were thick —most likely to ensure aristocrats weren't spotted bedding the establishment's occupants. The man's soul remained in his body but was wavering, moaning to get out.

Grimm snatched the lamp and stepped closer, his boots smearing blood and spittle on the floor. He bent down and held the light to the dying man's face. He'd never seen him before— not that he recalled.

Grimm knew he looked horrifying, composed of tattered skin and old bones. Death incarnate. For the first time, he was glad for it. Usually, he kept his hood up, aching to be a dealer of peaceful death for these tortured souls, wishing not to frighten but to soothe, as Lady Death taught him. But not this man.

He'd found a way to manipulate the sacred Book of the

Dead. He'd scared Mila to the point of solidifying from her ghostly form and resorting to violence. This man had painted Grimm as a target and learned secrets of him no one knew. He'd desecrated Lady Death. How, he didn't know. But so long as this man's soul was intact, Grimm was going to find out.

He reached toward him and yanked upon his essence, pulling it out just enough so he could see Grimm's form hovering over him. The man gasped and choked, trying to get away, but Grimm held him fast by the throat. He set the lamp down and pulled back his hood, revealing himself in all his grotesque glory. The fear that had been upon the man's face was nothing compared to what crossed it at the sight of the dealer of his death.

"Who are you, Pierre?" Grimm's voice dipped impossibly low and grating, reverberating against the dying man's bones.

He gasped and thrashed.

"*Who are you, Pierre?*" Grimm repeated. "Who sent you?"

"I—c—ca—"

Grimm's refrain permeated the room and Pierre's soul flickered.

With a snarl, he slammed him back down so hard that his skull cracked against the floorboards. Grimm thrust his hand toward the man's flickering soul and yanked with all his might. Pierre's essence tore from his body in a rush that pushed Grimm backward.

It jerked in his grip and he tightened his grasp on it. "*Who sent you?*" he demanded again. "I will not take you anywhere until you tell me. You can haunt this brothel until the end of time itself for all I care."

Pierre's soul flailed, restless and uneasy. "I cannot say. They ensured it," he whispered, attention darting around the room.

He wasn't of this realm any longer. Not even magic should keep him from speaking of anything. "How?"

"I never saw them. They were obscured."

Them. "What do they call themselves?"

"The Order," Pierre whispered, still looking around. Petrified, as if they could still reach him.

Grimm fought not to recoil. "The Order? As in The Order of *Hespa*?"

A heavy, tangible silence descended.

The room filled with darkness and the ominous chirping of birds. "Hello, my little one."

Grimm loosened his grip on Pierre's soul and bowed deeply. "My Lady."

Lady Death hovered above the floorboards in a gown of billowing midnight clouds. She shrouded Herself from Pierre but revealed Her face to Grimm, who choked back his emotion. He hadn't seen Her face since that day in the cave as a boy.

"Darling, this one was not yet ours. He would have survived." She caressed Grimm's cheek. "You must return him."

"My Lady, he altered Your Book."

"He did not. You must find out who did."

Grimm scowled. "He knows what I am. W*ho* I am."

"Do you think so little of my power? I watch over you. There is much for you to accomplish with your bride."

"What do you know of Agatha?" His heart was hammering against his exposed ribs.

Lady Death smiled lovingly. "My sweet Prince of Bone." She took his skeletal fingers and squeezed gently. "Remember. Remember her." Fog obscured the Goddess of Death's face until only a dark mist crowded the room. "Put Pierre back, darling."

His eerie refrain drifted off in the mist along with Her, and Grimm did as he was told. He took Pierre's essence by the ruff and brought it close to his monstrous face. For good measure, he smiled wickedly before slamming the soul back into its bleeding body with a roar.

Grimm bent down to examine the prone form at his feet. It was a brothel without his or anyone else's belongings within it, and he'd clearly come there to attempt to harm Grimm, but there was a very good chance he had *something* on him that could lend information. He turned out the man's pockets with nothing to show for it.

Grimm murmured curses, beginning to shift back into Thackery when he felt something in the man's coat. A hidden pocket tucked deep inside. Impatient, he ripped the fabric open and pulled out a small scrap of parchment. Pierre was beginning to stir, so Grimm shoved the parchment into his own pocket and cried out to alert the staff of a dying patron.

He was moving back at impossible speeds to the lighthouse when a thought struck him. If Pierre would have survived, how in the seven realms had they gotten his name into the Book of the Dead in the first place?

CHAPTER

TWENTY-TWO

I f only there were a place, bent by time and crumbling
with age, where one could escape wrong and right and
just be.

-Journal of Agatha Joubert

AGATHA

"GAIUS, no. I can't risk you being away from the castle right
now."

Agatha sipped her tea, listening to the bickering fight that
had been going on around Dulci's table for too long.

"We have to stop it somehow, Grimm, and you can't very
well leave."

"I *can*. That's what I'm telling you if you'd listen, you
buffoon." Grimm clamped his hand down on Dulci's relentlessly
drumming fingers and Agatha silently thanked him.

"I can keep an eye on the castle." They all turned to look at
Amira. "I can ensure nothing catastrophic happens."

"For all we know, you were the intended target, Amira. Isn't it time for you to head to Coronocco yourself?" Grimm asked.

"I do not believe I was the target. I don't think anyone was the target at all."

Dulci and Agatha exchanged a look.

"Explain," Grimm demanded.

She splayed her hands as if it were obvious. "It's an age-old trick, Grimm. Surely you're familiar with distraction and decoy."

Grimm's glowered. "That's a stretch. You really think setting off an explosion in the ballroom was just a distraction? That seems excessive."

"I've seen much worse." The empress folded her arms across her chest. "Your wedding distracted everyone from the making of so much draught, and the explosion has everyone worried for their own safety. All eyes are on the castle. No one will notice a strange shipment leaving."

"I'm not certain the people would have noticed a shipment leaving, anyway."

"You might have. Or Captain Dubois. There is no reason to believe the magus, or whomever he's working with, has any inclination you're aware of what they're about to do."

Grimm pinched the bridge of his nose before slamming his hand down on the table. "If you can handle this, truly, then Gaius will take the shipment by sea. Agatha and I will take the one by land."

"I don't like this, Grimm," Dulci broke in and set to drumming again.

"What choice do we have?"

"Wait." Agatha bit the inside of her cheek. "Grimm, can I speak to you alone?"

He rose and led her into Dulci's bedroom. Though it was small, the feel of *home* exuded from every wall. It was nothing extravagant, but it was filled with colour. Just like the vibrant pâtisserie below and the baker who owned it, the vivid space was worn by time, but energetic. There wasn't much by way of furniture, but there was a beautiful painting of a sailboat out on the black waves of Mer Noir. Beneath it, against the far side of the room, there lay a small cot.

"That was mine," Grimm told her, noticing where her gaze landed. She sat down on a chair in one corner and Grimm lowered himself to sit on the cot, its old hinges creaking under his weight. "Lady Death is the one that brought me here as a boy. She allowed me to use my time-altering abilities to leave my guards behind and come here. But only here." He smiled in a way that made him look years younger for a moment. "Dulci doesn't know what I am, but she knows I'm not quite...normal."

"She's never asked?"

"No. I tried to tell her once and she stopped me. She told me I'm *her Grimm*, and that's it. End of story."

"Denial?"

"Love. She thought it would put me at risk for anyone to know my secrets. She trusts me explicitly and loves me even more so."

"Mm." Agatha leaned back in her chair. "That must be nice. My parents died when I was a little girl."

Grimm's face fell. "I'm so sorry, Agatha. I can't imagine."

"It's difficult to miss what you never really knew, but somehow I've found a way to do so."

He let the silence hang briefly. "What did you need to tell me?"

"I—I think the elixir might be magical." Grimm stiffened at her words. "I can't sense anything specific from the small vials of it other than sheer malevolence, but I'm nearly certain. If I can get to where it's made—to a larger supply—I might be able to tell. Can you take me to it?"

"Agatha, they leave in less than a day, the place will be crawling with guards—"

"I can hide myself. Just get me close enough."

"No. I don't like this."

"Grimm, I think I can reverse it. If it's magical and I can get close enough to it, I can change its properties. At least spell it to be ineffective."

"Agatha—"

"It's a better plan than splitting off, trying to stop the shipments, and leaving the castle in the hands of someone we don't even know. I'm not *asking*. I'll find it with or without you. Your choice."

Grimm sighed and shook his head. "You are a clever witch."

"Just get me close."

THE MOON WAS bright in the sky before they had Amira and Gaius in place at the castle and made it into the woods.

Nearing the seaside warehouses storing the draught that would go out just after dawn, Agatha and Grimm tied their horses in the forest and traversed the rest of the way on foot, silenced by Agatha's magic. They huddled under a massive maple, ablaze with the last remaining red leaves of Autumn. In the dark, they looked less fiery and more like they were coated in congealed blood, Agatha thought, staring at the fallen leaves beneath her feet.

"If we're not back by dawn, Gaius knows where to find us." Agatha nodded resolutely and Grimm sighed. "I'm not sure about this."

"It's going to be fine, Grimm. I can't transport myself to a particular spot unless I've seen it. I don't know exactly where I'll end up, but I can cloak myself. I won't be seen or heard."

"If I explain the layout to you, will that help? I'd prefer you didn't land on the roof or somewhere you have to spend any more time there than necessary to find the vat."

Agatha nodded and Grimm gave her every detail he could think of. Eventually, she silenced him with a finger to his lips. It was the best they were going to do, and they were running out of time. "I'll be back."

In a blink of time and space brushing against her, Agatha stood just left of a giant vat of glowing golden elixir. Grimm's visual had been dead on. She inched closer, nausea settling in the pit of her stomach. It didn't feel right. Not at all. The vials from Anne and Eleanor had given her a rotten feeling, but there hadn't been a tangible presence of something sinister. Not like this.

Her magic recoiled within her, but she forced her feet forward and rested her hand upon the glass of the vat. Something pulsed against her palm and she gasped, snatching her hand back. Agatha gritted her teeth and pressed against it again, pushing her magic forward. It instantly warred with something. There was a tangle of properties born of their realm and something distinctly—*other*. She withdrew her hand, surprised by how heavily she was breathing. It could be handled, but she didn't think she was powerful enough alone.

"*Merde.*"

She willed herself back into the forest, the cool air welcomed against her flushed cheeks. Agatha watched, invisible, as Grimm paced under the maple tree, chewing on his lip. She removed her cloaking magic and snickered. "Afraid I'd get caught, were you?"

He frowned at her and came closer, eyes scanning, inspecting for any injuries and she laughed.

"I'm perfectly fine, reaper." Agatha pulled back and looked up at him. "I think I can do it. Alter the draught. But I need my Sister."

"We don't have the time to retrieve anyone."

She stepped away from him. "That's not really a problem. It's just that…"

One of Grimm's brows lifted. "It's just *what*?"

"We're forbidden from being together unless it's the Solstice or Equinox."

"Forbidden by whom?"

"Hespa." She grimaced.

Grimm blinked. "You're telling me you want to invoke the wrath of the Goddess Three." He shook his head. "This is a bad idea."

Perhaps it was, but her magic was quivering under her skin. The feel of that elixir was so sinister that her very bones wanted to cry out against it. Almost like the feeling of being watched; all senses alert and prepared to fight or flee.

This was not the magic of Hespa. It felt nothing like Her.

"I'm doing it. If Hespa is willing to let the minds of the people be poisoned—*controlled*—instead of bending the rules enough to allow two Sisters to come together and stop it, then She's not who I thought She was."

Grimm let out a long breath. "I'm inclined to agree. But we're running out of time." He looked at the sky. Dawn was not yet approaching, but they didn't have long.

"Summoning my Sister will take only a moment. Convincing her to help us will...take a little longer. I'm going to go to her. I'll be back."

Agatha turned away, but Grimm caught her by the wrist and pulled her to him. When her hips connected with his, she realised with a strange suddenness that she hadn't pictured Ira's face in days. Her heart cracked at the very same moment it healed.

Agatha stood on her toes and looked into Grimm's eyes for the briefest of moments, wrapping her arms around his neck. Never would she have guessed that the man who stood in the throne room that day, shouting that she was a peasant, could have caused her to feel this way.

The first Sisters had known, though. Hespa had known. It fueled her courage. Agatha brushed her lips against his, and, just for fun, vanished right from his arms.

THE SUDDEN JOLT from near freezing to the humid midnight air of Sorscha's treehouse made Agatha gag.

"Goddess' *teeth* it's so blasted stifling," she muttered, ripping her cloak off.

She noticed a shadow dance across one of the windows set high in Sorscha's tree.

"*Leviter.*"

Agatha's boots lifted from the ground, her raven-black skirts billowing out around her as she floated up to the open window. She sat upon the windowsill, arms around her bent knees, peering in at her Sister Spring. Sorscha dangled upside down, wrapped in crimson silk that hung from rafters crawling with ivy.

"What in the seven realms are you doing, Sister?"

Sorscha gasped and twirled down from the ceiling with exceptional grace. She landed on her toes without a sound and Agatha slipped inside.

"What do you think you're doing?" Her silken nightgown pressed against the outline of her body as she rushed forward. "Are you truly here?" Sorscha reached out to touch Agatha's cheek and jumped back when her fingers connected with flesh. "*What* are you doing here, Aggie?" She looked around frantically. "We could cause an earthquake or a—a—"

"Sorscha, calm yourself." Agatha rested her hands on either side of her Sister's face. "I'm here because I need your help."

Sorscha was already shaking her head and Agatha let go. "I don't think any disaster will befall us, Sister. Not from Hespa."

Sorscha scoffed. "That's not entirely a comforting statement, Aggie."

"Just listen. I truly need your help and I don't have much time. There is a draught that is given to the citizens of Merveille. It is magical but they believe it to be medicinal. It subdues them in some way. It blocks off some part of their mind and makes them do whatever they're told. I don't know all that it does yet but the magic in it is *vile*, Sorscha."

Her Sister still looked terrified. "What am I supposed to do about that?"

"It's being shipped out to the capital cities of Lyronia and Coronocco first, then I'm certain it will make its way here to Prilemia and spread through the rest of Midlerea. You have to help me alter its magic. I don't think I'm strong enough on my own—"

But Sorscha was backing up, shaking her head. "Just the two of us being in the same place is risky enough. We can't possibly combine our magic. We could kill the entirety of Merveille with one wrong move, Aggie."

Agatha stepped toward her Sister and took her hand. "Then we don't make a wrong move. We can do this, Sister. I know I sound mad, but I think we can do this, and I believe Hespa will help us. I think it's why I was sent here. Why I had to marry Grimm. I think this is what my Order means. At least in part."

"Then why didn't this fall on a night of the Solstice so we could safely handle it together?"

"I—I don't know. But I'm tired of causing pain with my magic. I don't think it's what I'm meant for. *Please*, just help me with this one thing. Help me make this right."

Sorscha blew out a breath, rubbing her temples methodically. "*Merde*. Alright. But if Hespa is going to smite us for this, I'm going to burn in a new dress."

She snapped and her nightgown was replaced with a scarlet gown edged in black lace. The bodice had the look of leather dyed with blood, and the ruffled skirt slit all the way up to her bare thigh.

"Goddess' teeth, Sorscha, you look like a bordello harlot."

"Thank you," she preened.

Agatha rolled her eyes and took Sorscha's hand. "Play nice," she warned.

Sorscha gasped. "Does that mean your princely plaything awaits us?" Her grin turned feline.

Agatha sighed and her magic carried them under the maple tree. When their boots hit the cold ground, she realised she'd left her cloak in Sorscha's meadow. At the same instant, she realised Sorscha might not have the quietest reaction to meeting Grimm. Agatha spelled sound-silencing magic around the three of them, just in time for Sorscha to screech. Grimm winced at the ear-piercing sound.

"*Aggie*," she purred, stalking forward and pawing at Grimm's chest. She turned to Agatha with wide eyes and a mad smile. "He is *exquisite*." Sorscha stepped forward and trailed a long nail down his cheek. Grimm withstood the entire thing frozen in place, a pleading in his eyes locked on Agatha's.

"Sorscha, keep your hands to yourself."

She reluctantly removed her hands with a pout and slid to Agatha's side. "Possessive, are we?" Agatha didn't answer and her Sister's eyes flashed. "You've fallen for him!" she whispered and put her hands up. "I'll keep my claws to myself, then."

Agatha turned Sorscha toward Grimm. She looked him up and down and Agatha pinched her.

"*What?*" she crowed. "I said my claws, not my *eyes*."

"Grimm, this is my second eldest Sister, Sorscha. Sister Spring."

Sorscha baulked. "You'll just give up any information for a

face like that, won't you?" She shrugged. "I suppose I would, too."

Grimm cleared his throat. "It's lovely to meet you, Sorscha. My wife has missed you terribly."

"*His wife?*" Sorscha whined, looking sidelong at Agatha. "He's too much, Aggie. I want one."

"Please stay focused." Agatha approached Grimm, Sorscha's gaze boring into them.

"Your Sister is terrifying," he whispered into her ear, eyeing Sorscha over her shoulder. He wrapped his hands around her waist. "Should I erase any qualms in her mind about the only witch I desire?" He smiled impishly and Agatha laughed.

"You're just as bad as she is. And we don't have time for this." The sky was shifting from black and star-studded to a bruised grey at the Estern seam.

"Please be careful." He kissed her gently. "If you think for a moment this won't work, or you'll be found—either of you—just come back. We'll find another way."

Agatha nodded and pulled away. She took Sorscha's hand, and in a breath they stood inside the warehouse that was filled to the brim with barrels of poison.

"Aggie." There was a tremor in Sorscha's quiet voice. They were cloaked in magic, but guards moved about the place in droves. "I can feel it."

"I know. It feels—"

"*Wrong.*" She trailed her hand along a barrel. "So utterly wrong." She looked at Agatha. "Who has magic like this?"

"I don't know, Sister. We're going to ruin this shipment, though, and figure that out."

Sorscha nodded and Agatha led her to the enormous vat of spinning elixir. They both reached out gingerly and touched the rotating glass. The glow of it lit Sorscha's face in ethereal beauty, and the contrast between her beloved Sister and the terrible magic they faced struck her like a blow.

"You're sure about this?" Agatha asked.

"Not at all."

They joined hands and interlaced their fingers, opposite hands still against the glass. "Ready?" Sorscha nodded, her throat bobbing as she swallowed.

Agatha closed her eyes, allowing her magic to guide her. It prodded at the potion, feeling the components of creation—the things that came from the soil and sea. Her magic drew near to them and she felt Sorscha's power brush against hers, examining the elixir as well. Their two forces—one of glimmering red and the other of silken black—intertwined and sifted through the unfamiliar ingredients within the potion.

Something slimy and twisted reached out toward their magic and sent it recoiling. Agatha pushed back against it, afraid if they had to begin again that they would run out of time. Sorscha's red band of magic cautiously wound itself around Agatha's once more, and together they pressed up against the unwelcomed serpentine coil. It felt cold. Slick. Like oil that had sprung up from the ground and pooled in the snow. It did not belong in their realm.

"*Être parti*," Agatha whispered.

Sorscha joined in, the deplorable magic thrashing against theirs as they chanted. Their palms grew slick with sweat, and a bead slid down Agatha's back. She felt the magic scream within her bones at the same moment Sorscha gasped. Violent light burst behind Agatha's mind's eye. With a hiss, the vile magic finally evaporated, screeching as it dissipated.

Panting, the Sisters regarded one another. Sorscha huffed a laugh and Agatha swore. The potion within the vat dimmed, and Sorscha jumped to bleed colour into it. They couldn't risk anyone discovering it had been tampered with. When she was done, it wasn't precisely the same hue of gold as before, but it would have to suffice.

"We need to do the same to each barrel of the draught,"

Agatha explained. "I couldn't really feel the magic in a small vial of it, so I don't think the barrels will be as formidable against our magic as the vat. Let's split up."

A few barrels in, Sorscha came up behind Agatha. "There are men taking the barrels out on the Estern side. Is the shipment leaving?"

Agatha cursed. Of course, if the ship was to leave just after dawn, they would have to load the cargo earlier. "Yes, there are two shipments. They must be loading the ship now. Let's get on board and get to as many barrels as we can. With any luck, we'll knock out the sea shipment at least."

"We could split up further and I could take the land shipment," Sorscha suggested.

Agatha sharply shook her head. "No. I don't trust this magic, Sister."

They moved through the space as quickly as possible and made it onboard the ship where it floated in the water outside the warehouses. The wind had picked up, and it felt almost warm, like the afternoon breeze of Spri—

Oh, gods.

"*Sorscha,*" Agatha whispered, her hair whipping across her face, each strand stinging her skin. "This is your wind."

Sorscha froze, eyes wide. "We need to hurry."

They weren't just hearth tales Winnie and the former Sisters used to scare them into submission, after all. Being together outside a Solstice or Equinox would truly cause catastrophe. The waves slammed into the ship, banging it brutally against the dock. Leaves of sienna, wine, and umber spun through the air wildly as the witches moved through the ship and down into the cargo hold.

"I'm going to be sick!" Sorscha yelled over the howling wind. Even without magic silencing their voices, Agatha doubted the guards could have heard her over the bedlam.

The rocking of the ship was jarring, worse where the sea

clawed at the boat's sides near their eye level. Agatha was not overly fond of being *under* the sea. "Let's just get this done."

They moved as swiftly as possible on their sea legs, rushing from barrel to barrel as the guards brought them aboard. Out of nowhere, the wind stopped abruptly, and the ship gave one final, heaving rock before settling in the water as if there had never been so much as a ripple.

The Sisters looked at one another. "That should have only gotten worse." Sorscha deftly wound her hair around and back in place.

All Agatha could think was that Hespa had intervened on their behalf.

When the last barrel came aboard, Agatha was dead on her feet but rested her hand upon it anyway and pushed against the malevolence. Sorscha came up next to her, and Agatha took her Sister's hand, leading them back into the warehouse.

"Let's get to as many as we can," she huffed as the guards scurried about like ants, moving the barrels the Sisters had already tampered with to where they'd be loaded for the shipment by land.

By the time barrels began to be taken right out from under their hands, both Sisters were gasping for air. Agatha was dripping sweat and Sorscha looked the same. She seized her Sister's hand once more and thought of Grimm. In a blink, they collapsed in front of him, a massive pile of leaves crunching on the forest floor.

Grimm dropped to his knees next to Agatha, and Gaius knelt before Sorscha. The maple, so full of Autumn's beauty, was stripped naked, and Gaius' cheeks were chapped like he'd ridden through that monstrous wind to get to them.

"Another beautiful boy has come to play," Sorscha breathed.

Agatha ignored her. "Gaius, this is my Sister. We couldn't get to all the barrels. The ship is loaded. I think we made it to all the ones moving by sea, but I can't be certain."

Grimm wrapped his cloak around her and stood. "Gaius, send someone to monitor the shipment by sea. We'll inform the palace that my wife and I will be taking our honeymoon."

"Grimm. You can't possibly—"

"We *will*." He reached down and helped Agatha up. "It looks like we're headed to Lyronia, little witch."

Sorscha feigned a faint. "*Goddess,* take me home first."

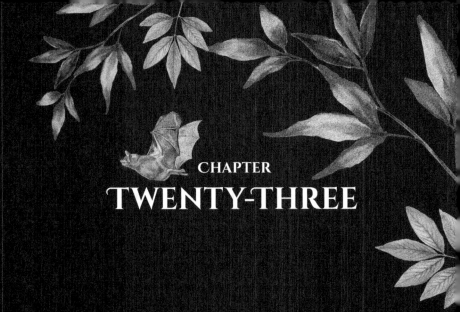

CHAPTER
TWENTY-THREE

L ight might, at times, resemble the darkness. It is not the
sinister thing it appears.
-Sacred Texts of the Order of Hespa

AGATHA

SORSCHA VANISHED, and the three of them ran for their horses
hidden in the thick woodlands.

"Agatha," Grimm shouted as she threw magic up around
them while they ran. "Slow down, we have some time."

"We don't. That shipment will be leaving any moment and
we need supplies to follow them." It was just like Grimm to
think things through to such an irritating extent.

He put a gentle hand on her arm and she reluctantly halted,
Gaius skidding to a stop next to them. "Just take a second,
Agatha."

Gaius led them off the trail and into a copse of trees, tucked away from view. Agatha didn't bother reminding him she'd already hidden them with magic.

The cool night air was clinging to her like a second skin, along with the gritty sand that had stuck in her sweat as the wind blew on the boat. She twisted her bedraggled tresses round and round, unable to sit still. She was itching to *move* and to keep moving until this whole blasted draught was eradicated. Looking up at Mother Moon's waning light, Agatha inhaled deeply and forced herself to listen to the sounds of the woods that slowed her racing heart. As soon as the adrenaline eased in her veins, the full extent of energy lost to her magic crept in its wake.

"I can't transport myself to where they are if I haven't seen it. Their carts are too similar to every other cart in existence, and we don't know exactly where they're taking the draught. We'll have to go by horseback and we need to *hurry*."

"*Wait*, Agatha." Grimm rubbed his tired eyes. "You need to rest. You look like Hades." She scowled at him. "They're a large party, slow with all those barrels. We can easily catch up before they get to Lyronia, even if we leave tomorrow. We need to make sure the castle is safe."

Agatha cursed colourfully. "Fine."

"Like Hades you're going, Grimm," Gaius snapped, and both of them turned toward him. "I'll send Augustus to the ship, but you can't leave, and you know it. We're not leaving the castle in the hands of Empress Amira. She very well could be playing us all."

"You can keep a close watch on her," Grimm countered.

"The damned castle was just *attacked,* and we don't know what in the seven realms Pierre and The Order have to do with all this. The magus could be in leagues with them!" She'd never heard Gaius shout before. Thankfully, she had her wards up. "It would be foolish for you to leave. That's what I keep trying to tell you but you're too damn stubborn to listen."

Grimm ground his teeth, but Gaius had a point.

"I'll go alone." The pair of them stared at Agatha as if she had just grown a second head.

"Absolutely not," Grimm said at the same time as Gaius said, "I'll go with you."

Grimm gave Gaius a look so sharp it could slice iron into ribbons. "*No.*"

Gaius made a derisive noise and Grimm bristled. An argument ensued, but Agatha heard nothing, their harsh words slipping in with the rustling leaves as a realisation descended upon her. *Amira.* Something about what Gaius said was tugging at her. She'd thought the empress' actions were odd but…

Agatha flung around to face the arguing men. "Amira's a witch." They both halted their fussing and gaped at her. "Think about it. It makes sense." Bolstered, she walked forward, hands moving as she spoke. "Amira left her guards without them protesting it. She looks like a goddess come to earth, and yet no one stopped her in the city proper. She knew there was something wrong with the elixir. She knew to trust Alestair. And she knows about the prophecy. A different version than either of us have."

"Wait. There are different prophecies?" Agatha and Grimm ignored Gaius' question.

"Why do you think it differs from ours?" Grimm asked.

"She called you Prince of Bone—no mention of gems, and she called me Autumn Daughter. I think it's a different version of the same thing."

"You still can't go, Grimm," Gaius said, stepping toward him. "*Especially* if Amira is a witch. We can't just leave her unattended at the palace."

Agatha could see the war behind Grimm's eyes and the subsequent defeat just before he growled.

"He's right," she said softly. "You need to stay within Merveille to keep an eye on Amira and learn more about Pierre and the attack." His jaw clenched tighter with every word she spoke. "It will take a matter of days, and then we can take down the Merveille supply. But in order to do that, you need to be here to locate it and we need to ensure you're safe, too." Agatha took his hand, lacing their fingers together. "There is someone after *you*, Grimm. Time is running out, and there is too much at stake for you to leave."

"At least take Sorscha," Grimm responded, a hand up to ward off Agatha's temper before it began. "It would be faster with her and less tolling on you."

She shook her head. "*No*. Our magic is formidable when it comes together outside of the Solstice or Equinox. That's what that wind was—*us*. Tonight, Hespa allowed us an exception and stopped it, but we don't know that She will again. We can't risk it. I'll go in on my own each time the party halts."

"You're completely drained right now, Agatha," Grimm protested. "You can't handle that entire shipment on your own."

"I have to. I'll split it up. I can follow them, cloaked during the day, and then at night, when they halt for sleep, I'll go in and reach as many barrels as I can. When I tire, I'll retreat until the following night."

She could tell by his frown that he wasn't fond of the idea, but he finally nodded wearily. "Gaius, keep her safe."

Gaius' brows rose at Grimm's relenting before he nodded. "Of course."

Agatha glowered at them both. "This is all very chivalrous, but I'm not asking permission from either of you, and I don't need protection. I'm a goddess damned witch and I can wield my own sword."

Gaius smirked at her but Grimm smouldered. "For the love of the goddess could you not be so obstinate for *one* moment?"

"What he means is—" All three of them jumped, shock roiling through them as Eleanor stepped out from behind the trees. "He's scared you'll get hurt and it will make him feel better if someone goes along with you."

"How did you find us?" Agatha wanted to be angry, but she was more panicked than anything.

"I followed you." Eleanor crossed her arms. "I lost you for a while, but then I heard voices."

But Agatha had wards up...

Her magic was too weak. Grimm was right. She needed to rest. "We need to get out of the woods. Now."

Grimm

EVERYTHING about this predicament was setting him on edge. Agatha was exhausted, dead on her feet, and she was packing a bag to leave with Gaius and take on an entire shipment of that poison *by herself*. Deep down, he knew she was more than capable. He knew the plan they'd set in motion while racing back to the castle was a good one. But he did not like it.

"Eleanor," she was saying, "you mustn't tell anyone about me. You can't."

"Oh, take the stick out of your arse, Highness. I won't tell anyone." Eleanor waved her off and disappeared into Agatha's closet.

When Eleanor returned, Agatha muttered, "Witches don't actually ride brooms."

Eleanor blinked at her, unimpressed as she stuffed more items in a knapsack.

"You didn't seem shocked in the woods." Agatha's eyes were narrowed, and Eleanor shrugged.

"My gran is a witch. The one I told you about in the slums. It wasn't difficult to figure out if you know what to look for." She snatched Agatha's hand. "Black chalk under your nails, crystals everywhere, herbs in your pockets…"

Agatha swore and Grimm snorted.

"I really didn't think so many witches could still exist after the Trials," Gaius broke in. "We all thought magic had been dead for hundreds of years."

Agatha shook her head. "That's just what The Order and the magi want you to believe. It's easier to control your flock if they don't think for themselves or practise magic. There aren't many witches left, but they're around. Hedge witches mostly. My coven was one of the last known, and they all burned nearly three hundred years ago."

Grimm squeezed her hand at that. He hadn't connected the Burned City of Helsvar with the loss of her coven—her family. She gave him a grateful smile as if to say she'd tell him more later.

"If she really is a witch, perhaps Amira comes from a long line of warlocks and witches. That could be how they've survived for so long—in secret."

"The Witch Trials were rampant in Coronocco as well," Grimm offered.

"What better way to conceal what you are than to hang or burn your own kind?" She shrugged half-heartedly, her eyes full of sadness. "It's what occurs in this palace, is it not?"

She wasn't wrong. The Seagovian royalty in Merveille dripped with duplicity. Nationalities of all kinds could be found within the palace walls, but they never extended a hand to those they saw as *lesser* of their kind. The court prided themselves on declaring that Seagovia had done away with the horrors of the past—the slaying of innocents over their origins. And yet, they did the very same thing with social class.

"Do you think Amira is the one who spelled the draught, then?"

Agatha considered this for a long moment, but it was Eleanor who spoke first. "I could be wrong, but I think that level of power would take more than one witch."

"She's right," Agatha agreed. "But it doesn't mean Amira's working alone, if it is her. Whatever it is, it's dark magic, and we need someone here to keep searching for answers."

Grimm ran a hand through his hair. "I still don't fancy the idea of you going alone."

"She's not going alone," Gaius said. Grimm clenched his fists but remained silent. "We all agree then. Agatha and I will go after the shipment. Grimm will stay here and investigate Amira and the draught."

"I want to come, too." They all looked at Eleanor.

Thank the goddess.

Grimm clapped his hands together. "I think that's a wonderful idea, Eleanor." She preened. "If you all leave at first light, you should be able to catch up with the shipment in a couple of days." He lifted a brow at Agatha. "I propose we take the rest of this morning to let Agatha rest." Her lip curled. "Then, little witch, we sneak you into Captain Dubois' quarters and the barracks to alter their draughts before you leave. They might have their supplies replenished by the time you return, but it could give them a level head long enough for me to find where the magus is hiding the draught stores supplying Merveille."

Agatha frowned. "I don't relish waiting to leave, but you're right. We have to cut off the head by any means necessary. I could also go into the slums and reach as many people as I can."

"No, I don't think that's wise."

Agatha crossed her arms. "If I have the capability to fix this for the people, I won't sit idly by and let them remain controlled."

She had the worst timing with her temper.

"Agatha, I don't like it any more than you do, but we don't know what it will be like for the people coming off the draught. Especially with the level of rebellion you have managed to incite in them *despite* the control. Clearly they're incredibly restless, even beneath its power. The result of their minds collectively returning to themselves. It could be catastrophic. They can wait a few more days while you deal with the shipment. Dubois needs a level head, and as many guards as we can manage to get to before you leave."

"And Anne."

Grimm sighed. "And Anne."

Agatha gasped and turned to Eleanor. "Did you already know before tonight? Your drawer is full of a large supply. You don't take it, do you?"

She rolled her eyes. "I'm not a fool. It was pretty clear the elixir isn't what they say. My gran threw hers out and I never took mine again."

"What about Anne?"

Gaius' face lit with pride. "Anne's are lessened dosages. I made her several dupes that I mixed with her supply. We're weaning her off until she takes completely false ones. Augustus changes them out when no one is around."

Agatha brightened. "That's why Anne is growing bolder."

"And why you couldn't detect much of the magic in her vials," Grimm interjected.

Eleanor's face scrunched up. "So, you traded Anne's out but just left mine?"

"Calm down—yours were lowered dosages, too."

Agatha tapped her foot impatiently. "We have to get moving."

"You need to rest first," Grimm snapped.

When Agatha turned on Grimm with wide eyes and her hands on her hips, Gaius and Eleanor exchanged a look and left in a hurry.

AGATHA

RESTING WAS FUTILE. Agatha couldn't sit *still*. She tossed and turned until her blankets were a knotted mess. With an exasperated snarl, she ripped them off, shoved her feet into a pair of black satin slippers, and shuffled over to one of her spelled hiding places.

"*Révéler.*"

The teetering stack of books revealed itself. Agatha ran a finger down the worn leather spines, a small smile creeping onto her lips. A stack of books never failed to soothe her soul. She selected the one she'd stolen from the magus' hidden study in the library. When she'd last looked at it, the tome seemed innocuous enough, but perhaps she was just missing something. If she had to try and *rest*, she could at least search for some answers about who the magus was working with and who attacked the castle.

Agatha returned to the extravagant bed, settling under the covers with her slippers still on. Propping the book on her bent legs, she flipped it open to where the magus had marked it, who knew how long ago.

The language was antiquated and her head ached as she tried to piece together the ancient dialect. She ran her finger along the words, only grasping possible phrases here and there until an entire sentence stuck out like a stark white rose in a sea of red.

Afer mahn sur, coreg ah lur, olren fahn bre ankhur.

Agatha gasped. She'd seen that sentence before—many times —word for word. Tossing the book onto the other side of the bed, she launched herself out of the blankets and toward the stack of tomes. She grabbed her father's journals so quickly that everything else—including the Grimoire—tumbled to the floor.

"Where is it, where is it, where is it?" She flipped furiously, looking for a specific passage her father had written that always stuck out to her and never quite made sense. "*Merde*." She slammed the journals shut, remembering exactly which one it was in. And she didn't have it.

It was a foolish and reckless idea. Completely imbalanced after what happened when she and Sorscha had been together, but Agatha needed that journal and her Sister Summer had it.

The Spring wind hadn't come to war with Autumn's until they'd used their magic. She could visit Seleste, just for a moment, to get the journal. Aside from transporting herself there, she would use no magic.

Agatha muttered curses and left in an imperceptible wisp of spell.

She opened her eyes, shielding them from the offensive sunlight. Seleste and Sorscha and their blasted sun. Agatha didn't see Sister Summer, but the entire island was hers; she could be anywhere. Her bungalow rested in the perfect centre, surrounded by lush palms and wild vines. It was as good a place to start as any.

Sand relentlessly filled her useless slippers and Agatha grumbled as she sat down under a towering palm—its coconuts littering the ground—to dump them out.

"*Aggie?*" Agatha's attention darted to her ethereal Sister Summer. Seleste dropped a basket of sunflowers and peaches to the sand at her feet and rushed over.

Goddess, Seleste was a vision, especially in her island glory. She resembled their father so very much that it hurt to look at her. Her hue was only a shade lighter than his rich carob skin. Their eyes were uncannily the same; their shape—tilted up ever so slightly at the edges; their colour like fresh gingerbread. Even their full lips were identical.

Agatha might have her father's blood in her veins, but she was his opposite in every way. She had the pallor of her mother's skin and the gloom of her mother's heart. Seleste alone carried the goodness of their father within her. Winnie and the previous Sisters had told them their mother was a heretic. That she had been the reason their coven burned. It felt to Agatha like she had inherited their mother's wickedness, though she wished with all her might to be like her father—that strong and kind soul.

Seleste's many golden bracelets *tinked* as she ran toward Agatha. Her vibrantly orange and yellow wrap swishing around her hips, the sea a cacophony of sound behind her. She dropped to her knees in front of Agatha, coiling her hundreds of tiny braids around to fall over one shoulder. The movement was so familiar, so like Agatha and Sorscha's own habit, that she sobbed, launching herself at Seleste. They fell backwards in a heap that coated every inch of Agatha in the offensive sand, but it was worth it.

Seleste simply held Agatha to her chest, swathed in only that thin strip of bright chiffon. She could feel her Sister's heart beating calmly, a complete contrast to Agatha's violent pulse.

Seleste took Agatha's hand, running an elegant thumb over her onyx ring. "You look like death incarnate on this beach all clad in black, Sister."

Agatha snorted a laugh and pulled back. "I know I shouldn't be here."

Sister Summer tucked a strand of hair behind Agatha's ear. "Are you alright?"

Seleste would never fault her for coming, even if it meant a tidal wave would come dash her home to pieces. She would never accuse Agatha of being reckless. When it came to Seleste, if Agatha needed her, she needed her, and that would be the end of it. This was the first time Agatha had been daring enough to go to her outside of a Solstice or Equinox, though.

"I need Father's journal. The one you have."

Seleste's colossal monarch butterfly, nearly as large as Mabon, floated down on the breeze to land on Agatha's arm, her beautiful wings opening and closing in greeting.

Seleste smiled. "Litha has missed you as much as I." She stroked Litha's magnificent wings gently. "Has something happened?"

"Much, but I haven't the time to explain."

Seleste made a melodic sound of understanding and looked down at her lap as a book materialised in it. She handed their father's journal to Agatha. "You've not responded to any of my letters, Sister."

"I know. I'm sorry for that. A lot has taken place since the wedding. It's a horrible disaster all throughout the continent, but especially in Merveille."

Seleste nodded. "And your husband?"

Agatha's cheeks turned pink from more than just the goddess-awful sun. "He's not so bad."

Seleste's sing-song laugh filled Agatha's soul. "Not the torture you thought Hespa was bringing to you, after all?"

"Grimm is not." Agatha twirled her onyx ring. "But it's all such a twisted mess."

"Mm. Sorscha told me that the Grimoire changed Sisters' handwriting in the middle of your Order." Seleste summoned a pineapple into her outstretched palm. With a snap, it hovered in the air and sliced itself. She plucked a piece from where it floated and handed it to Agatha. She might hate Summer, but Agatha would never deny fruit. "It happened to me once."

Agatha choked on her bite. "*What*?" Litha fluttered onto her pineapple, and she set it down for her to enjoy.

Seleste nodded. "Do you remember my Summer boy?"

"Of course." That Summer came after Agatha had been sent to set fire to a monastery and poison an army's food supply. She hated Seleste that year. Very nearly hated Hespa. It never made sense why the Goddess Three would send Seleste into a blissful

Summer of passion and Agatha into an Autumn of horrors. It was the first time she'd entertained the idea that the Grimoire might not be what they once thought.

"That Order began in Monarch's hand and finished in Talan's."

Time felt like it was repeating itself. A similar occurrence had happened with three of the Sisters, then. "But wasn't it a wonderful Summer?"

Seleste nodded, her gaze far off. "It was."

A cold wind hit them like a battering ram out of nowhere. The waves grew restless and wild. Seleste had used magic with the pineapple...and the journal. "I have to go."

Seleste ran a ring-clad finger down Agatha's cheek, not the least bit ruffled. "Of course, Sister."

CHAPTER
TWENTY-FOUR

T*he greatest facet of our Goddess Three will always be Love.*
        -Writings of Ambrose Joubert

AGATHA

GRIMM HAD EXPLAINED CAPTAIN DUBOIS' quarters to her four times, but she still found herself magicked into a room that clearly belonged to someone else. Agatha cursed bitterly. She was already running on the dregs of her energy, let alone magic, and didn't want to risk another try. If she used up all her power, she wouldn't be able to reach the barracks and the guards' vials, or make it back to her rooms.

Agatha had only burnt herself out once before, when she was sent to rid a village of disease. It was the only time she'd been Ordered to do something truly heroic. Though, it was she who'd set the plague on them in the first place, doing the bidding of the Grimoire. The people suffered and died within that village—cut off from all humanity—for a year as Agatha watched. Once the plague had been released, she couldn't bring herself to leave. It was torturous to stay, a permanent scar marring her soul, but there had been no other option in her mind. Agatha had tended to them day in and day out, posing as a healer who had survived the disease and was therefore immune.

When an Order came within the Grimoire from Belfry to heal them magically, Agatha threw every ounce of herself and her magic into healing the survivors immediately. On day three, with the last little child smiling up at her with clear eyes and smooth skin no longer covered in sores, Agatha lost consciousness. It took several days for her to even summon a small flame. That was how the Sisters learned they could reach the bottom of their magic reserves.

She couldn't very well burn out in the middle of the barracks, and they had a long road ahead of them. That thought in mind, Agatha sighed. She needed to conserve all the energy she could. And that meant sneaking through the chamber and into the hall as a mortal. Mercifully, it was empty and she slipped out into the corridor. She'd hardly closed the door when Queen Fleurina and her attendants were upon her.

"Queen Fleurina." Agatha hid her jump of surprise with a bow.

The queen's brow furrowed as her attention settled on the door Agatha had just exited through. "Have you gotten lost?"

"No, Your Majesty. Eleanor needed help with some linens that were to be delivered and I offered to be of service."

"How quaint." The queen's lips pursed. "My son has informed me you must travel to an ill family member in Drifthollow."

Grimm hadn't said how he was explaining her absence for the next several days, just that he would take care of it. "Yes, I should only be gone a few days."

The queen regarded her momentarily. "Mind yourself on this journey, Agatha. It is a strange time to leave the city proper."

With that, she turned and walked away. Her words swarmed in Agatha's mind. It almost sounded like a warning, but she had no time to consider it. The queen only traversed her own quarters of the castle, which were nowhere near Dubois' or the barracks.

By the time Agatha made it to the correct wing of the castle, she had invented several colourful new curses Grimm would have been immensely proud of. The thought put a small smile on her face. Thankfully, she didn't have to guess which room was Dubois', because the captain exited the third door on the left, right before her eyes.

"*Cacher.*"

She disappeared just before he turned in her direction. It was far too close. Breathing a sigh of relief, she scanned the hall for any others, then used her bat brooch to pick the lock of Dubois' door.

Pointless skill for a witch to learn, Winnie had said. *Just spy with magic*, Sorscha had said. *I hope you never have need of that skill,* Seleste had said. Agatha liked learning new skills, and to be prepared for any such need for them.

The lock made a satisfying *click* and she entered, shutting the door behind her. Dubois' rooms were as tidy and rigid as he was. There was hardly anything that didn't have a distinct use, unlike the room she'd found herself in earlier, full of pointless baubles and trinkets.

Good. It would make finding his store of draught simple. That proved wonderfully true as she found four vials within his nightstand.

Agatha took the vials in her hand and let her magic seek out the twisted force within the elixir. It felt weaker in such a small portion of the draught, but it was still stronger than her guttering magic. She found success at last, though she was at a loss for breath and felt desperately tired. Placing the vials back inside the drawer and sliding it shut, she thought of Grimm. In the span of a breath, she was back in their rooms, stumbling into his arms. He deftly picked her up and laid her on the bed.

"You didn't rest while we were preparing, did you?"

Mabon awoke and squeaked, flying to lay beside her on the pillow.

Agatha smiled sheepishly and Grimm frowned. "I think I need to reserve my magic for the shipment." She hated to not make it to the guards' vials, but she couldn't be daft. "I'm sorry."

"No." Grimm sat down next to her on the bed. "No apologies necessary. I won't see you harm yourself for this. If your well-being is on the line, we will find another way. This is already just a temporary fix at best."

"I'll be fine. I just need to conserve my magic. I'll have to do things like a regular boring mortal."

Grimm laughed and she felt their shared tension ease, if only slightly. "Poor little witch." He bent over her, resting his arms on either side of her hips, hands pressing into the mattress.

She leaned closer. "I know there is so much going on, but I'm still worried about whoever is after you. Pierre was just a pawn for The Order, and we don't know who else is. Amira? The magus? It all has to be combined somehow, and—"

Grimm cut her off with a gentle brush of his lips against her forehead. "I'm not invincible, but you know I'm quite difficult to harm. I'll be fine. I have Augustus, and you have Eleanor." He snorted at how ludicrous it sounded for two mortals to be their protectors.

Agatha rolled her eyes. "I'm not sure taking Eleanor is wise."

Grimm tensed slightly. "I think it's necessary."

"I would have much preferred Anne." She made a disgusted face and Grimm chuckled.

"Anne isn't quite ready for something like this. Eleanor is... difficult, but she's of a tough mind and she does know how important it is to keep our secrets safe." Grimm looked away briefly. "She does still hold a lot of contempt for me, I'll admit."

"But not for Gaius?"

Grimm brushed his thumb over Agatha's cheek as if counting her freckles. "Gaius' mother was much more tolerant than mine. If I broke the rules when we were children and found Eleanor, I would be shut up in the castle for a fortnight. Eventually, I stopped trying to see her." He looked down. "It was my fault. I should have tried harder. But Gaius found a way, constantly. By the time she was employed in the castle, she wouldn't even look at me anymore, but the two of them remained friends." He lifted one shoulder. "To be fair, she hardly tolerates Gaius, really."

"Yet he still took pains to ensure Eleanor would be weaned off the draught."

Grimm smirked. "Love, even between friends, is a peculiar thing, isn't it?"

He leaned in, kissing her gently, tender and sweet. Most likely because he didn't wish to see her energy used up. Alas, it was only filling her with *too much* energy. She pressed into the kiss, wrapping her arms around his neck. Her lips parted and his tongue found its way to hers. When his hand slid to her hip, she sucked in a breath and Grimm groaned, pulling back.

"That's not resting." He set his forehead against hers and loosed a breath.

Gaius cleared his throat from the doorway, face solemn, and Agatha barely caught the wicked glint in the prince's eye before he tucked it away.

"It's time to go."

AGATHA

GUINEVERE'S FLANK twitched beneath Agatha, her tail coming around to swat at whatever insect had hovered to taunt her, and Mabon huffed at the horse for nearly swatting him. They'd left the city of Merveille behind just after teatime. After covering a good amount of distance, they were still quite a ways behind the shipment party and wouldn't catch up for another day. It wasn't long before they would need to camp for the night, either.

"Our horses need rest," Gaius announced as if reading her thoughts.

"There's an inn not far from here," Agatha offered. "The Midnight."

"I think it's better if we camp. We can't risk you being seen at an inn when you're supposed to be headed toward Drifthollow in the opposite direction."

Eleanor grumbled under her breath and Agatha wondered for the thousandth time why in the seven realms they'd agreed to bring the bitter maidservant. "Camping doesn't suit your delicate taste, Eleanor?" The words were out before she could stop them. She was too damn tired to control her tongue.

Gaius turned abruptly in his saddle and stifled a snort.

Eleanor stuck her tongue in her cheek. "I might be a maidservant, but I've never been a *peasant*, Your Highness."

Snide little wench. Agatha opened her mouth to say as much, but Gaius reached across with his foot and kicked hers, shaking his head.

She bared her teeth at Eleanor anyway when Gaius wasn't looking. Her maid just rolled her eyes and the three of them trudged on toward a place to set up camp.

No one had thought to bring tents—they were miserable castle-dwellers and had never suffered a day in their insufferable lives. Thus, three almost-flat bedrolls were laid out around a small fire. They didn't want to risk a large one since Agatha couldn't waste her slowly rising store of magic on a shield for them, not with the greater need for it still ahead. Though Gaius could wield a sword and bow with the best of them, and Agatha was no stranger to a blade herself, they needn't risk drawing unwanted attention. Especially considering their attire. Now that she paid attention, it occurred to her how ridiculous they all looked.

"Do any of us have clothing not worth a year's wages? We're begging for trouble looking like puffed-up fish."

Gaius laughed, his green eyes twinkling, and Agatha thought he seemed much happier outside the castle walls, deep within the forest. "We'll rough them up a bit after supper." He slung a quiver across his back. "I'm going to hunt. Don't stray far from the fire. With any luck, I'll return with a rabbit or two to skin."

Eleanor grimaced.

"Gods, you are a frilly thing, Eleanor."

"And you are of a terrible temperament."

"I am very tired. And very hungry." Agatha sneered and slid a bite of pumpkin bread in her mouth. "Do you know how to cook?"

Eleanor baulked. "I work *upstairs*, not in the kitchens."

Agatha blinked at her. She shoved the bread into her knapsack and stood, wrinkling her nose at Eleanor before stomping off into the trees. Scouring the brush and surrounding wooded area, Agatha began to collect what she could, resting it in her skirts she held out as a makeshift basket. Lost in a menial task, she pondered their predicament.

Grimm was no doubt still in countless meetings with the royal council and Grand Magus, who'd just been sent in the king's stead to lead the investigation of the attack. For the most part, Grimm and Captain Dubois had been sent to the side and no one was listening to their input by the time Agatha left. The plan was to leave Dubois to worm his way back in while Grimm,

Mila, and Augustus would use the magus' busy schedule as an opportunity to search his quarters. With any luck, they would learn anything they could about his connection with the attack and where the kingdom's stores were.

Mabon tittered and landed on Agatha's shoulder in an ill temper. "Just go home, Mabon. Go back to the cottage, it's not so far off from here. I'll retrieve you in a couple of days."

He huffed at her but took off at breakneck speed. At least with him away Eleanor would have one less thing to complain about. Pleasantly surprised by all she'd managed to forage, Agatha returned to where Eleanor sat next to the fire and dumped it all out in front of her.

"Help me wash and prepare these. You might need to know how to cook one day."

Eleanor frowned but obliged. As they washed her findings with water from a nearby stream and prepared them for the pot, Agatha explained what they each were.

"This is a groundnut. It tastes more like a vegetable than a nut, almost like a potato. Use this to slice them into slivers." She stripped her dagger from where it had been strapped to her thigh and handed it to Eleanor.

"You carry this with you?" She took it in between the tips of her fingers, her face twisted in disgust.

Agatha flashed her teeth. "Always. You would do well to do the same, you frilly thing."

Eleanor handled the knife as if it was still coated in the blood of Agatha's last kill, but she began slicing and Agatha moved on. "These are mushrooms."

"I know what mushrooms are."

"Do you know which will kill you? Which will make you hallucinate until you wished you were dead? Which will cause you to vomit uncontrollably?" Eleanor stared at her. "I didn't think so." Agatha lifted a mushroom. "You want to look for puffy, round mushrooms—or these." She selected another that hardly resembled a mushroom at all.

"That looks like a flustered chicken."

Agatha laughed. "It does. It's safe. But these"—she pulled out a mushroom she'd tucked in her pocket, just for this particular lesson—"will make you very ill if they don't kill you, and they're likely to do that to someone so accustomed to fine foods as yourself." She threw the toxic mushroom far into the tree line and washed her hands from a water skin. "Anything with a parasol shape should be avoided."

Agatha showed Eleanor the rest of her loot and explained how to collect water from the stream by filling the pot with water flowing over rocks without moss. "The rocks help purify it. Some forms of moss can as well, but unless you know which mosses are acidic and which aren't, it's best not to try it. You'll want to let it boil for a good while over the fire with a bit of salt."

While the soup stewed, they both sat in the waning light and let silence fall, watching sparks fly off the flames.

"Why did you really want to come, Eleanor?" Agatha observed her maidservant. The ever-present frown that drew the corners of her mouth down, the flames highlighting the haughty set of her jaw and glinting off her blonde hair.

Eventually, Eleanor spoke, staring into the fire. "I wanted to keep an eye on you."

Agatha recoiled. "Keep an eye on me? Like a wayward child?"

Eleanor turned sharply toward her. "Yes. We're lucky Grimm hasn't been killed for taking you as his wife. And what if anyone finds out you're a witch? They'll hang you *and* Grimm."

The truth of her statement hit Agatha like a blow to the chin. Grimm very well could be a target for taking her as a wife—prophecy or not. And Eleanor had retained love for Grimm, even after their years of societal separation and the loss of their friendship.

"Do you truly think the two of you are making a difference?" she went on. "You're making a *spectacle* of us all."

"How is that?" Agatha could at least hear her out. Wasn't it what she was there for, even if Eleanor drove her mad?

"Agatha, no one less than a prince can defy royal mandates, or tradition. Even if you think you're paving the way, you're just giving everyone false hope. Nothing will ever change."

"I don't believe that's tru—" Agatha's words were abruptly cut off when she saw a spark of flame off in the tree line. No, not a spark—a reflection. A flame glittering across a blade.

In an instant, Agatha had a ward around Eleanor and she was stalking toward the trees. The maidservant tried to shout something, but it was muffled by the spell. She could feel Eleanor banging on the invisible wall of her magic, but she did not turn back.

"Who's there?" Only a cricket's song sounded in the woodland, followed by the soft hoot of an owl. The twisted part of her dark heart arose from slumber, crawling its way up until violence unfurled, skittering out and slithering down her spine.

"Won't you come out and play?" she cooed, wrapping her fingers around the hilt of her knife. Her magic coiled, ready to spring forward at any moment. A twig snapped to her right and Agatha whirled, sending a plume of magic in that direction. It stretched and clawed at the area, slinking out to seek the pursuant. One side of Agatha's lips slid up. A killing calm flowed over her like a shadowed gown of the purest spider silk. She twisted her barbed hand, summoning a black orb of magic. With a flick of her wrist, she sent it shooting toward her stalker. When her effort was met with a grunt and a heavy *thud* on packed dirt, Agatha sent a look back at Eleanor—wide-eyed with her fist against the ward—and tore off through the trees.

Her magic hovered above the prone form of a large, leather-clad man, illuminating him in its milky onyx glow. He was far too well-dressed—with a solid gold chain around his neck—to be a common thief. With a moan, he began to stir, but Agatha shoved him back down with her boot on his chest. When his head hit the ground, leaves crunching, she held her dagger to his throat. "Who sent you?" she growled.

The man began to chuckle, the vile laugh breaking away into a hacking cough.

"*Who sent you?*" She dug the edge of her blade in, drawing a hiss from the man. He only sneered at her, his leather jerkin groaning under her weight. "Last chance," Agatha purred, a trickle of his blood dripping onto her fingers.

"I'll never tell you, *witch*." He thrust his head forward and jerked his neck across Agatha's blade with incredible force. She gasped, dropping the knife. Drawing back quickly, she clutched at the cords of his jerkin, but it was too late. The man gurgled, sputtering his last breath.

Agatha cursed and shoved him down, anxious to get back to Eleanor. It was doubtful this man had travelled alone.

Just at the edge of the tree line, stepping into the warm light of the fire, she heard something behind her. She turned, angled for another fight, only to find a man wide-eyed and slack-jawed, a sword poised to stab her. And an arrow protruding from his throat. He fell to his knees, then face-first into the dirt. Gaius stood behind him, a wild look in his eyes, bow still raised in hand, staring at Agatha.

Grimm

"WHAT, pray tell, have I done to warrant a visit from the prince this late at night?" Tindle leaned up against the wooden archway between his foyer and drawing room in his silk dressing robe, candlestick in hand.

Though he'd been stripped of his shop, good name, and elegant home on the dark day he'd been Blacklisted, Tindle had clawed his way up from the mire. His home was nothing like the extravagant one he'd once owned in the wealthiest part of the city, but he had painstakingly made it his own. The modest house screamed his name with its evergreen walls and fine velvet furniture. Every nook and cranny was meticulously designed and equally in order.

Grimm hung his coat on the rack next to the door and loosened his collar. "I've not had any luck locating the draught stores." He walked past Tindle into the drawing room and set down a book on the side table before rolling up his sleeves. "A new round should be going out to the markets in a day or so," he said as he bent to light the fire. "I've sent Augustus to keep watch and follow the delivery wagon back to where it came from."

Tindle shrugged casually. "Sounds like something you should have done from the start."

Grimm paused his fire stoking and frowned at Tindle over his shoulder. "Thanks for that."

"And you're here, why? Because your bride is away and you're feeling restless?"

Tindle's eyes crinkled at the edges when Grimm levelled him with a stare. "Agatha came across this book." He rose and moved to pick it up.

Tindle pushed off the wall and traded him the candlestick for it. "What am I looking at here?"

"I'm not entirely sure. It's in the ancient dialect of Coronocco, and Agatha could only piece together bits."

Tindle raised an eyebrow. "Our peasant princess can read ancient Coronoccan?"

Grimm ignored the question. "I thought perhaps you could lend a bit more insight."

Leafing through the pages, Tindle blew a long breath past his lips. "I haven't studied this dialect in a very long time. Dulci would be able to tell you much more than I can."

"Yes, well, Dulci is currently keeping a close eye on Amira. I don't have a vast amount of trust for the empress at present."

Tindle eyed him but said nothing. He knew quite well that Grimm only dealt out information when he was good and ready to do so. Instead, he reclined in a wingback chair and studied the book. In turn, Grimm studied him.

Without raising his gaze from the pages, Tindle exhaled. "If you don't stop staring at me, I will shut this book and kick your pretty arse out."

Grimm snorted and took a seat opposite the fire. He couldn't shake the feeling that something wasn't right with Agatha, or Amira. It was driving him mad. After being told by von Fuchs to leave yet another meeting concerning the attack, he'd been on edge. But just before he left the castle to come to Tindle's, a sickening feeling had dropped in and unfurled within his gut.

"Stop fidgeting, Grimm," Tindle censured, eyes glued to the book. He reached over, scooping up a pair of spectacles, and balanced them on his nose. "I'm certain Princess Agatha is fine. Gaius would never let anything happen to her."

After a few moments of agonising silence, Tindle removed his spectacles, a deep crease drawing his brows together. "Where did you say Agatha found this?"

"I didn't."

A knowing glint sparked in his eye. "There is no way in all the realms she *stumbled* upon this book."

"What is it?"

Tindle ran his fingers along the length of his chin. "It's diffi-cult to make sense of it all, but these are definitely accounts of war."

Grimm sat forward, elbows resting on his knees. "A war between whom?"

"All of Midlerea."

The prince stood, shoving one hand in his pocket and cutting the other through the air as he spoke. "But we haven't been at war of that scope in four centuries. The dates I saw recorded there only went back two."

Tindle nodded. "That's correct. From what I can piece together, this was some kind of underground holy war around the time of the Witch Trials. We never would have known about it. Not even you, prince. It's not something that would have been written down for anyone outside of The Order to read."

Grimm chewed on his lip, pacing. "What do you know about The Order, Tindle?"

The dressmaker huffed through his nose. "What does anyone know about the shadow regime dispersed throughout the realm, masquerading as Hespa's Holy Order and dutiful magi."

Heart pounding at Tindle's bold, mocking response, Grimm stopped pacing and faced his friend, a dangerous question poised on his tongue. "What if the magi still possess magic?"

"Oh, dear boy. For a wise young prince, you are wholly blind if you think magic ever left this realm."

He might as well have slapped him. "You knew magic still existed and just sat on that information?"

Tindle stood. "Grimm, it's not that I *knew*, it's that I've lived long enough to realise much of what we're taught, especially by magi, is a farce protecting their own arses and their own power." He came forward and rested a hand on Grimm's shoulder. "Magic *is* power."

Gods, he'd been a damned fool. He'd been so blind. "Doesn't

this all seem to be tangled together? An underground holy war within the last two centuries—just after the Witch Trials—magic being covered over, a draught controlling the people of this continent…"

The wheels of Tindle's sharp mind were nearly visibly spinning and he nodded, tapping a finger to his cheek. "What did Agatha discover in this text?"

Grimm froze. He trusted Tindle to his core, but it was already too much that Gaius and Eleanor knew Agatha's secrets. He spoke before Tindle could read his face. "It's there, where the marker is. *Afer ma…*something…"

Tindle's mouth fell open. He sat slowly and recited from memory, "*Afer mahn sur, coreg ah lur, olren fahn bre ankhur?*"

Grimm nodded mutely, his pulse quickening.

"*Bind the light, keep it from sight, to come forth in new life,*" Tindle translated.

"What is that?"

Tindle touched a closed fist to his lips and blew out a breath. "It's a mantra. It belonged to the mages of old in ancient Coronocco."

AGATHA

"WE NEED to scan the perimeter to be sure there aren't any more of them."

Gaius nodded his agreement, then silently stalked toward the tree line. Agatha moved to search the opposite direction but caught sight of Eleanor, deathly pale. She let down her magic and Eleanor sagged forward.

"Stay with me. And for the love of the goddess, keep your mouth *shut*. Do as I say without asking questions." A tremor raked over Eleanor's body, but she agreed.

They searched the woods for a long while, jumping at every deer or skittering rabbit in a thicket.

Gaius looked over his shoulder every few breaths. "I think we need to keep moving."

They were all exhausted, but he was right. "I agree. But I think we should bury the bodies first."

Eleanor went a bit green and Gaius looked at his feet.

"Eleanor, I'm going to wrap my magic around you again." Agatha caught Gaius' eye. "Come with me to dig."

Gaius dipped his chin, walking toward the thick of the woods without a word.

Agatha could feel agitation radiating from him, but she addressed Eleanor again. "If anyone approaches, bang on the wall of my magic like it's the last thing you'll do. I'll feel it."

She caught up with Gaius just a few paces from their camp but waited until they were under the cover of the forest to speak. "Are you alright?" She laid a gentle hand on his arm.

"I'm fine." But his too-rapid breaths were clouding the cold air in front of him.

"Gaius…"

He moved away from her and swung his sword into a tree trunk with such force it stuck there. He growled and slumped down onto a rock. "I've trained how to wield a sword and shoot a bow for my entire life." Running a hand over his close-cropped hair, he closed his eyes. "But I've never even truly wounded a man, let alone…"

Agatha knelt beside him and put her hand on his arm again. "Many will tell you that the first is the hardest, and that it gets easier." Tears pricked the back of her eyes. "But the truth is it doesn't. Or it shouldn't." She squeezed his arm. "Gaius, that man could have killed you, or Eleanor. Potentially all three of us. But that truth won't keep your nightmares at bay. This will be a painful road, and I'm here to walk it with you, should you need a friend."

Gaius looked at her then, and his throat bobbed as he swallowed. "Thank you, Agatha."

She offered him a wan smile and stood, brushing off her riding pants. "Now, I'm afraid we have the gruesome task of burying these men in a shallow grave. They might have been pricks trying to kill us, but a life is a life. We can offer them that much."

Gaius nodded and yanked his sword free from the tree.

After depositing the unnamed men in an unmarked grave, they headed out, riding without sleep. By the time they'd caught up to the draught shipment, the sun stood almost directly above them. Gaius went ahead of them, scouting the area to ensure it was the correct travelling party and came back to confirm. When the shipment party stopped for the night, they set up camp.

"You need rest first, Agatha." Gaius threw a bundle of sticks down at his feet.

She shook her head vehemently, tugging on a pair of black leather gloves and donning her hood. "We don't have time for that."

"There's nothing I can do?"

Agatha rolled her eyes at him. "Did you become a warlock whilst we travelled?"

He scowled. "Just—be careful."

Agatha turned wordlessly and slunk through the darkening forest toward her target. She was tired and so very drained, but hope and the distinct feeling of doing something *good* with her magic pushed away her doubts and propelled her forward.

Upon entering their camp, Agatha set her sights on the barrel closest to her. She removed her gloves and rubbed her hands together to stave off the chill before pressing her magic against the darkness beneath the wood and steel.

By the sixth barrel, she was breathless and wobbling. The cloaking magic she'd wrapped around herself was taking too much of her waning energy. Despite how foolish it might be, she needed to drop the protection ward.

It was incredibly dark. If she was light on her feet, she could possibly reach most of the barrels undetected. With a slew of whispered curses, Agatha dropped to the ground behind a cart and let her shield fall. Unprotected but determined, she slunk through the sea of barrels, magic pulsing.

She soon fell into a rhythm, sending tendrils of her magic into each barrel, locating the dark magi and driving it out, then invisibly marking each one as completed. It went far more swiftly than the night on the ship—no altercations—and when the final cart of barrels loomed before her, Agatha almost sagged with relief. She was nearly there.

"Oy!" Someone shouted, and Agatha's heart stopped. "Who goes there?"

She dropped to her knees and threw her wards up, but they flickered. She'd have to choose between altering the last cart of barrels and staying hidden. Footsteps sounded in the leaves to her right, and Agatha squeezed her eyes shut, trying to *think*.

Still hidden, she moved around to the far side of the cart. She could at least get to some of the barrels. Agatha dropped her protection shield and moved as quickly as she could, the guard inching closer. With one barrel left, his boot came into view, and Agatha used the last of her magic to transport herself to their camp.

As soon as her boots hit the ground and Eleanor's panicked face came into view, she fainted, Gaius running to catch her.

Grimm

"Where are the two of you headed in such a rush?" Mila crossed her arms, red-painted lips puckered.

Augustus looked away from her abruptly and Grimm stifled a snort. Young men were often taken with Mila. She was beautiful, but her allure was wrapped up in her mystery. Everyone wanted her, yet no one had been confirmed to have truly had her.

She was such a pain in his arse sometimes, but he had to admit he did not envy her lot in the Afterlife. Mila could materialise to a certain extent—enough to feel fully present—but not in a way that allowed her a chance to truly participate in this life. She was barely a woman when she'd died, so little life behind her, and now she was destined to haunt the castle halls as the untouchable courtier. Grimm suddenly felt dreadful for how little time he'd spent with her since Agatha's arrival. No wonder she hated his wife.

"We're going to market. Would you like to join us?"

To his surprise, Mila smiled prettily. "I'd be delighted. But only briefly. I'm to have dinner with Lord Covington."

Grimm raised a brow at her. Another evening spent making a man want her all the more for lack of having her. Another evening for her to cry her ghostly tears alone once it was over. "Are you certain that's wise, Mila?"

The tops of her cheeks coloured, and she glanced sharply at Augustus before a cavalier façade fell over her. "He buys me pretty things." She shrugged. "Let me retrieve my shawl."

Mila bustled into her room just down the hall. Augustus sidled up to Grimm, speaking out the side of his mouth. "I'm not certain that was the best decision, Highness. How can we spy with her around?"

Grimm waved him off. "Mila knows all about the draught. Besides, she will become distracted by some pointless bauble, and then we'll send her off in the carriage to her dinner. That will give our driver a reason to go back to the castle without us since we need to go the rest of the way on foot."

Augustus frowned. "Also not something I agree with."

Grimm clapped the guard on the back. "I'm glad you speak up now, Augustus."

"Does that mean you'll listen?"

"Not a chance."

It took no time at all for Grimm to be proven correct. Though, he'd not expected an argument about Agatha to ensue before they even left the carriage.

"You're spending an awful lot of time with her." Mila looked sidelong at him, batting her eyelashes like she hadn't just tried to poke a slumbering bear.

Grimm took a measured breath, overlooking how obviously Augustus was attempting to feign ignoring them. "She's my wife."

The carriage pulled to a stop and Mila froze in place, hand on the door. "Is she, though?"

Grimm clenched his jaw. "*Yes*," he hissed through his teeth.

Something akin to pain flashed across her face and Mila threw open the carriage door, storming off in a huff to a clothier. Grimm sighed. At least he and Augustus were left to the task they'd gone to market for in the first place.

"Wait for Mademoiselle Mila, please, Luc," he instructed the driver. "We won't be needing the carriage any longer."

"Ya' sure, Your Highness?"

Grimm smiled at the kind man and climbed out. "Fresh air will do me some good. I have Augustus here to keep me safe." He made doe eyes at the guard and the driver laughed.

"The way I hears it, ya' could best any of the guards, Highness." He winked at Augustus.

"Yes, well"—Grimm leaned in conspiratorially—"not

everyone has to know that." He tapped the top of the carriage with his palm twice and nodded farewell.

They meandered around the market for a time with hoods up, concealing their faces, pretending to peruse. When they came upon a cart of a new delicacy made of spun sugar, Augustus' eyes grew wide and Grimm purchased some for him.

"This is delicious. It just melts right on your tongue."

His mouth was covered in the remnants of his treat, giving him the appearance of an elderly man with a white beard. Out of nowhere, he thrust out an arm so hard that Grimm grunted when he ran into it.

"Just there." Augustus pointed, swiping at his sugar-coated face. "They're all carrying amber vials, coming out of that apothecary."

"That's the one. Shipment was right on time. Let's sneak around back."

Augustus discarded his spun sugar and followed Grimm. To avoid suspicion, they kept a normal pace and Augustus prattled on about Anne casually. Rounding the corner to the back of the stone apothecary, they feigned interest in a shop across the way, Grimm's eyes darting to the three wagons in the alley.

"This is where we get on the wagons?"

"It is, indeed, Augustus."

"I still think this is the worst plan you've had yet."

Grimm's eyes crinkled at the edges. "That's why it'll work. Come on."

When no one was looking, they climbed up into the cart at the back of the line and pulled a thick wool blanket over themselves. They huddled in the hay for only a few moments before voices echoed off the stones. Several men—far too many for a simple elixir delivery—clambered up onto the carts and whipped the horses unnecessarily.

Grimm gritted his teeth. He hated the mistreatment of beasts as much as he hated that of the people. Augustus was stiff next to him and he turned his head, unable to make out much more than his profile underneath the blanket. "Nervous?"

The guard scoffed. "Aren't you?"

"I'm pleased to be handling something myself for once, instead of sending you all out for me," he whispered.

Augustus was quiet for a moment. "You have a lot of power as prince, but you're really more locked up than we are most of the time."

His friend's words hit him square in the gut. Grimm spent the rest of the ride listening to the creak of the axles and crunching of the wheels over gravel, contemplating the truth of what Augustus had said.

A long time later, the cart finally rolled to a stop. The sun was setting, and the sky was heavy with the promise of torrential rain. They waited several moments after the last man dismounted and took the horses into the stable before slipping from under the blanket and taking in their surroundings.

There was a large, haphazardly structured wooden building and a small stable. One lantern lit the entrance to the stable, and there was a dim glow coming from two torches hanging at the front of the larger building. Aside from that, there were no lights, no fires, and no structures as far as the eye could make out in the darkness.

"I'm going in there." Grimm gestured to the building. "Keep watch out here."

"I don't like this..." Augustus fidgeted.

"I've done a lot more sleuthing than you know. I'll be fine."

Grimm crouched and moved on nimble feet up to the building where he pressed himself against the side to listen. Six men had ridden out into the wilderness and four of them had entered the building. The other two were still in the barn. It would take them several minutes to brush the horses down, but they may not do that at all if they didn't have their own sleeping quarters on site.

Grimm slid along the rough side of the building, the smell of oncoming rain pushing him to move more quickly. When he rounded the corner to the far side, the sliver of moon peeking behind the clouds illuminated a small window. He lifted a whispered thanks to the goddess and slunk to peer through it.

Much like the seaside storeroom, the centre of the space was home to a large spinning vat, illuminating everything in a golden glow. It wasn't nearly as large as the one Agatha had contended with, and a surge of hope washed over him. Even if they had to come every fortnight for moons, Agatha could easily tamper with an amount that size. It was a temporary solution, but still a step forward.

Grimm chewed on his lip, sinking down below the window to think. They did need a more permanent solution. And to come up with that, they needed the formula for the elixir. He heard voices and peered back through the window. Several robed figures moved about the warehouse, the window too thick or their voices too low for Grimm to make out their words. Nor could he see any of their faces cast in deep shadows.

Grimm cursed and snuck his way back to where Augustus was frozen in place, hand on the hilt of his sword, scanning the area. It was a wide-open field, far too flat and bare to be anywhere near Merveille. Judging by that and the time they spent in the back of the wagon, Grimm estimated they'd made it halfway to Vorren.

"We're out in the open," Augustus mirrored his thoughts. "I don't like it."

Grimm yanked on his arm, and they crouched behind a horse trough. "I still need to get in the building. Did the men leave the barn?"

Augustus shook his head. "Haven't seen anyone come in or out."

That meant there were at least nine men on site. Seven or more in the main building and two in the barn. "Watch the barn. I have to get in there before this rain begins or I won't be able to hear anything."

Augustus' face soured. "Yes, Your Highness."

Grimm snorted and moved back toward the building.

Just before he reached the side with the window, he bent down to grab a large stick and slammed it against the side of the building. He darted around, hunched down, and waited. The voices inside were raised with alarm, and he knew they must be looking out into the darkness to discern where the sound had come from. He counted three breaths and rose to peer in, exhaling with relief when seven cloaked figures rushed out the door. Clearly they weren't trained soldiers to all leave their post at once.

Grimm tested the window, finding it was unlocked. In just a few moments, they would all be upon him. He thrust the window open and deftly slipped inside, sliding it down and closing the latch. There was a great possibility there was still a guard posted and he could be found at any moment. Grimm searched for a place to hide, but there were none.

The inside of the building was wide open and empty of any barrels or cases of the draught. All that remained was the vat of elixir in the centre. Off to one side was a small room with the door closed. A supply closet most likely, or…

Grimm sprinted across the space, unsheathing his dagger. The door was locked, and he had no way of knowing what awaited him on the other side, but he kicked it in anyway. There was no time for the doubts peppering his mind.

The door crashed in to reveal a small office. Vials stood in holders along one wall and alchemical jars and tubes littered another shelf. On the desk sat an orderly journal, pages filled with notes Grimm would need Gaius to sort out. He was considering taking the entire thing when a parchment nailed to the wall caught his eye. It was a list of specific measurements of some items he knew and many he did not. Temperatures and instructions were also scrawled in numerical order. *The formula.*

Just as the front door of the building slammed open, Grimm ripped it down and shoved it into his pocket. He closed the office door and threw the lock. Frantically, he turned every which way, stomach sinking when he realised he was trapped. Prepared to fight his way out, but not overly fond of his odds against seven or more men, he desperately scanned the room again. There, partially hidden behind a shelf, was a narrow alcove. Situated in it...

"Goddess bless me, I might just return to the Church for this."

Grimm shoved the shelf aside, cursing when a beaker crashed to the floor, glass shards scattering. He threw open the child-sized window, struggling with all his might to squeeze through it. His shirt ripped and he felt his skin tear with it on a loose nail. Stifling a reaction, he pushed and pulled, just slipping through—a gash on his abdomen to show for it. He hit the soft earth with a thud and heard the door to the room he'd just fled crash open.

At the same moment, a flash of lightning and clap of thunder shook the sky. Grimm rolled away, backing up against the opposite side of the warehouse when the skies opened and the awaited downpour began her torrential weeping. Another blessing from the goddess.

Grimm made it to Augustus, nearly slipping in his haste. The guard had his sword out, wide-eyed and frantic.

"Damn you, Grimm!"

"We don't have time for that. *Run.*"

When they'd run for what felt like ages with no sign of pursuit, they slid to a stop in a copse of trees. Heaving, and covered in mud from crown to heel, Grimm pointed up a steep, mud-slick hill. "There's an inn just up the way there." They were soaked to the bone and the trek back to the castle would still be long. "We'll get a bowl of stew and wait out the rain."

The heat from the tavern was such an instant balm that Grimm almost groaned. Hoods pulled low, they took the first table available near the fire and hoped they wouldn't draw any unwanted attention.

"Caught out in the rain were ya', lads?" A woman stood next to their table, hand on her hip as she examined them with keen eyes.

"Aye." Grimm didn't miss a beat. "Have you any stew left?"

"There's a dribble at the bo'om o' the cauldron, I wager."

Grimm kept his chin down but faced the woman, hidden in the shadows of his wet cloak. "You've a room?"

"Aye. Go' a couple left. Fancy an ale?"

"Two, please."

The buxom woman banged her palm on the table and bustled away. Augustus began to say something in a hushed tone, but Grimm held up a finger. There was a familiar voice coming from the table behind him, followed by another with a thick Lyronian accent.

"Who is that behind me?"

Augustus' eyes darted past Grimm's shoulder and landed back down on the table, still wide. "Highn—"

"Not here," Grimm cut him off sharply. "No names, either."

"Right." He cleared his throat. "It's the magus."

Grimm froze. "Who is he speaking with?"

"A—a man in a cloak. I can't see his face."

The prince fixed every iota of his attention on the murmured conversation behind him, but only caught a few fragments.

Attack...suspect...Rashidi...clear.

"*Dammit.*"

"Everything alright lads?" The serving woman set down two meager bowls of stew and two dark ales.

"Fine, madame," Augustus answered for them both. She shrugged and walked away without another word.

"Would you walk past their table and spill your ale?" Augustus blanched at Grimm's suggestion. "I need to see who that man is."

The guard groaned, but stood and casually went to the bar top, then over to a group of men playing cards. He said something and they all laughed heartily. Augustus clapped one of them on the back and made his way across the room as if headed to the lavatory. As tasked, he tripped just before the magus' table and sent his ale flying, splattering on the cloaked man.

Grimm turned to see the commotion with the rest of the inn's patrons. The stranger's hood fell back. He was unfamiliar, but clearly Lyronian with his olive skin and thick beard. He stood abruptly, gesturing to what Grimm realised were robes, not a cloak. A sleeve fell back to reveal a peculiar marking on his skin —the numeral eight, flat and lying on its side. Grimm knew he'd seen it before but couldn't place it. Augustus' profuse apologising provided the perfect segue for the man to curtly bid the magus farewell and rush for a room up the stairs. Augustus successfully shielded himself from the magus and took the opportunity to flee to the lavatory.

Grimm rose slowly, heading in the opposite direction toward the door. He hovered near it until the magus—astonishingly dressed in plain clothes—muttered something to himself and bolted toward the staircase. Grimm pushed his hood back from his face and strode in the same direction, acting as if he'd just arrived. He looked over his shoulder to feign saying something to the barkeep and barreled into the magus.

Von Fuchs hissed and Grimm let his hood fall away entirely. The shock that darted across the magus' face had an intriguing edge to it before he smoothed it over with his usual sneer.

"I almost didn't recognise you in plain clothes, von Fuchs."

"Haven't you strayed a bit far from the castle, *Your Highness*?"

Grimm smiled placidly. "I wasn't aware I had limitations in my own lands. Haven't you selected an interesting place for a Grand Magus to haunt?"

Von Fuchs grinned as if dealing with nothing more than a petulant child. "I don't believe I'm the one doing any *haunting*, my boy." He pushed past Grimm, bumping him in the shoulder. "But even a Grand Magus needs a night away on occasion." He shifted up onto the first step, his gaze flicking over Grimm to the full room behind him. "Tread lightly, dear prince."

The draught's formula weighed heavily in his pocket as the magus meandered up the stairs, and the sight of the mysterious marking on the robed Lyronian's arm burned in his skull. The entire endeavour should have felt like the massive stride forward that it was, but Grimm couldn't help feeling that something was amiss.

CHAPTER
TWENTY-FIVE

I cannot shake the notion that all my lives coalesce.
      -Journal of Thackery Peridot III

AGATHA

THEY'D DONE IT. They'd caught up with the shipment in only a few days and had reached every single barrel, save for one. Though that one barrel niggled at the back of her consciousness, Agatha felt nearly euphoric.

Judging by glimpses of Eleanor's rare smiles, and the jaunty hop in Gaius' step, her travelling companions were feeling the same. They were only a day's ride from Merveille when Eleanor and Gaius were occupied in conversation and Agatha vanished into her thoughts. There was so much left to sort out. The attack on the castle, Merveille's draught stores, the magus' involvement, The Order's strange pursuit of Grimm, and how Empress Amira fit into the entirety of it all. But when Gaius and Eleanor's

341

eyes grew heavy and they retired to their bedrolls, Agatha left what little magic she could to protect them and prayed to Hespa that they'd be safe. Then, she slipped into the night.

Grimm

GRIMM AWOKE WITH A START, a hand on his shoulder. He reared back from the desk he'd fallen asleep on in the lighthouse and fumbled for his dagger. A familiar form materialised next to him and he sagged with relief, the knife clattering to the floor as he stood.

"You're back." He rushed around the desk to her.

"It's only been a few days, reaper," she teased.

"Don't care," he murmured and brushed his lips against hers, pulling her body toward him with the force of all his restlessness. Agatha returned his kiss with an urgency Grimm didn't fully comprehend. Though, with her lips on his and the feel of her in his hands, he didn't care if she came bearing good or horrible news. He didn't care about the magus and his draught. He didn't care who attacked the castle or who hunted him.

She untangled herself from him, just as breathless as he was, and grinned mischievously. Grimm raised an eyebrow at her and she held a finger to her lips, taking his hand.

He blinked, a peculiar rush of air washing over him like waves, and his eyes opened to total darkness. Suddenly, thousands of dim, flickering lights lit in unison. They danced against the shadows of Agatha's face, her lips turned up in the most astounding smile—unlike any he'd seen from her.

"Is this your home?"

It was a ridiculous question. He was standing in a lush meadow of gravestones, somehow a good five shades darker than the rest of the meadows in existence and littered with *pumpkins*. The vibrancy of the leaves was equally more vibrant and more diminished than any copse of Autumn trees he'd ever seen. At the edge of a shadowed path lit with faerie light sat a solid black cottage befitting none other than Agatha.

She didn't answer. She only led him down the path.

When they reached the portico, Grimm halted her. Damn his logic and duty. "Before we enter, I need to know how it went."

Agatha took a deep breath, and Grimm stiffened. "We got to all but one barrel. We found two men following us, too well-dressed to be simple thieves."

His hand formed a fist at his side. "You escaped them? Is everyone alright?"

Agatha looked down and he lifted her chin gently. He searched her face for answers, worry etched in his brow. When she still didn't answer, he stroked his thumb across her cheek.

"I killed one, and Gaius killed the other."

Grimm's hand stilled. His friend had never so much as harmed a fly. "Is he alright?"

"He will be." She offered him a sad smile. "It's best if we get back to them soon."

Grimm's eyes narrowed. "You're not back in Merveille?"

"We're still a day's ride from the city," she confessed. "I just needed to see you. Just for a moment."

It was reckless, but he couldn't bring himself to deny her. "Are they safe?"

She nodded and he bent down to brush his lips against hers again. The draught shipment was dealt with and plans to stop Merveille's supplies were underway. They could finally take a moment—even if only a brief one.

Something fuzzy flew at Grimm's face and he darted back.

"Mabon. Behave yourself," Agatha chastised. The tiny

assailant settled himself on Grimm's shoulder and licked his ear. "Little traitor," she mumbled.

Grimm gave Mabon a generous scratch behind his ears. "Well,"—he gestured toward the door, ignoring the knot of worry at the back of his mind—"what are we waiting for?"

Agatha took out an obnoxious ring of old skeleton keys that she'd not had moments ago and set to unlocking the front door, the keys clanking together noisily. Grimm—quite aware of what Agatha was capable of—knew she did not need *keys* to open a door. He suspected she summoned them just to have the satisfaction of using them.

When they stepped inside, Agatha sent flames frolicking onto the wicks of countless taper candles. Some hung from the ceiling, others lined the walls and disappeared up a set of stairs. Even more lined window sills, dotted full bookshelves—some even floated mid-air. Mabon left Grimm's shoulder and hung upside down from a rafter, squawking at Agatha. She flicked her finger and an apple floated—suddenly peeled—beneath him. Mabon set to licking the fruit, and Grimm marvelled at Agatha's life. Her *real* life.

He wasn't quite prepared for the depth of heavy guilt that came to land on his shoulder where Mabon had left it. This place was so utterly *Agatha*. And he had taken her from it. She would argue it was Hespa, a prophecy, a Grimoire, or all three. She would never blame him. But he still blamed himself, and this cottage was a testament to the truth in the blame. Agatha deserved *this* life—the one that had set the contented smile she wore upon her lips. He watched her run a finger along the spines of her books and wipe the dust off a shelf lined with potion bottles and spices.

He should have fought harder for her to escape.

Suddenly feeling impossibly weary, Grimm sank into a worn chair—obscenely comfortable for how dreadful it looked—and watched the little witch murmur a few words as she stirred something in a cauldron over the fireplace.

"Eye of newt?" he teased.

Her playful smile made his heart ache even more. She was herself in her cottage. He'd seen glimpses as if looking behind a curtain, but nothing like this. He'd fallen for her through those glimpses. The ones that appeared when she was angry, or teasing him, or defying his mother with some macabre fashion choice. She turned to him with a goblet of mulled wine and he thought he'd burst. No—what he thought he'd felt for her did not hold a candle to *this*. He was irrevocably, desperately in love with her.

The realisation settled into his bones, filling him with restlessness. Something about it struck him as familiar, but he'd never once felt like this about anyone. Not in this lifetime, anyway. He stood and strode to a row of books, itching to touch them; to open each one and read its contents.

"Any History?" He smirked at her, and she plucked one off the shelf for him. Grimm set his goblet on the mantel and flipped through the yellowed pages. "*The History of Magic*." He raised an impressed eyebrow at her. "I'm taking this one with me."

Agatha snickered. "I'll put a spell on it so you don't get *caught* with it, then."

"Much obliged." He tucked it under his arm and picked another volume at random. It was a novel of some sort about ships. When he opened it, his pulse stuttered at the name scrawled at the bottom of the title page: *Ira Laughlin*. He'd asked about him on their wedding night, and though he'd not expected at the time to fall in love with Agatha, he still wanted to hear of him—of what she had lost.

"Will you tell me about him?" Grimm's voice was raw and he hoped she wouldn't notice.

"Who?" Her beautiful face scrunched up in confusion.

"Ira."

She paled, looking every inch like she'd just seen a ghoul. "That isn't a pleasant story."

Grimm set the books on a side table and approached her, taking her hands. "I'd still like to know. I want to know all parts of you, Agatha."

When her eyes climbed up to meet his, they were heavy with moisture. "Are you certain? I have a monstrous life inside of me."

Grimm swiped his thumb across her cheek just as a tear fell to meet it. "I'm absolutely certain."

"How did you know his name?"

"You used to have nightmares. Every night you thrashed and cried out. Sometimes I would take your blankets off and open the window, just to see if cooling you off would help, but it never did. I began bringing in extra blankets in hopes that would calm you. It never worked, either. Eventually, you stopped having the nightmares." Grimm shrugged. "But every time you did, you always said one name. Ira. It didn't really take a lot of thought to realise he was the one you briefly spoke of on our wedding night."

Agatha nodded. "Before I tell you what happened to him, I need you to know why I no longer have nightmares." She placed her palm on his cheek and another tear slid down the side of her face. It took every ounce of strength he possessed not to do something, *anything,* to take away her sadness. "You chased them away, Grimm. After a hundred years of nightmares, *you* chased them away."

Grimm swallowed hard, his heart cracking. He swiped at her tears, letting her cry. When she finally took a deep, shuddering breath, he kissed her gently. "Tell me what happened, love."

"I met Ira in Merveille. I'd just completed a horrible Order from the Grimoire and then reversed it the next Autumn." She shook her head. "I needed to be away from the Forest of Tombs, where my actions only haunted me. I needed to be somewhere I couldn't lose myself in all that I'd done. Sorscha had spoken so highly of Merveille's coast and wine. I hadn't been in ages, and decided since the royal library had always been a dream of mine to visit, that I would go. Clear my mind in the city."

Agatha twirled her hair around and set it over her shoulder. He knew that nervous habit like the back of his hand and intertwined her fingers with his.

"Ira was from Coronocco. I met him while he was working at the docks that Winter. I was reading on a rock by the coast, and he came to say I was the only person he'd ever seen willingly sit out in the cold to read."

That certainly sounded like Agatha.

"We were fast friends, talking of books. Ira wanted to be a writer. Eventually, we became lovers. It was a tedious thing because some people were still against the interrelations of those so different, as we were. You see me." She gestured to herself, pale and lovely. "Ira was the night." A wistful smile lit her face. "He used to call me his moon."

She looked away. "King Caliban ruled at the time. He was a *good*, honest man. He worked tirelessly to rid Merveille and all of Seagovia of such vile views of humanity—that there could ever be a difference in a human's worth because of their skin, or origin, or preferences, or social status." Agatha spat the words and Grimm could not have agreed more. "But…" She trailed off and stood, backing away from him. "But the Grimoire. I was Ordered—" Her voice broke, hardly even a whisper, and she closed her eyes. "I killed King Caliban." She brought her hand to her mouth like she'd never said the words out loud before.

A violent memory slammed into Grimm and he reached up to touch his temple. A beautiful woman all dressed in black. The begging last words of a good man. The remorse of a killer. A slice. Blood hitting wood and leather. And a soul slamming into him. "I—I think I was there…"

Agatha nodded, tears streaming down her face. "I think that

you were. That's where I'd heard the song before, the one you played on the piano. The one I heard the night of the Eve of Hallows ball."

It made sickening sense. Grimm knew all about the History of Seagovia. Caliban's death was shrouded in mystery—his tyrannical cousin that assumed the throne, and the horrors that followed. In truth, if it weren't for the death of Caliban, Grimm would not be in line for the throne himself. "What happened to Ira? To you?" His heart was hammering against his ribs. He remembered it—a story. One that had caused him to vomit when he'd found it by accident in a History book as a boy. A book he was not supposed to have. It had belonged to Professor Ludwig, and he'd stolen it. It couldn't have been his Agatha, not the woman in that terrifying story. *Goddess,* tell him it hadn't been her.

"We were tied by our feet to the legs of a warhorse."

No...*no.*

"The king commanded that the horse be whipped relentlessly, dragging us through the streets and past the gates of Merveille until my back was ripped to the spine and—" Her words choked off, and Grimm launched himself at her, wrapping her in his arms, her ear pressed against his chest. "I had to watch him, Grimm. I had to watch, screaming, as his skin was ripped from his bones. Even as his skull shone through the gore, he never let go of my hand. Until the moment he lost consciousness he kept telling me it was okay—that I was going to be okay."

Agatha buried her face in Grimm's chest and he fought a phantom pain pulsing at the back of his head, his back, thinking of what Agatha and Ira had suffered.

"I thought he was dead," she whispered against him before pulling back. "How could any mortal survive that? When they came to untie us, I pretended I was dead until they weren't looking, and I transported myself here." She pushed away from Grimm and sat hard in a chair. "He wasn't dead. I could have helped him. He died from his injuries later that night." She put her head in her hands and sobbed. "Why didn't I protect him?"

She looked up at Grimm with more sorrow than he could stand. Kneeling before her, he held her in his arms as she wept.

When she slowly began to calm, Grimm rammed steel into his nerves and stood. "I want to show you who I really am."

"I know who you really are, Grimm. I won't flinch away from you in your true form or any other."

Gods, the sincerity in her eyes. He had to do it before he lost his nerve. "Are you certain?"

"More certain than I have ever been about anything in my three hundred years, reaper."

Grimm swallowed hard. *"Thanasim."*

Agatha's mouth fell open. She stood slowly, her eyes never leaving him as she approached. At first, he thought it was horror written across her face, but he realised with knee-trembling relief that it was awe.

She raised a hand to his chest, her fingers grazing the exposed bone—ribs bursting out of his decrepit skin. Agatha ran a finger down the length of his arm, sinew and muscle shrouded in billowing black smoke. His darkness reached out to caress her and she leaned into it, letting it envelope her. When she reached his skeletal hand, she lifted it to her cheek, his bony fingers curling around the nape of her neck to rest precisely where he held her when their lips met. She took his other hand and wrapped it around her, setting it to rest on the small of her back.

Agatha reached up, standing on the tips of her toes, and took his hood in her fingers. He knew she could physically see every beat of his decaying heart right in front of her. Still, she slowly removed his hood and explored the bones of his face.

"Prince of Bone," she whispered in wonder. Her gaze roved over his grotesque skeleton, bones cleaved apart by shadows, and settled on his eyes. Agatha took her hand and placed it on his ribs, just over his heart. "This is who I am inside, too."

"You are not a monster, Agatha."

"And neither are you, *Thanasim*."

Grimm shuddered, shifting back into his body in an instant, and he crushed her mouth with his. It was wild and desperate, filled with the pain of the horrors they'd faced apart and the incomprehensible relief of being seen. Before he even realised what he was doing, Grimm had her by the waist, hauling her onto him. Agatha threw flickers of flame into candles as he climbed the stairs with her in his arms, never breaking from their ravenous kiss.

He found her room without guidance—another mystery he hadn't the mental fortitude to traverse. Not with her breath against his ear as his lips roamed her neck, her legs wrapped around his waist. Grimm laid her gently on the bed and pulled back. "Are you certain?"

"Whatever you're made of, I am too," she breathed against his lips and kissed him softly. "I'm *immensely* certain, reaper."

AGATHA

GRIMM TASTED OF IMMEASURABLE *GOODNESS*. The feel of his lips felt more like coming home than the moment she'd walked through her own front door.

But then he moved those lips, that tongue, to her collarbone, her earlobe, her neck, and all senses faded. Her mind was a muddle of want, need, and *more*. His hands roved over the bodice of her dress, and he growled as she arched her back, sending her heaving chest into his lips. He kissed lower until his mouth was grazing the tops of her breasts and she needed to feel him against her. Anything that barred him from her needed to vanish—namely her dress.

Agatha ran her fingers through his hair, her breaths coming in quick bursts as his hands found her backside through her skirts, his chest rumbling with pleasure. *Goddess*, if he didn't touch her skin she was going to combust. His lips found hers again and she scrabbled at the buttons of his shirt. Her hands were useless and he chuckled, the sound landing deliciously low in her belly as he pulled back to undo them himself. When the last button came undone, Agatha reached up to gingerly touch his olive skin. The smooth plane of his abdomen and the trailing line of dark hair just below the muscle dip at his hips felt divine beneath her fingertips, and her body reacted in kind.

Grimm slowly lifted her up to her knees and untied the laces of her dress. Agatha held the front in place until she turned to face him, overjoyed that she'd elected to leave her corsets behind in Merveille. She dropped her hands and let the dark fabric fall away, sliding down her breasts. Grimm's breath shuddered and he pressed his mouth to hers once more, snaking an arm around her waist and gently laying her down. His hand found the curve of her breast and Agatha gasped. He moved his tongue to her neck and carved a tantalising line down to her hip, sliding her dress and underthings ever lower as he did so.

She pulled at his belt until he unclasped it and slipped out of his pants. He lay down beside her, his calloused hand exploring her hips, her firm nipples, and he kissed her deeply. When his fingers slid up her skirts to the honeyed, silken warmth between her legs, he sucked in a breath and Agatha moaned, reaching for him. She needed to feel him closer, within her. Her hand stroked the hard length of him and Grimm cursed, his breath hot against the tender skin of her neck, his strong fingers digging into her backside. He nipped at her ear, his unsteady breathing as she ran her thumb over him making her ache. He pulled her closer, her body flush with his.

"Mm, little witch," he murmured against her lips, his fingers between her thighs and her hands gripping his muscled back. She couldn't take it any longer.

There was the tearing of fabric as her skirts landed in a heap on the floor next to the bed. For a moment, he pulled back to drink her in. The hunger and adoration in his eyes left her both blissful and deeply in need. He recognised her desire the moment she shifted her hips, desperate, and he gave her the smirk he reserved only for her. In one fluid movement, he had her legs spread and his tongue found her wetness. Her back arched and he slid his hands up to her hips, holding her in place to better taste her.

"*Please*," she breathed, her nails digging into his shoulders, and Grimm's remaining self-control evaporated. Moving to let himself rest right where he knew she needed friction, he teased her for a moment until she nearly begged. With a wicked kiss, he slipped into her, and the world erupted into sparks. It was unlike anything Agatha had ever experienced, even in her three hundred years. It was as if Grimm's very soul was inside hers, intertwining until they were indistinguishable.

When it was over—twice—they laid in the tangled sheets, blissful beyond compare. Grimm ran an idle finger up and down Agatha's arm, and her head rested on his chest—the perfect fit.

"How did you know which souls to collect, and which to not at the Eve of Hallows ball?" she whispered, simply wanting to hear his voice.

"I had to rely on touch." His voice was scratchy in the intimate way of lovers in the dark, and Agatha feared she would need to feel him within her again very soon. "In instances so devastating, names often don't appear in the Book of the Dead until the event is occurring. Even if I'd been looking at the Book, it might not have given me any time. I had to touch each person —feel their essence—to know if it was their time or not."

Agatha considered his words, tracing a circle on his stomach. "I suppose it wasn't my time, then."

Grimm's chest rumbled under her ear. "I don't know, actually. I saved you for last because it didn't matter if it was your time or not. There was no way in Hades I was going to collect you."

Agatha sat up on her elbow to look into his eyes. "You were going to defy the Book? Lady Death?"

Grimm nodded once. "For you, yes."

Agatha resumed her position on his chest and considered the kind of courage and love it took to do something like that.

"This is going to sound strange..." Grimm broke into her thoughts. "But I can sense you, within."

Agatha shot up to sitting. "You feel that, too?" She thought it was some delusion after subconsciously wanting him so badly for moons and finally tasting him. An intensity after being alone for so long.

Grimm gave her a wild, bewildered smile. "Is this a witch thing?"

Agatha laughed outright. "No! I thought I was going mad. It's as if we're..."

"Entangled," he said at the same instant she said, "Intertwined."

Grimm nodded, dumbfounded. "That's exactly it. I can *feel* you—your essence, in mine."

They regarded each other for a heartbeat longer before Grimm became distracted by the sheet slipping to reveal her breast. It was a long time later, and only due to parched thirst, that they rose from the bed and padded downstairs.

Grimm

HE COULDN'T STOP STARING at her. The freckles dusting her cheeks that he'd so pleasantly found dotting her stomach as well. The ample curves of her backside and her breasts unbound and outlined in her thin nightgown, taunting him as she prepared something for them to eat. He could still feel those soft curves. Still taste her, every inch. Still hear her breathe his name. The feel of her teeth snagging on his bottom lip, her nails dragging down his back, his hands on her hips, pulling her closer—

Grimm shook his thoughts loose before he took her right there on the kitchen table. They needed to make sure Eleanor and Gaius were safe and get back to Merveille right away. It struck him then that they could repeat that evening over and over if they wanted to. She was his wife.

"Coin for your thoughts, husband?" Her lips tipped up in a coy smile he could *feel* reflected inside him.

That inexplicable entanglement. It was odd, but it felt so right. Like a missing piece finally set in place. *Gods*, he would rip the world apart for her. Until the end of time.

"I'm only marvelling at the fact that you are my wife, little witch."

"Mm." She dried her hands with a linen and perched on his lap, wrapping her arms around his neck. "I am that, reaper."

He kissed her until she pulled back, sniffing the air and cursing. He chuckled as she launched off of him and toward her burning pastries. Grimm strolled over to the bookshelf again, inspecting some of the other trinkets she had along the shelves. When he saw a locket that appeared as old as time itself, he picked it up and his breath caught.

"Agatha, what is this?"

She looked over her shoulder at his hand. "Oh, that's a locket that belonged to my mother. The only thing I have of hers, other than my armlet."

He brought it over to her in the kitchen. "This detailing on the top, it's identical to the sketch I found on the parchment in Pierre's pocket. The man falsely in the Book of the Dead."

Agatha recoiled. "I'm not sure what connection could be there…"

Grimm's mind took a turn, contemplating the locket, the parchment, and The Order. The web grew more complex by the moment.

Agatha laid the rescued pastries on the table and beckoned for him to come and sit again. She took a seat herself, resting her bare feet on Grimm's lap as they nibbled. There wasn't time for a moment like this. Not when Gaius and Eleanor were in the woods alone with possible pursuers. Not when things were growing only more complicated, but… He looked at Agatha, so at ease in her home; alive in such a simple, peaceful moment. It was so gods damned *normal*. He couldn't bear to take it from her.

"What have you seen coming at the end of all your scheming and faction-raising, hm?" she asked around a bite.

Another secret he would lay at her feet. "Overthrowing the monarchy."

Agatha choked. "You plan to *what*?" She withdrew her feet from his lap and leaned over the table. "I thought you didn't want to be king."

Grimm's eyes danced with mirth. "I didn't say overthrow the king and queen. I said overthrow the *monarchy*, which includes me. And you."

Her face blanched, but something akin to an impressed thrill fluttered through their new entanglement toward him. "And you mean to leave Seagovia in the hands of…whom?"

"The people." He let his response hang in the air between them. "Seagovia does not need a kind ruler. She does not need a strong ruler. What she needs is the chance to govern *herself*. To make her own choices. The *people* deserve to lead Seagovia."

Agatha's mouth opened, and she might have begun to say something, but Grimm spun in his chair, attention drawn sharply to the middle of the room where, a heartbeat later, Mila materialised with panic flaring in her eyes.

"I'm so sorry," Mila gasped and Grimm launched toward her. She held out the Book of the Dead, hand trembling. "It—it's Dulci."

Grimm locked eyes briefly with Agatha and flipped the Book open. A name stared back at him, and his heart lodged in his throat.

DULCIBELLA AMIN.

A tremor coursed through him, making his hands shake. From horror or fear, he couldn't determine. Breathing was becoming difficult and he couldn't think.

DULCIBELLA AMIN.

Her name went in and out of focus the further the news sank into him. Dulci had one day before Grimm was to collect her soul. It took all his strength not to double over. It screamed of malfeasance. His head swam with fury and his vision with it, everything coated in red and blurred at the edges.

"What do you know, Mila?" he asked through clenched teeth, blinking rapidly.

The wraith shook her head. "Nothing. Things have been calm since you left. Dulci and Amira have been holed up in the castle. She's been playing the empress' distant cousin as you set in place. Nothing has appeared amiss."

"I moved them back to Dulci's," he breathed, running a hand over his beard, shock coursing through him. "Mila, find out anything you can. Get into every room you can think of and *listen*."

She nodded once and evaporated.

Grimm turned to Agatha. "We have to get back to Gaius and Eleanor."

Agatha snapped her fingers and every fire and candle flame went dark. She whispered and they were both dressed in old riding clothes. Taking his hand, she transported them back to the woods.

When their feet hit the dirt, Grimm saw Gaius pacing and he stepped out from behind the tree line. The moment Gaius saw them, he launched himself at Agatha. "Do you have *any* idea how worried we've been? Where in the seven realms have you *been*?"

Grimm stepped between them, but Agatha spoke calmly. "I'm sorry Gaius, I've been away. But we have to go. Now."

Gaius' jaw unclenched at the fear he registered in Grimm's eyes and he deflated. "What's happened?" he asked, looking between them.

Grimm held up the Book of the Dead. "It's Dulci."

Gaius swore. "When?"

"A day." Gaius' brow furrowed and Grimm's mind continued to spin. The Book had never given him a soul with a day left. At best it was hours. Usually, it was mere moments. Something wasn't adding up.

Agatha stepped closer and gently put her hand on his arm. Eleanor was approaching and Grimm knew they needed to *go*, to get back to Merveille, but he felt as if he were moving through mud, unadulterated wrath filling him to the point of overflowing.

"What are you thinking?" she whispered, leading him away as Gaius intercepted Eleanor.

Grimm ran a hand down the length of his tired face. He could feel Agatha, with that strange entanglement—her concern, her fear, and something else that felt like defiance. It fueled the spark that was growing inside of him.

A *whoosh* shot by his ear and Agatha gasped. A leather tome from another age landed in her hands, humming and glowing. Her fingers trembled as she lifted a page marker and opened it.

"Is that the—"

"Grimoire," she whispered.

AGATHA

THE REST of her Order had finally come.

Her lungs felt as devoid of life as an exhumed tomb. Logically, she knew her chest must be heaving, but she was suffocating. Grimm looked at her with fear in his eyes, saying something, but her ears were only ringing with a piercing sound drowned in water.

She couldn't do this. She wouldn't.

But Sorscha. She'd lose Sorscha if she refused.

Agatha sank to sit on the ground, the Grimoire falling into the leaves.

Grimm knelt beside her and gingerly picked up the Book, seeing only blank pages. "*Agatha*, what does it say?" he pressed, as if he'd already said it many times.

Her voice stuck in her throat like she'd swallowed sand. "I— I'm to poison anyone who refuses the draught."

Grimm's lips parted but it seemed words had failed him. She rose on trembling legs, and he followed.

"Aren't you *tired* of this, Grimm?" Her lip wobbled and she splayed a hand out toward the forest—the world—around them. "Aren't you tired of doing the bidding of gods and man?" Her chest heaved, fury building. It wasn't until Grimm spoke that she realised it wasn't hers alone.

"*Of course I am.*" Anger flowed from them both like a torrent. "You know better than anyone how true that is. How damn weary I am. But this—" He closed the Grimoire, holding it up. "How do we fix this?"

She took his face in her hands, their breath mingling as she looked up at him. She could still sense his insurgence, but his dread was louder. Agatha knew it was her terror that lit her own face. "Grimm, I think this is it. The prophecy." He'd never believed in that blasted thing, but it all made sense to her now. "The two of us, coming together to change the course of all things."

Grimm backed away, scrubbing at his eyes. "You're suggesting we fight this? These demands made of us?"

Agatha seethed. "People we care about are going to die!" Her voice echoed through the trees, birds flying out in a rush.

But Sorscha. A sob tore from her throat, followed by hot tears that slid down her cheeks. Grimm shot forward and rubbed his hands up and down her arms.

"If I defy my Orders, I lose Sorscha forever." A gash opened in her heart, bloody and seeping poison. But Agatha knew what she had to do.

Grimm must have felt every ounce of her tumult of emotion, because he swallowed hard and ran his thumb across her cheek, collecting tears. "Which path do you want to take?"

The tether between them was chaotic and hard to decipher, but one thing was very clear. She could *feel* that Grimm was prepared to fight the demands made of them, yet he stood there silently waiting. He was leaving the decision of what *she* would do up to her alone.

"Neither." Agatha squared her shoulders. "I say we follow neither path. We follow *ourselves*. We follow *us*. Surely there is a place outside of rightdoing and wrongdoing. A place of peace and not of Orders, duties, and punishments dictated so severely by men playing at being gods. What if Lady Death and Hespa *are* who we know them to be, not what this damned Book and The Order have made them out to be?"

Grimm's jaw flexed, eyes blazing with the heat of the inferno between them. "We do what we feel is right with what we've been given, to the best of our ability."

Agatha' gusto ran out and her shoulders slumped. "The problem is that what we've been given has been dealt at the hands of *them*—Hespa and Lady Death."

Grimm growled. "*Fuck.* Then let them take it back!"

Her chin lifted as she let his defiance bolster hers. "We will do what we can until they pry it from our cold, dead bodies."

TWENTY-SIX

F rom my earliest memory, I recall a gaping void. Not one
that always was, but one of something ripped from me
before I was yet born.
　-Journal of Agatha Joubert

AGATHA

THEY RODE IN UTTER SILENCE. Despite the growing distance
between them, Grimm's urgency intermingled with her own
unease as he travelled ahead. Agatha thought she'd scream at
any moment.

"What are the two of you not telling me?" Eleanor
complained from behind Agatha. "Why did Grimm ride ahead of
us? Why do you both look as if you've seen a ghost?"

She'd surrendered Nuit back to Grimm. Agatha was content
to let her walk, but Gaius insisted she ride Guinevere with her. If
she didn't send a sharp elbow into the maid's stomach, it would

be a ridiculous miracle The Order could have their congregations misguidedly worship for ages to come.

No one answered Eleanor and she huffed. "I did not come on this journey just to learn about mushrooms and lay out bedrolls."

Agatha's brittle control snapped. "We don't have time for your petty grievances, Eleanor!"

Silence descended upon them once more and Agatha focused on the growing bond inside of her: a tangle of emotions, intent, and overall essence. Some things were obvious, like Grimm's fury and urgency. Her trepidation and unease. Other things were muddled.

There was no way he'd make it there in time, not on horseback. She'd warned him as much and offered to transport him, but Grimm refused. He didn't want her involved in the slightest and wasn't strictly able to bend time himself until it was needed for collection. Thus, he rushed far ahead and she rode along at snail pace with Gaius and Eleanor, keeping watch over them. "Can we pick up the pace even a little?"

"No," Gaius ground out. She didn't need a bond with *him* to feel his irritation. "We make camp and prepare."

Grimm

THE WIND WAS icy against his chapped cheeks. It wouldn't be long, perhaps a fortnight, until snow covered the ground, and he hoped to have Dulci settled somewhere safe before that happened.

Nuit raced through the fallen leaves at breakneck speed, but

Grimm knew the beast was growing tired. He would have to let him rest soon.

Agatha was right. He wasn't going to make it there in time, not without killing Nuit. He had already travelled for days with Eleanor. Grimm swore and pulled the horse's reins, letting him walk.

He would have to get as close as he possibly could and tie Nuit in the woods, then use the window of time opened for Dulci's death to get to her. It would be risky, but it was the only way. If he arrived even a breath too late—

Grimm shook those thoughts loose and dismounted to walk next to Nuit. He needed to *move*. Agatha's anxiety swam within him, but he couldn't sort through that peculiar bond at the moment. He needed to remain focused. With a deep breath, he quieted his wife's presence as best he could before mulling over what he knew.

Mila had said Merveille was still calm. He'd only been away a handful of hours. The plan to have Dulci pose as Amira's distant cousin was going well, but he and Tindle had tucked Amira away at Dulci's for the night after the run-in with the magus—just in case. It was possible someone had followed them and gone into Dulci's when he'd left for the lighthouse.

If he got to her in time, some of his questions might be answered. That was, if the killer didn't send a mercenary after her. In Grimm's experience, most planned murders were not dealt by the person who planned them. It was highly probable that whoever sent the men after Agatha was also responsible for Dulci's impending doom. Someone had been watching them and gone completely undetected.

Grimm's frustration grew, Agatha's worry fueling his own. He growled and it swiftly turned into an outright roar. The birds rushed from their nests above him and Nuit looked at him sidelong.

"Apologies, boy." He rubbed the horse between his eyes.

"We need to get moving faster again." Nuit huffed through his nose.

"YOU HAVEN'T SAID anything in a long time, *princess*."

Agatha didn't respond to Gaius or his attempt at humour.

"We'll stop and make camp just over that hill. I recall a cave with a stream not too far off from here. It'll be as good a place as any. The air is getting colder and more rain is coming."

Agatha dipped her chin.

"Agatha. I know you're worried, I am too, but you have to hold it together."

"It's not that. Yes, I'm worried about Grimm and Dulci but —" She glanced behind them to where Eleanor walked in bitter silence, tired of riding with Agatha. Fine by her. "Has Grimm explained the Grimoire to you?"

Gaius nodded. "It's filled with prophecies and words from Hespa, spelled out for you and your Sisters by the First Sisters, yes?"

"You're a quick study, Lord Gaius."

He snorted. "One has to be with Grimm as his friend."

Agatha smirked, overwhelmed by the depth of warmth— pride even—that filled her when she thought of Grimm. She pushed it out at him through their new entanglement, hoping he could feel it and know she was with him. "I think—"

Someone fell out of the air onto Gaius' horse, and the forest erupted in screams.

Grimm

Nuit flew through the trees, sensing Grimm's urgency. If they didn't stop again, he could get the horse close enough, and hidden long enough, for him to return with Dulci. It would take time to get to the city on foot and traverse it without being seen. But if he managed it, Grimm could wait until nightfall and reach Dulci well before the intended attack. He might even have time to position Dubois in place to watch for an assailant.

A force burst within him and bled sweetness into his core. It was Agatha and it felt every inch like her kiss. He closed his eyes, relishing the brief moment, but it was choked out—crushed by a violent jolt. Something was wrong.

"*Merde.*" He pulled Nuit to a grinding halt, looking forward toward Merveille and back to the road behind—toward Agatha.

The woodlands suddenly erupted in darkness around him, clouds of the blackest night billowing in like a roiling fog. Nuit pranced underneath him and he measured his breaths, waiting.

"My Lady?" Grimm's hands began to shake. She must have known he planned to steal Dulci away. To go against the Book. Against Her.

Lady Death's clouds churned, swirling and enveloping his body in thick, inky night. Nuit whinnied and bucked until Grimm fell off, landing hard on the ground with a grunt. He looked up to find Her watching him like a panther. He'd never once seen Her furious. She was utterly terrifying. Lightning lit in the clouds around Her, thunder rumbling the ground beneath him.

Grimm stood, willing his body not to tremble.

"You plan to defy Me."

Grimm's throat went dry. It pained him when he swallowed and he nearly choked. The most he could muster was honesty—a small nod.

Rage met him. Rage unlike anything he'd ever seen. The Goddess of Death was *crackling* with fury as She stalked toward him.

AGATHA

GAIUS JERKED in his saddle while Eleanor screamed bloody murder in the middle of the trail.

"Eleanor, *enough!*" Agatha shouted back at her.

Sorscha giggled. "Wrong horse." She shrugged and wrapped her arms around Gaius' middle.

He bristled but said nothing.

Agatha stared daggers at her Sister Spring. "Goddess' teeth, Sorscha. You could have frightened Eleanor to death."

Sorscha looked at Eleanor's horrified face. "Gods, she's trembling. Pale, too." She let out a low laugh. "*Mortals.*" She rested her cheek on Gaius' back and he grumbled. "I sent a crow, but the damn thing got lost."

Merde. Gaius shook his head, muttering his own curses. Sorscha giggled again, kissing Gaius on the cheek, but he jerked away. She laughed and turned back to Agatha.

They halted in unison, and Agatha promptly hauled her Sister off the horse and into the twilight woodlands.

"What are you doing here, Sorscha?" she asked around the

lump in her throat. She hadn't been prepared for this. She'd planned to visit Sorscha at her treehouse for a proper goodbye.

"Seleste wrote to me that you visited her. She said you told her Belfry's Order ended in Talan's hand and that she informed you hers had changed once, too—begun in Monarch's and ended in Talan's. Seleste said it also happened to Winnie at least once. About fifty years ago, and maybe before. Talan started an Order and Belfry concluded it."

"And you mentioned it's happened to you as well? Hissa began it and Talan finished it?"

Sorscha nodded with her arms crossed, all traces of humour gone. "I think something is very wrong, Sister."

Grimm's anxiety twisted in Agatha's gut, making it hard to think.

"There's something else." Sorscha looked back toward the path. "I didn't think it wise to write it." The wind howled through the trees, warm and cold combining at dangerous speeds. "The boy that was consumed outside my village... I did some more digging." She shifted uncomfortably. "I—well...I *dug up* his grave to be precise. He was eaten in a very specific, ritualistic fashion. By people."

Agatha blanched. "A ritual sacrifice?" Harsh shock filled her low whisper.

"A ritual *consuming*. And there's more, Aggie. He was a young warlock."

"I thought he was training to be a mage?"

"He was."

"But the magi wouldn't accept a warlock—" He must have kept it hidden. The wind howled, the sound almost deafening. Through it, Agatha heard the horses beginning to whinny, spooked. Her beautiful Sister was to be ripped from her at any moment—for good.

Agatha took in Sorscha, fresh tears filling her eyes. Confusion contorted Sister Spring's face and she rushed forward, taking Agatha's hands in hers. "Aggie, what is it?"

Her throat was nearly too thick to speak. "I have to defy my Orders," she choked out.

Sorscha paled. "Aggie…"

Agatha ripped her hands free and backed away, the rising wind sending her hair lashing against her face. Sorscha stood in place, hand still outstretched toward her Sister.

"I have to protect Merveille and her people. The Grimoire has Ordered me to do a terrible thing and I—I can't go through with it. So many innocents will die, and I can't go on like this, slaying and spreading horrors…"

"But, Aggie, your Sanction. You cannot mean to—"

"It's you." Agatha's voice broke off and she sobbed openly. "It's you. You're my Sanction," she shouted through the tears. "Hespa will take you from me forever." Her words were garbled, but she saw them hit Sorscha square in the chest. "I won't even see you on the Solstice or Equinox. Never again."

Sorscha's own eyes glossed over and she stepped forward, gaze locked with Agatha's. "If that is your Sanction, then *enough is enough*, Aggie." She looked away and Sorscha put a hand to her chin, turning her face. "Look at me." Agatha met her Sister's eyes, lip trembling. "If anyone can change this world, it's you. If this is the time to put an end to the horrors, let it be so." Sorscha's tears finally slipped free, running down to drop into the swirling leaves. "You can survive losing me, Aggie. You are strong, and you know—beyond a shadow of a doubt—that I will *never* stop trying to get back to you."

A tree cracked in the wind, drawing their attention upward. A large branch fell, crashing to the ground and sending a plume of leaves spraying. Sorscha ran her hand down Agatha's cheek. "No matter what it takes, Aggie."

Agatha blinked and Sorscha was gone.

Her knees buckled and she hit the dirt, unable to control the sobs that wracked her body. It was a pain unlike any she'd ever faced. Her precious Sister was *gone.*

In her absence, the twilight air calmed—as if formalities and doctrine were right and the heart was wrong. As the breeze returned to cold, the leaves slowly falling to settle on the ground, Agatha cursed it. Cursed Hespa. Cursed the Grimoire. Cursed The Order.

She curled into a ball in the leaves, their beauty mocking her, and wept.

A twig snapped, and Agatha expected to hear Gaius' footsteps as he came to check on her. When she was only met with silence, she opened her eyes to make sense of the twig snapping.

The air left her lungs when she saw a woman standing in the tree line, ethereal and glowing like the moon. She shifted in and out of focus like wind through a fog, revealing three separate forms. One of youth—vibrant and full. One of a mother—glowing cheeks and swollen belly. One of a crone—ancient and wise. All three pairs of eyes, shifting as they were, bore into Agatha's very soul.

"*Who are you?*" Agatha breathed, scrabbling up onto her feet.

"You know,"

"Who we,"

"Are."

Agatha's legs trembled. The Goddess Three. *Hespa* in Her Three Forms stood before her.

"Agatha Peridot,"

"Princess Witch,"

"Daughter of Autumn."

She couldn't breathe. Couldn't move. "You took my Sister, then?" She couldn't stop the tremble in her lip, or her voice.

"Agatha,"

"It wounds Us,"

"That you should,"

"Think such,"

"A thing."

"We,"

"Are,"

"Immensely proud."

"We would never,"

"Take Sister Spring from you."

Agatha's legs gave out and she collapsed in the dirt again, fresh tears streaming down her cheeks.

"Sister Autumn,"

"You know,"

"Us."

"Look at Us,"

"Sister Autumn."

"You've,"

"Been,"

"Lied to."

"You know Us."

Agatha raised her weeping eyes to Hespa.

"You,"

"*Know,*"

"Us."

She clutched her chest, certain she would burst. Her mind screamed that she should feel terror, but she only felt an incomprehensible love. *Mercy.*

"Why did you make me do all those horrible things?" The words were hardly audible, strangled by her traitorous emotions. Hespa bent down before her, Agatha's skin glowing silver in such close proximity to the Goddess Three.

The maiden put her hand to Agatha's heart. "Our words have been twisted. Tainted. You *know* Us."

She shifted into the mother, placing her hand on Agatha's cheek. "Our people have gone astray. Gone wrong. You *know* Us."

The crone took Agatha's hands and helped her rise. "You *know* Us. Remind them who We are, Agatha Peridot. You and your Prince of Bone."

"Tell your Sisters."

"Burn,"

"The Grimoire."

The Goddess Three dissipated, Her hand sliding down Agatha's cheek in tender departure.

Alone in the woods, Agatha could do nothing but weep anew. For the things she'd done. For the mercy of Hespa. For the terrifying Order that had sprung forth from Hespa's own lips. For the thought of burning the First Sisters' words. For the responsibility of moving forward without it.

Grimm

GRIMM DASHED THROUGH THE FOREST. He jumped over logs, slapping away tree branches that sliced his arms and face as he went. Time was running out.

When the trees began to thin, he slid to a stop in the slick leaves. The Autumn rains were upon them, and frost would soon follow. He set the hood of his cloak in place and thanked Hespa for the sound of the rain concealing any noise he might make.

Stalking through the forest just outside the city, he waited for his chance, inching forward toward the thick walls of Merveille, slinking along the shadows. Too many moments passed before he caught sight of a guard wobbling on his feet and sipping not-so-discreetly from a flask.

Grimm waited until the drunk guard turned his head and he

seized his moment. Rushing up on silent feet, he slammed his elbow into the man's temple. When he verified the guard was out cold, Grimm deftly climbed the stone wall, hopped down, and landed in a crouch.

He was suddenly immensely grateful for Gaius and Augustus' training sessions. Regardless, he would hardly be able to walk on the morrow. But he couldn't think of tomorrow when he didn't yet have Dulci's safety guaranteed.

Moving forward through the slums, the reek of alcohol and vomit assaulted his nose. The door to a pub opened, the light spilling out along with raucous laughter. Grimm forced himself to stroll, leaning to one side and tripping on occasion, slipping on the wet cobblestones—just another drunk in the dark. He wasn't as familiar with the slums anymore, and he chastised himself for not making his way there more often. It's what he stood for after all—equality. Instead, he'd told himself Mer Row was enough. Seeing the faces of his people, he knew how erroneous—how pompous—he'd still been.

After a few wrong turns, his heart started pumping quickly. Cursing colourfully, he spun in a circle trying to catch his bearings in the rain-obscured city. He smelled night jasmine just before feeling a whisper of breath at his ear. He froze, listening.

"*Hurry.*" She urged him forward. "There isn't much time, *Thanasim.*"

Grimm ripped apart with a roar, soaring through time. In a jolt, his boots landed hard on the floor of Dulci's upstairs apartment. He heard a small gasp and swung around.

"Prince of Bone," Empress Amira mused, eyes wide.

Grimm growled and stalked toward her where she stood in Dulci's small kitchen. She raised her chin and the sound of breaking glass came from the other side of the room. Dulci stood in the doorway of her bedroom, slack-jawed and horrified.

"Dulci, it's me." Grimm raised his skeletal hands and cursed at the sight of them. "*Thanasim,*" he spoke, hardly a whisper.

Dulci staggered against a wall as he shifted back into Thackery, and he rushed forward to catch her. Once she was steady on her feet, Grimm pulled out his dagger, pointing it at the Empress. "If you so much as think of harming her—"

"I've already made myself clear that I am a *friend* and not a foe, prince," Amira snarled. She held up her hands. "Just listen to me."

Grimm did not lower his dagger, but gave her a curt nod. "Speak, then."

"The attack on the castle. At first, I thought it was the Grand Magus, as we all did, but I began to look more closely. Dulci and I sent in a man of my own and discovered a cloaked figure had met with the magus, demanding he look the other way and distract the king. I don't believe the magus knew exactly what was coming."

Grimm squeezed the hilt of his dagger but lowered it when Dulci pushed his arm down and stepped up to his side. "It's true. We found out just this evening, after you brought us here."

Amira came forward. "Grimm, listen. There is a man, in the pass of the Sacrée Mountains, he told me of you—of your wife. I believe he can help us. All of us." She put one palm to her chest. "*I am on your side.* I can take you to him, but I need you to trust me."

Grimm growled again and faced Dulci. They didn't have time for this. "Someone wishes you harm, Dulc—" A strangled gasp choked off his words.

He realised slowly, so slowly, that it had been his own. He looked at Dulci. Her brows were pulled together in confusion, then her hand was moving toward her mouth in shock. Gradually, he watched as her face melted into horror. It was then that he saw the hand materialising at his side, holding the hilt of a dagger near his heart. He couldn't see the blade. It was buried too far into him. That's when the pain struck between his ribs.

"I'm sorry, Grimm."

He looked up, his consciousness moving like sand funneling through an hourglass, to find Mila with her hand on the hilt of the dagger, a tear sliding down her cheek. His lips parted, but nothing came out.

Why hadn't he known she was there?

A searing heat flooded his wound as Mila slid the knife out of him.

Suddenly, Dulci screamed, a spray of his blood slashing across her chest as Mila turned the dagger on her. Through his swimming vision, Grimm saw Mila's arm shoot forward and Dulci began to crumple.

Grimm dropped to his knees, one hand clutched at his ribs, the blood slick on his fingers. Amira was screaming for help, things in the kitchen clattering as she tried to find a weapon of her own.

Dulci hit the ground in front of him with a sickening thud. Each movement sent agonising pain coursing through him as he clawed his way toward her, fingernails tearing on the wooden floorboards.

All Grimm could see were Mila's heeled shoes as she stepped over Dulci and stalked toward Amira. A pungent smell filled the room and Grimm heard Amira struggle, cursing in her mother tongue. Then, everything went quiet—too quiet.

He finally reached Dulci, pulling her as close as he could through the pain. An obsidian fog filled the room just as Grimm caught sight of Mila pulling Amira out the door by her ankles.

And everything went dark.

A *fer mahn sur, coreg ah lur, olren fahn bre ankhur. Bind the light, keep it from sight, to come forth in new life.*
-Writings of Ambrose Joubert

AGATHA

AGATHA POKED at the fire just to see the sparks fly. It was a balm to her frayed soul. The air had dipped below freezing and Eleanor shivered in her sleep. With a sigh, she rose and dropped a few more logs onto the fire, the flames licking dangerously high. Eleanor soon settled on her bedroll. Worried the bonfire would draw unwanted attention, Agatha spelled an extra ward around their camp and set to drawing protection symbols in the dirt.

She'd spent the journey back toward Merveille feeling empty. Everything she'd been taught since she was a child was a lie. If the encounter with Hespa had been real, and not just a figment of her exhausted imagination, Agatha would still have Sorscha, and that was all that kept her from breaking.

Tell your Sisters. Burn the Grimoire.

Her Orders had been vicious and vile. They'd made her life a miserable existence for three hundred years. But what was she without them?

Agatha couldn't imagine an existence with freedom. It seemed too good to be true. This new path would hold a plethora of deconstruction, should she choose to take it.

Her stick snapped in her hand and she doubled over in sudden, excruciating pain. Agatha struggled for air, gasping— horrifying sounds coming from her throat—and Gaius sprang from his bedroll.

"What is it? What's happened?" He gripped her by the shoulders and searched her for injuries.

"It's Grimm," she gasped out. "Something is terribly wrong."

Agatha doubled over once more in agony, willing the pain to cease.

The fire guttered out, waking Eleanor. Billows of dark clouds surrounded their campsite, almost glittering as the three of them looked on in terror. Beneath the dim light of the moon, the smog had a celestial gleam to it. One not of their realm. Like a scattering of stars fallen down to earth. As quickly as it had come, the strange fog dissipated and the fire relit in monstrous flames to reveal Grimm in a heap on the ground, soaked in blood and clutching Dulci to his chest.

Agatha rushed, skidding to a stop next to them. Gaius was on her heels, taking Dulci from Grimm's arms. She looked over his face—there were cuts everywhere and he was soaked through with blood. His own, and Dulci's. She ran her hands down his chest, his abdomen—he flinched when she reached his ribs, near his heart, and found consciousness, gasping and cursing. Agatha screamed at Eleanor to get her pack.

"*Grimm.*" She ripped open his shirt and shouted for Eleanor to hurry. "I'm going to fix this. Hang on and breathe."

He sucked air sharply through his teeth, shivering as he lost far too much blood.

"Dulci is unconscious, but her injury looks to have missed anything vital," Gaius clarified.

"Bring her here."

Gaius did as he was commanded and laid Dulci gently next to Grimm. Eleanor brought the pack and Agatha instructed her to look for a jar of green mud. As she waited for Eleanor to find it, she rested one hand on Grimm and the other on Dulci.

"This is going to hurt, my love."

Grimm gritted his teeth and nodded once, sweat soaking his hair.

"Gaius, hold them down the best you can."

When Gaius did as he was commanded, Agatha began chanting. She threw down the wards surrounding the camp in order to send every ounce of strength she had into willing their wounds to seal. She could feel Dulci's knitting itself together with the tendrils of her magic, but Grimm's was slower. Too slow.

"*Merde!*" she spat. "Gaius, get the poultice on Dulci. I need all of my magic on Grimm."

Agatha leaned over her husband, tears welling in her eyes, and whispered in his ear, "*Look at me.*" She pulled back to see his ashen face. Agatha could feel him fighting in their entanglement to look at her—to live. His eyes slid open—just barely—and met hers. "Don't you dare leave me here, reaper. If I'm alive, so are you. Our grave will be dug as one, and we'll climb in *together*. Do you understand me?"

The barest of laughs echoed in her soul, and she threw everything she had into him, from within and from without. Grimm's back arched as he writhed in pain. For too long, he trembled all over, his chest and face glistening with sweat and blood in the firelight.

Finally, she felt it. The viscera beneath his ribs binding together. The muscle knitting. The skin beneath her hand tugging, the two jagged edges of the wound reaching for one another.

When the wound closed enough for a spelled poultice to suffice, Agatha lost consciousness.

Grimm

AGATHA AWOKE WITH A GASPING BREATH, screaming his name with the next and frantically searching for him.

"Shh, little witch," Grimm calmed her. "I'm right here." He gently pulled her back down against him, where Eleanor and Gaius had set up a pallet for them. Her heart was hammering so fiercely he could see it in the hollow of her throat. Resting his hand over her chest, he realised she hadn't known whether he'd lived or died and nightmares had probably plagued her while she was unconscious.

Tears leaked from her eyes, landing on his tattered shirt and soaking through to his skin. "I've never been so afraid in my entire life, Grimm."

He held her close with one arm, unable to move much. "I know. I could feel it."

"Who did this?"

She wasn't prepared. He half expected her to set the whole damn world on fire when he told her. Perhaps she should. "It was Mila."

Agatha shot up and stood. He watched her chest rise and fall rapidly, teeth bared. He didn't need their entanglement bond to feel the fury rolling off of her in waves.

"I didn't sense her coming into the room. I—" He ran a hand through his hair, trying to sit up. It was his fault. "Mila knew I would protect Dulci. She was just the decoy."

"Who was the target, then?"

"Empress Amira. Just before Mila showed herself, Amira was telling me of a man in the Sacrée Mountains that knew of you and I both. She said she would take us to him. Mila stabbed me, then Dulci, then she took Amira. Lady Death brought us here Herself. She met me in the woods, rage incarnate because someone had tampered with Her Book and plotted to kill me."

He thought Agatha had been livid before, but that was a mere tug in the bond compared to the ire that came flooding in at his words. "That makes two of us."

Grimm watched in awe as she silently turned toward the fire, the flames responding to her wrath. They danced impossibly high as they lit the planes of her face, sending deep shadows under her bones and rendering her skeletal. Gaius and Dulci stirred, awoken by the brightness of the flames. Eleanor sat up at Gaius' shake of her shoulder, and they all watched in stunned silence as Agatha raised her face to the moon and spread her arms wide.

In a breath, a white-haired beauty stepped from the midnight air and walked toward the fire, never missing a step.

Across the flames, her polar opposite stepped forth with unimaginable grace, golden bracelets tinkling.

Agatha looked across the fire to the only remaining empty space, and Sorscha sauntered forward, hips swaying. Grimm felt a pang of desperate relief shoot through their bond at the same time Agatha laid eyes on Sorscha.

The white-haired one opened her mouth. "*Aggie*—"

"Silence, Winnie." Agatha looked to each of her Sisters— regal, bold, and dangerous. "Something wicked is lurking. It's threatening our realm from all sides." She paused to let her words sink in. "Those people, those *organisations*, we trusted, are proving to not be what they claim." Agatha shifted on her feet. "But there is more. Hespa has come to me directly. The Goddess Three stood before me this very night and declared that it is our duty to burn the Grimoire and move *forward*."

Wendolyn sucked in a breath. Seleste's lips parted. Sorscha lifted a brow.

"Have you gone *mad*?" Wendolyn spoke again, irate.

"No," Agatha snapped, eyes darting to her eldest Sister. "I believe I am of sound mind for the first time in my entire life."

"Hespa hasn't shown Herself to anyone in a thousand years. How can you possibly be certain of what you saw?" Wendolyn challenged, hands splayed. "It could have been anything. A dream, an illusion—"

Agatha held up her palm to the moon and the Grimoire appeared, cutting off Wendolyn's words. "This Grimoire has commanded us for centuries. It has bent us to its will, cloaking itself as Hespa, when it is *not*." She breathed hard, the fire crackling and reflecting off her hair, tangible magic coursing through the woods. "I have been made to *sit* and *obey* out of fear for the last time. I will never again be convinced that what I *know* to be true is a falsehood." She held the Book in front of her, locking eyes with each of the Sisters individually. "I am sending it into the flames, with or without you. But I cannot make this decision in your place. If you would like to leave, and not be a part of this, now is your chance."

"I'm with you," Sorscha spoke, and all the Sisters turned to her.

"You cannot be serious!" Wendolyn shouted, a murder of crows startling out of a briar.

"I am," Sorscha shot back, fists clenched at her sides. "I've spent these last moons searching into the sacrificial *slaughter* of a young warlock. Not because the Grimoire told me to, but because *you* told me to." She stabbed a finger toward Wendolyn. "That Grimoire had me planting goddess damned *poppies* in a field *leagues* away while that boy was brutally murdered right near my treehouse." When she was done speaking, her lip was quivering and she mirrored the rage filling Agatha. "Something dark is at work here, Sisters."

"We've seen it, Winnie." Agatha's voice was deadly calm this time. "We've felt it with our own magic."

Seleste broke in, "I'm with you as well." Sorscha grinned and relief coursed through Grimm as it filled Agatha.

Wendolyn threw her hands in the air. "Oh, for *fuck's* sake!"

A manic laugh bubbled out of Sorscha at the same time Seleste gasped and Agatha's eyes bulged.

"*Winnie*," Seleste censured.

"I can't very well let you three walk into damnation all on your own, now can I?" Wendolyn shrieked. "*Well*." She gestured roughly to the fire. "Go on then."

Agatha locked eyes with her eldest Sister, voice wavering as she spoke, "*More than magic, or duty, or blood, may love be what binds us.*"

She tossed the Grimoire into the flames, and all four Sisters gasped in unison. Wendolyn reached out as if she might stop it, and it struck Grimm that she probably could have. Yet, she had not.

Suddenly, each of the Sisters was lifted off her feet, back arched and chest raised to the night sky as if a string were wrapped around her breastbone and tied to the stars. When the flames finally overtook the tome, they each floated down to the ground, faces glowing with the pale illumination of the moon.

Agatha spoke once more, her voice steady with the strength of a ruler. "The Empress of Coronocco has been taken. And it is up to us to find her. We must locate a man in the pass of the Sacrée Mountains who holds precious information concerning the state of our realm. And us."

A beat of silence followed her words, and the only sign of Agatha's nerves was within Grimm, for her face read only courage.

"So be it," Wendolyn spoke first, and Grimm felt another fierce pang of Agatha's relief like lightning. "I'm with you."

"I am as well." Seleste bowed her head.

"Whatever it takes." Sorscha smiled coyly.

Agatha flashed a wicked grin. "Then let us change History, Sisters."

EPILOGUE
AGATHA

"Alright. Explain it to me one more time."

Winnie scrunched up her face at Eleanor before glancing impatiently at Agatha. "Is she daft? Are you giving me the daft one?" She turned back to Eleanor without waiting for an answer. "It's not that complicated."

Eleanor sneered. "Excuse me, but I'm not exactly a *witch* like you."

Winnie turned to her youngest Sister, pointing a lackadaisical finger at Eleanor. "You trust this mortal?"

"I do," Agatha answered, surprising herself. She lifted a shoulder. "She's spent most of her adult life in a castle."

"Ah. There we have it." Winnie waved her hand dismissively.

"And what am I to do, then?" Gaius spoke up. "I'm not letting Eleanor go with her alone."

Winnie baulked.

As did Eleanor. "I don't need you to go with me, Gaius." She stepped toward him and they began arguing.

Winnie moved, quick as lightning, landing between the two

of them. "*Pardon.*" Startled, they both jumped back from her. "If there's anything between you two"—she waved a long fingernail between them—"you're *not* both going with me."

"That doesn't matter," Gaius bit out. "I'm not sending you off with someone you've known all of an hour."

"You're not my protector, Gaius. For goddess' sake."

Winnie turned to Agatha, still gesturing at Eleanor and Gaius. "Do you hear this? I don't have time for this, Aggie."

"I'll take him," Sorscha cooed, sauntering forward.

"Not if you'll devour him whole," Seleste teased, her plum lips turned up deviously.

"Hush, you."

Seleste snickered, then turned to Agatha. "Aggie, I believe our grace period for being together has reached its end." She pointed to the sky.

"The sun shouldn't be rising for hours yet," Grimm mused.

"Nor should the leaves on the ground be turning *green*." Winnie shot Sorscha a glare.

"Oh, like it's *my* fault, Winnie."

Agatha watched the ground beneath their feet change from crimson and russet to the startling, lush hues of spring. "Alright," she spoke, bringing their attention back to her. "Eleanor, you go with Winnie to her home in the mountains. Gaius, you go Ouest with Sorscha to Prilema."

Sorscha giggled, stepping too close to Gaius—who stiffened —and Agatha frowned.

"*Behave yourself.*" She turned to Sister Summer. "Seleste, get Dulci to your Isle. Keep her safe."

She put a hand to her chest, bracelets tinkling. "You have my word."

"You can take our horses as far as you need to. Grimm and I must return to Merveille for now. We will reconvene in a fortnight at Winnie's home in the mountains." They all began to stir.

"And Sisters, *move quickly.*" She pointed to ice forming too rapidly over the green grass, barreling toward them.

"How quickly can you ride?" Sorscha sidled up to Gaius.

"Very quickly."

"Come along then, you pretty thing."

To be continued...

FROM THE AUTHOR

Dearest Reader,

It is my sincerest hope that you find yourself within these pages and it feeds your soul with the truth that you are irreplaceable—for *exactly* who you are, *right now*. May you never let anyone put you in a corner or tell you to heel. Fight your way forward and don't look back—there is nothing for you there. Your only trajectory is forward. When things turn rocky and rough, and you feel you cannot go on, I hope the Sisters whisper in your ear that *you.are.enough.*

I adore connecting with my readers. I do so mostly through my email list which you can sign up for at jlvampa.com, or through Instagram, @jlvampa.

I hope to see you on the rest of this journey with the Sisters Solstice.

WINTER OF THE WICKED COMING 2023

Best Wishes & Dark Tidings,

J.L.

ACKNOWLEDGMENTS

Mama–Every book I write, I write for you. Thank you for teaching me how to fight my way forward and never give up.

Alyse Bailey–My editor; my prose cheerleader; my throat-punching Plot Coach. I meant it when I said this book should be dedicated to you. The work and heart you poured into this manuscript truly brought the magic to life.

A.E. Kincaid–My Write or Die. You know this already, but without you in my corner, I might have quit long ago. Thank you for being there for the wins and losses, and everything in between.

K.C. Smith–The Ron to my April. Thank you for reading early drafts and telling me when they sucked. Thank you for being there to hate everything with me when I need to.

KayleighAnne–My HLM. You are my forever and my always.

Jac–"If I'm alive, so are you. Our grave will be dug as one, and we'll climb in *together*." Thanks for being the only lovers left alive with me.

Bram & Wren–Thank you for solving plot holes with me. Thank you for being the most incredible humans I've ever met.

Thank you for being who you are. I love you just the way you are, no matter what.

Manon—Thank you for adding such helpful pages of kitty gibberish to my manuscript. And for all the late night snuggles as I write.

Mr. Tramel—You'll be in every Acknowledgements section until I die. Without that encouragement in the produce aisle of a market that I doubt you remember, I might never have penned another word.

My Writing Coven—Amy, Katelyn, Autumn, Michelle, Christianna, Liz… Always there for check-ins, accountability, fun reels, jokes, coffee, trading words, venting, laughing, pumping each other up. You are all the epitome of what a coven should be and I adore each of you.

ABOUT THE AUTHOR

Jane Lenore (J.L.) Vampa is an author of Dark Fantasy and Victorian Gothic fiction. She also owns a macabre-style bookish shop, Wicked Whimsy Boutique, and teaches writing courses via the Vampa Writing Academy. She lives in Texas with her musician husband and their two littles who are just as peculiar as they are.

Printed in Great Britain
by Amazon

60271867R00234